The Naiads
The Beauty and the Beast

The Naiads
The Beauty and the Beast

by
Madame de Villeneuve

Translated, annotated and introduced by
Brian Stableford

A Black Coat Press Book

ISBN 978-1-61227-626-7. First Printing. June 2017. Published by Black Coat Press, an imprint of Hollywood Comics.com, LLC, P.O. Box 17270, Encino, CA 91416.
Printed in the United States of America.

TABLE OF CONTENTS

Introduction

"La Belle et la Bête" by Madame de Villeneuve, here translated as "The Beauty and the Beast, was first published in 1740 as by far the longest item in a two-volume collection entitled *La Jeune Américaine et les Contes marins*, signed "Madame de ***" and bearing a title-page alleging that it had been printed in La Haye [The Hague]. Although it is not impossible that it really had been published in The Hague, the attachment of title-pages bearing false places of publication was commonplace at the time for works printed in Paris without the benefit of the royal license necessary for licit publication, and the likelihood is that it was really published in Paris.

The collection was incomplete, the frame story containing the included tales breaking off with a long way still to go and the number of stories included being fewer than the number advertised in the prefatory note. In 1865, however, some years after the author's death, the two earlier volumes were reprinted, as the first two items in a five-volume collection entitled *Contes de Madame de Villeneuve*, similarly bearing title-pages claiming publication in the Hague but also giving a Paris address from which the volumes could be purchased.

The three new volumes did not contain the material missing from the earlier collection. Although the frame narrative is continued in a rather tokenistic fashion, the additional volumes are almost completely taken up by a single novel, "Les Nayades," here translated as "The Naiads." That collection too is manifestly incomplete, the final page advertizing the imminent continuation of the series of tales with one entitled "L'Empire du temps et le pouvoir de la patience" [The Empire of Time and the Power of Patience], which never materialized (the 1768 book entitled *Le Temps et la Patience* bearing her signature is simply a reprint of *La Jeune Américaine*.) Presumably, the author had intended to work on that continuation before her death but was unable to do so.

Madame de Villeneuve (1685?-1755) began life as Gabrielle-Suzanne Barbot, born in Paris to Protestant parents from La Rochelle. Although there is some uncertainty about her birth-date, which contemporary bibliographers were unable to discover, modern sources claim that she was born in the same year that Louis XIV revoked the Edict of Nantes and thus rendered French Protestants vulnerable to relentless and savage persecution. In 1706 she was married to Jean-Baptiste Gallon de Villeneuve, of Poitou, a lieutenant-colonel in the infantry, but she requested a legal separation of their assets within six months, her husband already having squandered most of their combined fortune. In 1711 she was widowed; she had apparently given birth to a daughter, but all historical trace of her was lost and she probably had not survived infancy.

Soon reduced to penury, Madame de Villeneuve returned to Paris in search of gainful employment, where she met the playwright Prosper Jolyot de Crébillon (1674-1762), subsequently known as Crébillon *père* in order to differentiate him from his son, also a writer, and eventually moved in with him and lived with him until her death. Crébillon *père* served as a crown censor licensing publications, so Madame de Villeneuve became familiar not only with the requirements for obtaining such licensing but also the procedures that could be followed in their absence. She published four more books after *La Jeune Américaine* during her lifetime, one of which was another collection of tales, *Les Belles solitaires* (1745) and the other three being naturalistic novels, one of which, *La Jardinière de Vincennes* [The Gardener of Vincennes] (1753), was moderately successful. Although there is no formal record of who it was that arranged for the posthumous publication of the 1765 *Contes*, and Crébillon *père* was already dead by then, the likeliest candidate seems to be Crébillon *fils* (1707-1777), also a royal censor, who might have inherited the manuscript of "Les Nayades" along with his father's property.

A further naturalistic novel published after Madame de Villeneuve's death, in 1757 is widely attributed to her, but the author of her entry in the 1827 *Biographie universelle* published by Louis Gabriel Michaud flatly denies that attribution and also denies her authorship of several other tales wrongly attributed to her by various sources, although he does not question her authorship of "Les Nayades," in spite of its belated date of publication. Nor had Joseph de La Porte, who included a long synopsis of the novel in the account of the author contained in his *Histoire littéraire des femmes françoises* (1769), although he was careful to say that the other posthumous novel was only "attributed" to her, without endorsing her authorship of it.

Madame de Villeneuve owes such posthumous fame as she still retains primarily to an abridged adaptation of "La Belle et la Bête," which was published by Jeanne-Marie Leprince de Beaumont (1711-1780) in her *Magasin des Enfants*—not a magazine but a kind of educative manual for parents and teachers—in 1743. The shorter adaptation became far more famous than Madame de Villeneuve's original, and is the version that has been reprinted, copied and adopted relentlessly ever since. Although it is not inconceivable that Madame de Villeneuve gave her permission for the adaptation, the overwhelming probability is that it was simply plagiarized, Leprince de Beaumont knowing full well that, as the original was an unlicensed publication, there could be no legal grounds for complaint.

Although Madame de Villeneuve's authentic version was reprinted by Charles-Joseph de Mayer in his forty-one-volume collection of *Le Cabinet de fées, ou Collection choisie des contes de fées et autres contes merveilleux* [The Fays' Cabinet, or selected Collection of Tales of Enchantment and Other Marvelous Tales] (1785-1789), which was similarly unlicensed and bore title pages claiming publication in Amsterdam, it virtually disappeared from view thereafter and remained difficult to find for the next two hundred years, prior to a 1996 reprint of the story. It was, however, translated into

English by James Robinson Le Planché (1796-1880), supplying by far the longest item in his volume *Four and Twenty Fairy Tales* (1858), and Le Planché also adapted the story for the stage; his rather mannered version has been reprinted recently and is currently in print, but I thought it worth doing a new translation to accompany "The Naiads," because the juxtaposition of the two tales adds interest to both.

The Leprince de Beaumont version of "La Belle et la Bête" was also translated into English, and became the basis for numerous further adaptations, of which the best known during the 19th century was probably a retelling in verse published as an anonymous booklet in 1811, generally credited to Charles Lamb—although Andrew Lang doubted that attribution, and challenged it when he reprinted the poem in 1887. It is at least arguable, however, that the principal interest of Madame de Villeneuve's original story is not so much the basic narrative that was plagiarized by Leprince de Beaumont as the two supplements ignored in the abridged version, in the first of which the re-metamorphosed Beast explains how he came to be transformed into the monster and why it was forced to act in the fashion it did in regard to the Beauty; in the other, the fay who has contrived the Prince's liberation from his curse then fills in a further back-story, which explains how and for what motives an evil rival placed her in that elaborate necessity. The second back-story contains an original account of the organization and internal politics of the world of Faerie that is of considerable interest in itself, as well as completing the explanatory schema of the enigmatic fundamental tale.

The corrupt version of "La Belle et la Bête" included in the 1743 *Magasin des Enfants* is illustrated, and the illustrations depict the Beast as a large dog, but the story lends no encouragement to that depiction, and it does not correspond at all with the only four specific details contained in the original story, which are that the Beast is equipped with something resembling an elephant's trunk, has scales that rattle, has paws instead of hands and is extremely heavy. Later images that equip the creature with an animalesque head but a more-or-less human body—including the illustrations in Le Planché's *Four and Twenty Fairy Tales*—have no warrant in either version. The *Magasin des Enfants* version is also harsher in its moral judgments, punishing the Beauty's jealous sisters (reduced to two from the original five) by turning them into statues rather than forgiving them and treating them kindly—a moral policy taken to an unusual extreme in "Les Nayades."

It is not immediately obvious to a modern reader why "La Belle et la Bête" was published without a royal license, especially given that the author had a close liaison with a censor able to hand out such licenses. In fact, that might have been the problem, and Crébillon *père* might well have thought that if he or anyone else granted a license to a book written by his mistress—his Protestant mistress—it might render him vulnerable to criticism, and perhaps to attack. It is unlikely that the mere fact that the Beast continually asks Beauty point-blank whether she will permit him to *couche* [go to bed] with her would have caused difficulties, but what might well have done is the fact that although the story is explicitly set in the present rather than the vague legendary past in which most *contes de fées* are set, albeit a long way from France, it contains absolutely no mention of religion, and is thus literally ungodly.

That might be considered from a distance as a delicate diplomatic omission on the part of a Protestant writer working in a sternly Catholic country, but the representatives of the Catholic Church would undoubtedly have seen the matter differently. The absence of religion from the *Magasin des Enfants* version is less obvious, and that version is, in any case, contained within a stubbornly pious frame narrative, which includes numerous versions of stories from the Old Testament retold in a manner to which no Catholic clergyman would have objected.

"Les Nayades," which is set in a vague distant past, addresses the diplomatic problem of godliness differently, the author equipping her fictitious realm with a pagan religion honoring "divinities" based on elemental spirits; it might nevertheless have been regarded with a similarly jaundiced eye by censors who were supposed to be defending the Church as well as the State from seditious notions. Although the King who is one of the story's main characters advocates and practices a hyper-Christian forgiveness of his enemies, relentlessly turning his other cheek to the most vicious slaps, he does not do so in Christ's example, and the underlying rhetoric of the narrative calls that policy somewhat into question—without, however, resorting to the crude and brutal principle of talion featured in the *Magasin des Enfants* version of "La Belle et la Bête."

Although *contes de fées* of the length of "Le Belle et la Bête" were not unknown by 1740, although not very common—the Mayer *Cabinet des fées* contains several similar items—"Les Nayades" is perhaps unique in being more than twice as long, extending to approximately 94,000 words. It is, in consequence, one of the earliest "fantasy novels" that can be readily assimilated to the modern genre that was belatedly given that label in the 1970s. Like "La Belle et la Bête," it uses several of the stock motifs of *contes de fées*, featuring a Prince Perfect who falls in love with a shepherdess, unaware that she is really a Princess, as well as an exceedingly wicked stepmother and a grotesquely exaggerated ugly sister to supply the beleaguered heroine with an excess of persecution, but, like its predecessor, it is conscientiously concerned to "look behind" those motifs and provide them with much more elaborate explanatory schemas than was then conventional. The embedded story of the strange custodian of the Mill of Misfortune and the explanation of Prince Perfect's true identity provided by the gnomide queen are addenda as interesting as the supplements in the earlier novella.

Madame de Villeneuve has suffered the fate to which numerous female writers of her era were subjected—including some who had fewer prejudicial strikes against them than she had—in being largely ignored by historians and critics, and her fantasies have faded almost entirely for view. They were somewhat handicapped in attracting the attention of anthologists by their length—those in the totally neglected *Les Belles solitaires* are also long—but in terms of their content, the author was certainly as enterprising and as interesting as any of the other writers in her problematic genre, and more so, from a modern viewpoint, than many of those whose greater orthodoxy facilitated licensed publication.

Modern feminists have not taken up her cause, some of them, in fact, asserting that "Le Belle et la Bête"—which they tend to know only in the corrupted version—sends entirely the wrong message to girls in need of future liberation from masculine bestiality, but she is a more complicated and more sophisticated writer than that superficial reading of the Beauty/Beast motif implies, and the source of vigor, enterprise and moral fortitude featured in her work is always female, albeit mostly associated on the side of virtue with fays, naiads, hamadryads and gnomides, who lend their support to human women whose actions are hesitant no matter how strong their resilience might be.

Madame de Villeneuve's main strength as a writer, however, and the main interest she retains for modern readers, does not lie in her politics or her sexual politics, which are admittedly and understandably old-fashioned now, even though they were not devoid of challenge in their epoch, but in the nature and intensity of her imagination. She was one of a number of eighteenth-century writers whose involvement with *contes merveilleux* was inquisitive and analytical, interested in experimenting with the deployment of narrative implements of such tales, studying their logic and extrapolating their use. Such work has been done with far more sophistication and expertise by modern writers, but that does not detract from her status and achievements as a pioneer, who helped lay groundwork on which countless future writers were to build, and whose endeavors remain enjoyable as well as fascinating.

The translation of "La Belle et la Bête" was made from the 1996 reprint published by Le Cabinet des Lettres, edited by Jacques Cotin and Élizabeth Lemirre. The translation of "Les Nayades" was made from the version of the 1865 *Contes* reproduced on Google Books. The latter version has a very small amount of text missing because one of the pages in the scanned book was badly torn, so I have adjusted the text slightly at that point in order to maintain its continuity. The original version of "Les Nayades" contains a few interruptions and supplementary annotations by the supposed teller of the tale, some of which I have omitted on the grounds of their redundancy.

Although Cotin and Lemirre retained some of the eccentric features of the typesetting of the original, I have modernized the presentation of the both texts, introducing the quotation marks that are, in any case, necessary in all English translations of French texts. The original texts do not contain any text breaks apart from the entirely arbitrary breaks between volumes and the bracketing of the Beast's story in the novella, but I have introduced text-breaks for the convenience of readers, mostly where there are changes of scene or viewpoint that would usually be accompanied by text breaks in modern works. The layout of the original texts, including the distribution of paragraph breaks will have been determined by the typesetter, not the author; as it does not represent authorial intention, it did not seem to me to be inappropriate to modify it slightly in order to make the text more comfortably readable.

Brian Stableford

THE BEAUTY AND THE BEAST

In a country far away from this one there is a great city in which flourishing commerce is abundant. It once counted among its citizens a merchant fortunate in his enterprises, over whom good fortune, at the whim of his desires, had always spread its finest favors. But if he had immense wealth, he also had a great many children. His family was composed of six boys and six girls. None of them was established. The boys were young enough not to be in any hurry. The girls, too proud of the great wealth on which they were used to counting, could not easily settle on the choice that they had to make, although their vanity was flattered by the assiduities of the most brilliant young men.

A reverse of fortune that they did not expect came to trouble the comfort of their life. Their house caught fire. The magnificent furniture that filled it, the books of tales, the banknotes, the gold, the silver and all the precious merchandise that composed the merchant's wealth were enveloped in that disastrous conflagration, which was so violent that very little was saved.

That first misfortune was only the forerunner of others. The father, for whom everything until then had prospered, also lost, whether by virtue of shipwreck or piracy, the ships that he had at sea. His correspondents rendered him bankrupt; his agents in foreign countries betrayed him; and in sum, from the greatest opulence, he suddenly fell into frightful poverty.

All that remained to him was a small country residence situated in a deserted location more than a hundred leagues from the city, which became his ordinary abode. Constrained to find a refuge far from the tumult and the noise, it was there that he took his family, in despair at such a revolution.

The unfortunate man's daughters, especially, only envisaged with horror the life that they were going to lead in that sad solitude. For some time, they flattered themselves that when their father's intention became known, the suitors that had sought their hand would be overjoyed that they had would soften their attitude. They all imagined that the honor of their preference would be eagerly sought. They even thought that they had only to wish it to obtain husbands.

They were not left in such a pleasant error for long. They had lost the finest of their attractions in seeing their father's brilliant fortune disappear like a flash of lightning, and for them, the season of choice had passed. The eager host of admirers disappeared at the moment of their disgrace. The power of their charms could not retain any of them.

Their friends were no more generous than their lovers. As soon as they were in poverty, all of them, without exception, ceased their acquaintance. One even pushed cruelty so far as to impute the disaster that had overtaken them to their own fault. Those to whom the father had been the most obliging were the most eager to calumniate him. They suggested that he had attracted his misfortunes by his bad conduct, his profusions, and the foolish expenditures that he had made and allowed his children to make.

In consequence, therefore, the unfortunate family was unable to make any other decision than to abandon a city where everyone made it a pleasure to insult their disgrace. Having no other resource, they confined themselves in their country house, situated in the middle of an almost impracticable forest, which might well have been the saddest abode on earth. How much chagrin they had to endure in that frightful solitude! It was necessary to resolve to labor at the most difficult tasks. Unable to have anyone to serve them, the sons of the unfortunate merchant shared the domestic chores and labors between them. All of them were endlessly occupied in what the countryside demands of those who want to extract their subsistence therefrom.

The daughters, for their part, had no lack of employment. Like peasants, they were obliged to make their delicate hands serve for all the functions of rural life. Only wearing woolen clothing, no longer having anything to satisfy their vanity, only able to live on what the local land could furnish, limited to simple necessity, but still having a taste for refinement and delicacy, the young women regretted the city and their charms incessantly. The memory of their early years, rapidly passed in the midst of laughter and games, was their greatest torture.

However, the youngest of them showed the most constancy and resolution in their common misfortune. She was seen to play her part generously, with a firmness far above her age. It was not that she had not given signs of veritable sadness at first—oh, who would not be sensible to such misfortunes?—but after having deplored her father's misfortunes, could she do any better than to resume her original gaiety, embrace by choice the sole estate in which she found herself and forget a society in which she had her family had experienced ingratitude, on the amity of which she had been so completely convinced that it was necessary not to count in adversity?

Attentive to consoling her father and her brothers by the mildness of her character and the cheerfulness of her spirit, what did she not imagine in order to amuse them agreeably? The merchant had spared nothing for her education and that of her sisters. In those testing times she obtained all the advantage from it that she desired. Playing several musical instruments very well, which she accompanied with her voice, she invited her sisters to follow her example, but her cheerfulness and patience only made them sadder.

Those young women, whom such great disgrace rendered inconsolable, found in the conduct of their younger sister a pettiness of mind, a baseness of soul, and even the weakness of living gaily in the estate to which Heaven had reduced them.

"How happy she is!" said the eldest. "She is made for coarse occupations. With sentiments so base, what would she have been able to do in society?"

Such comments were unjust. The young women would have been as able to shine as any of them. A perfect beauty ornamented her youth; an even humor rendered her adorable. Her heart, as generous as it was compassionate, was visible in everything. As sensible as her sisters to the revolution that had overwhelmed her family, by virtue of a strength of mind that is not ordinary in her sex, she was able to hide her dolor and rise above adversity. So much constancy passed for insensitivity, but a judgment born of jealousy is easily summoned.

Known by enlightened persons for what she was, everyone hastened to give her preference. In the midst of her greatest splendor, if her merit had caused her to stand out, her beauty had caused her to be given, in particular, the name of "the Beauty."[1] Merely in being known by that name, what more was necessary to augment the jealousy and hatred of her sisters?

Her charms, and the general esteem she had acquired, should have enabled her to hope for an establishment more advantageous than her sisters, but, only touched by her father's misfortunes, far from making any effort to delay his departure from a city in which she had had so much pleasure, she devoted all her care to hasten its execution. That daughter gave evidence in solitude of the same tranquility that she had had in the heart of society. To soothe her cares, in her hours of

---

[1] Many adaptations drop the definite article from this name, and preserving it every time the author employs it does lead to some awkward constructions, but it is notable that none of the characters in the story is named, even though that refusal creates difficulties in later scenes in which more than one character is defined as "the Queen," "the fay," etc. The policy is presumably intended to imply a kind of archetypal quality with regard to the central characters, so I have only dropped or varied the articles when the original text does.

relaxation, she ornamented her head with flowers, and as with the shepherdesses of olden days, rustic life allowed her to forget what had been the most flattering in the midst of opulence, and procure her days of innocent pleasure.

Two years had already gone by, and the family was beginning to be accustomed to leading a rural life, when the hope of a return came to trouble their tranquility. The father received information that one of his ships, which he had thought to be lost, had just arrived in harbor richly laden. It was added that it was to be feared that his agents might abuse his absence, selling his cargo at a low price, and, by virtue of that fraud, profiting from his goods.

He communicated that news to his children, who did not doubt for a moment that they would soon be able to quit their exile. The daughters, in particular, more impatient that their brothers, believing that it was not necessary to wait for anything more positive, wanted to depart immediately and abandon everything. But the father, more prudent, begged them to moderate their enthusiasm. Necessary as he was to his family, especially at a time when rural labors could not be interrupted without considerable prejudice, he left the care of the harvest to his sons and made the decision to undertake such a long journey on his own.

All his daughters, with the exception of the youngest, no longer had any doubt that they would soon see themselves returned to their original opulence. They imagined that even if their father's wealth did not become considerable enough for them to return to the great city, their birthplace, it would nevertheless be sufficient to allow them to live in another town, less flourishing. They hoped to find good company there, to obtain suitors, and to take advantage of the first establishment that was proposed to them.

Already giving hardly any thought to the difficulties they had been enduring for two years, believing themselves to be already transported, as if by a miracle, from mediocre fortune to the bosom of a agreeable abundance, they dared—for solitude had not caused them to lose the taste for luxury and vanity—to heap their father with foolish commissions. He was charged with making purchases for them of jewels, clothes and hats. Envy of one another caused each of them to ask for more, and the entire product of the father's pretended fortune would not have been enough to satisfy them.

The Beauty, whom ambition had not tyrannized and who had only ever acted prudently, judged at a glance that if he fulfilled her sisters' commissions, her own would be futile. But the father, surprised by her silence, interrupted his insatiable daughters said to her: "And you, the Beauty, don't you desire anything? What shall I bring you? What do you want? Speak boldly."

"My dear Papa," the lovable daughter replied, embracing him tenderly, "I desire one thing more precious than all the apparel that my sisters are asking of you. I will limit my request to that, and will be only too happy to see it fulfilled. That is the joy of seeing you return in perfect health."

That response, marked so clearly with the stamp of disinterest, covered the others with shame and confusion. They were so angry that one of them, responding for them all, said with bitterness: "That girl is putting on airs, and imagines that she is distinguishing herself by that heroic affection. Assuredly, nothing is more ridiculous."

But the father, softened by his sentiments, could not help manifesting his joy, and, touched by the wish to which the youngest daughter had limited herself, wanted her to ask for something, and to soothe his other daughters' resentment of her, he told her that such an insensibility to adornment was not appropriate at her age, and that there was a time for everything.

"Well, my dear father," she said to him, "since you order me to do so, I beg you to bring me a rose. I love that flower passionately; since I have been in this solitude, I have not had the satisfaction of seeing a single one."

That was in order to obey him, while wanting at the same time that he should not go to any expense for her.

The day came, meanwhile, when it was necessary for the worthy old man to tear himself away from his numerous family. As promptly as he could, he went to the great city to which the appearance of a new fortune summoned him.

He did not find the advantages there for which he might have hoped. His ship really had arrived, but his associates, who believed him to be dead, had taken possession of it, and all the effects had been dispersed. Thus, far from entering into the full and peaceful possession of that which ought to belong to him, in order to sustain his rights, it was necessary to endure all imaginable chicanery.

He overcame the difficulties, but after more than six months of trouble and expense, he was no richer than before. His debtors had become insolvent, and he was scarcely reimbursed for his expenses. That was where his chimerical wealth terminated. To complete his displeasure, in order not to hasten his ruination, he was obliged to depart in the most inconvenient season and in the most frightful weather.

Exposed on his route to all the insults of the air, he nearly perished of fatigue, but when he found himself a few leagues from his house, from which he had not expected to emerge to run after such foolish hopes, which the Beauty had rightly scorned, he recovered his strength.

It would take several more hours to traverse the forest, and it was late, but he wanted to continue his journey. Surprised by the night, however, penetrated by the sharpest cold, and, so to speak, buried beneath the snow along with his horse, not knowing in the end in which direction to go, he thought he was reaching his final hour. There was no hut on his route, although the forest was filled with them. A tree hollowed out by rot was all the shelter that he could find, glad of being able to hide himself within it.

That tree, in protecting him from the cold, saved his life; and the horse, perceiving another hollow lair not far from its master, was led to take shelter there by instinct.

In that condition the night appeared to him to be extremely long; furthermore, persecuted by hunger, frightened

21

by the howling of wild beasts that incessantly passed close by, how could he remain tranquil for an instant?

His difficulties and anxieties did not end with the night. He no sooner had the pleasure of seeing the daylight than his embarrassment was great. On seeing the ground extraordinarily covered with snow, what route could he take? No footpath presented itself to his eyes. It was only after long fatigue and frequent falls that he was able to find a path of sorts long which he could walk more easily.

While advancing without knowing where, hazard drew his steps into the avenue of a very fine château, which the snow appeared to have respected. It was composed of four rows of extremely tell orange-trees laden with flowers and fruits. Statues could be seen there, placed without order or symmetry, some in the road and others between the trees, all made of an unknown substance. They were of human size and color, in different attitudes and in various attire; the greater number of them represented warriors.

Having arrived at the first courtyard, he saw there, once again, a large number of other statues. The cold that he was suffering did not permit him to pay close attention to them.

A staircase of agate with a banister of sculpted gold was the first thing offered to his sight. He went through several magnificently furnished rooms. A mild warmth that he breathed in enabled him to recover from his fatigue. He had need of some nourishment, but to whom could he address himself? The vast and magnificent edifice only appeared to be inhabited by statues. A profound silence reigned there, and yet it did not give the impression of an old palace that had been abandoned. The halls, the rooms and the galleries were all open, but no living being appeared in such a charming place.

Weary of moving through the apartments of the vast dwelling, he stopped in a drawing room in which a large fire had been lit. Presuming that it had been prepared for someone who would not take long to appear, he approached the fireplace in order to warm himself; but no one came.

Sitting while he waited on a sofa placed by the fireside, a gentle slumber closed his eyelids, and rendered him incapable of seeing whether anyone might come in to surprise him.

Fatigue had caused his repose; hunger interrupted it. For more than twenty-four hours it had been tormenting him; even the exercise he had had since entering the palace had augmented his needs further. When he awoke, he was agreeably surprised on opening his eyes to see a table, delicately served. A light repast could not content him, and the sumptuously prepared dishes invited him to eat everything.

His first concern was to thank aloud those to whom he owed so much benefit, and he resolved thereafter to wait tranquilly until it pleased his hosts to make themselves known.

As fatigue had put him to sleep before the meal, nourishment produced the same effect, and rendered his repose longer and more peaceful, with the result that he slept that second time for at least four hours.

When he awoke, instead of the first table, he saw another, made of porphyry, on which a benevolent hand had set out a collation composed of cakes, dried fruits and liqueur wines; again, it was for him to make use of it. So, profiting from the generosity that was being testified to him, he ate everything that could flatter his appetite, his taste and his delicacy.

Meanwhile, seeing no one to whom to speak and to tell him whether the palace was the abode of a man or a god, fear took possession of his senses, for he was naturally fearful. He made the decision to go back through all the apartments, heaping blessings there upon the genius to whom he owed so many benefits, and by means of respectful appeals he solicited him to show himself. All his urgent requests were futile. No domestic staff appeared, no retinue that allowed him to know that the palace was inhabited.

Wondering profoundly about what he ought to do, the thought occurred to him that, for reasons he could not penetrate, some Intelligence was making him a present of the dwelling, with all the riches with which it was filed.

23

That thought appeared to him to be an inspiration, and without delay, making a further review, he took possession of all those treasures. More than that, in his thoughts, he regulated the share that he destined for each of his children, and marked the separate lodgings that might be suitable for them, congratulating himself on the joy that such a journey would cause them. He went down into the garden where, in spite of the winter, he saw, as in the middle of spring, the rarest of flowers exhaling a charming odor. A mild and temperate air was respired there. Birds of every species were mingling their songs with the confused sound of fountains, forming an admirable harmony.

Ecstatic at so many marvels, the old man said to himself: *My daughters will have little difficulty, I think, in becoming accustomed to this delightful abode. I cannot believe that they will regret the city, or that they would desire it in preference to this abode.*

In an uncommon transport of joy, he exclaimed: "Let's go, let's leave immediately. I know in advance the felicity of seeing theirs; let's not delay the enjoyment of it."

When entering the château so cheerfully, he had taken care, in spite of the great cold by which he was penetrated, to unsaddle his horse and take it to a stable that he had noticed in the first courtyard. A pathway furnished with palisades formed by arbors of rose-bushes led to it. He had never seen such beautiful roses. Their odor reminded him that he had promised one to the Beauty.

He picked one of them, and was about to continue to make six bouquets, but a terrible noise caused him to turn his head. His fear was great when he perceived a horrible Beast by his side, which, with a furious expression, placed on his neck a kind of trunk similar to that of an elephant and said to him, in a terrible voice:

"Who gave you the liberty to pick my roses? Was it not enough that I have tolerated you in my palace with so much generosity? Far from being grateful for that, brazen individual,

I find you stealing my flowers. Your insolence will not remain unpunished."

The fellow, already utterly terrified by the unexpected presence of the monster, thought he would die of fright at that speech and, promptly throwing away the fatal rose, he prostrated himself on the ground. "Oh, Monseigneur," he cried, "Have pity on me. I do not lack gratitude. Penetrated by your generosity, I did not imagine that such a little thing could be capable of offending you."

The Monster, extremely angry, replied to him: "Shut up, accursed orator; I don't care about your flatteries, nor the titles you give me; I'm not a Monseigneur, I'm the Beast, and you shall not avoid the death that you deserve."

The merchant, consternated by such a cruel sentence, believing that the policy of submission was the only one that could protect him from death, told it with a veritably touching expression that the rose that he had dared to take was for one of his daughters, called the Beauty. Then, because he hoped either to delay his doom or to touch his enemy with compassion, he told it the story of his misfortunes, and the reason for his journey. He did not forget the little present that he had promised to make the Beauty, adding that the thing to which she had restricted herself, while the riches of a king would hardly have been sufficient to fulfill the desires of his other daughters, had given birth when the opportunity presented itself to the desire to satisfy it, which he had thought himself able to do without consequence, and that, in any case, he begged pardon for that involuntary fault.

The Beast meditated for a moment. Then, resuming speaking in a less furious tone, it spoke as follows: "I'm willing to pardon you, but only on condition that you give me one of your daughters. I need someone to repair that fault."

"Just Heaven, what are you asking of me?" said the merchant. "How can I give you my word? If I were inhuman enough to want to ransom my life at the expense of that of one of my children, of what pretext would I make use for making her come here?"

"No pretext is necessary," the Beast interrupted. "I want whichever of your daughters that you bring to come here voluntarily, or I don't want one at all. See if there is one among them courageous enough to be willing to risk herself in order to save your life. You have the appearance of being an honest man; give me your word to return here in one month, if you can persuade one of them to come with you; she will remain in this place and you will return home. If you cannot, promise me to return here alone after having said goodbye to them forever, for you will be mine.

"Do not think," the monster continued, clicking its teeth, "of accepting my proposal in order to run away. I warn you that if you think in that fashion, I will come to find you, and I will destroy you, along with your family, even if a hundred thousand men present themselves to defend you."

The fellow, although fully convinced that he would attempt the amity of his daughters in vain, nevertheless accepted the monster's proposition. He promised him to return, at the appointed time, to surrender himself to his sad destiny, without the necessity of coming in search of him.

After making that assurance, he thought he might be able to withdraw and take his leave of the Beast, the presence of which could only afflict him. The mercy he had obtained was slight, but he feared that even that might be revoked. He made his desire to depart known to it, but the Beast replied that he could only depart the following day.

"You will find," it said to him, "a horse ready at daybreak. It will take you home in a short time. Go to supper, and await my orders. Adieu."

The poor man, more dead than alive, retraced his steps to the drawing room in which he had had such good cheer. Facing a large fire, his supper, already served, invited him to sit down at table. The delicacy and sumptuousness of the dishes had nothing any longer to attract him. Overwhelmed by his misfortune, if he had not feared that the Beast might be hiding somewhere and observing him, and if he had been sure of not exciting his anger by the scorn he would have shown its gifts, he would not have sat down at the table. To avoid a further disaster, he made a momentary truce with his dolor, and as much as his afflicted heart would permit, he tasted all the dishes sufficiently.

At the end of the meal a loud noise became audible in the neighboring apartment; he had no doubt that it was his formidable host. As he was not the master of avoiding its presence, he tried to suppress the fear that the sudden noise caused him.

Immediately, the Beast, which then appeared, asked him whether he had supped well.

The fellow replied, in a modest and fearful tone that he had, thanks to its attentions, eaten a great deal.

"Swear to me," the monster said, "to remember the promise you have given me, and to keep it as a man of honor, by bringing one of your daughters."

The old man, who was not amused by that conversation, swore to execute what he had promised and to return in a month, alone or with one of his daughters, if he found one of them who loved him enough to come with him, on the conditions that had been proposed to him.

"I warn you again," said the Beast, "to be careful not to surprise her with regard to the sacrifice that you must demand of her and the danger that she will incur. Describe to her my appearance, such as it is. Let her know what she is going to do; above all, let her be firm in her resolution. There will no longer be time to make reflections when you have brought her here. It is necessary that she not go back on her word; you would both be doomed without her having the liberty to return."

The merchant, stunned by such a speech, reiterated his promise to conform with everything that had just been prescribed to him. The monster, content with that response, ordered him to go to bed and not to get up until he saw the sun and heard the ringing of a golden bell.

"You will have breakfast before leaving," it said to him then, "and you can take a rose for the Beauty. The horse that will carry you will be ready in the courtyard. I expect to see you again in a month, as long as you are an honest man. Adieu; if you lack probity, I shall render you a visit."

For fear of prolonging a conversation that was already very burdensome for him, the fellow bowed profoundly to the Beast, which also told him not to worry about the route for his return; at the appointed time, the same horse that it would show him in the morning would be at his door, and would suffice for his daughter and for him.

However little desire the old man had to sleep, he dared not disobey the orders he had received. Obliged to go to bed, he did not get up until the sun began to shine into his room.

His breakfast was prompt; then he went down into the garden to pick the rose that there Beast had instructed him to take away. How that flower caused his tears to flow! But for fear of attracting further misfortunes, he constrained himself without delay to seek out the horse that had been promised. He found a warm, light cloak on the saddle. He was much more comfortable there than on his own.

As soon as the horse felt him seated, it departed with incredible speed. The merchant, who lost sight of the fatal palace in an instant, felt as much joy as he had felt the previous evening on perceiving it, with the difference that the pleasure of going away was poisoned by the cruel necessity of returning there.

To what have I engaged myself? he said to himself, while his courser carried him with a promptitude and lightness that is only known in the land of tales. *Would it not have been better for me to become at a single stroke the victim of that monster thirsty for the blood of my family? By the promise that I've made, as unnatural as it is indiscreet, my life has been prolonged. Is it possible that I have been able to think of saving my days at the expense of those of one of my daughters? Could I be barbaric enough to bring her, doubtless to see her devoured before my eyes...*

Suddenly interrupting himself however, he exclaimed: *Oh, wretch that I am, what ought I to fear the most? When I am able to silence in my heart the voice of blood, will it de-pend on me to commit that cowardice? It is necessary that she knows her fate and that she consents to it; I see no appearance that she will want to sacrifice herself for an inhuman father, and I ought not to make her that proposition; it is unjust. But if the affection that they all have for me engaged one of them to devote herself to it, would not the mere sight of the Beast destroy her constancy, without me being able to complain of it?*

Oh, too imperious Beast, he said to himself, vehemently, *you have done it deliberately; by putting an impossible condi-tion on the means you have offered me to escape your fury and obtain pardon for such a slight fault, you have added insult to injury.*

But it's too much to think about, he continued. *I shan't hesitate any longer, and I would rather expose myself without deflection to your rage than attempt a futile rescue by which parental amour is frightened.*

Let's retrace, he went on, *the road to that fatal palace, disdaining to purchase so dear the residue of a life, which could only be miserable, before the month that has been ac-corded, let's go back to terminate our unfortunate days today.*

With that thought, he tried to turn back, but it was im-possible for him to make his horse return.

Allowing himself to be carried along in spite of himself, at least he made the decision not to make any proposition to his daughters. Already, he could see his house in the distance, and fortifying himself increasingly in his resolution, he said:

I shall not mention to them the danger that threatens me. I shall have the pleasure of embracing them one last time. I shall give them my final advice; I shall beg them to live well with their brothers, whom I shall instruct not to abandon them.

In the midst of those reveries, he arrived home. His horse, which had returned the previous evening, had made his family anxious. His sons, dispersed in the forest, had searched for him in all directions, and his daughters, impatient to have news of him, were at the door in order to ask everyone who passed by whether they had seen him. As he was mounted on a magnificent horse and enveloped in a rich cloak, how could they recognize him? At first they mistook him for a man who had come on his part, and the rose that they perceived attached to his saddle completed their tranquility.

When the afflicted father came closer they recognized him. They thought of nothing but showing him the satisfaction they had in seeing him return in good health. But the sadness painted on his face and his eyes filled with tears that he strove in vain to hold back changed their delight into anxiety. They all hastened to ask him the reason for his distress. He made no response except to tell the Beauty, while presenting her with the fatal rose: "This is what you asked of me; you will pay dearly for it, as will the others."

"I knew it," said the eldest, "and I assured everyone just now that she would be the only one to whom you would bring what she requested. To force the season, it must have been necessary for you to give no less than you would have employed for the rest of us put together. That rose, by all appearances, will have withered by the end of the day, but at no matter what price, you wanted to satisfy the fortunate Beauty."

"It's true," the father said, sadly, "that that rose cost me dear, and dearer than all the apparel you wanted would have cost—but not in money, and I wish to Heaven that I had bought it with all the wealth that remains to me."

That speech excited the curiosity of his children, and cased the resolution he had made not to reveal his adventure to vanish. He told them about the poor success of his voyage, the trouble he had had in running after a chimerical fortune, and everything that had happened in the monster's palace.

After that clarification, despair took the place of hope and joy.

The daughters, seeing all their plans annihilated by that thunderbolt, uttered frightful cries; the brothers, more courageous, said resolutely that they would not allow their father to return to the fatal château, and that they were courageous enough to free the land from that horrible Beast if it had the temerity to come to search for them.

Meanwhile, they searched for expedients to save his life. Those young men, full of courage and virtue, proposed that one of them go to offer himself to the wrath of the Beast. But the latter had explained itself positively in saying that it wanted one of his daughters and not one of his sons. Those brave brothers, annoyed that their good will could not be put into execution, did what they could to inspire the same sentiments in their sisters; but their jealousy against the Beauty was sufficient to mount an invincible obstacle to that heroic action.

"It isn't just," they said, "that we should perish in a frightful fashion for a fault of which we are not guilty. That would be to render ourselves victims of the Beauty, to whom everyone would be very glad to sacrifice us, but duty does not demand such sacrifices of us. This is the fruit of the moderation and moralities perpetuated by that wretch. Why did she not ask for jewels and clothes like us? If we have not had them, at least it cost nothing to ask for them, and we do not have to reproach ourselves for having exposed out father's life by means of indiscreet requests. If she had not wanted to distinguish herself by an affected disinterest, and as she is, in addition, more fortunate than us, he would doubtless have found enough money to satisfy her. But it was necessary, by virtue of a singular caprice, for her to be the cause of all our woes. It is her that attracted them to us, but it is on us that they have rebounded. We will not be dupes. She has caused hem, let her remedy them."

The Beauty, from whom dolor had almost taken away consciousness, silenced her sobs and sighs, and said to her sisters: "I am culpable of his misfortune; it is up to me alone to repair it. I confess that it would be unjust for you to suffer for my fault. Alas! It was, however very innocent. Could I foresee that the desire to have a rose in the middle of summer would be punished by such a torture? The fault has been committed, however; whether I am innocent or guilty, it is just that I expiate it. It cannot be imputed to anyone else.

"I shall expose myself," she continued, in a firm tone, "In order to extract my father from his fatal engagement. I will go to find the Beast, only too glad in dying to conserve the life of the man from whom I received it, and to put an end to your murmurs. Have no fear that anything can deflect me from it. But please, during this month, give me the pleasure of no longer hearing your reproaches."

So much firmness in a girl of her age surprised them greatly, and her brothers, who loved her tenderly, were touched by her resolution. She had infinite attentions for them, and they sensed the loss that they were about to suffer; but it was a matter of saving a father's life. That pious motive closed their mouths, and, quite convinced that it was a matter resolved, far from thinking of opposing such a generous design, they were content to shed tears and to give their sister the praise that such a noble resolution merited, all the more so because, being only sixteen years old, she had a right to regret a life that she intended to sacrifice in such a cruel fashion.

Only the father did not want to consent to the decision that his youngest daughter had made. But the others reproached him insolently, saying that the Beauty alone touched him, that in spite of the misfortunes she had caused, he was annoyed that it was not one of her elders who was paying for her imprudence.

Such unjust speeches forced him no longer to persist. In any case, the Beauty came to assure him that if he did not agree to the exchange, she would make it in spite of him, since she would go alone to seek out the Beast and doom herself without saving him.

"Who can tell?" she said, striving to give evidence of more tranquility than she had. "Perhaps the frightful fate that is destined for me hides another, as fortunate as it seems terrible?"

Her sisters, on hearing her say that, smiled maliciously at that chimerical thought; they were delighted by what they believed to be her error. But the old man, vanquished by all her arguments, and, remembering an ancient prediction, by which he had been told that that daughter would one day save her life and that she would be the source wellbeing for the entire family, ceased to oppose the Beauty's determination. Gradually, they began to talk about her departure as an almost indifferent matter.

She it was who set the tone of the conversation, and if in their presence she appeared to be counting on something fortunate, it was uniquely to console her father and brothers, and not to alarm them further. Although discontented by the conduct of her sisters in her regard, who seemed impatient to be rid of her and found that the month was passing too slowly, she had the generosity of dividing between them all the petty possessions and jewels that she had at her disposal.

They received that further proof of her generosity gladly, without their hatred being diminished. An extreme joy took possession of their hearts when they heard the whinny of the horse sent to carry away a sister whom black jealousy prevented them from finding lovable. Only the father and the afflicted sons could not hold firm against that fatal moment; they wanted to cut the horse's throat, but the Beauty, conserving all her tranquility, showed them on that occasion all the absurdity of that design and the impossibility of carrying it out. After having taken her leave of her brothers, she kissed her insensible sisters, making them an adieu so touching that it drew a few tears from them, and they believed for the space of several minutes that they were almost as afflicted as their brothers.

During those brief and belated regrets, the fellow, pressed by his daughter, mounted the horse, and she set herself on its rump with the same urgency as if it had been a matter of a very pleasant journey.

The animal appeared to fly rather than walk. That extreme diligence was not at all uncomfortable; the gait of the singular horse was so smooth that the Beauty felt no other agitation that that originating from the breath of zephyrs.

In vain, on the route, her father offered a hundred times over to set her down and go to meet the Beast alone

"Think, my dear child," he said to her, "that there's still time. That monster is more frightful than you can imagine. However firm your resolution might be, I fear that it will fail at the sight of it. Then it will be too late and you'll be doomed, and we'll both perish."

"If I were going to seek this terrible Beast," the Beauty replied, prudently, "with the hope of being fortunate, it would not be impossible that hope would abandon me on seeing it; but as I expect an imminent death and believe it to be certain, what does it matter to me whether the one that gives it to me is agreeable or hideous?"

While they were conversing thus, night fell, but the horse continued its progress nevertheless in the obscurity. By virtue of the most surprising spectacle, the darkness suddenly dissipated. There were rockets of all sorts, fire-pots, windmills, sunbursts, sprays all that artificial fireworks can invent of the most beautiful, which came to strike the gaze of the two travelers. That agreeable and unexpected light, illuminating the entire forest, spread a gentle warmth in the air, which was beginning to be necessary, because the cold, in that region, made itself felt more keenly by night than by day.

By the favor of that charming brightness, the father and daughter found themselves in the avenue of orange-trees. As soon as they were there, the firework display ceased. Its light was replaced by all the statues, which had lighted torches in their hands. Furthermore, countless lanterns covered the entire façade of the palace; placed symmetrically, they formed love-knots and crowned figures, in which were seen paired LLs and paired BBs. On entering the courtyard they were regaled with salvos of artillery, which combined with the sound of a thousand various musical instruments as many soft as martial, made a charming harmony therewith.

"The Beast must be very hungry," said the Beauty, in jest, "to rejoice so much at the arrival of its prey."

In spite of the emotion caused by the imminence of an event that, according to appearances, was to be fatal for her, however, in giving all her attention to so many magnificences succeeding one another, and presenting her with the most beautiful spectacle that she had ever seen, she could not help saying to her father that the preparations for her death were more brilliant than the nuptial pomp of the greatest king on earth.

The horse stopped at the foot of the perron. She got down lightly, and her father, as soon as he had set foot on the ground, led her through a vestibule into the salon where he had been entertained so well. They found a large fire there, lighted candles that spread an exquisite perfume, and also a table splendidly laid.

The man, familiar with the fashion in which the Beast nourished its guests, told his daughter that the meal was destined for them and that it was appropriate to make use of it. The Beauty made no difficulty about that, convinced that it would not advance her death. On the contrary, she imagined that it would make known to the monster the scant repugnance that she had had in coming to find it. She flattered herself that her frankness might be capable of softening it, and even that her adventure might be less disastrous than she had feared at first.

The frightful Beast with which she had been threatened did not show itself; everything in the palace respired joy and magnificence. It appeared that her arrival had given birth to it, and it seemed implausible that it was the preparation for a funeral celebration.

Her hope did not last long. The monster made itself heard. An awful noise, caused by the enormous weight of its body, the terrible rattle of its scales and frightful howls announced its arrival. Terror took possession of the Beauty. The old man, kissing his daughter, uttered piercing cries. However, having mastered her senses in an instant, she recovered from her agitation. On seeing the Beast approach, which she could not envisage without shivering internally, she advanced with a firm step, and curtsied very respectfully to the Beast in a modest fashion.

That step pleased the monster. After having considered her in a fashion that, without seeming wrathful, could have inspired terror in the boldest, it said: "Good evening, sir," to the old man and, turning to the Beauty, it similarly said to her, "Good evening, the Beauty."

The old man, still apprehensive that something sinister was going to happen to his daughter, did not have the strength to reply. The Beauty, however, unmoved and in a soft and confident voice, said: "Good evening, the Beast."

"Have you come here voluntarily," asked the Beast, "and do you consent to let your father go without following him"

The Beauty replied that she had no other intention.

"What do you think will become of you after his departure?"

"Whatever pleases you," she said. "My life is at your disposal, and I submit blindly to whatever fate you order for me."

"Your docility satisfies me," said the Beast, "and since you have not been brought here by force, you shall stay with me. As for you, fellow," it said to the merchant, "You will leave tomorrow at sunrise; the bell will warn you. Do not delay after your breakfast; the same horse will take you home.

"But," it added, "when you are in the midst of your family, do not think of seeing my palace again, and remember that it is forbidden to you forever. You, the Beauty," the monster continued, addressing her, "take your father into the nearby wardrobe; choose there everything that either of you think might please your brothers and your sisters. You will find two trunks; fill them. It is just that you send them something of great enough value to oblige them to remember you."

In spite of the monster's liberality, the imminent departure of her father touched the Beauty sensibly and caused her an extreme chagrin. However, she set about obeying the Beast, which quit them after having said to them, as it had said on entering: "Good evening, the Beauty; good evening, sir."

When they were alone, the man, embracing his daughter, never ceased weeping. The idea that he was about to leave her with the monster was the cruelest of tortures for him. He repented of having brought her to that place. The doors were open and he would have liked to take her away, but the Beauty reminded him of the dangers and consequences of such a design.

They went into the wardrobe that had been indicated to them. They were surprised by the riches that they found there. It was filled with garments so superb that a queen could not have wished for anything finer or in better taste. No boutique was ever so well stocked

When the Beauty had chosen the adornments that she thought the most appropriate, not to the present situation of her family but proportionate to the wealth and liberality of the Beast that was making such gifts, she opened a cupboard whose door was rock crystal mounted in gold. Although she had expected to find rare and precious treasure there, at the sight of such a magnificent exterior, she saw a heap of precious stones of every sort of which her eyes could scarcely sustain the glare. In a spirit of submission, the Beauty casually took a prodigious quantity of them, which she did her best to sort into each of the lots she had made.

On opening the final cupboard, which was nothing other than a cabinet filled with gold coins, she changed her plan.

"I think," she said to her father, "that it would be more appropriate to empty these trunks and fill them with coins; you can give to your children whatever you please. By that means, you will not be obliged to have anyone in on your secret, and your riches will be yours without danger. The advantage that you would obtain from the gems, although their value would be much more considerable, might not be so convenient for you. To enjoy them, you would be obliged to sell them, and to confide them to people who would only look at you with envious eyes. Your confidence might even prove fatal to you, whereas gold coins," she continued, "would shelter you from any unfortunate event, by giving you the facility to acquire land and houses and to buy precious furniture, jewels and gems."

Her father approved her idea, but, wanting to take his daughters adornments and garments, in order to make room for the gold he wanted to take, he took out of the trunks what he had chosen for his own usage. The large quantity of coins that he put into them almost filled them. They were equipped with pleats, which relaxed as they were filled. He found room for the jewels that he had removed, and in the end the trunks contained more than he wanted.

"So many coins," he said to his daughter, "will enable me to sell my gems at my ease. Following your advice, I'll hide my wealth from everyone, even my children. If they knew that I was as rich as I shall be, they'd torment me to abandon the rural life, which, however, is the only one in which I've found pleasure and in which I haven't experienced the perfidy of the false friends with which the world is full."

But the trunks were so heavy that an elephant would have succumbed under the weight, and the hope that had come to him of satisfying himself appeared to him to be a dream and nothing more.

"The Beast is mocking us," he said. "It pretended to give me wealth that it has made it impossible for me to carry away."

"Suspend your judgment," replied the Beauty. "You have not provoked its liberality by any indiscreet request or by any avid and interested gaze. The mockery would be insipid. I think, since the monster has invited you to take it, that it will find a means to enable to enjoy it. We have only to close the trunks and leave them here. Apparently, it knows by what vehicle it can send them to you."

One could not think more prudently. In conformity with the advice, the fellow went back into the drawing room with his daughter. Both sitting on a sofa, they saw breakfast served. The father ate with the better appetite than he had the previous evening. What had just happened diminished his despair and caused his confidence to be reborn. He would have departed without chagrin if the Beast had not had the cruelty of making him understand that he was no longer to think of seeing the palace again and that it was necessary to bid his daughter an eternal adieu.

No evil without remedy is known save that of death. The fellow was not absolutely afflicted by that decree. He flattered himself that it might not be irrevocable, and that hope enabled him to depart quite content with his host.

The Beauty was not so satisfied. Unconvinced that a fortunate future was prepared for her, she was apprehensive that the rich presents with which the monster had heaped her family might be the price of her life and that it would devour her as soon as it was alone with her; at the least she feared that an eternal prison was destined for her and that she would have a frightful Beast for her unique companion.

That reflection plunged her into a profound reverie, but a second chime of the bell warned them that it was time to separate. They went down into the courtyard, where the father found two horses, one charged with the two trunks and the other destined uniquely for him. The latter, covered with a good cloak, and its saddle equipped with two bags full of refreshments, was the same one that he had already ridden. Such great attentions on the part of the Beast were about to furnish further matter for conversation, but the horses, whinnying and pawing the ground, made it known that it was time to part.

The merchant, for fear of irritating the Beast by his slowness, bid his daughter an eternal adieu. The two horses departed more rapidly than the wind, and the Beauty lost sight of them in an instant.

In tears, she went back up to the bedroom that was to be hers, where she made even sadder reflections for a few moments. However, overwhelmed by drowsiness, she wanted to seek a repose that she had lost for more than a month. Having nothing better to do, she was about to lie down when she saw a cup of chocolate prepared on the night table. She took it, while half-asleep, and her eyes having closed almost immediately, she fell into a tranquil sleep, which had been entirely unknown to her since the moment she had received the fatal rose.

During her slumber she dreamed that she was on the bank of a canal extending as far as the eye could see, the two sides of which were ornamented by two rows of orange-trees and flowering myrtles of prodigious height, where, entirely occupied with her sad situation, she deplored the misfortune that condemned her to spend her days in this place without the hope of ever emerging from it.

A handsome young man, like a depiction of Amour, with a voice that went to her heart, said to her: "Don't believe, the Beauty, that you are as unfortunate as you appear to be. It is in these places that you are to receive the recompense that has been unjustly refused to you everywhere else. Activate your penetration to disentangle me from the appearances that disguise me. Judge, in seeing me, whether my company is despicable, and ought not to be preferred to that of a family unworthy of you. Wish, and all your desires will be fulfilled. I love you tenderly; alone, you can make my happiness by making your own. Never struggle. Being as far above other women by virtue of the qualities of your soul as you are superior to them in beauty, we shall be perfectly happy."

Afterwards, that charming phantom appeared to her at her feet, combining the most flattering promises with the most tender speech. He pressed her in the most ardent terms to assent to his happiness, and assured her that she was entirely his mistress.

"What can I do?" she said to him, urgently

"Follow the slightest impulses of gratitude," he replied, "do not consult your eyes, and above all, don't abandon me, and extract me from the frightful punishment that I'm enduring."

After that first dream, she thought she was in a magnificent cabinet with a Lady whose majestic air and surprising beauty gave birth in her heart to a profound respect. That Lady, in a caressant fashion, said to her: "Charming Beauty, don't regret what you have just quit. A more illustrious fate awaits you, but if you want to merit it, refrain from allowing yourself to be seduced by appearances."

Her sleep lasted for more than five hours, during which she saw the young man in a hundred different places, and in a hundred different fashions.

Sometimes he entertained her splendidly, sometimes he made her the most tender protestations. How agreeable her slumber was! She would have liked to prolong it, but her eyes, opened to the light, could not close again, and he Beauty believed she had only had the pleasure of a dream.

A clock that chimed twelve by repeating her name musically twelve times obliged her to get up. First she saw a dressing table garnished with everything that might be necessary to ladies. After having adorned herself with a sort of pleasure, the cause of which she could not divine, she went into the drawing room, where her dinner had just been served.

When one eats alone, a meal is soon taken. On returning to her bedroom, she threw herself on to a sofa; the young man of whom she had dreamed came to present himself to her thoughts

I can make his happiness, he said to me, Apparently, the horrible Beast who reigns here is keeping him imprisoned. How can he be freed from it? The advice has been repeated to me not to trust appearances. I don't understand any of it, but how foolish I am! I'm amusing myself seeking reasons to explain an illusion that sleep has formed and wakefulness has destroyed. I ought not to pay any attention to it. It's necessary to occupy myself with my present fate, and seek amusements that will prevent my succumbing to ennui.

Some time later, she began exploring the numerous apartments of the palace. She was enchanted by them, having never seen anything so beautiful. The first one into which she entered was a large hall of mirrors. She saw herself there everywhere. First, a bracelet, and then a girandole, came to catch her eye. She found the portrait of a handsome cavalier on the bracelet, like the one she had seen while sleeping. How could she have failed to recognize him? His features were already too forcefully engraved in her mind, and perhaps in her heart. With a hasty joy, she put the bracelet on her wrist, without reflecting as to whether the action was appropriate.

Having passed from that room into a gallery filled with paintings, she found the same portrait there, life-sized, which seemed to be looking at her with such tender attention that she blushed, as if the painting had been what it represented, or that it had been witness to her thoughts.

Continuing her stroll, she found herself in a room filled with various musical instruments. Knowing how to play almost all of them, she tried a few of them, preferring the harpsichord to the others because it accompanied her voice better.

From that room she entered a gallery other than the one with the paintings. It contained an immense library. She loved learning, and since her sojourn in the country she had been deprived of that pleasure. Her father, because of the disturbance of his business affairs, had been forced to sell his books. Her great liking for reading could easily be satisfied in his place, and the protection from ennui in her solitude.

The day passed without her being able to see everything. At the approach of night, all the apartments were illuminated by perfumed candles placed in chandeliers in which different colors were transparent, not of crystal but of diamonds and rubies.

At the usual hour the Beauty found her supper served with the same delicacy and the same neatness. No human face was presented before her; her father had warned her that she would be alone.

That solitude was beginning no longer to trouble her when the Beast made itself heard to her ears. Not having yet been alone with it, ignorant of how that conversation would go, even fearing that it was only coming to devour her, how could she not tremble? But when the Beast arrived, which at first did not manifest any fury, her terrors disappeared.

The monstrous colossus said, roughly: "Good evening, the Beauty." She returned its greeting in the same terms, with a soft but slightly tremulous expression.

Among the various questions that the monster asked her, it asked her how she had amused herself. The Beauty replied: "I spent the day visiting your palace, but it's so vast that I didn't have time to see all the apartments and the beauties they contain."

The Beast asked her: "Do you think you will be able to accustom yourself to being here?"

The girl replied politely that she could live without difficulty in such a beautiful abode.

After an hour of conversation on the same subject, the Beauty easily distinguished, through its frightful voice, that it was a tone compelled by the organs, and that the Beast was inclined more toward stupidity than fury.

It asked her without circumlocution whether she would allow it to go to bed with her. At that unexpected request, her fears were renewed, and, uttering a terrible scream, she could not help saying: "Oh Heaven! I'm doomed."

"Not at all," said the Beast, tranquilly. "But respond as necessary, without fear. Say precisely yes or no."

The Beauty replied, tremulously: "No, the Beast."

"Well, since you don't want to," replied the docile monster, "I'll go. Goodnight, the Beauty."

"Goodnight, the Beast," said the frightened girl, with a great satisfaction.

Extremely content with not having to fear violence, she went to bed tranquilly and fell asleep.

Immediately, her dear Unknown returned to her mind. He appeared to say to her tenderly: "How glad I am to see you again, my dear Beauty, but how much harm your rigor causes me! I know that it will be necessary for me to remain unhappy for a long time."

Her ideas changed their object; it seemed that the young man presented her with a crown. Sleep made her see him in a hundred different fashions. Sometimes, he appeared to her to be at her feet, sometimes abandoning himself to the most excessive joy, sometimes shedding a torrent of tears, by which she was touched to the utmost depths of her soul.

That mixture of joy and sadness lasted all night. When she awoke, having her imagination struck by that dear object, she sought out his portrait in order to confront it again and to see whether she was not mistaken. She ran to the gallery of paintings, where she recognized him even more clearly. How much time she spent admiring him! But, ashamed of her weakness, she contented herself with looking at it at arm's length.

To put an end to her tender reflections, however, she descended into the gardens, the fine weather inviting her to take a walk. Her eyes were enchanted; they had never seen anything so beautiful in nature. The arbors were ornamented with admirable statues and countless fountains, which refreshed the air, the extreme height of which almost extended out of sight.

What surprised her most was that she recognized the places where, in her sleep, she had dreamed about the Unknown. Above all, at the sight of the great canal bordered with orange-trees and myrtles, she was only able to think about that dream, which no longer appeared to her as a fiction.

She believed that she found the explanation of it by imagining that the Beast was retaining someone in its palace. She resolved to clarify the matter that very evening, and to ask the monster, another visit from which she was expecting at the usual hour.

As much as her strength permitted, she walked for the rest of the day, still without being able to consider everything.

The apartments that she had not seen the previous day merited her gaze no less than the others. Apart from the musical instruments and curiosities by which she was surrounded, she found something else to occupy in another room. It was equipped with bags, shuttles for making knots, scissors for cutting and frameworks set up for all kinds of needlework—in sum, everything was there. A door of that charming room allowed her to see a superb gallery, from which one could discover the most beautiful landscape in the world.

In that gallery, care had been taken to place an aviary filled with rare birds, which all performed an admirable concert when the Beauty arrived. They also came to alight on her shoulders, and some of those tender animals approached her very closely.

"Lovable prisoners," she said to them, "I find you charming, and I am mortified to see you so far away from my apartment; I would have liked the pleasure of hearing you often."

How surprised she was when, as she spoke those words, she opened a door and found herself in her bedroom, which she had thought far away from that beautiful gallery, in which she had only arrived by circling through a series of apartments that composed the building. The partition that had prevented her from perceiving the vicinity of the birds opened, and was very convenient for blocking out the sound when one did not have the desire to hear it.

Continuing her route, the Beauty perceived another plumed troop, of parrots of every species and all colors. All of them, in her presence began to chatter. One of them said "Good day" to her, another asked her for breakfast, a third, more gallant, begged for a kiss. Several sang operatic arias, other declaimed verses written by the best authors, and all of them offered to amuse her. They were as mild and gentle as the inhabitants of the aviary. Their presence gave her a true pleasure. She was very glad to find something to talk to her, for silence, to her, was not a pleasure. She interrogated several of them, which responded to her like very witty animals. She chose one of them, which pleased her the most. The, others jealous of that preference, complained dolorously. She appeased hem with a few caresses, and by the permission that she gave them to come and see her whenever they wished.

Not far from that place, she saw a numerous troop of monkeys, of all sizes: big ones, small ones, capuchin monkeys, monkeys with human faces, others with blue, green, black or golden beards.

They came toward her at the entrance to their apartment, to which hazard had led her. They made reverences to her, accompanied by countless capers, and testified to her by their gestures that they were sensible to the honor that she was doing them. In order to celebrate the occasion they performed rope-dances and acrobatics, with unparalleled skill and lightness.

The Beauty was very satisfied with the monkeys, but she was discontented to find nothing that gave her news of the handsome Unknown. Giving up hope of finding any, regarding her dream as a chimera, she did what she could to forget him, but her efforts were vain. She petted the monkeys, and said while stroking them that she wished she had some that wanted to go with her to keep her company.

Instantly, two large she-monkeys clad in court costumes, which seemed only to be awaiting her orders, came gravely to place themselves by her sides. Two alert little monkeys picked up her dress and served her as pages. An ape comically dressed as a Spanish squire presented her with a properly gloved hand. Accompanied by that singular cortege, the Beauty went to take her meal. For as long as it lasted the birds chirped like musical instruments and accompanied accurately the voices of the parrots, which sang the most beautiful and most fashionable songs.

During that concert, the monkeys that had been given the right to serve the Beauty, having regulated their ranks and charges instantaneously, commenced their functions and served her ceremoniously, with the dexterity and respect with which queens are served by their officers.

When she left the table another troop wanted to regale her with a new spectacle. They were actors of a sort, who performed a tragedy in the rarest fashion. Those aristocratic monkeys and she-monkeys in theatrical costumes covered with embroidery, pears and diamonds, made gestures appropriate to the words of their roles, which the parrots pronounced quite distinctly and appositely, with the result that it was necessary to be sure that those birds were hidden under the wigs of some and the mantles of others to perceive that those actors of novel manufacture were not speaking themselves.

The play seemed to be expressly designed for the actors, and the Beauty was delighted by it. At the end of the tragedy, one of them came to pay the Beauty a very fine compliment, and thanked her for the indulgence with which she had listened to them. None of the monkeys remained except those of her household and those destined to amuse her.

After her supper, the Beast came, as usual, to visit her, and after the same questions and the same responses the conversation concluded with a "Good night, the Beauty."

The she-monkey ladies-in-waiting undressed their mistress, put her to bed and had the attention to open the window of the aviary in order that the birds, by means of a song less strident than that of the day, could provoke sleep, soothe the senses and give her the pleasure of dreaming of her attractive lover.

Several days passed without her getting bored. Every moment was marked by new pleasures. In three or four lessons the monkeys each contrived to train a parrot that, serving as an interpreter, responded to the Beauty with as much promptitude and accuracy as the monkeys had in their gestures. In sum, the Beauty only found it annoying to be obliged to sustain every evening the presence of the Beast, the visits of which were brief—and it was doubtless by its means that she had all the pleasures imaginable.

The mildness of the monster sometimes inspired in the Beauty the design of asking it for some enlightenment on the subject of the man she saw in her dreams; but, sufficiently informed that it was in love with her, and fearing to awaken jealousy by that request, she prudently kept quiet and dared not satisfy her curiosity.

She had visited all the apartments of the enchanted palace several times, but one gladly sees rare, curious and rich things again.

The Beauty directed her steps toward a large drawing room that she had only seen once. The room was pierced by four windows on each side; only two were open and only gave a somber daylight. The Beauty wanted to give it more light, but instead of the daylight she believed she would let in, she only found an opening overlooking an enclosed location. That area, although spacious, appeared to her to be obscure, and her eyes could only perceive a distant glimmer, which only seemed to be reaching her through an extremely thick crepe.

While she was wondering what the purpose of that place might be, a bright light suddenly dazzled her. The curtain was raised, and the Beauty discovered a brightly illuminated theater. In the stalls and the boxes she saw everything that one could see of the most handsome and beautiful of either sex.

Instantly, a soft symphony, which began to make itself heard, only ceased in order to give actors other than the monkeys and parrots the liberty to perform a very beautiful tragedy, followed by a brief play that, in its genre, was the equal of the first.

The Beauty loved spectacles; it was the only pleasure that she had regretted on quitting the city. Curious to see what fabric decorated the box next to her own, she was prevented from doing so by a mirror that separated them, which let her know that what she had thought to be real was only an artifice, which, by means of that crystal, reflected objects and sent them to her from above the most beautiful theater in the world. It was the masterpiece of optics to transmit reverberations from so far away.

After the comedy she remained in her box for some time to watch the beautiful society going out. The obscurity that spread through the location obliged her to take her reflections elsewhere. Content with that discovery, of which she promised herself to make frequent use, she went down into the gardens. Prodigies were beginning to become familiar to her; she sensed with pleasure that they were only being produced for her benefit and to procure her pleasure.

After supper, the Beast, as usual, came to ask her what she had done during the day. The Beauty gave it an exact account of all her amusements, telling it that she had been to the theater.

"Did you like it?" the heavy animal said to her. "Wish for anything that would please you, and you shall have it; you are very pretty."

The Beauty smiled internally at that gross fashion of being honest with her; but what did not make her laugh was the customary question, and that "Would you like me to go to bed with you?" caused her to lose her good humor. She got out of it by responding "No," but its docility during that latest conversation did not reassure her at all. The Beauty was alarmed by it.

Where is all this going? she wondered internally. *The request that it makes me every time as to* whether I want to go to bed with it *proves to me that it still persists in its amour. Its benefits confirm that. Although it is not obstinate in its demand, and testifies no resentment at my refusals, how do I know that it will not become impatient and that my death might be the cost of that?*

These reflections rendered her so pensive that it was almost daylight when she went to bed. Her Unknown, who was only waiting for that moment to appear, made her tender reproaches for her lateness. He found her sad and distracted, and asked her what could have displeased her in this place.

She replied that nothing displeased her except the monster, but that she saw it every evening. She could become accustomed to that, but it was in love with her, and that amour made her apprehensive of some violence.

"By the stupid compliment it paid me, I judge that it would like me to marry it. Would you advise me," said the Beauty to her Unknown, "to satisfy it? Alas, even if it were as charming as it is frightful, you have rendered access to my heart inaccessible for it, as for any other, and I do not blush to confess that I cannot love anyone but you."

A confession so charming could not help flattering him; he only responded to it by saying: "Love whom you love; do not allow yourself to be surprised by appearances and release me from prison."

That speech, repeated continually without any further explanation, put the Beauty in an infinite difficulty. "How do you expect me to do that?" she said to him. "I would like, at any cost, to be able to render you liberty, but that good will is useless to me as long as you do not furnish me with the means of putting it into practice."

The Unknown replied to her, but it was in a fashion so confused that she could not understand any of it. A thousand extravagances passed before her eyes. She saw the monster on a throne brilliant with gems, which appealed to her and invited her to place herself at its side. A moment later, the unknown made it descend precipitately and put himself in its place. The Beast getting the upper hand again, the Unknown disappeared in his turn. Someone spoke to her through a thick veil, which changed the voice and rendered it frightful.

The entire time of her slumber passed in that fashion, and in spite of the agitation that it caused her, she nevertheless found that it ended too soon for her, since her awakening deprived her of the object of her tenderness. On emergence from her dressing-room, various items of needlework, books and animals occupied her until it was time for the play. The time came for her to go to it, but she was no longer in the same theater, it was that of the opera, which commenced as soon as she had taken her place. The spectacle was magnificent and the spectators no less so. The mirrors represented it distinctly, down to the smallest items of clothing in the stalls. Delighted to see human faces, several of which were known to her, it would have been a great pleasure for her to speak to them and make herself heard.

More satisfied with that day than the preceding one, the remainder was similar to what had happened since she had been in the palace. The Beast came in the evening; after its visit she retired, as usual. The night was similar to the others—which is to say, filled with pleasant dreams. When she awoke, she found the same number of domestics to serve her.

After her dinner, her occupations were different. The previous day, on opening another window, she had found herself at the opera; in order to diversify her amusements, she opened a third, which procured her the pleasures of the Foire Saint-Germain,[2] even more brilliant then than it is today. But as it was not the time when good company presented itself, she had time to see everything and examine everything. She saw the rarest curiosities there, the extraordinary productions of nature, and works of art; the most trivial bagatelles fell before her eyes. Even the marionettes were an amusement not unworthy of her, while awaiting something better. Comic opera was in its splendor. The Beauty was very content with it.

At the exit from the spectacle she saw all the stylish individuals strolling among the merchants' stalls. She recognized professional gamblers there who went to the place as if to their studio. She remarked some who, losing their money because of the expertise of those against whom they were playing, went out with countenances less joyful than those they had had on going in. The prudent players, who did not stake their fortune on games and played in order to take advantage of their talent, could not hide their trickery from the Beauty. She would have liked to warn the parties suffering from the wrong that was being done to them, but, more than a thousand leagues distant from them, she could not do it.

She could hear and see everything very distinctly, without it being possible for her to make her voice heard, or even to be perceived. The reflections that brought to her what she could see and hear were not sufficiently perfect to do the same in reverse. She was placed above the air and the wind; every-

---

[2] The Foire Saint-Germain was an annual event held for the benefit of the abbey of Saint-Germain-des-Prés. In the eighteenth century it opened in early February and closed on Palm Sunday. Although the fair and its theater featured the full range of conventional fairground exhibitions, it became particularly famous for its development of the tradition of *opéra-comique* [comic opera] and vaudeville, which was in its heyday there in the early eighteenth century.

thing arrived as far as her in thought. She made that reflection, which prevented her from making futile attempts.

It was after midnight before she thought that it was time to retire. The need to eat would have been able to instruct her as to the time, but she had found in her box liqueurs and baskets filled with everything necessary for a snack.

Her supper was light and brief. She was in a hurry to get to bed. The Beast perceived her impatience and came simply to wish her good night, to leave her the time to sleep and the Unknown the liberty to reappear.

The following days were similar. In her windows she had inexhaustible sources of new amusements. One of the other three gave her the pleasure of the Comédie-Italienne,[3] another a view of the Tuileries, where all the most distinguished and best-looking people in Europe went. The last window was not the least agreeable; it furnished her with a sure means of learning everything that was happening in the world. The scene was amusing and diversified in all sorts of ways. It was sometimes a famous ambassador that she saw, an illustrious marriage, or a few interesting revolutions. She was at that window during the latest revolt of the Janissaries;[4] she witnessed it all the way to the conclusion.

---

[3] The Comédie-Italienne was the name given to the *commedia dell'arte* troupe established in the Hôtel de Bourgogne in 1680, which also became known as the Théâtre-Italien, just as the Comédie-Française was also known as the Théâtre-Français. The names and the contrast they embodied continued to be applied in common parlance even after the Comédie-Italienne merged with the Opéra-Comique in 1762, but the distinction was much sharper when the present story was written.

[4] Presumably a reference to the Janissaries' revolt of 1730, associated with the beginning of the Turko-Persian War of 1730-36, during which the Janissaries switched sides after initially backing the rebels against Ottoman rule, and massacred their former allies.

Whatever time she was there, she was certain of finding an agreeable occupation there. The ennui that she had felt in the early days while waiting for the Beast had entirely dissipated. Her eyes were accustomed to seeing its ugliness. It had asked its stupid questions, and if the conversation had been more extensive, perhaps she would have seen it with more pleasure, but four or five remarks, always the same, spoken coarsely, which only furnished yes or no answers, were not to her taste.

As everything seemed eager to anticipate the Beauty's desires, she took more care in her attire, although she was certain that no one was going to see her—but she owed herself that indulgence, and it was a pleasure for her to dress in the various costumes of all the nations of the world, all the more easily because her wardrobe furnished her with everything she could desire, and presented her with something new every day. In her various adornments, her mirror informed her as to the taste of all nations, and her animals, each in accordance with its talents, imitated her incessantly, the monkeys by their gestures, the parrots by their speech and the birds by their songs.

Such a delightful life ought to have fulfilled all her desires, but one wearies of everything; the greatest joy becomes insipid when it is continual, when it always involves the same things, and one finds oneself exempt from dread and hope. The Beauty experienced that. The memory of her family came to trouble her in the midst of her prosperity. Her happiness could not be perfect, so long as she did not have the satisfaction of obtaining information about her relatives.

As she had became more familiar with the Beast, either by virtue of the habit of seeing it or the mildness she found in its character, she thought she might be able to ask something of it, but she only took that liberty after having obtained a promise from it that it would not become angry.

The question that she asked it was whether the two of them were alone in the château.

"Yes, I affirm it," replied the monster, with a kind of vivacity. "I assure you that you and I, the monkeys and the other animals, are the only living beings in this place."

The Beast said no more, and left more abruptly than usual.

The Beauty had only asked that question in order to try to ascertain whether her lover was not in the palace. She would have liked to see him and talked to him; it was a joy that she would have bought at the price of her liberty, and even all the pleasures that surrounded her. The charming young man no longer existing except in her imagination, she regarded the palace as a prison, which would become her tomb.

Those sad ideas came back to overwhelm her by night. She thought she was on the edge of a great canal. She was afflicted when her dear Unknown, very alarmed by her sad state, said to her while pressing her hands tenderly in his:

"What's the matter my dear Beauty? What can displease you and what can be capable of harming your tranquility? In the name of the amour that I have for you, deign to explain yourself. Nothing will be refused to you. You are the unique sovereign here, everything is submissive to your orders. Whence comes the ennui that is overwhelming you? Is it the sight of the Beast that causes you chagrin? It is necessary to deliver you from it."

At those words, the Beauty thought she saw the Unknown draw a dagger and prepare to cut the throat of the monster, which made no effort to defend itself, and even offered itself to his thrusts with a submission and docility that made the Beauty apprehensive that the Unknown might execute his design before she could raise any obstacle to it, even though she had got up to run to its aid as soon as she realized his intention.

In order to anticipate the effects of her protection she shouted with all her might: "Stop, Barbarian, don't offend my benefactor or give me death."

The young man, who persisted in trying to strike the Beast in spite of the Beauty's cries, said to her angrily: "You don't love me anymore, then, since you take the side of this monster, which opposes itself to my happiness."

"You're an ingrate," she said, still holding him back. "I love you more than life, and I would lose it rather than cease to love you. You are everything to me, and I will not do you the injustice of putting you in parallel with all the wealth of the world. I would renounce all that without difficulty to follow you into the most savage deserts. But those tender sentiments cannot do anything to my gratitude. I owe everything to the Beast; it anticipates my desires; it is the Beast that has procured me the benefit of knowing you, and I will submit to death rather than endure your submitting it to the slightest outrage."

After such combats, the objects disappeared, and the Beauty thought she saw the Lady she had already seen several nights before, who said to her:

"Courage, the Beauty; be the model of generous women; show yourself to be as good as you are charming, and do not hesitate to sacrifice your inclination to your duty. You are taking the true road to happiness. You will be happy, provided that you are not prevented by deceptive appearances."

When the Beauty had woken up she paid attention to that dream, which began to appear mysterious to her. But it was still an enigma for her.

During the day the desire to see her father again prevailed over the anxieties that the monster and the Unknown has caused her during sleep. Thus, neither tranquil by night nor content by day, although in the midst of the greatest opulence, she had nothing to calm her annoyances but the pleasure of spectacles.

She was at the Comédie-Italienne, which she left as soon as the first scene began in order to go to the opera, but she left again with the same promptitude. Her ennui followed her everywhere, she often opened the six windows more than six times each without finding a moment of tranquility there. The nights that she spent were similar to the days; incessantly, in the agitation, sadness took a violent grip upon her, and on her attractions and her health.

She took great care to hide the dolor that was overwhelming her from the Beast, and the monster, which had surprised tears in her eyes several times, on which occasions she told him that she had a slight headache, did not push its curiosity any further. But one evening, her sobs having betrayed her, and no longer able to dissimulate, she said to the Beast, which wanted to know the reason for her chagrin, that she desired to see her relatives again.

At that proposition, the Beast fell, unable to sustain itself, and uttering a sigh—or, rather, a howl capable of causing someone to die of fear—it replied:

"What! You want to abandon an unfortunate Beast, the Beauty! Must I believe that you would have so little gratitude? What do you lack in order to be happy? Ought not the attentions I have for you protect me from your hatred? Unjust as you are, you prefer your father's house to me; you would rather go look after flocks than enjoy the pleasures of life here. It's not by virtue of tenderness for your relatives, it's because of antipathy toward me, if you want to go away."

"No, the Beast," the Beauty replied to him, in a timid and flattering manner, "I don't hate you, and I'd be sorry to lose the hope of seeing you again, but I can't vanquish the desire I have to embrace my family. Permit me to absent myself for two months, and I promise to come back gladly to spend the rest of my life with you, and never to ask you for any other permission."

During that speech, the Beast, lying on the ground with its head extended, only made it known that it was breathing by its dolorous sighs. It replied to the Beauty in these terms:

"I cannot refuse you anything, but it might cost me my life. No matter. In the cabinet nearest to your bedroom you will find four crates; fill them with anything you please, either for yourself or for our relatives. If you break your word you will repent of it, and you will be sorry about the death of your poor Beast when it is too late. Come back at the end of two months and you will find me alive. For your return you have no need of a carriage; simply take your leave of your family in the evening before you go to bed, and when you are in bed turn the stone in your ring inwards and say in a firm tone: 'I want to return to my palace to see my Beast again.' Good night; don't worry about anything, sleep tranquilly; you'll see your father very soon. Adieu, the Beauty."

As soon as she was alone, she hastened to fill her crates with all imaginable gallantries and riches. They were only full when she wearing of putting things into them. After all her preparations, she went to bed. The hope of seeing her family kept her awake incessantly throughout the time that she ought to have been asleep, and sleep only attained her at the hour when it would have been necessary for her to get up. While asleep she saw her lovable Unknown, but he was no longer the same; lying on a bed of grass, he seemed penetrated by the most acute dolor.

The Beauty, touched by seeing him in that state, thought that she could extract him from that profound melancholy, and asked him the reason for his chagrin. But her lover, gazing at her with an expression full of languor, said: "Can you ask me that question, inhuman creature? Do you not know, since you're leaving, and that departure is my death-sentence?"

Don't abandon yourself to dolor, dear Unknown," she replied. "My absence will be brief; I only want to disabuse my family regarding the cruel destiny to which they think I have been subjected; I'll return to the palace immediately. I won't quit you again. How could I abandon an abode that pleases me so much? Furthermore, I've given my word to the Beast to come back, and I can't break it. But why is it necessary for this journey to separate us? Be my guide. I'll put off my journey until tomorrow, in order to obtain the Beast's permission. I'm sure that it won't refuse me. Accept my proposition; we won't quit one another, we'll come back together; my family will be delighted to see you, and I count on their having all the regard for you that you merit."

"I cannot yield to your desires," the lover replied, "unless you are resolved never to return here. That is the only means by which I can leave. See what you want to do. The power of the inhabitants of this place is not great enough to force you to return. Nothing can happen to you except causing grief to the Beast."

"You don't know," said the Beauty, with vivacity, "that it has told me that it will die if I break my word."

"What does that matter to you?" replied the lover. "Would it be a misfortune if, for your satisfaction, it only cost the life of a monster? What use is it to the world? What would be lost by the destruction of a creature that only appears on the earth in order to horrify nature entire?"

"Oh!" cried the Beauty, almost in anger. "Know that I would give my life to preserve its own, and that that monster, which is only so in its form, has a humor so humane that it ought not to be punished by a deformity to which it has made no contribution. I cannot repay its generosity with such black ingratitude."

The Unknown, interrupting her, asked her what she would do if the monster tried to kill him; and if one of the two had to cause the other to perish, to which would she accord her aid?

"I love you uniquely," she said, "but although my tenderness is extreme, it cannot weaken my gratitude to the Beast, and if I found myself in that disastrous situation, I would forestall the dolor that the consequences of that combat might cause me by killing myself. But what is the point of such nasty suppositions, even though they are chimerical? The very idea chills my senses. Let's change the subject."

She set the example by saying to him everything that a tender lover can say to flatter her swain. She was not held back by proud decorum, and, slumber leaving her the liberty to act naturally, she revealed sentiments that she would have constrained in making perfect use of reason.

She slept for a long time, and when she woke up she feared that the Beast might not keep his word.

58

She was in that uncertainty when she heard a sound of human voices that she recognized. Precipitately opening her bed-curtains, she was surprised to find herself in a bedroom that she did not know, the furniture of which was not as superb as that of the Beast's palace.

That prodigy made her hasten to get up and open the bedroom door. She did not recognize anything in the apartments.

What astonished her even more was to find the four crates there that she had packed the previous evening. The transport of her person and her treasures was a proof of the power and generosity of the Beast, but where was she?

She still did not know when, finally, hearing her father's voice, she went to throw her arms around his neck.

Her presence astonished her brothers and her sisters. They looked at her as if she had arrived from another world. All of them embraced her with demonstrations of the greatest joy, but her sisters, in the depths of their hearts, only saw her with pain. Their jealousy had not diminished.

After many caresses on either side, the old man wanted to see her in private in order to know the circumstances of such a surprising journey and to inform her as to the state of his fortune, in which she had played such a large part.

He told her that on the day when he had left the Beast's palace he had reached home that evening without any fatigue, that on the way he has thought about the means to hide his trunks from the knowledge of his children, wanting them to be taken into a little cabinet adjacent to his bedroom, to which he alone had the key. He had regarded that desire as impossible, but as he set foot on the ground the horse carrying the trunks having fled, he had suddenly found himself discharged of the embarrassment of hiding his treasures.

"I confess to you," the old man said to his daughter, "that those riches, of which I believed myself to be deprived, cased me no chagrin; I had not possessed them sufficiently to regret them greatly. But that adventure appeared to me to be a cruel prognostication of your destiny. I did not doubt that the perfidious beast would act in the same fashion with you, and I feared that its benefits in your regard were not durable.

"That idea caused me anxiety; in order to dissimulate it, I pretended to need repose, but that was only to abandon myself without constraint to dolor. I thought your loss certain, but my affliction did not last. At the sight of the trunks that I believed to be lost, I took it as a good augury for your wellbeing. I found them placed in my little cabinet precisely as I had wished. The keys, which I had forgotten on the table of the drawing room where we had spent the night, were in the locks.

"That circumstance, which gave me new evidence of the goodness of the ever-attentive Beast, filled me with joy. It was then, no longer doubting that your adventure would have advantageous consequences, that I reproached myself for the unjust suspicions I had had against the probity of that generous monster, and I begged its pardon a thousand times for the insults that my dolor had caused me to address to it internally.

"Without informing my children of the extent of my fortune, I contented myself with giving them what you had sent them, and showing them jewelry of a mediocre value, I pretended thereafter to have sold it and to have employed the money to procure us a more comfortable life. I bought this house; I have slaves who dispense us from the labors to which necessity had subjected us. My children enjoy a life of ease; that's all that I desired. Ostentation and luxury once attracted envy, and I would attract it again if I put on the face of a rich millionaire.

"Several suitors, the Beauty, having presented themselves for your sisters, I shall marry them soon, and your fortunate arrival will prompt me to do so. Having given them the share that you judged appropriate that I make them of the wealth that you have procured for me, rid of the care of their establishment, we shall live, my daughter, with your brothers, whom your presents have not been capable of consoling for your loss; or, if you prefer, the two of us can live together."

The Beauty, touches by her father's good will and the evidence that he rendered her of the amity of her brothers, thanked him tenderly for all his offers, and thought that she ought not to hide from him that she had not come in order to stay with him. The fellow, although chagrined by not having his daughter for support in his old age, did not try to deflect her from a duty that he recognized as being indispensable.

In her turn, the Beauty told him the story of what had happened to her during her absence. She talked to him about the fortunate life that she led. The fellow, delighted by the charming details of his daughter's adventures, heaped the Beast with blessings. His joy was even greater when the Beauty, opening her crates, showed him immense riches, and told him that he would have the liberty of disposing those that she had brought in favor of his children, having enough of these latest evidences of the Beast's generosity to live agreeably with his sons.

Finding in that monster a soul too beautiful to be lodged in such a vile body, he thought he ought to advice his daughter to marry it, in spite of its ugliness. He even employed the strongest arguments in order to persuade her to make that decision.

"You ought not," he told her, "to rely upon your eyes. You have been exhorted incessantly to allow yourself to be guided by gratitude. By following the movements that it inspires in you, you have been assured that you will be happy. It's true that you have only received that advice in dreams, but those dreams are too sequential and too frequent to be attributed merely to hazard. They promise you considerable advantages; that's enough to vanquish your repugnance. Thus, when the Beast asks you if you want it to go to bed with you, I advise you not to refuse. You admit to being loved tenderly by it. Take the appropriate measures for your union to be eternal. It's more advantageous to have a husband with a good character than one whose only merit is a handsome appearance. How many young women have been married to rich Beasts more

61

bestial than the Beast, which is only so in form and not by sentiment or actions?"

The Beauty agreed with all these arguments, but to resolve to take for a husband a monster horrible in form, with an intelligence as material as its body, did not appear to her to be possible.

"How," she replied to her father, "can I determine to choose a husband with whom I cannot keep company and whose appearance will not be repaired by amusing conversation? No objects will be able to distract me and spare me from that unpleasant commerce. Not to have the pleasure of being sometimes distanced from it; to limit all my pleasure to five or six questions regarding my appetite and my health; to see that bizarre conversation finish with a 'Good night, the Beauty,' a refrain that my parrots know by heart and which they repeat a hundred times a day…it is not in my power to make such an establishment, and I would rather die suddenly than die every day of fear, chagrin, disgust and ennui. Nothing speaks in its favor except the attention that the Beast has in making me one brief visit and only presenting itself before me every twenty-four hours. Is that enough to inspire amour?"

The father agreed that his daughter was right. But, seeing in the Beast so much complaisance, he did not believe it to be so stupid. The order, abundance and good taste that reigned in its palace were not, in his view, the work of an imbecile. In sum, he found it worthy of his daughter's attentions; and the Beauty would have felt a liking for the monster if her nocturnal lover had not raised an obstacle to it. The comparison she made between the two lovers could not be advantageous to the Beast.

The old man was not unaware himself of the great difference that had to be put between one and the other. However, he tried by all sorts of means still to vanquish her repugnance. He reminded her of the advice of the Lady, who had warned her not to be guided by what she could see, and who, in her speeches, had appeared to try to make her understand that the young man could only render her unhappy.

It is easier to reason about amour than to vanquish it. The Beauty did not have the strength to yield to her father's reiterated arguments. He left her without having been able to persuade her. The night, already well-advanced, invited her to take repose, and the daughter, although charmed to see him again, was not sorry when he left her the liberty to go to bed.

She was delighted to find herself alone. Her heavy eyes made her hope that in going to sleep she was about to see her cherished lover again. She was impatient to savor that sweet pleasure. A tender urgency marked the joy that her tender heart might feel in such beautiful commerce. But her afflicted imagination, in representing to her the places where she ordinarily had charming conversations with the dear Unknown, was not sufficiently powerful to make her see him as she had desired.

Several times she woke up, several times she went back to sleep, but amours did not flutter around her bed; to tell the truth, instead of the night full of sweetness and innocent pleasures which she had counted on passing in the arms of sleep, that night was for her extremely long and filled with anxiety. She had never had one like it in the palace of the Beast, and the daylight that she saw appear with a sort of satisfaction and impatience was a welcome release from her cruel irritations.

He father, enriched by the Beast's liberalities, had quit the country residence in order to procure establishments for his daughters. He lived in a large city, where his new fortune had procured him new friends, or rather, new acquaintances. The news that his youngest daughter had returned soon spread among the people he saw. Everyone displayed an equal eagerness to see her, and everyone was as charmed by her intelligence as by her person.

The tranquil days that she had spent in her deserted palace, the innocent pleasures that sweet sleep lavished incessantly upon her, a thousand amusements that had succeeded one another in order that ennui did not enter into her heart—in sum, all the attentions of the monster—had contributed to render her even more beautiful and charming than she had been when her father had quit her. She won the admiration of those who saw her. Her sisters' suitors, without deigning to color their infidelity with the slightest pretext, fell in love with her, and, attracted by the force of her charms, did not blush to abandon their former mistresses. Insensible to the overly marked attentions of a host of idolaters, she neglected nothing to deter them and to make them return to their original objects, but in spite of all her cares, she was not sheltered from the jealousy of her sisters.

Those flighty lovers, far from dissimulating their new flames, invented some fête every day in order to pay their court to her. They even begged her to give a prize that could animate the games that they wanted to hold in her honor. The Beauty, who could not ignore the chagrin she was causing her sisters, but who did not want entirely to refuse the grace that was requested of her with so much instance and in such a gallant fashion, found a means to content all of them by declaring that her sisters and she would give prizes successively to the victors. What she promised was only a flower or something similar; she left her sisters the glory of giving in their turn jewels, diamond crowns, expensive weapons or superb bracelets: presents with which her liberal hand furnished them, and of which she did not want to claim the honor.

The treasures that the monster had lavished upon her left her wanting for nothing. She divided between her sisters all that she had brought of the rarest and most gallant. Giving nothing herself but trifles, and leaving them the pleasure of giving a great deal, she counted on engaging that youth by amour as much as by gratitude. But those lovers only wanted her heart, and what she gave them was more precious to them than all the treasures that the others lavished.

The pleasures that she savored in the midst of her family, although much inferior to those she enjoyed in the home of the Beast, amused her sufficiently for her not to be bored. However, the satisfaction of seeing her father, whom she loved tenderly, the pleasure of being with her brothers, who testified the extent of their amity in a hundred different ways, and the joy of conversing with her sisters, whom she loved even though they did not love her, could not prevent her from regretting her agreeable dreams. In her father's house—what a chagrin for her!—her Unknown did not come into the milieu of her sleep to hold the most tender discourse with her. The eagerness that her sisters' lovers showed did not compensate her for that imaginary pleasure. Even if her character had permitted her to flatter herself with such conquests, she was able to put a great difference between their attentions and those of the Beast and her lovable Unknown.

Their assiduities were only repaid with the greatest indifference, but the Beauty, seeing them in spite of her coldness stubbornly determined to demonstrate the most passionate amour to her, thought that she ought to let them know that they were wasting their time.

The first that she tried to undeceive was the lover of her eldest sister, whom she told that she had only come to the family to attend the marriages of her sisters, especially that of the eldest, and that she would beg her father to hasten its execution. The Beauty did not find a man smitten with her sister's attractions. He no longer sighed for anyone but her, and neither coldness, disdain, nor the threat of departure before the two months had expired, was capable of putting him off.

Very afflicted by not having succeeded in her project, she gave the same speech to the others, in whom she was chagrined to find similar sentiments. To complete her sadness, her unjust sisters, who regarded her as a rival, conceived against her an aversion that they could not dissimulate, and while the Beauty deplored the excessive effect of her charms, she had the dolor of learning that her new admirers, in the idea that they were harming one another and that each of them was the cause of another not being favored, wanted, by virtue of the greatest extravagance, to fight one another.

All those disagreeable circumstances caused her to form the design of departing sooner than she had originally resolved.

Her father and her brothers neglected nothing to retain her, but, a slave to her word, firm in her resolution, neither the tears of the one nor the pleas of the others could win her over. All that they obtained was for her to defer her departure as much as she could.

The two months went by, and every morning she formed the resolution to bid her family adieu without having the strength to take her leave of them in the evening. Torn between sentiments of tenderness and gratitude, she could not incline toward one without doing injustice to the other.

In the midst of her embarrassment, it required nothing less than a dream to seal her determination. She believed that in sleeping at the Beast's palace, she found herself in a deserted pathway, at the end of which was a fort filled with undergrowth, which hid the opening of a cavern, from which frightful groans were emerging. She recognized the voice of the Beast and ran to help it. The monster, which appeared to her in her dream lying on the ground and dying, reproached her for having put it in that sad state, and that she had only repaid his amour with the blackest ingratitude.

Afterwards she saw the Lady that she had seen before while sleeping, who told her in a severe manner that she was doomed if she delayed fulfilling her promises any longer; that she had given her word to the Beast to come back in two months, that they had expired; that if she delayed for one more day the Beast would die; that the disorder that she was causing in her father's house and her sisters' hatred ought to engage her to leave, all the more gladly as everything in the palace of the Beast was designed to give her pleasure.

Frightened by that dream, and fearing that she might be the cause of the death of the Beast, the Beauty woke up with a start, and without further ado declared to her entire family that she did not want o defer her departure any longer.

That news caused different reactions. He father allowed his tears to speak, the sons protested that they would not let her leave, and the despairing lovers swore not to abandon her house. Only the daughters, far from seeming afflicted by their sister's departure, did nothing but praise her good faith, even claiming that virtue for themselves, daring to assure her that if, like the Beauty, they had given their word, the form of the Beast would not make them waver in such a just duty, and that they would already have returned to the marvelous palace. It was thus that they wanted to disguise the cruel jealousy they had in their hearts. However, the Beauty, charmed by their apparent sentiments of generosity, no longer thought about anything but convincing her brothers and her lovers of the obligation she had to leave them.

Her brothers, however, loved her too much to consent to her departure, and the lovers, too infatuated, could not be made to listen to reason. All of them were ignorant of the means by which the Beauty had arrived in her father's house, however, and, having no doubt that the horse that had carried her to the Beast's house the first time would come to fetch her, all resolved collectively to raise obstacles to it. The sisters, who only had the appearances of a pretended good faith to hide the joy that they felt internally at seeing the moment of their sister's departure approaching, feared more than death that they might delay its execution.

The Beauty, however, firm in her resolution, knowing where duty summoned her, and having no more time to lose in order to prolong the days of the Beast, her benefactor, took her leave of her entire family and those interested in her destiny as soon as night fell. She assured them that whatever attention they paid to preventing her departure, she would be in the Beast's home the following morning before they were awake, that all their measures would be futile and that she wanted to return to the enchanted palace.

She did not forget, on going to bed, to rotate her ring.

She slept for a long time, and only woke up when the clock, striking twelve, caused her to hear her name in music. By that sign, she knew that her wishes were accomplished. When she had indicated that she no longer wanted to sleep her bed was surrounded by the animals that were eager to serve her. All of them gave evidence of the satisfaction they had on her return, and made known to her the dolor that her long absence had caused them.

That day appeared longer to her to her that all those she had spent in that place before. Not that she regretted the company that she had left, but she was impatient to see the Beast again, and to spare nothing in her justification. Another hope also animated her, which was of having tender conversations in her sleep with the Unknown, a pleasure of which she had been deprived during the two months that she had just sent with her family, and which she could only savor in the enclosure of the palace.

In sum, the Beast and the Unknown were, alternately, the subject of her reveries. At one moment she reproached herself for not having returned for a lover who, under a monstrous form, caused such a beautiful face to appear. At another, she was sad to have abandoned her heart to some fantastic image who had no other existence that was lent to it by her dreams. She doubted whether her heart ought to prefer a chimera to the real love of a Beast. The dream that made her see the handsome Unknown warned her incessantly not to rely on her eyes. She feared that it might only be a vain illusion to which the vapor of sleep gives birth and awakening destroys.

Thus, still irresolute, loving the Unknown but not wanting to displease the Beast, only seeking to occupy herself with pleasures, she was at the Comédie-Française, which she found incomparably insipid. Closing the window abruptly, she thought she could compensate herself at the Opéra; the music appeared to her to be pitiful. The Italiens also lacked the talent to amuse her. She found their play devoid of wit, intelligence and direction. The ennui and distaste that followed her would not allow her to find pleasure anywhere. She could obtain no relief in the gardens. Her court sought to please her, but some wasted their capers, others their pretty speech and others their twittering.

She was impatient to receive the visit of the Beast, the noise of whose approach she thought she could hear at every minute, but the time so desired arrived without the Beast appearing. Alarmed, and as if angered by that lateness, she did not know what the reason for that absence might be. Suspended between dread and hope, her mind agitated, her heart prey to sadness, she went down to the gardens, determined not to go back into the palace until she had found the Beast.

In all the places she went she could not find any trace of it. She called out, but only the echo repeated her cries. Having spent more than three hours in that disagreeable exercise, overcome by weariness, she sat down on a bench.

She imagined that the Beast was dead, or that it had abandoned the place. She found herself alone in the palace, without the hope of getting out of it. She regretted the Beast's conversation, although it was not diverting for her, and what appeared extraordinary to her was to find so much sensibility for the monster. She reproached herself for not having married it. Regarding herself as the author of its death—for she feared that her overlong absence had caused it—she made herself the harshest and bloodiest reproaches.

In the midst of those sad reflections, she perceived that she was in the very pathway where, during the last night that she had spent in her father's house, she had represented the monster dying in an unknown cavern. Convinced that she had not been led to that place by pure hazard, she directed her steps toward the fort, which she did not find impracticable. She saw a hollow den there that appeared to be the same one that she had seen in the dream. As the moon was only providing a feeble light, the monkey pages appeared hurriedly with a number of torches sufficient to illuminate the lair, and allowed her to see the Beast lying on the ground, which she believed to be asleep.

Far from being frightened by the sight of it, the Beauty was very glad, and. approaching it boldly, she put her hand on its head, calling to it several times. But, feeling it cold and motionless, she no longer doubted that it was dead, which caused her to utter dolorous cries and say the most touching things in the world.

The certainty of its death, however, did not prevent her from making efforts to recall it to life. On putting her hand over its heart she felt, with an inexpressible joy, that it was still breathing. Without amusing herself by caressing it further the Beauty emerged from the cavern and ran to a fountain, from which she drew water with her hands and came back to throw it over him. But as she could only carry very little, and as she spilled it before getting back to the Beast, her help would have been ineffective without the assistance of the monkey courtiers, who ran to the palace and came back with so much diligence that she had a vase for drawing water in an instant, and fortifying liquors.

She made it drink and swallow, which produced an admirable effect, giving it some movement, and shortly afterwards it recovered consciousness. She animated it with her voice, and stroked it so much that it pulled itself together.

"How much anxiety you have caused me," she said, obligingly, to the Beast. "I did not know to what extent I loved you; the fear of losing you has made me realize that I was attached to you by stronger bonds than those of gratitude. I swear to you that I would only have thought of dying if I had not been able to save your life."

At those tender words the Beast, feeling entirely relieved, replied in a voice that was as yet still feeble: "You are good, the Beauty, to love such an ugly monster, but you do well; I love you more than my life. I thought that you would not come back again. I would have died of it. Since you love me, I want to live. Go and repose, and be certain that you will be as fortunate as your good heart merits."

The Beauty had not yet heard the Beast pronounce such a long speech. It was not eloquent, but it pleased her by the quality of tenderness and sincerity that she thought she could detect within it She had expected to be scolded by it, or at least to receive reproaches. She had from then on a better opinion of its character; no longer finding it so stupid, she even regarded its curt responses as something like a hint of prudence; and, increasingly prejudiced in its favor, she retired to her apartment with her mind full of the most flattering ideas.

Extremely fatigued, the Beauty found all the refreshments there of which she had need. Her heavy eyes promised her pleasant slumber. Asleep almost as soon as she had laid down, her dear Unknown did not fail to present himself. How many tender things he said to her to express the pleasure he had in seeing her again! He assured her that she would be happy; that it was no longer a matter of anything but following the impulses dictated to her by the generosity of her heart.

The Beauty asked him if that would be in marrying the Beast. The Unknown replied that there was only that sole means. She felt a sort of resentment at that, and even found it extraordinary that her lover was advising her to render his rival happy.

After that first dream, she thought she saw the Beast dead at her feet. An instant afterwards, the Unknown appeared and disappeared at the same time to let the Beast take his place. What she remarked most distinctly was the Lady, who seemed to say to her: "I am content with you. Always follow the movements of reason, and don't worry about anything; I will take charge of the care of rendering you happy."

Although asleep, the Beauty appeared to discover her inclination for the Unknown and her repugnance for the monster, which she did not find lovable. The Lady smiled at her scruple and told her not to worry about her tenderness for the Unknown, that the impulses she felt had nothing incompatible with the intention she had to do her duty, that without resistance, she could follow it, and that her happiness would be perfect in marrying the Beast.

That dream, which finished with her slumber, was for her an inexhaustible source of reflections. In the last and in the others she found more foundation than dreams commonly have; that is what determined her to consent to the strange hymen. But the image of the Unknown came incessantly to trouble her. That was the only obstacle, but it was not mediocre. Still uncertain of what she had to do, she went to the

71

Opéra without putting an end to her embarrassment. After the spectacle she sat down at table; only the arrival of the Beast was capable of conforming her determination.

Far from making her reproaches with regard to her long absence, the monster, as if the pleasure of seeing her had made it forget its past irritations, appeared, on coming into to the Beauty's apartment, only to be in haste to know whether she had been well amused, if she had been well received, and whether her health had been god.

She replied to those questions, and added that she had purchased dearly all the pleasures that she had enjoyed by its cares, that they had been followed by cruel pains by virtue of the state in which she had found it.

The Beast thanked her laconically, after which, wanting to take its leave of her, it asked her, as usual, whether she wanted it to go to bed with her.

The Beauty took some time to respond, but, finally making her decision, said to it, trembling: "Yes, Beast, I would like that, provided that you give me your faith, and that you receive mine."

"I give it to you," said the Beast, "and promise never to have any other wife."

"And I," replied the Beauty, "receive you as my husband, and swear to you a tender and faithful love."

Scarcely had she pronounced those words than a volley of artillery was heard, and in order that she could not doubt that it was a sign of rejoicing, she saw the windows all ablaze with the illumination of more than twenty thousand rockets, which was renewed for more than three hours. They formed love-knots; gallant cartouches represented the monogram of the Beauty, and the legend was legible in distinct letters: LONG LIVE THE BEAUTY AND HER HUSBAND.

That charming spectacle having lasted sufficiently long, the Beast indicated to its new wife that it was time to go to bed.

However scant impatience that the Beauty had to find herself next to that singular spouse, she went to bed. The lights were extinguished at that moment.

The Beast, approaching her, caused the Beauty the apprehension that the weight of its body might crush their bed, but she was agreeably astonished to sense that the monster placed itself at her side as lightly as she had just done. Her surprise was even greater when she heard it snoring almost immediately, and that by its tranquility, she had a certain proof that it was sleeping profoundly.

In spite of her astonishment, accustomed as she was to extraordinary things, after having given a few moments to reflection, she went to sleep, as tranquilly as her husband, not doubting that the sleep would be mysterious, as with everything that happened in the palace.

Scarcely had she fallen asleep than her dear Unknown came, as usual, to render her a visit. He was more cheerful and more elaborately adorned than he had ever been.

"How obliged I am to you, charming Beauty," he said to her. "You have delivered me from the prison in which I have been groaning for such a long time. Your marriage to the Beast will render a king to his subjects, a son to his mother and life to his kingdom. We shall all be happy."

At that speech, the Beauty felt a violent resentment, seeing that the Unknown, far from giving evidence of the despair into which the engagement she had just made should have cast him, was making an excessive joy shine in his eyes. She was about to express her discontentment to him when the Lady appeared in the dream in her turn.

"Now you are victorious," she told her. "We owe you everything, the Beauty, you have just preferred gratitude to any other sentiment; there not many who, like you, would have had the strength to keep their word at the expense of their satisfaction, or to risk their own life to save that of their father; in recompense, there are not many who can hope to enjoy for ever a happiness similar to that which your virtue has enabled you to attain. You only know the least part of it at present. The return of the sun will tell you more."

After the Lady, the Beauty saw the young man again, but lying down as if dead. The entire night passed in making different dreams. Those agitations had become familiar to her, and they did not prevent her from sleeping for a long time. It was broad daylight than woke her up. It shone in her bedroom even more than usual; her she-monkeys had not closed the curtains—which gave her the opportunity to cast her eyes upon the Beast.

Initially taking the spectacle that she beheld for an ordinary sequel of her dreams, and believing than she was still dreaming, her joy and surprise were extreme when she had no more grounds to doubt that what she saw was real.

The previous evening, on going to lie down, she had placed her herself on the edge of her bed, thinking that she could not leave too much room for her frightful spouse. It had snored at first, but she had ceased to hear it before falling asleep. The silence that it maintained, when she woke up having made her doubt that it was beside her, and imagining that it had got up quietly, in order to know the truth, she had turned over with as much precaution as was possible for her, and was agreeably surprised to find, instead of the Beast, her dear Unknown.

That charming sleeper appeared to her a thousand times more handsome than he had been during the night; in order to be certain that he was really the same, she got up and went to take from her dressing-room the portrait that she usually wore n her arm. But she could not be mistaken. Occupied with the marvelous nature of that torpor, she spoke to him in the hope of putting an end to it. As he did not awake at her voice, she tugged him by the arm. That second attempt was also futile, and only served to make her aware that there was enchantment in it, which made her resolve to let the charm, which probably had a prescribed term, pass.

As she was alone, she did not fear scandalizing anyone by the liberties she might take with him. In any case, he was her husband. That is why, giving free rein to her tender sentiments, she kissed him a thousand times and then made the decision to wait patiently for the end of that species of lethargy.

How charmed she was to be united with the only object that had forced her to hesitate, and to have by duty what she would have wanted by taste. She no longer doubted the happiness that she had been promised in her dreams. It was then that she knew that the Lady had told her the truth, in representing to her that it would not be incompatible to have, simultaneously, amour for the Beast and for her Unknown, since the two of them were only one.

However, her husband did not wake up. After a little nourishment, she tried to distract herself by her ordinary occupations, but they appeared insipid to her. Not being able to resolve to leave her bedroom, in order not to remain idle there, she took up a musical instrument and began to sing. Her birds joined in with her in a concert all the more charming because the Beauty always hoped that it would be interrupted by the awakening of her spouse, for she had flattered herself that she might destroy the enchantment by the sound of her voice.

It was destroyed, in fact, but not in the fashion that she had hoped. The Beauty heard the unfamiliar noise of a chariot rolling under the windows of her apartment, and the voices of several people approaching her bedroom. At the same moment, the ape who was captain of the guard announced the ladies via the beak of his parrot interpreter.

The Beauty, looking through the window, saw the chariot that had brought them. It was of an entirely new model, and an unparalleled beauty. Four white stags with golden antlers and hooves, superbly harnessed, were pulling the rig, the singularity of which augmented the desire she had to become acquainted with those it had brought.

By the noise that was becoming louder she knew that the ladies were drawing nearer and that they must be close to the antechamber. She thought she was obliged to go to meet them.

She recognized in one of the two the Lady whom she was accustomed to see in dreams. The other was no less beautiful; her aristocratic and distinguished bearing testified clearly enough that she was an illustrious person. That unknown woman had passed her first youth but she had an air so majestic that the Beauty did not know to which one to address her compliment.

She was in that embarrassment when the one she already knew, and who appeared to have some superiority over the other, addressing her companion, said to her: "Well, Queen, what do you think of this beautiful young woman? You owe your son's return to life to her, for you'll agree that the deplorable fashion in which he was enjoying it cannot be called living. Without her, you would never have seen the Prince again, and he would have remained in the horrible form into which he had been transformed if he had not found a unique person in the world whose virtue and courage equaled her beauty. I believe that you will see with pleasure the son that she is rendering to you, having become his. They love one another, and at present nothing is lacking their perfect happiness but your consent; will you refuse it to them?"

At these words the Queen, embracing the Beauty tenderly, exclaimed: "Far from refusing them my consent, I put my sovereign felicity into it. Charming and virtuous young woman, to whom I have so much obligation, tell me who you are, and the name of the sovereigns fortunate enough to have given birth to such a perfect princess."

"Madame," replied the Beauty, modestly, "I have no longer had a mother for a long time. My father is a merchant well known in society for his good faith and his misfortunes, who by his birth..."

At that sincere declaration the astonished Queen took two steps back. "What! You are nothing but the daughter of a merchant...! Oh, great fay...!" she added, with a mortified expression, looking at her. She fell silent after those few words, but her expression revealed clearly enough what she was thinking, and her discontentment was expressed in her eyes.

"It seems to me," said the fay, proudly, "that you are not content with my choice. This young woman's condition excites your scorn. She was, however, the only person in the world capable of fulfilling my project and rendering your son happy..."

"I am very grateful," replied the Queen, and added: "But, powerful Intelligence, I cannot help representing to you the bizarre assemblage of the finest blood in the world, of which my son is the issue, with the obscure blood from which the person you want to unite him emerges. I confess to you that I am scarcely flattered by the pretended happiness of this Prince, if it is necessary to purchase it by an alliance so shameful for us and so unworthy of him. Would it have been impossible for him to find in the world a person whose virtue equaled her birth? I know the names of so many estimable Princesses; why will it not be permissible for me to have the pleasure of seeing him possess one of them?"

As they reached that point the handsome Unknown appeared. The arrival of his mother and the fay had awakened him, and the noise they had caused had had more effect than all the Beauty's efforts; the order of the spell determined it thus.

The Queen held him in her embrace for a long time without saying a word. She had rediscovered a son whose fine qualities rendered him worthy of her tenderness. What joy for that Prince to see himself liberated from a frightful form and an even more dolorous stupidity, that it had affected, and which had not obscured its reason. He had recovered the liberty of appearing in his ordinary form thanks to the object of his amour, which rendered her all the more precious to him.

After the initial transports that blood had inspired in him for his mother, the Prince interrupted them in order to follow the duty and the gratitude that pressed him to render thanks to the fay. He did so in the most respectful and briefest terms, in order to have the liberty of turning his urgency in the direction of the Beauty.

He had already made it known by his tender gaze, and to confirm what his eyes had said, he was about to add to it in the most touching terms when the fay retained him and indicated to him that she took him as a judge between his mother and her.

"Your mother," she said to him, "condemns the engagement that you have contracted with the Beauty. She finds that her birth is unworthy of yours. For myself, I believe that her virtues cause the inequalities to disappear. It is for you, Prince, to decide which of us is thinking in accordance with your taste. In order that you have an entire liberty to make us know your true sentiments, I declare to you that it is permissible for you not to constrain yourself; even though you have given your faith to this attractive individual, you may take it back. I am certain that the Beauty will return it to you without any difficulty. Although you have recovered your natural form thanks to her kindness, I assure you that her generosity will push disinterest as far leaving you the liberty of disposing of your hand in favor of the person to whom the Queen will advise you to give it..."

"What do you say, the Beauty?" the fay went on, turning toward her. "Am I mistaken in explaining your sentiments? Would you want a husband who would regret it?"

"Certainly not, Madame," replied the Beauty. "The Prince is free; I renounce the honor of being his wife. When I accepted his faith, I believed that I was granting mercy to something less than human. I only engaged himself to him with the design of doing him a signal favor. Ambition played no part in my intentions. Thus, Great Fay, I beg you to demand nothing of the Queen in a circumstance in which I cannot criticize her delicacy."

"Well, Queen, what do you say to that?" said the fay, in a disdainful and piqued tone. "Do you think that Princesses who are only so by the caprice of fortune merit the high rank in which fate has placed them any more than this young woman?

For myself, I think that she ought not to be held responsible for an origin above which her virtue elevates her sufficiently..."

The Queen responded, with a kind of confusion: "The Beauty is admirable; her merit is infinite, nothing is above it. But Madame, can we not find other means of recompensing her? Can I not do it without sacrificing my son's hand?

"Yes, the Beauty," the Queen said to her, "I owe you so much than I cannot measure it; I put no limit on your desires. Wish boldly; I will grant you anything except that one point. But the difference will not be very great for you. Choose a spouse in my court. No matter how great a Lord he is, he will have reason to esteem himself fortunate, and in your consideration I will place him so close to the throne that there will be hardly any difference."

"I thank you, Madame," the Beauty replied to her, "but I have no recompense to demand of you. I am amply rewarded by the pleasure of having put an end to the enchantment that was stealing a great Prince from his mother and his kingdom. My happiness would be perfect if it were to my Sovereign that I had rendered that service. All that I desire is that the fay will deign to return me to my father."

The Prince, who, by order of the fay, had maintained silence throughout this discourse, was not the master of retaining it any longer, and his respect for orders so inconvenient was no longer capable of holding him back. He threw himself at the feet of the fay and his mother, and begged them with the most ardent insistence not to render him even more unhappy than he was by sending the Beauty away and depriving him of the happiness of being her husband.

At these words the Beauty, looking at him with a gaze filled with tenderness, but accompanied by a noble pride, said to him: "I cannot hide from you, Prince, the sentiments that I have for you; your disenchantment is the proof, and I would try in vain to disguise them. I confess, without blushing, that I love you more than myself. Why should I dissimulate it? One only ought to disavow criminal impulses. Mine are filled with innocence, and are authorized by the consent of the generous fay, to whom you and I owe so much. But if I was able to renounce them when I believed that my duty ordered me to sacrifice it to the Beast, you must be persuaded that I would not belie myself on this occasion, when it is no longer a matter of the interest of a monster, but yours.

"It is sufficient for me to know who you are, and who I am, to renounce the glory of being your wife. I even dare say that if, vanquished by your prayers, the Queen granted you the consent you desire, she would be doing nothing for you, since in my house and in my amour itself you would find an insurmountable obstacle. I repeat, the only favor for which I ask is that of returning to the bosom of my family, where I will conserve an eternal memory of your generosity and your amour."

"Generous Fay," cried the Prince, putting his hands together in a suppliant fashion, "please prevent the Beauty from departing, and render me instead my monstrous form. On that condition I would remain her husband; she has given her faith to the Beast, and I prefer that advantage to all those that she is procuring me, if I cannot enjoy them without paying so dearly."

The fay made no reply. She looked fixedly at the Queen, who was touched by so many virtues, but whose pride was not shaken. Her son's dolor afflicted her, without making her forget that the Beauty was the daughter of a merchant and nothing more. However, she was apprehensive of the anger of the fay, whose expression and silence marked her indignation clearly enough. Her embarrassment was extreme. Not having the strength to say a word, she feared seeing a conversation by which the protective Intelligence was offended finish in a disastrous fashion.

No one spoke for several moments, but the fay finally broke the silence, and, darting an affectionate gaze at the lovers, she said to them: "I find you worthy of one another. One cannot think without crime of separating so much merit. You will remain united; I promise you that. I have power enough to execute it."

At those words the Queen shivered; she had opened her mouth in order to utter a few protests but the fay prevented her from doing so, saying to her: "As for you, Queen, the scant value you place on a virtue devoid of the vain ornaments that alone command your esteem authorizes me to make you bitter reproaches. But I pardon that sin of pride, which is inspired in you by the rank you hold, and I will not take any other vengeance that that I take from the petty violence I am doing you, and for which you will thank me before long."

At those words the Beauty kissed the fay's knees, and cried: "Oh, don't expose me to the dolor of hearing myself reproached all my life for being unworthy of the rank to which your generosity wants to raise me; remember that the Prince, who believes at present that his happiness consists of the gift of my hand, might perhaps think like the Queen before very long."

"No, no, the Beauty, have no fear," said the fay, "the misfortunes that you anticipate cannot arrive. I know a sure means of preserving you from them, and if the Prince is capable of scorning you after having married you, it will be necessary for him to find another reason than the inequality of condition. Your birth is not inferior to his. Indeed, the advantage is very considerable on your side, since the truth is," she said, proudly, to the Queen, "that this is your niece, and what ought to render her respectable to you is that she is mine, being the daughter of my sister, who was not, like you, the slave of a dignity of which virtue made the principal luster.

"That fay, able to estimate true merit, did the King of the Fortunate Isle, your brother, the honor of marrying him. I have protected the fruit of their amour from the fury of a fay who wanted to be her mother-in-law. Since she was born I have destined her to be your son's wife. In concealing the effect of my good will from you, I wanted to give your confidence time to burst forth. I had some reason to believe that you could have had more in me. You could have relied on my cares with regard to the destiny of the Prince. I have given evidence of taking sufficient interest in that, and you ought not to have been apprehensive that I would expose him to anything shameful for you or for him." She continued with a smile that still had a hint of bitterness: "I am convinced, Madame, that you will not take disdain any further, and that you will be eager to honor us with your alliance."

Nonplussed and confused, the Queen could only respond. The sole means of repairing her fault was to make a sincere confession of it and to give evidence of a true repentance. "I am culpable, generous Fay," she said to her. "Your good will ought to have been a sure guarantee that you would not allow my son to make an alliance that would dishonor him. But please pardon the prejudices of an illustrious birth. I was told that royal blood could not be misallied without shame. I would merit it, I confess, if, to punish me, you gave the Beauty a mother-in-law worthy of possessing her, but you take too generous an interest in my son to render him the victim of my fault.

"As for you, dear Beauty," she continued, kissing her, "you ought not to hold my resistance against me. It was only caused by the desire to give me son to my niece, whom the fay had assured me was alive in spite of the appearances to the contrary. She had painted me a picture of her so charming that, without knowing you, I loved you tenderly enough to expose myself to the indignation of the Intelligence in order to conserve the throne and my son's heart for you."

In saying that, she recommenced her caresses, and the Beauty received them with respect. The Prince, for his part, delighted by that agreeable news, marked his joy by his gaze.

"Now we are all content," said the fay, "and to conclude this happy adventure, we only lack the consent of the King, the father of the Princess, but we shall soon see him in person."

The Beauty begged her to permit that the man who had raised her, and to whom she had believed she owed life, be present at her good fortune.

"I like that concern," said the fay. "It is worthy of a beautiful soul, and since you wish it, I shall take charge of informing him."

Then, taking the Queen by the hand, she took her way under the pretext of showing her the enchanted palace. That was to allow the newlyweds the liberty of conversing for the first time without constraint and without the aid of illusion. They tried to follow them but she forbade them to do so.

The happiness that they were about to enjoy penetrated them with an equal joy, and they were unable to doubt their mutual tenderness. The confused and inconsequential conversation, and the protestations renewed a hundred times over, were for them a more certain testimony than a discourse full of eloquence would have been.

After having exhausted what amour could say on such an occasion to persons whose hearts are veritably touched, the Beauty asked her lover by what misfortune he had been so cruelly metamorphosed into the Beast. She then asked him to inform her of all the events that had preceded his cruel metamorphosis. The Prince, who was no less ardent to obey her for having changed his face, and not wanting to defer it any longer, spoke in the following terms.

The Beast's Story

My father, the King, died before I came into the world. The Queen could not have been consoled for her loss if the interest of the child she was carrying had not combated her grief. My birth caused her an extreme joy; it was to the pleasure of bringing up the fruit of the amour of a spouse so dearly beloved that the good fortune of dissipating her affliction was reserved.

The cares of my education and the fear of losing me occupied her uniquely. She was seconded in her views by a fay of her acquaintance, who showed her nothing but the ardor of preserving me from all sorts of accidents. The Queen was infinitely grateful to her, but she was not content when she asked her to put me in her hands. That Intelligence did not have the reputation of being good; she was reckoned to be capricious in her favors; she was feared more than loved, and even when my mother had been convinced of her good will, she could not be determined to lose sight of me.

However, for fear of enduring the disastrous effects of the vindictive fay's resentment, she was advised by prudent individuals that she should not refuse flatly. In yielding me to her voluntarily, there was no appearance that she might do me any harm. Experience suggested that she only delighted in harming those she thought had offended her. The Queen agreed with that, but was still reluctant to see herself deprived of the pleasure of gazing at me continually with a mother's eyes, with enabled her to discover graces in me that I only owed to her prevention.

She was still irresolute as to what to do when a powerful neighbor believed that it would be easy for him to take possession of the estates of a child governed by a woman. He had entered my kingdom with a formidable army. The Queen raised one in haste, and with a courage superior to her sex, she put herself at the head of her troops and went to defend our frontiers.

It was then that, being obliged to quit me, she could not dispense with confiding the care of my education to the fay. I was placed in her hands, after she had sworn the oath most sacred to her that she would return me to the Court without any difficulty as soon as the war was over, which my mother counted on being concluded in a year at the most.

In spite of all the advantages she obtained, however, it was not possible for her to see our capital again so soon. In order to profit from her victory, after having expelled the enemy from our estates, she pursued him in his own. She took entire provinces, won battles, and finally reduced the vanquished to requesting a shameful peace, which he only obtained under very harsh conditions.

After that fortunate success, the Queen departed triumphantly, and savored in advance the pleasure of seeing me again. Having learned *en route*, however, that against the faith of the treaties, the unworthy enemy had had our garrisons murdered and had retaken almost all the places that he had been obliged to cede, she was constrained to retrace her steps. Honor took precedence over the eagerness that recalled her to my presence, and she formed the resolution not to end the war until she had rendered her enemy incapable of committing further treasons.

The time that she employed in that second expedition was very considerable. She had flattered herself that two or three campaigns would be sufficient, but she had to combat an adversary who was as clever as he was treacherous. He strove to make entire provinces revolt or to debauch entire battalions, which forced the Queen not to distance herself from her army for fifteen years. She did not think of summoning me to her side; she always imagined that she was in her final month of absence and on the point of seeing me again.

Meanwhile, the fay, conforming to her word, had devoted every care to my education. Since the day when she had taken charge of me in my kingdom she had remained with me and had never ceased to give me marks of her attention with regard to my health ad my pleasures. By my respect, I showed her how sensible I was of her generosity; I had the same regard for her and the same urgency that I would have had for my mother, and gratitude inspired me with sentiments as tender in her favor.

For some time, she appeared satisfied by that, but she undertook a journey of several years, the secret of which she did not communicate to me, and on her return, admiring the effect of her cares, she conceived for me a tenderness different from that of a mother. She had permitted me to give her that name, but now she forbade me to employ it. I obeyed, without enquiring about the reasons she might have, nor suspecting what she required of me.

I could see clearly that she was not content, but how could I suspect the reason for the complaints she made incessantly about my ingratitude? I was all the more surprised by her reproaches because I did not believe that I merited them. They were always followed or preceded by the most tender caresses. I did not have enough experience to understand them. It was necessary that she explain herself, and she did so one day when I gave evidence of a chagrin mingled with impatience regarding the tardiness of the Queen.

She made me a few reproaches, and when I assured her that my tenderness for my mother did not diminish in any way that which I owed to her, she replied that she was not jealous, although she had done a great deal for me, and had resolved to do even more. But she added that in order to give free rein to the designs she had made in my favor, it was necessary that I marry her, that she did not want to be loved by me as a mother, but as a lover, that she had no doubt that I would receive her proposal with gratitude and that I would have a great deal of joy in accepting it; that it was henceforth only a matter of abandoning myself to the pleasure that the certainty of possessing such a powerful fay ought to cause me, which would preserve me from all dangers and procure me a life full of charms and heaped with glory.

At that proposal I was embarrassed. Educated in my own land, I knew enough about the world to have observed among married couples that some were happy by virtue of a conformity of age and humor, and that others had much of which to complain because different circumstances had put an antipathy between them that could be their torture.

The fay, old, ugly and of an arrogant character, did not give me any hope of a destiny as agreeable as the one she was promising me. I was very far from feeling for her what it is necessary to feel for a person with whom one wants to spend one's life agreeably. I did not want, in any case, to engage myself at such an early age. I had no other passion than that of seeing the Queen again and distinguishing myself at the head of her armies. I sighed after my liberty; that was the only thing that could satisfy me, and the only one that she refused me.

I had often begged her to permit me to go to share the perils into which I knew the Queen had hurled herself for the sake of my interests, but my pleas before that day had been futile. Pressed to respond to the astonishing declaration that she had made me, I was embarrassed; I reminded her that she had often told me that it was not permissible for me to dispose of myself without my mother's orders, and during her absence.

"That is how I understand it," she said. "I do not want to oblige you to do otherwise; it is sufficient for me that you refer the matter to the Queen."

I have already said, beautiful Princess, that I had not been able to obtain from the fay the liberty to go to find my mother, the Queen. The desire she had to have her consent, which she expected to obtain, obliged her to grant me, without even asking her, what she had always refused me. But she put a condition on it that was not agreeable to me, which was that of accompanying me. I made efforts to dissuade her, but it was impossible, and we departed, accompanied by a numerous escort.

We arrived on the eve of a decisive affair. The Queen had arranged things so well that the following day would decide the enemy's fate, who no longer had any resources if he lost the battle. My presence, causing an extreme pleasure in the camp, only augmented the courage of the troops, who took my arrival as a favorable augury for the victory. The Queen thought she might die of joy.

After that first transport, however, the pleasure that it had caused gave way to the most intense alarms. While I was flattering myself with the pleasant hope of acquiring glory, the Queen shivered at the thought of the danger to which I was about to expose myself. Too generous to want to divert me, she begged me, in the name of all her tenderness, to spare myself as much as honor would permit. She begged the fay not to abandon me on that occasion.

Her solicitations were unnecessary; the overly susceptible Intelligence was as apprehensive as the Queen, because she had no secret with which to preserve me from the hazards of war. At any rate, by inspiring me instantaneously with the art of commanding an army and the prudence necessary for such a great employment, she did a great deal. The most experienced leaders admired me.

Having become master of the battlefield, the victory was complete; I had the good fortune to save the life of the Queen and prevent her from being made a prisoner of war. The enemies were pursued with so much vigor that they abandoned their camp, lost their baggage and more than three-quarters of their army, while we had only suffered very mediocre losses.

A slight wound that I received was the only advantage of which the enemy could boast. But, that event having made the Queen fear that, if the war continued, greater misfortunes might overtake me, in spite of the devotion of the entire army, whose pride had been redoubled by my presence, she made peace on terms more advantageous than those for which the vanquished had dared to hope.

Shortly thereafter, we resumed the road to the capital, which we entered in triumph. The occupations of the war and the eternal presence of my aged conquest had prevented me from warning the Queen about that incident. She was entirely surprised when the harpy said to her, without circumlocution, that she was resolved to marry me immediately. That declaration was made in this very palace, not as superb as it is today. It was the pleasure-house of the late King, of the embellishment of which a thousand occupations had not permitted him to think. My mother, who cherished that which he had loved, chose it for preference in order to relax there from the fatigues of war.

At the fay's declaration, unable to render herself mistress of her first reaction, and not knowing the art of dissimulation, she cried: "Can you think, Madame of the bizarre assortment that you are proposing to me?"

It is true that it impossible to think of one more ridiculous. In addition to the fay's advanced age, almost decrepitude, she was so ugly as to inspire fear. It was not the years that had made her ugly—if she had been beautiful in her youth she might have conserved it with the aid of her art—but being naturally ugly, her power had been unable to give her an artificial beauty for more than one day every year, and when that day was past she reverted to her original condition.

The fay was surprised by the Queen's declaration. Her self-regard had hidden from her everything that was frightful about her, and she expected that her power ought to substitute for the attractions of which she was deprived.

"What do you mean," she said to the Queen, "by the term *bizarre assortment*? Remember that there is an imprudence in making me remember when I deign to forget. You ought only to think of congratulating yourself for having a son lovable enough for me to prefer him to the most powerful elemental spirits, and since I deign to lower myself as far as him, receive with respect the honor that I have the generosity of offering you, without giving me time to take it back."

The queen, as proud as the fay, had never understood that there was a rank above the throne. She did not think much of the pretended honor that the Intelligence was offering her. Having always commanded everyone who approached her, she was not ambitious for the advantage of having a daughter-in-law to whom it was necessary to render respects. Thus, far from responding, she remained as if motionless, and contented herself with fixing her eyes upon me. I was as surprised as she was, and was looking at her with the same expression with which she was looking at me; it was not difficult for the fay to discern that our silence expressed naively sentiments very different from the joy that she wanted to inspire in us.

"What is the significance of what I see?" she said, bitterly. "How comes it that the mother and the son are saying nothing? Has this pleasant surprise taken away the use of your tongues, or are you blind enough and reckless enough not to accept my offers? Speak up, Prince," she said to me, "will you be sufficient ingrate and imprudent to scorn my generosity? Will you not consent immediately to give me your hand?"

"No, Madame, I assure you," I said, precipitately. "Although I am sincerely grateful for everything I owe to you, I cannot resolve to acquit myself in that way, and, with the Queen's permission, I do not want to lose my liberty so soon.

Give me any other means of recognizing your generosity, and I would not find it impossible. But dispense me from employing the one you propose to me, if you please, for..."

"What, paltry creature," she interrupted me, furiously, "you dare to resist me? And you, stupid Queen, see such pride without indignation? What am I saying, without indignation? It's you who are authorizing it, since it is from your insolent gaze that he has taken the audacity of his response."

The Queen, already piqued by the scornful expressions of which the fay had made use, was no longer able to contain herself, and, chancing to dart her gaze at a mirror before which we were standing during the time that the malevolent fay was still pressing her, she said: "Can I tell you that you ought not to represent yourself thus? Deign to consider without prejudice the objects that that mirror presents to you, and it will answer for me."

The fay understood easily what the Queen meant. "It's the beauty of your precious son, then, that renders you so vain, and that's what has exposed me to a shameful refusal. I appear to you to be unworthy of him. Well, then, she continued, raising her voice in a furious tone, "after having devoted all my cares to rendering him so charming, it's necessary that I crown my work and give you both a substance as new as it is sensible, to remind you of what you owe me. Go, wretch" she said to me, "and boast of having refused me your heart and your hand, and make the sacrifice of them to someone you find more worthy of them than me."

As she spoke those words, my terrible admirer struck me on the head. The blow was so heavy that I fell face down on the ground, and thought that I had been crushed by the fall of a mountain. Angered by that insult, I tried to get up again, but it was impossible. The weight of my body was so great that it prevented me from doing so. All that I could do was sustain myself on my hands, which had instantly become horrible paws, the sight of which caused me to perceive my transformation. Immediately, I cast my gaze upon the fatal mirror, and it was no longer possible for me to doubt my cruel and sudden metamorphosis.

The dolor that I felt rendered me immobile. At that tragic spectacle, the Queen was beside herself. To put the final seal on her barbarity, the furious fay also said to me, in a mocking tone: "Go make illustrious conquests, more worthy of you than an august fay. And as one has no need of intelligence when one is so handsome, I order you to appear as stupid as you are frightful, and to wait in that condition, in order to resume your original form, until a beautiful young woman comes voluntarily to find you, even though she is convinced that you will devour her.

"It is also necessary," she continued, "that after she no longer fears for her life, she acquires a sufficiently tender affection for you to offer to marry you. Until you encounter that rare individual, I want you to be a subject of horror for yourself and for all those who see you.

"As for you, excessively fortunate mother of such a lovable child," she said to the Queen, "I warn you that if you tell anyone that this monster is your son, his form will never change. It is without the aid of interest, ambition and the charms of his intelligence that he must quit it. Don't be impatient, you won't have to wait for long. He's dainty enough to encounter a remedy for his woes soon. Adieu."

"Oh, cruel Fay!" cried the Queen. "If my refusal has offended you, avenge yourself on me. Take my life, but don't destroy your work, I implore you..."

"You can't think so, Great Princess," said the fay, in an ironic tone. "You're lowering yourself too much; I'm not beautiful enough for you to deign to converse with me. But I'm firm in my determination. Adieu, Powerful Queen. Adieu, Handsome Prince, it's unjust for me to weary you further with my odious presence. I shall retire, but the charity still remains to me of warning you"—she turned to me—"that it's necessary to forget who you are. If you allow yourself to be flattered by vain respect, or ostentatious titles, you are doomed without recourse, and you are also doomed if you dare to make use of your wit to please in conversation."

After those words, she disappeared, and left the Queen and me in a state that can neither be described or imagined. Plaints are the consolation of the unfortunate; that was too feeble an aid for us. My mother took the decision to stab herself and I to throw myself into the nearby canal. We were both about to execute such fatal designs, without communicating them to one another, but a person of majestic stature whose expression inspired a profound respect came to let us know that there is cowardice in succumbing to the greatest accidents, and that with time and courage, there is no misfortune that cannot be vanquished.

The Queen was inconsolable, however; her eyes shed abundant tears and, not knowing how to tell her subjects that their sovereign had changed into a horrible beast, her only resource was a terrible despair. The fay—for she was one, the same one that you see here—knowing her dolor and her embarrassment, made her remember the indispensable obligation she had to conceal that frightful adventure from her people. She remonstrated with her that, without abandoning herself to despair, it would be better to seek a remedy for her woes.

"Is there any powerful enough," the Queen cried, "to prevent the will of a fay from being executed?"

"Yes, Madame," the fay replied. "There are remedies for everything. I am a fay, like the one whose fury you have just experienced; I have no less power. It is true that I cannot repair immediately the harm that she has done to you, for it is not permitted to us to oppose ourselves directly to one another's will. The one who has caused your misfortune has lived longer than me; among us, antiquity is a respectable title. As she was unable to prevent herself from imposing a condition that might break the deadly charm, I shall make use of it. I confess that it is difficult to terminate this enchantment, but it does not appear to me to be impossible. By devoting all my cares to it, let us see what I can do for you."

Then she took a book from her robe, and after having taken a few mysterious steps, she sat down at a table and read for a considerable time with an application that made her sweat. Afterwards, she closed her book and meditated profoundly. She had an expression so serious that it gave us reason to believe for some time that my misfortune was irreparable. But, having returned from her trance, and her physiognomy recovering its natural beauty, she told us that she had a remedy for our woes.

"It will be slow," she told me, "but it will be certain. Keep your secret, so that it does not leak out, and do not let anyone know that you are hidden under that horrible disguise, for you would rob me of the power to deliver you from it. Your enemy flatters herself that you will divulge it; that is why she has not taken the power of speech away from you."

The Queen thought that condition impossible, because two of her women had been present at the fatal adventure and had gone out, terrified, which would not have failed to excite the curiosity of the guards and courtiers. She imagined that the entire court would be informed of it, and that her kingdom, sad even the world, would soon hear the news. But the fay knew a means of preventing the mystery from being exposed. She made a few gestures, sometimes gravely, sometimes precipitately; she combined them with words that we did not understand, and ended up by raising in the air the hand of a person who commands with absolute power.

That action, combined with what she had pronounced, was so powerful that everything alive within the château became immobile, changed into statues. They are still in that state; they are the forms that you see in various places, in the same attitudes in which the fay's urgent order surprised them.

The Queen, who cast a glance into the great courtyard at that moment, perceived the transformation of a prodigious number of people.

The silence that suddenly succeeded the agitation of a great people gave birth in her heart to surges of compassion for so many innocents who were losing their lives because of

93

me, but the fay reassured her by saying that she would only leave her subjects in that state for as long as their discretion was necessary. It was a precaution that it was necessary to take. But she promised that she would compensate them, and that the time they passed thus would not be counted against their days.

"They will be rejuvenated proportionately, so let your pity cease," said the fay to the Queen. "Let us leave them here with your son. They will be safe here, because I have raised up fogs in the environs of the château so dense that it will only be possible to penetrate here when we judge it appropriate." She continued: "I will take you back to where your presence is necessary; you have maneuvers to fear on the part of your enemies. Be careful to publish that the fay who has raised your son has retained him with her for an important purpose, and that she has kept all the people who followed you."

It was not without shedding tears that my mother found herself obliged to quit me. The fay renewed her assurances to watch over me continually, and protested that I had only had to wish in order to see my desires accomplished. She added that my woes would end, provided that neither my mother nor I raised any obstacle to it by some imprudent act.

All those promises were incapable of consoling my mother; she would rather have remained with me and left to the fay, or whomever she judged most worthy, the care of governing her kingdom. But fays command imperiously and want to be obeyed. My mother, fearing to augment my misfortunes by a refusal and deprive me of the help of that benevolent Intelligence, consented to everything that was asked of her.

She saw a beautiful chariot arriving, drawn by the same white deer that brought her here today. The fay made the Queen climb in next to her; she scarcely had time to embrace me; her interests summoned her elsewhere, and she was warned that a longer sojourn in this place might harm me.

She was taken with an extraordinary celerity to where her army was camped. They were not astonished to see her arrive in that carriage. Everyone thought that she was with the old fay, because the one who accompanied her did not make herself known, and left again immediately. That was to return to this palace, which she instantly embellished with everything that her art and imagination could furnish.

The obliging fay permitted me to add here everything that would give me pleasure, and, after having done everything for me that she could, she left me, exhorting me to have courage and promising to come back from time to time to inform me of the hopes that she had conceived in my favor.

I appeared to be alone in the palace; however, I was only so in terms of the eyes; I was served as in the midst of my court, and my occupations were almost the same as those that you had subsequently. I read, I went to spectacles, I cultivated a garden that I had made while amusing myself, and success followed me in everything that I undertook. Whatever I planted took no more than a day to acquire its perfection. It needed no more to produce the rose arbor to which I owe the good fortune of seeing you here.

My benefactress came to see me frequently; her promises and her presence soothed my pains. By her intermediary, my mother had news of me and I had news of her.

One day, I saw the fay arrive, with joy shining in her eyes. "My dear Prince," she said to me, "the day of your happiness is drawing nearer."

Then she told me that the man you believed to be your father had spent a very bad night lost in the forest. She gave me a brief account of the adventure that had put him on the path, without informing me of the verity of your birth. She told me that the fellow had been forced to seek a shelter from the evils that he had endured for twenty-four hours.

"I will give orders for his reception," she said. "It's necessary that it be agreeable. He has a charming daughter; I intend that it should be her who will liberate you. I have paid attention to the conditions that my cruel companion has put on your disenchantment. It is fortunate that she has not ordered that the one who must liberate you come here for love of you.

On the contrary, she has said that she must fear death, and even expose herself to it voluntarily. I have imagined a means to oblige her to that step. That will be to make her believe that her father's life is in danger and that she has no other means of saving it.

"I know that, in order not to cause the old man any expense, she only asked him for a rose, while her sisters heaped him with indiscreet commissions. When he finds a favorable opportunity, he will satisfy her. Hide in the arbor, seize him as soon as he has begun picking roses and make him fear that death will be the punishment for his audacity unless he gives you one of his daughters—or, rather, that she gives herself, in accordance with the order prescribed by our enemy. The man has five other daughters in addition to the one I intend for you, but none of them will be generous enough to ransom their father's life at the price of their own. Only the Beauty is capable of that great action."

I carried out the fay's orders exactly. You, know, Beautiful Princess, how successful that was. The merchant, to save his life, promised me what I demanded of him. I saw him depart without being able to convince myself that he would return with you. I desired it, but dared not flatter myself that he would.

How many woes I suffered throughout the month for which he had asked me! I only desired to see the end of it in order to be more certain of my misfortune. I could not imagine that a young, beautiful and lovable person would have the courage would come in search of a monster whose prey she believed she would be. Even if she had sufficient firmness, it was necessary that she live with me, without it being permissible for her to repent of her step, and that appeared to me to be an invincible obstacle. Besides which, how would she be able to support my presence without dying of fright?

I spent my miserable life in the midst of those sad reflections, and never had more of which to complain. However, the month went by, and my protectress announced your arrival. You doubtless remember the pomp with which you were received. Not daring to mark my joy by speech, to give you evidence of it I borrowed the assistance of magnificence. The fay, full of attention for me, forbade me to make myself known, whatever fear I might inspire in you or whatever kindness you showed me. It was not permitted to me to seek to please you or show you any mark of amour—in sum, to reveal myself. I could only retrench myself in an excessive generosity, for, fortunately, the malign fay had forgotten to forbid me to give you evidence of that.

That law appeared harsh to me, but it was necessary for me to subscribe to it, and I formed the resolution only to present myself to you for a few moments every day, and to avoid intimate conversation in order to prevent my heart from yielding to tenderness.

You arrived, Charming Princess, and the first glance I cast at you produced an effect in me entirely opposite to the one that my monstrous form must have produced in you. To see you and to love you instantaneously was the same thing for me. Only entering into your apartment tremulously, my joy was excessive on seeing you sustain the sight of me in a more intrepid manner than I sustained it myself. You gave me an infinite pleasure when you declared that you were willing to live with me. By an effect of self-esteem, which followed me even into the most frightful form, I believed that you did not find me as hideous as you had expected.

Your father left, content. But my dolor was redoubled when I thought that I could only please you by the sole bizarrerie of your taste. Your conduct and your speech, as sage as it was modest, everything about you made me understand that you only acted in accordance with the principles that reason and virtue dictated to you; that is what permitted me to flatter myself with the hope of a happy captive. I was in despair at being unable to employ with you any other terms than those that the fay had dictated to me, and which she had chosen expressly because they were base and puerile.

In vain I told her that it was not natural that you would accept the proposal to 'go to bed with me.' To that she only responded: 'Patience, perseverance, or all is lost.' In order to compensate you for my ridiculous conversation, she assured me that she would give you all sorts of pleasures, and give me the advantage of seeing you continually without frightening you and without being forced to say impertinent things to you. She rendered me invisible, and I had the satisfaction of seeing you served by spirits, which were similar, or which showed themselves to you in the form of animals.

Much more than that, in directing your dreams, the fay enabled you to see my face in imagination by night and during the day by way of my portraits, and enabled me to talk to you, via the voice of dreams, in the way that I thought, and as I would have talked to you myself, You sensed my secret confusedly, and the hopes that it invited you to fulfill, and by the means of a constellated mirror I was witness to your conversations and I saw there everything you imagined yourself saying or what you were thinking.

That situation was not sufficient to render me happy; I was only there in a dream, and my misfortunes were real. The extreme love that you had inspired in me obliged me to lament the constraint in which I was living. But my condition was much sadder when I perceived that these beautiful places had no more charms for you. I saw you shed tears, which pierced my heart, and thought myself doomed. You asked me if I was alone here; it would not have taken much for me to abandon my feigned stupidity and make you oaths to assure you of it. They would have been in terms by which you would have been astonished, and they would have made you suspect that I was not as coarse as I wanted to appear.

I was about to make it known to you when the fay, invisible to you, offered herself to my gaze. By her menacing expression, which frightened me, she found the secret of making me remain silent. Of what means, O Heaven, did she make use in order to impose silence on me! She approached you with a dagger in hand, and made me a sign that the first word I pronounced would cost you your life. I was so frightened that I

98

naturally resumed the stupidity that she had ordered me to affect.

I was not at the end of my troubles. You expressed the desire to go to your father's house. I gave you permission without hesitation. Could I refuse you anything? But I regarded your departure as the death-blow, and without the cares of the fay I would have succumbed to it. During your absence, that generous Intelligence did not abandon me. She preserved me from my own fury, to which I would have yielded, not daring to flatter myself that you would come back. The time that you had spent in the palace rendered my initial state more insupportable than it had been before, since I found myself the unhappiest of all men, without the hope of being able to let you know it.

The sweetest of my occupations was visiting the places where you had gone most often, but my chagrin was redoubled on no longer seeing you there. The evenings and the hours when I had had the pleasure of conversing with you momentarily redoubled my affliction and were even more cruel for me. Those two months, the longest of my life, finally ended, and I did not see you return. It was then that my unhappiness entered its final period, and the fay's power was too weak to prevent me from succumbing to my despair.

The precautions she had taken to prevent me from attempting my life were futile. I had a sure means that exceeded her power, and that was no longer to take any nourishment. By the force of her art she still had the power to sustain me for some time, but when she had exhausted all her secrets on me, I gradually weakened. In the end, I had no more than a moment to live, when you came to snatch me from death.

Your precious tears, more efficacious than all the cordials of the disguised spirits, retained my soul, ready to depart. Recognizing by your laments that I was dear to you, I tasted a perfect felicity, and it reached its peak when you accepted me as a husband. However, it was not yet permitted to me to reveal my secret, and the Beast was obliged to lie down next to you without daring to reveal the Prince to you. I was scarcely in your bed than my impatience ceased. You know that I immediately fell into a lethargy which only ended with the arrival of the fay and the Queen. On awakening, I found myself such as I am now, without being able to say how my change had taken place.

You have been witness to the rest, but you have only been able to judge imperfectly the dolor caused me by my mother's obstinacy in opposing a marriage so just and so glorious for me. I was resolved, Princess to become the Beast again rather than lose the hope of being the husband of such a virtuous and charming person. If the secret of your birth had still been a mystery to me, gratitude and amour would have made me sense no less that, in possessing you, I would be the most fortunate of all men.

The Prince finished thus, and the Beauty was about to respond to him when she was prevented from doing so by the sound of loud voices and martial instruments, which, however, announced nothing sinister. They put their heads out of the window, and the fay and the Queen, who had returned from their stroll, did likewise.

That noise proceeded from the arrival of a man, who, according to appearances, must have been a King. The escort that surrounded him had all the marks of royal dignity and he, in his person, made visible an air of majesty that was not belied by the magnificence by which he was accompanied. That Prince, perfectly well made although he was not in his first youth, showed that he could have had few equals in the spring of his age. He was followed by a dozen guards and a few courtiers in hunting costumes, who appeared to be as astonished as their master to find themselves in château unknown to them. The same honors were rendered to him as if he had been in his own estates, and all by invisible beings, for they heard cries of joy and fanfares, but they did not see anyone.

On seeing him appear, the fay said to the Queen: "Here is the King your brother, and the Beauty's father; he does not expect the pleasure of finding you here. He will be all the more satisfied because, as you know, he believes that his daughter has been dead for a long time. He still regrets her loss as much as that of his wife, of whom he conserves a tender memory."

That discourse augmented the impatience that the Queen and the young Princess had to embrace that Prince; they arrived promptly in the courtyard at the moment when he descended from his horse. He saw them without knowing them, but, not doubting that they were coming to meet him, he did not know what compliment to pay them, nor what terms to use, when the Beauty threw herself at his knees, embraced him and called him "Father."

The Prince raised her to her feet and held her tenderly in his arms, without understanding why she was giving him that name. He imagined that she might be an oppressed orphan Princess who was coming to implore his protection, and who was only making use of the most touching terms in order to obtain the effect of her request. He was ready to assure her that he would do everything in his favor that depended on him when he recognized he Queen his sister, who embraced him in her turn and introduced her son to him. She told him a part of the obligations that she and he had toward the Beauty, and did not hide from him the frightful adventure that had just terminated.

The King was praising the young Princess and wanted to know her name when they fay interrupted and asked him whether it was necessary to name his relatives, and whether he had ever known anyone who resembled her enough to reveal them to him.

"If I judged by her features," he said, looking at her fixedly and not being able to hold back a few tears, "the name she has given me would be legitimately due to me, but in spite of those signs and the emotion into which the sight of her throws me, I dare not flatter myself that this might be my daughter, whom I have mourned ever since I saw the certain evidence that he was devoured by savage beasts.

"However," he continued, considering her again, "She bears a perfect resemblance to the tender and incomparable spouse that death has stolen from me, How agreeably flattered I am by the hope of seeing once again in her the fruit of a charming hymen, whose chains were broken far too soon for me."

"You can, Sire," said the fay. "The Beauty is your daughter. Her birth is no longer a secret here. The Queen and the Prince know who she is. I have only enabled to you come in order to inform you, but we are not in a convenient place for recounting the detail of that adventure. Let us go into the palace; you can rest there for a few moments and then I will tell you what you desire to know. After the joy that you will have experienced on rediscovering such a beautiful and virtuous daughter, I will make you party to another item of news, to which you will be no less sensible."

The King, accompanied by his daughter and the Prince, was conducted by the monkey officers to the apartment that the fay had destined for him.

The Intelligence took that time to render to the status the liberty of speaking about what they had seen. As their fate had attracted the compassion of the Queen, she wanted it to be by her hands that they would sense the joy of seeing the light again. She gave her wand to her, with which the Queen described seven circles in the air, and pronounced in a natural voice the words: "Animate yourselves, your King is saved." All the immobile figures stirred, and began to walk and act as before, only remembering confusedly what had happened to them.

After that ceremony, the fay and the Queen returned to the King, whom they found in conversation with the Beauty and the Prince. Alternately, he gave them caresses, especially his daughter, whom he asked a hundred times over how she had been saved from the ferocious beasts that had carried her away, without making the reflection that she had replied to him the first time he asked that she had no idea, and had even been ignorant of the secret of her birth.

For his part, the Prince spoke without being heard, repeating a hundred times the obligations be had to the Beautiful Princess. He would also have liked to inform the monarch of the promises that the fay had made him in granting him possession of her, and to beg him not to refuse an agreeable consent to his alliance. That conversation and his caresses were interrupted by the arrival of the Queen and the fay.

The King, who had rediscovered his daughter, knew the entire extent of his happiness, but he did not know yet to whom he was obliged for that precious advantage.

"It is to me," the fay told him. "And it is me alone who owes you an explanation of the adventure. I shall not limit my benefits to telling you the story; I have other news to announce to you that is no less agreeable. So, Great King, you can mark this day among the happiest of your life."

The company, knowing that the fay was preparing to speak, made it known by their silence that they would give her great attention. To respond to their expectation, this is the discourse that she addressed to the King:

"The Beauty, Sire, and perhaps the Prince, are the only ones here who do not know the laws of the Fortunate Isle. It is for them that I shall explain them. It is permitted to all the inhabitants of that isle, even the King, only to consult their taste in the person that each ought to marry, in order that no one opposes their happiness. It was by virtue of that privilege that you chose a young shepherdess, whom you encountered while hunting. Her charms and her goodness caused you to find her worthy of that honor.

"Anyone but her, even daughters raised in dignity, would have accepted gladly and eagerly that of being your mistress, but her virtue made her disdain such an offer. You elevated her to the throne and gave her a rank from which the baseness of her birth seemed to exclude her, but which she merited by the nobility of her character and the beauty of her soul.

"You can remember that you always had reason to praise your choice. Her mildness, her kindness and her tenderness for you equaled the charms of her person. But you did not enjoy the pleasure of seeing her for long. After she had made you the father of the Beauty, you found yourself obliged to undertake a voyage to your frontier to prevent an appearance of revolt of which you had been informed. During that time, you suffered the loss of that dear wife, which touched you all the more because you combined with the tenderness that her attractions had inspired in you the most perfect esteem for her rare qualities. In spite of her great youth and the scant education that her birth had given her, you found in her a consummate prudence, and your most skillful advisers were astonished by the sage advice that she gave you, and the expedients she found to enable you to succeed in all your projects."

The King, who had always conserved his grief, and to whom the death of that worthy spouse was still present, could not hear that narration without giving further evidence of sensibility, and the fay, who perceived that the discourse was affecting him, said to him:

"Your sensibility proves to me that you merited that happiness; I shall not remind you any further of a memory that can only sadden you; but I ought to tell you that that pretended shepherdess was a fay, and my sister. Informed that the Fortunate Isle was a charming land, knowing its laws and the mildness of your government, she had desired to see it.

"The garb of a shepherdess was the only disguise that she borrowed, in order to enjoy the rural life for a time. You encountered her during that sojourn. Her graces and her youth touched you. She abandoned herself without constraint to the desire to know whether you had as many charms in your intelligence as she found in your person. She was proud of her quality and her power as a fay which would shield her when she wished from your eagerness if it went as far as importunity and if the condition in which she appeared enabled you to presume that you could lack respect for her without consequence.

"She had no fear of the sentiments that you might inspire in her, and, convinced that her virtue was sufficient to protect her from the traps of amour, she attributed what she felt for you to the simple curiosity of knowing whether there were still men on earth capable of loving virtue deprived of foreign ornaments, which render it more brilliant and more respectable to the vulgar than its own quality, and whose baleful assistance has often given its name to the most abominable vices.

"Abused by that idea, far from retiring to our general refuge as she had initially planned, she wanted to live in a little hut that she had made in the solitude, where you encountered her with a fantastic figure who was represented as her mother. Those two individuals seemed to live on the products of a pretended flock that had no fear of wolves, being in fact nothing more than spirits in disguise. It was that place that she received your cares. They produced all the effect that you could have desired. She did not have the strength to refuse the offer that you made her of the crown. You know the full extent of the obligation that you owed to her, in the time when you believed that she owed you everything, and when you wanted to leave her in that error.

"What I am telling you is a tangible proof that ambition had no part in the consent that she gave to your desires. You are not unaware that we regard the greatest kingdoms as property of which we make a present to whoever pleases us. But she was attentive to your generous procedure and, believing herself to be fortunate to unite herself with a man as virtuous, she was dazed by that engagement to the extent that she did not make any reflection as to the danger in which she was about to precipitate herself. For our laws directly prohibit any alliance with those who do not have as much power as us, especially before we have sufficient antiquity to have authority over others and enjoy the right to preside in our turn.

"Before that time we are subordinate to our elders, and in order that we do not abuse our power, we only have that of disposing of our persons in favor of an Intelligence or a sage whose power is at least equal to our own. It is true that after achieving that veteran status, we are mistresses of making whatever alliances we please, but it is rare for us to use that right and it is never without the scandal of the order, which only receives that insult rarely, and only on the part of a few aged fays who almost always pay dearly for their extravagance, for they marry young men who scorn them. Although they are not punished directly, they are sufficiently so by the bad conduct of their spouses, on whom it is not permissible for them to avenge themselves.

"That is the only penalty that we impose in them. The unpleasant results that almost always follow the follies they have committed take away their desire to reveal our advantageous secrets to the profane from whom they might hope for regard and concern. My sister was not in any of those circumstances. Endowed with all the qualities appropriate to make herself loved, she only lacked age; but she only consulted her amour. She flattered herself that she would be able to keep her marriage secret, and she succeeded in that for some time.

"We scarcely have the custom of seeking information about what those who are absent are doing. Everyone occupies herself with her own affairs, and we spread out in the world to do good or evil in accordance with our inclinations, without being obliged, when we return, to render an account of our actions, unless we have done something that causes talk about us, or a few benevolent fays, touched by unfortunates unjustly persecuted, bring complaints. Finally, some unexpected adventure is necessary for which the general book is visited, in which we have the thing engraved spontaneously at the moment when it happens. Except on those occasions, we only have to appear at the assembly three times a year, and as we travel very easily, that is only matter of a presence of two hours.

"My sister was 'obliged to enlighten the throne'—that is what we call that chore—when it was necessary; she prepared for you some time in advance a hunt or a pleasure trip, and after your departure she affected some inconvenience in order to remain alone, locked in her cabinet, where it was supposed she had a need to write, or to rest. It was not perceived in your palace, or by us, that she had anything of interest to hide.

"That mystery was not one for me. The consequences of it were dangerous; that is what I told her, but she loved you too much to repent of what she had done. Even wanting to justify it in my eyes, she asked that I come to see you. Without paying you a compliment, I confess, Sire, that if the sight of you did not make me approve of her weakness entirely, at least it diminished it and augmented the zeal with which I tried to keep it hidden.

"Her prevarication was unknown for two years, but in the end, it was discovered. We are obliged to make a certain number of benefits in the general extent of the universe, of which we have to render an account. When my sister was obliged to render hers, she could only show favors in the Fortunate Isle and for the Fortunate Isle.

"Several of our ill-humored fays criticized her procedure; that is what made our Queen demand for what reason she limited her beneficent humor to that small part of the world, since it is not permitted to be unaware that a young fay ought to travel a great deal in order to make the acquaintance of the universe that is our power and our will.

"As that law was not new my sister had not reason to murmur about it and no pretext to refuse to obey it. She promised to conform to it. But the impatience to see you again, the fear that her absence might be perceived and the impossibility of carrying out secret actions on the throne did not permit her to go way for long enough and often enough to do her duty, and at the following assembly, she could scarcely prove that she had spent a quarter of a hour away from the Fortunate Isle.

"Our Queen, irritated against her, threatened her with destroying the island in order to prevent her from violating our laws any longer. That threat troubled her so much that the least clairvoyant of our fays realized the extent to which your wife bore a sensibility for that fatal isle, and the evil fay who had given this Prince the monstrous form that he had perceived her disturbance, and deduced that by opening the Great Book, an important subject would be found there capable of exercising her malevolent inclination.

"'It's there,' she cried, 'that the truth will be discovered, and we shall learn the truth about her conduct.'

"With those worlds, she made the entire assembly see all that had happened in the last two years, and read it out in a loud and distinct voice.

"All the fays made a strange noise on learning of that misalliance, and heaped my sad sister with the cruelest reproaches. She was degraded from our order and condemned to remain a prisoner among us. If the punishment for her fault had only consisted of the first of those penalties she would have consoled herself, but the second chastisement, more terrible than the first, made her feel the rigor of both. The loss of her dignity did not matter to her much, but, loving you tenderly, she asked, with tears in her eyes that they be content to degrade her without depriving her of the joy of living as a simple mortal with her husband and her dear daughter.

"Her tears and supplications touched the young veterans, and I saw, by the murmur that they made, that if a vote had been taken instantly she would surely have got away with a remonstration. But one of the most ancient, who was known because of her decrepitude as the Mother of Time, did not give the Queen the leisure to explain herself and to make it known that pity had taken possession of her heart, like those of the others.

"'This crime must not be tolerated,' that detestable old crone cried, in a hoarse voice. 'If it is not punished, we will be exposed to the same insults every day. The honor of the order is absolutely at stake here. This wretch, attached to the earth, does not regret the loss of a dignity that raises her a hundred times further above kings than they are above their subjects. She tells us that her affection, her fears and her desires are turned toward her unworthy family. It is in that regard that it is necessary to punish her. Let her spouse regret her. Let her daughter, the shameful fruit of loose amours, marry a monster in order to make her expiate the laxity of a mother who has had the weakness to allow herself to be charmed by her father's fragile and despicable beauty.'

"That cruel sentence brought back to rigor many of those who were leaning toward clemency. The small number of those who had been touched by pity not being sufficiently considerable to oppose the general deliberation, it was executed rigorously, and even our Queen, whose physiognomy appeared to be turned to compassion, resumed her severe expression.

"However, my sister, who sought to have such a cruel edict revoked, in order to touch the judges and excuse her marriage, made such a charming portrait of you that she inflamed the heart of the fay who was the governess of the prince—the one who had opened the Book—but that nascent amour only served to redouble the hatred that the unjust fay already had for your sad wife.

"Unable to resist the eagerness she had to see you, she colored her passion with the pretext of knowing whether you merited a fay making the sacrifice that my sister had made for you. As she was responsible for the prince and had had that tutelage approved by the assembly, she would not have dared to abandon him if ingenious amour had not inspired her to put a protective spirit beside him and two invisible subaltern fays to answer for him in her absence. After that precaution she only thought of following her desires, whose took her to the Fortunate Isle.

"Meanwhile, the women and officers of the imprisoned Queen, astonished by the fact that she had not emerged from her cabinet, were alarmed by that. The express order they had been given not to interrupt her caused them to let the night pass without knocking on her door, but, impatient taking the place of any other consideration, they knocked urgently, and when no one answered, they broke down the door, no longer doubting that some accident had occurred.

"Although they expected some kind of disaster, they were nevertheless consternated not to find her. They called to her and searched or her in vain. Nothing emerged to soothe the distress that her absence caused. A thousand hypotheses were made, each as absurd as the others. They could only suspect that her escape was voluntary. She was all-powerful in your kingdom, the sovereign power that you had left her not being contested by anyone. Everyone obeyed her joyfully. The tenderness that you had for one another, the love that she had for her daughter and for the subjects whose delight she was, prevented anyone from accusing her of flight. Where could she have gone that was better? On the other hand, what man would have dared to abduct a Queen from the midst of her guards and the depths of her palace? They would have known the route that the kidnapers had taken.

"The misfortune was certain, although the circumstances of it were hidden. There was another to be feared. That was, Sire, the fashion in which you would receive that fatal news. The innocence of those who were responsible for the person of the Queen did not reassure them against the effects of your just wrath. It was either necessary to determine to flee your estates, and by that flight declare themselves guilty of a crime they had not committed, or to find the secret of concealing the misfortune from you.

"After much deliberation, they could imagine no other plan than persuading you that she was dead. That was immediately carried out. A courier was sent to inform you that she had fallen ill. A second, who departed a few hours later, took you the news of her death—that was in order that you did not come diligently; your presence would have defeated all the measures that were ensuring general safety. She was given a funeral worthy of her rank, your affection and the regrets of a people who had adored her and who mourned her as sincerely as you did yourself.

"That cruel adventure was always a secret for you, although there was no one in the entire Fortunate Isle was unaware of it. The initial surprise had rendered the misfortune public. The dolor that you sensed at that loss was proportionate to your affection; you only found relief from it in summoning your daughter the Princess to you. The innocent caresses of that child were your only consolation. You did not want to be separated from her. She was charming, and presented you incessantly with a living portrait of her mother the Queen.

"The enemy fay who had been the original cause of all the disorder, by opening the Great Book in which she had discovered my sister's marriage, had not come to see you without paying for her curiosity. Your presence had produced in your heart the same effect as on that of your spouse, and without that experience causing her to excuse her, she ardently desired to commit the same sin. Invisible by your side, she could not resolve to quit you.

"Seeing you inconsolable, she did not flatter herself with the possibility of a success in her amours, and, fearing to add the shame of your scorn to the futility of her designs, she dared not make herself known to you. On the other hand, judging that it was necessary to appear, she thought that by a trick of her mind she might accustom you to seeing her and perhaps to loving her. But it was necessary to get close to you, and in order to have the means, she meditated so much on the trick that she would play in order to present herself before you with decency that she found it.

"There was a neighboring Queen who had been expelled from her estates by a usurper who had murdered her husband; that sad Princess was traveling the world in search of a refuge and an avenger. The fay kidnapped her, and, having put her in a safe place, put her to sleep and assumed her appearance. You saw that disguised fay, Sire, throw herself at your feet and implore your protection in order, she said, to punish the murderer of a husband she regretted as much as you regretted the Queen. She protested to you that conjugal love was the unique motive that made her act, and that she renounced wholeheartedly a crown that she would offer to anyone who avenged her dead husband.

"The unfortunate have pity on one another. You entered into her dolor, all the more so because she was mourning a cherished spouse, and, mingling her tears with yours, she talked to you incessantly about the Queen. You accorded her your protection, and it did not take you long to reestablish her in her pretended kingdom, punishing the rebels and the usurper as she seemed to desire. But she did not want to return or to quit you. She begged you, for her security, to reign over her kingdom in her name, since you had too much generosity to accept the gift of it that she wanted to make to you, and to permit her to live at your Court.

"You could not refuse her that further favor. She appeared to you to be necessary to raise your daughter, for that adroit harpy was not unaware that the child was the unique object of your affection. She feigned an extreme tenderness for her, and held her in her arms continually. Anticipating the request that you were going to make of her, she asked you eagerly to permit her to take charge of her education, saying that she did not want any other heirs than that dear daughter, who would be her own, and the unique object of her amour, because, she said, she reminded her of the one she had had with her husband, who had perished with him.

"Her proposition appeared to you to be so advantageous that you did not hesitate to hand the Princess over to her, and even to render her absolute mistress of her upbringing. She acquitted her responsibilities perfectly; by virtue of her talents and her affection, she had your entire confidence, and you gave her your amity as to a beloved sister. That was not enough for her, all her cares only tending toward becoming your wife. In order to reach that goal she neglected nothing. But when you had been the husband of the most beautiful of the fays, she was not made to induce amour. The face she had borrowed could not enter into comparison with that of the person whose place she sought to obtain. Extremely ugly, and being naturally so herself, she was unable to borrow beauty for more than one day per year.

"That scarcely flattering experience made her understand that, in order to succeed, it would be necessary for her to have recourse to other means than beauty. She conspired secretly to oblige the people and the aristocracy to solicit you to take a wife, and to have herself designated. But certain ambiguous remarks that she had made to you in order to sound your dispositions allowed you to guess easily where the urgent solicitations originated with which you were being importuned.

"You testified clearly that you did not want to hear talk of giving your daughter a stepmother, or putting you in that position, subordinating her to a Queen and robbing her of the first rank in your estates, along with the certain expectation of succeeding you on the throne. You also made that false Princess understand that she would give you pleasure by returning to her own land quietly and without delay. When she had returned there you promised to render her all the good offices that she could expect of a faithful friend and a generous neighbor, but you did not hide from her that if she did not make that decision with a good grace, she would run the risk of being forced to do it.

"The invincible obstacle that you opposed to her amour threw her into a terrible wrath; however, she feigned such a great indifference in the matter that she succeeded in persuading you that the attempt was an effect of her ambition and the fear that you might subsequently take possession of her estates, preferring, in spite of the eagerness that she had testified in order to make to accept them, to let you believe that she had not offered them to you in good faith than to let you know her true sentiments.

"Her fury was no less violent for being hidden. Having no doubt that it was the Beauty, more powerful in your heart than politics, that was making you renounce the advantage of augmenting your empire in such a glorious fashion, she conceived a hatred for her as powerful as that she had had against your spouse, and made the resolution to get rid of her, not doubting that if she were dead, your subjects, renewing their pressure, would force you to put yourself in a state to leave successors. The crone was scarcely of an age to provide any, but that deceit was nothing to her. The Queen who resemblance she had taken was still young enough to have many, her ugliness not being an obstacle to a royal and political marriage.

"In spite of the authentic declaration that you had made, it was thought that if your daughter died, you would yield to the continual representations of your council. It was not even doubted that your choice would fall upon the pretended Queen, which attracted countless creatures to her. Thus, with the aid of one of her flatterers, whose wife had a soul as base as him and who was as wicked as her, her plan was made to get rid of your daughter. She had made her the governess of the little Princess.

"They arranged between them to stifle her and to say that she had died suddenly, but for greater security they agreed to commit the murder in the nearby forest, in order that no one would surprise them during that barbaric execution. They were counting on no one having the slightest knowledge of it, and that it would be impossible to criticize them for not having asked for help before she died, having for a legitimate excuse that they were too far away.

"The husband of the governess proposed that he come in search of her after the child was dead, and, in order that no one should suspect anything, he would appear surprised to find her beyond all help when he returned to the place where he had left the tender victim of their fury; and he studied the dolor and astonishment that it was necessary to affect.

"When my miserable sister found herself deprived of her power and condemned to the rigors of a cruel prison, she recommended me to console you and to watch over the security of her daughter. It was not necessary for her to take that precaution; the union there was between us and the pity I felt for her would have been sufficient to attract my protection, and her recommendation did not make me fulfill her desires with any more zeal.

"I saw you as often as I could, and as much as prudence permitted, without running the risk of arousing the suspicions of our enemy, who would have denounced me as a fay in whom fraternal affection prevailed over the honor of the order and who was protecting a guilty race. I neglected nothing to convince all the fays that I had abandoned her to her unfortunate fate, and by that means, I counted on conserving a greater facility to be of service to her.

"As I was attentive to all the steps of your perfidious lover, as much in person as by way of the spirits submissive to me, her frightful intention was not hidden from me. I could not oppose open force to it, and although it would have been easy for me to annihilate those to whose hands she had abandoned the little creature, prudence prevented me from doing so; and if I had removed your child, the malign fay would have recaptured her without it being possible for me to defend her. There is a law among us that obliges us to have a thousand years of antiquity before entering into dispute against our elders, or at least to have been a serpent.

"The perils that accompany us in that condition we call the 'terrible auspices.' There is none among us who does not shiver in thinking of undergoing it. We hesitate for a long time before resolving to expose ourselves to it, and without a very powerful motive of hatred, amour or vengeance, there are few who do not prefer to await the veteran status that comes with the assistance of time rather than anticipating it by that dangerous means, in which the greater number succumb. I was in that situation. It would require ten years for my thousand years to be completed, and I had no other resource than artifice. I employed it.

"I took the form of a monstrous she-bear and hid myself in the forest destined for the detestable execution. When the wretches came to carry out the barbaric order that they had received, I threw myself upon the woman who had the child in her arms, and over whose mouth she had already placed her hand. The fright she had obliged her to drop the precious burden, but she did not get away with it so cheaply, and the horror that her evil nature caused me inspired in me the cruelty of the animal whose form I had taken. I killed her, along with the traitor who had accompanied her, and I carried off the Beauty after having promptly stripped her and stained her garments with the blood of her enemies. I scattered them in the forest after having taken the precaution of ripping them in several places in order that no one would believe that the Princess had escaped, and I withdrew, very content at having succeeded so well.

"The fay believed that she had been served in accordance with her desires. The death of her two accomplices was an advantage for her; she became mistress of her secret, and the fate that I had just caused them to experience was the one that she had destined for them to recompense them for their culpable services. Another circumstance, which was even more advantageous, was that shepherds who saw that expedition from a distance ran to call for help, which arrived soon enough to find the wretches dying, and removed any suspicion on your part that she might have had any part in it.

"The same incidents were also favorable to my enterprise. They convinced the wicked fay of the same thing as the vulgar. The event appeared so natural to her that she no longer had any doubt about it. She did not even deign to employ her power to assure herself of it. I was delighted by her security. I would not have been strong enough if she had wanted to take the little Beauty back, because, in addition to the reasons that made her my superior, which I have explained to you, she had the advantage of having obtained the child from you; you had entrusted your authority to her, against which only you would have had power, and unless you removed her from her hands yourself, nothing could abstract her from the laws that she would have imposed in her until she was married.

"Freed from that anxiety, I found myself overwhelmed by another, in remembering that the Mother of Time had condemned my niece to marry a monster. But she was not yet three years old, and I flattered myself that by means of study I might find an expedient in order that that malediction would not be accomplished literally, and that I could make it equivocal. I had a long time to think about it, and I only occupied myself with the care of finding a place where I could put my precious prey in security

"Mystery was absolutely necessary to me. I dared not give her a château, nor make any magnificence of art for her; our enemy might have perceived it and conceived an anxiety whose consequences would have been fatal for us. I therefore preferred to put on a simple costume and confide her to the first individual I encountered who appeared to me to be a good man and where I could flatter myself that she would find all the comforts of life.

"Hazard soon favored my intentions. I found what suited me perfectly. It was a little house in a hamlet, the door of which was open. I went into the cottage, which appeared to me to be that of a well-to-do peasant. I saw by the light of a lamp three peasant women asleep next to a cradle, which I judged to be that of a nursling. It had nothing of the simplicity of the rest of the room; everything about it was sumptuous. I thought that the little creature was ill and that the sleep into which its guardians were plunged came from the fatigue they had experienced beside her. I approached silently with the design of giving relief, and took pleasure in advance in the surprise the women would have on finding their invalid cured, without knowing to what to attribute it. I hastened to take the infant from the cradle with the intention of breathing life into it, but my good will became futile, the child expired as soon as I touched it.

"That death instantly inspired in me the desire to profit from it and put my niece in its place, if luck determined that it was a girl. I was fortunate enough for my wish to be granted. Delighted by that occurrence, I made the exchange without delay and took the little corpse away, which I buried. Then I went back to the house, where I made a noise at the door in order to wake the sleepers.

"I told them in an affected patois that I was a stranger requesting a shelter for the night; they granted it to me with a good grace and went to look at their child, whom they found sleeping peacefully with every appearance of perfect health. They were joyful and surprised by that, because they were unaware of the deceit I had contrived by fascinating their eyes.

"They told me that the little girl was the daughter of a rich merchant; that one of them was her nurse, who had returned her to her parents when she was weaned, but that the child had fallen ill in her father's house, and he had sent her to the country in the hope that the fresh air would do her good. They added, with satisfied expressions, as they gazed at the child, that the experiment had succeeded, and that it had produced a better effect than all the remedies that had been employed before returning her to them. They resolved to take her back to her father as soon as it was daylight, in order not o delay the satisfaction that he would receive, and for which they counted on receiving a large recompense, because the child had become extremely dear to him, although the last of eleven.

"At sunrise they departed; for my part, I pretended to continue my route, applauding myself for having placed my niece so advantageously. In order to augment her security further and to engage the supposed father to attach himself to the little girl, I adopted the face of one of those women who tell fortunes and, finding myself t the merchant's door when they brought her back, I entered with them. He received them joyfully, and, taking the little girl in his arms, he was the dupe of the prejudices of paternal love, firmly believing that his entrails were stirred by the sight of her. It was only the stirring of a natural goodness, which he confused with those of nature. I took the opportunity of the moment to augment the tenderness he imagined that he felt.

"'Look after that child well, my good Sire,' I said to him in the ordinary language of the individuals whose costume I had adopted. "She will do you great honor in your family, will give you great wealth, and will save your life and those of all your children. She will be beautiful, so beautiful that she will be so named by everyone who sees her.' To recompense me for my prediction he gave me a gold coin and I withdrew, quite content.

"Nothing more remained that obliged me to reside with the race of Adam. To take advantage of my leisure, I returned to our empire, resolved to remain there for some time. I went tranquilly to console my sister, by giving her news of her dear daughter, and testifying to her that, far from having forgotten her, you cherished her memory with the same tenderness that she had had for your person.

"That, Great King, was our situation while you were penetrated by the new misfortune of being deprived of your daughter, which renewed the dolors that the loss of her mother had caused you to experience. Although you could not accuse the person to whom you had confided her of that accident, it was impossible for you to avoid looking at her with a hostile eye because, although it did not appear that she was culpable, she could not justify the negligence that the event had rendered criminal.

"After the first transports of your affliction, she flattered herself that there would no longer by any obstacle to prevent you from marrying her, and had the proposition renewed by her emissaries. But she was disabused, and her mortification was extreme when you declared that not only had you no more intention than before of remarrying but that, even if you changed your mind, it would never be in her favor. To that declaration with added an urgent order to leave your kingdom immediately. Her presence reminded you of the memory of your daughter and renewed your dolor; that was the pretext of which you made use, but the principal reason you had was that you wanted to put an end to the conspiracies that she continually made in order to achieve her goal.

"She was outraged by it, but it was necessary to obey without being able to avenge herself. I had engaged one of our ancients to protect you. Her power was considerable because she combined her veteran status with the advantage of having been a serpent four times. As there is an extreme danger in becoming one, there are also honors and a redoubling of attached powers. That fay, on my consideration, took you under her protection and made it impossible for your irritated lover to do you any harm.

"That setback was favorable to the Princess whose resemblance she had taken. She brought her out of her slumber, and, hiding the criminal usage she had made of her features, only wanted to make her see the good in all her actions. She did not forget to make the most of her good offices and the trouble she had spared her, and in order that she would continue to stay in character, she gave her salutary advice as to how to maintain it. It was then that, seeking to console herself for your indifference, she returned to the Prince and renewed her cares in his regard; she cherished him, loved him too much, and the fay, being unable to make herself loved, made him feel the terrible effect of her fury.

"Meanwhile, the moment of my veteran status had gradually arrived, and my power was augmented—but the desire to serve my sister and you persuaded me that I still did not have enough. My sincere amity disguising from me the peril of the 'terrible auspices,' I wanted to pass through them. I became a serpent, and got out of it successfully; that is what put me in a state to act without mystery for the service of those that our evil companions oppress. Although I cannot destroy 'evil spells' entirely on every occasion, I often have the power, and at least I am always the mistress of softening them by means of my power and my advice.

"My niece was one of those to whom I could not give entire favor. Not daring to reveal the interest that I had in her, it appeared to me more appropriate to leave her under the name of the merchant's daughter; I went to see her often in different guises, and always came back satisfied. Her virtue and her beauty equaled her intelligence. At fourteen years of age, she had already given evidence of an admirable constancy in the good and bad fortune that her pretended father had experienced.

"I was delighted to know that the cruelest reverse had not been capable of diminishing her tranquility. On the contrary, by means of her cheerfulness and the mildness of her conversation, she had made it a duty to rally her father and her brothers, and I had the pleasure of seeing that she had sentiments worthy of her birth. But that pleasure as mingled with the cruelest bitterness when I recalled that so many perfections were destined for a monster. I labored and occupied myself in vain, night and day, seeking to find the means to protect her from such a great misfortune, and I was in despair of being able to imagine any.

"That anxiety did not prevent me from making frequent visits to you. Your wife, who did not have that liberty, solicited me incessantly to go to see you, and in spite of our friend's protection, her alarmed tenderness always persuaded her that that the moments in which I lost sight of you might be the last of your life and those that our enemy might sacrifice to her fury. That apprehension troubled her so forcefully that she scarcely gave me time to rest. When I came to give her an account of the state you were in, she begged me with so much insistence to return that it was impossible for me to refuse.

"Touched by her anxiety and wanting to put an end to them rather than spare myself the difficulties they caused me, I made use against our barbaric companion of the same weapons that she had used against us and I had the Great Book opened. Fortunately, it was at the moment of the conversation that she had had with the Queen and the Prince, which had terminated with his metamorphosis. I did not miss a word of it, and my delight was extreme that, in order better to assure her vengeance, she had unwittingly destroyed the injury that the Mother of Time had done us in subjecting the Beauty to marriage with a monster. To complete the good fortune she put circumstances so advantageous upon it that it seemed that she had made them expressly, with the unique intention of obliging me, for she furnished my sister's daughter with the opportunity to demonstrate that she was worthy of emerging from the purest fay blood.

"A sign, the slightest gesture, expresses among us what the vulgar could not pronounce in three days. I only said one word with a scornful expression; that was enough to make the assembly know that the case against our enemy had been made by herself in the sentence that she had rendered ten years earlier against your wife. At the age of the latter it seemed more natural to have the weaknesses of amour than for a fay of the first order and a much greater age. I spoke about the base and evil actions that had accompanied that superannuated

121

amour; I represented that if so many infamies went unpunished, there would be grounds to say that fays were only in the world to dishonor nature and to afflict the human race.

"In presenting them with the Book I concluded my abrupt harangue with the single word: 'Look.' It was no less powerful for that; I also had young and veteran friends, who treated the amorous crone as she merited. She had not been able to marry you, and to that punishment was added the dishonor of being degraded from the order, and she was treated like the queen of the Fortunate Isle.

"That council was held while she was with you; as soon as she appeared the result was signified to her. I had the pleasure of witnessing it. After which, closing the Book again, I descended precipitately from the median region of the air, where our empire resides, in order to oppose the effect of the despair to which you were ready to abandon yourself; I employed no more time in making that journey than I had put into my laconic speech. I arrived soon enough to promise you my help. All sorts of reasons invited me to do that."

She turned to the Prince and said to him: "Your virtues and your misfortunes, the advantage I found in them for the Beauty, made me see in you the monster that I needed. You seemed to me to be uniquely worthy of one another, and I had no doubt that when you knew one another, our hearts would render one another a mutual justice.

"You know," she said to the Queen, "what I have done since in order to succeed in that, and by what means I obliged the Beauty to come to this place, where the sight of the Prince and his conversation, which I enabled her to enjoy in dreams, had all the effect that I could have desired. They inflamed her heart without shaking her virtue, and without that amour having had the power to weaken the duty and gratitude that she attached to the monster. In sum, I brought all things successfully to their perfection.

"Yes, Prince," the fay went on, "you no longer have anything to fear on the part of your enemy. She has been deprived of her power, and will never be able to harm you by means of further spells. You have fulfilled the conditions that she imposed on you exactly, for if you had not done so, they would still subsist in spite of her eternal disgrace. You have made yourself loved without the aid of your intelligence and your birth, and you, Beauty, have similarly acquitted the malediction that the Mother of Time had put upon you. You have voluntarily taken a monster for your husband. She has nothing more to demand; everything is henceforth directed toward your happiness."

The fay ceased speaking, and the King, throwing himself at her feet, said to her: "Great Fay, how can I thank you for all the favors with which you have deigned to heap my family? The gratitude that I have for your benefits is infinitely beyond all expression. But my august Sister," he added, "That name encourages me to ask you for yet more favors, and in spite of the obligations that I have for you, I cannot help telling you that I shall never be happy as long as I am deprived of the presence of my dear fay. What she had done, and what she is suffering for me, would increase my amour and my dolor if both were not already at the highest degree. Oh, Madame," he added, "can you not complete the measure of your benefits by letting me see her?"

That request was futile. If the fay had been able to render that good office, she would have been too zealous to wait for him to request it; but she could not destroy what the Council of Fays had ordered. The young Queen being a prisoner in the median region of the air, there was no appearance, action, or industry that would allow him to see her, and the fay was about to make him understand that gently, and to exhort him to be patient while awaiting unexpected events of which she promised to take advantage, when a delightful symphony made itself heard, and interrupted her.

The King, his daughter, the Queen and the Prince were entranced by it, but the fay had another sort of surprise. That music indicated the triumph of fays. She did not understand who the triumphant fay could be. Her ideas settled on the old fay, or the Mother of Time, who might perhaps have obtained in her absence, on the one hand, her liberty or on the other, permission to cause new difficulties for her lovers.

She was in that perplexity when she was agreeable extracted from it by the presence of her sister, the Queen of the Fortunate Isle, who suddenly appeared in the midst of that charming company. She was no less beautiful than when the King, her husband, had lost her. The monarch, who could not mistake her, surrendered the respect that he owed her to the amour that he had conserved for her and embraced her with transports and a joy that even surprised the Queen.

Her sister, the fay, could not imagine to what fortunate prodigy she owed her liberty, but the crowned fairy told her that she owed her good fortune entirely to her own courage, which had driven her to risk her life for another.

"You know," she told the fay, "that the daughter of our Queen was received into the order at birth, but that she did not obtain the light of day from a sublunar father, having received it from the sage Amadabak, whose alliance honors the fays and who is much more powerful than us by virtue of his sublime science. In spite of that, it is not arbitrary for his daughter to become a serpent at the end of her first hundred years. That fatal term has arrived and our Queen, a mother as tender for that dear child and as alarmed for her fate, as an ordinary creature might be, was unable to resolve to abandon her to the risk of the accidents that might make her perish in that state in her first youth, the misfortunes of those who gave succumbed therein having become only too common to authorize such dread.

"The dolorous situation that I was in took away all hope of seeing my tender spouse and lovable daughter again. I had a perfect disgust for a life that I had to spend separated from them; so, without hesitation, I made the decision to offer to crawl in order to disengage the young fay. I saw with joy a sure, prompt and honorable means of delivering myself from all the misfortunes with which I was heaped, by death or by a glorious liberty, which would render me mistress of my fate, permitting me to rejoin my husband.

"Our Queen had no more hesitation in accepting that offer, so flattering to maternal love, than I had had in making it to her. She embraced me a hundred times, and promised to reestablish all my privileges and render my liberty unconditionally if I were fortunate enough to escape that danger. I got through it without accident, the fruit of my difficulties has been attributed to the young fay in whose name I exposed myself; I have immediately recommenced my advantage. The fortunate success of my first ordeal encouraged me for the second, in which I also succeeded. That action has rendered me a veteran, and, in consequence, independent. I have not delayed in taking advantage of my liberty to some here and rejoin such a dear family."

When the fay Queen had finished informing her tender audience, the caresses recommenced. There was a charming confusion, they were made and rendered almost deliriously, especially on the part of the Beauty, delighted to belong to such illustrious parents and no longer having to fear dishonoring the Prince her cousin by causing him to make an alliance unworthy of him.

Although transported by the excess of her happiness, however, she did not forget the man she had believed to be her father. She reminded her aunt the promise she had made to enable him and his children to have the honor of attending her wedding. She was still talking to her about it when she saw from her window sixteen individuals appear on horseback, the majority of whom had hunting horns and appeared very embarrassed. The disorder of the troop was sufficient evidence that the horses had carried them away by force. The Beauty recognized them easily as the man's six sons, their sisters and their five lovers.

Everyone except the fay was surprised by that abrupt entrance. Those who made it were no less so on finding themselves, by virtue of the impetuosity of their horses, transported to a palace unknown to them. This is how the accident had happened: they had all been hunting when their horses, uniting in a squadron, had run with rapidity all the way to the palace, without it being possible to retain them, in spite of all the efforts they had been able to make.

Forgetting her present dignity, the Beauty hastened to go to meet them in order to reassure them. She embraced them all them with generosity.

The father also appeared, but without disorder. The horse had come to whinny and scratch at his door. He had not doubted that it had come to find him on behalf of his dear daughter. He made use of it without dread and, easily judging where his mount was taking him, he was not astonished to find himself in the courtyard of a palace, which he was seeing for the third time, and to whom he suspected that he was being taken in order to witness the marriage of the Beauty and the Beast.

As soon as he perceived her, he ran to her with open arms, blessing the happy moment that presented her to his eyes and heaping blessings upon the generous Beast that permitted his return. He looked in all directions with the design of rendering it very humble thanks for the kindnesses with which it had heaped his family, and especially his youngest daughter. He was sorry not to perceive it, and apprehensive that his conjectures might be false. However, the presence of his children gave him reason to believe that he had thought justly, and that they would not have been drawn to this place if it had not been a matter of a solemn celebration, such as the marriage ought to be.

That reflection made by the fellow internally did not prevent him from hugging the Beauty tenderly in his arms and moistening her face with tears that joy made him shed.

After having allowed him to savor the moment at his ease, the fay finally said to him: "That's enough, Fellow; you have lavished your caresses upon this Princess sufficiently. It is time to stop looking at her like a father; you will learn that that title does not belong to you, and that you presently owe her homage, as to your sovereign. She is the Princess of the

Fortunate Isle, the daughter of the King and the Queen that you see, and she is about to become the wife of this Prince. This is the Queen, his mother, the sister of the King. As for the Prince," she added, seeing that the fellow was staring at her, "he is better known to you than you think, but his form is different from the one you have previously seen; in a word, this the Beast itself."

On learning such surprising news, the father and the brothers were delighted, while the sisters felt a dolorous jealousy; but they disguised it under the appearances of a feigned satisfaction, by which no one was fooled. However, everyone pretended to believe that they were sincere. As for the lovers, whom the hope of possessing the Beauty had rendered inconstant, and who had only returned to their first bonds in despair of obtaining her, they did not know what to think.

The merchant could not help weeping, without being able to decide whether those tears originated from the pleasure of seeing the good fortune of the Beauty or the dolor of losing such a perfect daughter. His sons were agitated by the same sentiments. The Beauty, extremely sensible to the evidence of their tenderness, begged those on whom she now depended, as well as the Prince, her future spouse, to permit her to recognize such a tender affection. Her pleas testified too well to the goodness of her heart for them not to be heard. They were heaped with gifts, and with the kind permission of the King, the Prince and the Queen, the Beauty conserved for them the affectionate names of father, brothers and even sisters, even though she was not unaware that the latter had no more in their hearts than blood.

She wanted all of them to continue to make use of the same name by which they had called her when they believed her to be one of their family. The old man and his children would employ it in the Beauty's Court and would continually enjoy the good fortune of living with her at a rank sufficiently illustrious to be generally considered. As for the sisters' lovers, whose passion would have easily been reignited if it had not been futile, they would be very glad to unite themselves with the old man's daughters and marry persons for whom the Beauty conserved so much generosity.

All those she desired to be present at her marriage had arrived. It was not deferred any longer, and during the night that followed that happy day, the Prince was not struck by the soporific spell to which he succumbed on the Beast's wedding night. To celebrate that august fête, several days went by in pleasures. They only ended because the fay, the young bride's aunt, warned them that they ought not to delay quitting that beautiful solitude any longer and that it was necessary to return to their estates to show themselves to their subjects.

It was appropriate that she had them remember their kingdom and the indispensable duties that recalled them there. Delighted by the abode they inhabited, charmed with the pleasure that they had in loving one another and saying so, they had entirely forgotten sovereign grandeur, as well as the embarrassments consequent upon it. The newlyweds even proposed to the fay to renounce it and to consent to her disposing of their position in favor of whomever she judged appropriate, but the sage Intelligence represented to them ardently that they were obliged to fulfill the destiny that had charged them with the government of their people, in order that those same people would conserve an eternal respect for them.

They yielded to those just remonstrations, but the Prince and the Beauty obtained permission for them to come occasionally to that place, in order to relax from the burdens inseparable from their condition, and that they would be served there by the invisible spirits or the animals that had kept them company in the preceding years.

They took advantage of the liberty as much as was possible for them. Their presence appeared to embellish the place; everyone hastened to please them. The spirits waited for the impatiently and received them with joy, testifying to them in a hundred ways what they felt on their return.

The fay, whose foresight was attentive to everything, gave them a chariot pulled by twelve white stags with antlers and hooves of gold, like her own. The speed of those animals almost surpassed that of thought, and by their means, one could easily go around the world in two hours. In that fashion they wasted no time in their journey; they took advantage of every instant they could devote to their pleasure.

They also made use of that fine transport frequently to go and see the King of the Fortunate Isle, their father, who had been so prodigiously rejuvenated by the return of the fay Queen that he ceded nothing in beauty and wellbeing to his son-in-law the Prince. He was just as happy, being no less amorous nor any less eager than the Prince to give his wife continual evidence of his sentiments.

The latter, for her part, responded with all the love that had caused misfortunes for such a long time. She had been received by her subjects with transports of joy as great as the dolors caused to them by the sensible loss of her affection, and still loved her dearly. Nothing then opposed her power, and for several centuries she showed them all the marks of her good will that they could desire. Her power, combined with the amity of the Queen of the Fays, conserved the life, the health and the youth of her husband the King. Both of them only ceased to live because humans cannot last forever.

She and her sister fay had the same intention for the Beauty, her husband, his mother the Queen, the old man and his family, with the result that so much life had never been seen. The Queen, the Prince's mother, did not forget to have this marvelous story inscribed in the archives of that empire and in those of the Fortunate Isle, in order to transmit it to posterity. Relations of it were sent throughout the world, in order that there would be talk eternally of the prodigious adventures of the Beauty and the Beast.

THE NAIADS

Although our marine maps give us a geographical picture of all maritime lands, I nevertheless find myself obliged to ask you to excuse me from giving you the position of the land in which the adventures I am going to relate to you took place. All that I knew for certain is that in a place not far from China there is a kingdom that abounds in everything that can contribute to the wealth of a State.

A few centuries ago that fertile canton was obedient to a King who, by his virtues, merited the high rank in which Heaven had placed him. He loved his subjects as much as his own children, his only care was to render them happy, and, regarding peace as the fundamental basis of the happiness of peoples, he spared no effort to reach an understanding with his neighbors.

Although his inclination was entirely given to mildness, he had testified sufficiently that weakness played no part in that, having vigorously repelled an enemy jealous of his prosperity, whom ambition had persuaded that it would be easy for him to vanquish a King whose placid humor was a poor augury for his courage. That ambitious Prince was mistaken in his project, however, and the King, who combined with the love of peace a consummate valor and experience, triumphed without difficulty over that imprudent enemy.

Having pursued him all the way to his own land, where he could have made great progress, his rival's chimerical hopes were so disappointed that the Prince in question made accommodating proposals, which the King's pacific humor led him to accept. Content to have made it known that his conduct was an effect of wisdom and not fear, he returned everything that he had conquered, only applying himself consequently to ensuring the welfare of his subjects.

He enabled the arts to flourish, maintained the laws, protected commerce and justice, and although his principal concern was the avoidance of war, he nevertheless maintained military schools, so the young men who were educated there did not run any risk of being surprised by their ignorance in case he was obliged to break the peace. His generosity bore him to recompense magnificently the slightest advice that was presented to him when it tended to public advantage.

In sum, the monarch would have been a perfect model of all the virtues if he had been able to force his natural mildness to allow him to show a little more severity occasionally. Always ready to reward good deeds, however, he was not always prepared to punish the guilty and whatever crimes that they had committed, he could not resolve to refuse them mercy if they asked for it.

By virtue of that excess of generosity, and the impunity of which the guilty were almost certain, he authorized a license that often caused great disorder among his subjects, who represented to him in vain that his excessive clemency was costing honest people too dear. He was not offended by those remonstrations, but nor did he correct himself.

Far from that mildness—which might have passed for insensibility—being admired by those who abused it, it became the subject of a scorn that, passing insensibly from the Court to the people, caused him to be generally given the name of *gnan gnan gnaan pouii pouaa*—which is to say, in our language and pronounced slowly, Good and Better.[5]

(As the idiom of the country is not familiar to me, I shall tell you everyone's names in their language once, and then reduce them to French, which will be more convenient for me.)

---

[5] The original has *Bon et Rebon*, the second word being an improvisation implying "re-good" or "good again," but as George Orwell's "newspeak" has already co-opted "plusgood" and equipped it with particular connotations, it seemed preferable simply to use "better."

The generosity of the Prince was not a rule for his entire family, and he had a relative whose inclinations were very different. Like the King, he had all the necessary qualities to make a great Prince, but he had none of those appropriate to a good subject. By virtue of the proximity of blood and his master's benefits, he lacked nothing but wearing the crown, but he was not happy. The ambition that devoured him poisoned all the pleasures that he might have savored if he had been of a different humor, for Good and Better, who loved him dearly, did nothing without consulting him, and shared his authority with him. He took excess of facility as far as to have the same honors rendered to his person, because his penetration allowed him to know only too clearly the passion that agitated the Prince's heart, but he hoped to triumph over it by means of honors, believing, rather inappropriately, that the best means to contain him was to bring him so close to the throne that there was no longer any difference between the master and the subject.

The Prince's passion was so far from secret that he had already been nicknamed *Kaustrombihc*—which is to say, Ambitious. Nicknames were much in vogue in the realm, and he was soon only known by that one; far from being offended by it, he gloried in it. The King, seeing that he was flattered by it, left it to him.

Although the monarch lacked neither intelligence nor enlightenment, his great generosity deceived him, and he believed that by satisfying the vanity of Ambitious he would prevent him from becoming culpable; but he was mistaken, for the closer that pride came to the throne, the more the desire to reign was inflamed. Far from the honors that were heaped upon him putting limits of the fury that possessed him, they served to stimulate it, and he could not contain himself when he thought that all his grandeur was solely dependent on the benefits of a man whose power could destroy them at any time, with as little effort as it had required to bestow them.

Ambitious had a faithful friend who sought to soothe him in that kind of torture, representing to him that he was the only one who opposed his own happiness, since his ambition ought to be satisfied with the favors that Good and Better lavished on him, and that if he were wise, he would enjoy a fortune that he could not take any further without crime. Ambitious rejected that sound advice, however, responding proudly that it was unworthy of a heart like his to receive favors, that the word alone was sufficient to poison the happiness that was praised to him, and that only the power to give them in his turn could compensate him for having received them. He could not bear only wearing the odious title of subject, becoming firmer every day in the determination to shrug off that yoke.

He took measures to execute his design, and not only was he determined to dethrone his master, but also to take away his life, believing that it would be impossible for him to enjoy his usurpation while he allowed a respectable Prince, who had only occupied himself throughout his life with the welfare of his subjects, to go on breathing.

He took measures that he thought infallible to stab him during one of the strolls that Good and Better often took with him, adding to that frightful project that of abducting Princess Licmanekic (as that name is similar to that of Lisimene, I shall translate it thus). Princess Lisimene was the King's only daughter. The perfidious Ambitious wanted to put her in a place as secure as it was secret, where he would dispose of her fate, and, depending on the sentiments that the people testified in her regard, he would let her live, cause her to die or keep her in irons, as his interest required.

The execution of that criminal design did not seem to face any obstacle. Ambitious had more creatures than the King; he had inspired so much scorn for the good King in them that each of them believed that he was doing a noble deed in committing that parricide. The ingrate had also attracted to his party several people whose relatives had been murdered, or had experienced injustices of some kind and had been unable to obtain satisfaction, Good and Better's weakness preventing him from refusing the mercy for which the guilty parties had confidently asked.

It is true that to compensate those whose blood was crying out in vain for vengeance, he had lavished gifts and positions on them, but that means had not succeeded. Without rejecting their King's benefits, those culpable subjects had nevertheless conserved a violent desire to avenge themselves. Ambitious told them incessantly that the weakness of the Prince and the impunity of crimes exposed the State to a thousand disorders, and that there was no longer any security for property, life or even the honor of daughters, abductions being as common as murders.

Everything was already arranged to the liking of the perfidious Ambitious when one of the conspirators, who owed to the generosity of the King a mercy that he could not have expected from the law, penetrated by remorse and frightened by the horror of such a criminal action, unable to resolve to betray his master and benefactor, decided to disclose the plot into which he had entered.

That man, more culpable by virtue of misfortune than inclined to vice, not believing that it was permissible for him, without crime, to keep the secret of a plot in which he had been reluctantly engaged, addressed himself to the Prime Minister. By that means, he obtained a private audience, in which he exposed to the King all of Ambitious' intentions, named his accomplices, among whom were the greatest lords in the Court and even those he had heaped with the most benefits. Finally, he told him that the conspirators were to carry out their enterprise the following day.

The King's surprise was extreme on learning the circumstances of the infamous plot, but nothing was equal to the anger of the Prime Minister, whose wisdom had always opposed the King's indulgence, fruitlessly.

"Well, Sire," he said to him, vehemently, "will you defer yet again, in accordance with your custom, the punishment of these guilty men, and wait tranquilly for them to come and plunge a dagger into your breast? Forgive me if I say that you have already taken that indulgent weakness too far, that you can see the fruit it has borne, and that you would not be exposed to the danger that threatens you now if you had not spared from death subjects so worthy of receiving it." He added: "There is no longer any question of temporizing; I believe that you can see the consequences clearly enough not to oppose my assembling your guards and those subjects I know to be faithful to you, in order to arrest the guilty men, who cannot be subjected too soon to the punishment they deserve."

With these words, he tried to leave in order to carry out what the Prince could not help ordering him to do; but the Prince stopped him with an impatient phlegm. "Very well, Vizier," he said to him, "without raging against my indulgence, consider that if my life is in danger by virtue of the treason of those to whom I have accorded a mercy that they do not merit, it has been saved by a man loyal to me, to whom I have the same obligation today as he previously had to me. Thus, although you criticize the excess of my generosity, I cannot repent of it, since it has acquired me a grateful friend."

"What, Sire?" the Vizier went on, impatiently. "You want to leave these impious individuals the time and convenience to come and attack you, and it will be necessary for us to watch tranquilly as the vainglorious Ambitious stabs you before our eyes? Rather let him expiate his crime by the most frightful tortures! Is any cruel enough to punish such an atrocity?"

"Stop, Zulbach," said the King, holding him back. "It isn't just that after so often refusing my subjects the vengeance thy have demanded of me, I appear more ardent for my own interests that I was for theirs. They would then have a legitimate occasion to murmur against me, and to say that I have as much concern for threats against my life as I have indifference to save theirs; but you do not know me if you have been able to conceive that thought."

"Just Heaven!" cried Zulbach, overwhelmed by dolor. "Is it necessary that by virtue of such misplaced delicacy I shall see the most precious blood in the world spilled, and that it not be permitted for me to raise any obstacle to it?" He went on: "What is your plan, Sire; can you not conceive the error of this false magnanimity, which disguises the weakness with which you are abandoning your days to the favors of this parricide? Well, scorn life, abandon it without regret, along with your crime, but think of the state to which you will reduce the Princess, and to what horror you will leave her exposed after you have found the death to which you are running so ardently."

"You have not penetrated my design," the King replied. "No, my dear Zulbach, I don't want to abandon my daughter to the misfortunes you foresee, but there are gentler means than those you are offering me to prevent that effect. I don't intend to run to death, but I can't resolve either to preserve myself by that of Ambitious. I admit that he's culpable, but he's of my blood, and that privilege demands that I punish him in a manner other than the one I inflict on my common subjects. I'm preparing for him a punishment that is harsher for a heart like his than if I made him suffer a torture that would be as shameful for me as for him. Let him be summoned," he went on, "but secretly, for publicity might harm my project."

Without penetrating his master's design, Zulbach approved of the secrecy that he wanted to maintain, but not for the same motive. He only feared that the guilty Prince might escape if he suspected that his crimes were known.

(Zulbach signifies "immortal torch, model for the most faithful subjects," so I have left the name in the original language.)

An officer of the guard was detached in order to go and inform the Prince, simply, that the King had summoned him, and he took him to the monarch's apartment without knowing himself what was happening.

Ambitious, believing himself sure of the execution of his project, and fearful of arousing the King's suspicion if he did not go to see him, did so directly, affecting a very tranquil attitude. However, he could not help a pang of anxiety on seeing the guard changed and perceiving that it had been doubled in the places through which he passed—which the Minister, who feared that the Prince might escape, had done unknown to the King, convinced that the latter would have refused the order had he requested it.

The Prince's surprise increased on seeing Zulbach next to his master, and although the Minister and the guards surrounding him rendered him the same honors as they were accustomed to do, the cold and severe expression painted in Zulbach's eyes caused him to be apprehensive of some misfortune for himself.

As soon as he was in Good and Better's chamber, the Vizier, on the King's order, sent everyone else away, and remained alone with him. Having made Ambitious sit down, the King declared without anger that he knew about his design, without implying any hostility; on the contrary, he looked at him affectionately.

"My dear Ambitious," he said, before explaining himself, "I'm certain that you're unaware of the reason for which I've summoned you; I was unaware of it myself a quarter of an hour ago, and I would never have suspected it; but in sum, as the matter is urgent, I thought it necessary to interrupt your repose, and I didn't imagine that it was possible to delay, without peril, informing you that I'm sufficiently informed of the plan you've made to murder me tomorrow during our stroll. You see," he continued, "that I could not lose any time in order to let you know that your plan was known to me, without exposing you to committing an enormous crime, by steeping your hands in the blood of a King, your relative and your most faithful friend."

Far from this speech inspiring the slightest repentance in Ambitious, and not being touched by so much generosity, he stood up, denied everything, raging against the accusation as if a blatant injustice were being done to him. It would not have taken much for him to demand reparation, but Good and Better obliged him to sit down again, told him that he would spare him the trouble of defending himself; that he was too well informed for there to be any possibility of him refuting it by oaths, and that the only resource that remained to him was to rely on his amity."

"I can't believe," the King went on, "that you meditated such a crime purely by virtue of the motive of personal hatred against me. By what would I have merited it? I have never given you and grounds for complaint; on the contrary, I have always done everything possible to attract your amity as frankly as I have given you mine."

He went on: "Let's not talk about it anymore; I don't want to excite your animosity by longer reproaches, nor augment your confusion by forcing you to search for bad reasons to color the violence and injustice of your conduct. I can see only too clearly that it has no foundation except your ambition; that alone has drawn you into an enterprise so opposed to the sentiments of honor that you ought to have. I am convinced that, if you had been born to this throne, the unique object of your desires, you would have had no reluctance in choosing me for your favorite, and you would have been right, for I love you veritably, and I swear to you that if I could dispose of my crown without doing an injustice to my daughter, I would cede it to you with all my heart and I would not think that I had purchased your amity too dearly.

"Oh, my dear Prince," he continued, "it seems that the brightness of the object of your desires disguises the weight and the difficulties, and after having acquired it, on considering it at close range, you would detest it, if it had cost you your innocence. Think, then to what remorse and regrets the memory of my death would have exposed you. I repeat to you that if I were not a father, I would spare you the trouble of committing a crime in order to reign and abandon to you the throne that you are devouring internally; you would have the satisfaction of mounting it as a legitimate master. However, it is not just that in sacrificing everything to your desires I disinherit me daughter, whom I love, and whom I cannot deprive without injustice of the right she has to succeed me.

"However," he continued, after having thought for a moment, "although I cannot do everything in your favor that I would wish, I do not think that it is absolutely impossible for us to arrange matters by surrendering, you a part of your desires and me one of my rights. I think I have found a means of reconciling our hearts and out fortunes. This is it.

"You are a father, as I am, and if that reason prevents me from descending from the throne, it is perhaps, without your knowing it, the reason that excites you to want to mount it. Your ambition might well have for its foundation no other desire than enabling your son to reign, and it is perhaps the cause, as innocent as it is unknown, of your criminal projects. Don't form any more, therefore; rather have the son that is so dear come to my Court; you are of sufficiently high rank for no one to criticize the design I have formed to give him my daughter. Lisimene has beauty; although your son does not know her, I am convinced that the sight of her will not disrupt our design, and that he will fulfill without difficulty the treaty to which I invite you.

"Come on, Prince," he said, extending his hand to him benevolently, "think about it, and tell me without dissimulation whether you can, at a price that will make you my brother, resolve to stop hating me and let me live with the shadow of a crown that will be more yours than mine."

Zulbach and Ambitious were equally astonished by this speech. Although they knew their master's character they would not have dared to expect that excess of generosity; their surprise was so great that it had played a greater part than respect in the silence that they had both maintained while the King was speaking.

Ambitious did not know what to say. He saw that he was convicted, and if he tried to persist in denying the accusation, he had no doubt that, the King being so well informed of the names of the conspirators, a sufficiently large number of them would be forced to name him and sustain that he was their leader. He was known to them all; there was not one who did not have the conviction of the treaty written by his own hand, by virtue of the promises he had made in order to engage them in his interests. Those mute witnesses were too irreproachable for him to dare to accuse them of falsity.

On the other hand, he could not help admiring the grandeur of soul and generosity of an offended King who had him in his power, who could and perhaps ought to punish him according to all the rules of prudence, but who, instead of the torture that he clearly sensed was due to him, was asking him for peace and amity. He had not expected the favor that the King was doing him in offering him the hand of the Princess for his son, and he did not know how to respond.

Good and Better, who perceived his embarrassment, embraced him tenderly. "I don't want to hear either excuses or thanks," he told him. "I've already said everything that you could say to me by way of justification, and I can't at present imagine the terms that you might employ to thank me; so, without a longer speech, send for your son in order that we can judge whether Lisimene will please him.

"Oh, Sire," exclaimed Ambitious, who had finally recovered the use of speech, "my son doesn't merit the honor you want to do him. He's a young man—what am I saying? he's a child—that I have had raised among hermits, wanting them to form his mind to science and virtue before the dissipation of the Court could occupy him sufficiently to prevent him applying himself to the worthy possession of the grandeur that is destined for him."

"That won't be an obstacle," said the King. "He's fifteen years old and my daughter is only twelve, while perfecting himself in what it's appropriate for him to know, they'll make one another's acquaintance and learn to love one another; so, let him come without delay."

With those words, the King sent him away, ordering him to keep secret what had just occurred. "It isn't necessary," he added, "for the public to be informed of what happens within families. Only Zulbach knows, but he's wise and can keep a secret; in spite of the confidence I have in him, though, I would have kept him in the dark if he hadn't found out about it before me. Finally," he added, "to prove my sincerity, I'll pardon all the conspirators as a favor to you. Adieu, Prince, go and exhort them to be more faithful in future."

Ambitious retired, after bowed without response, leaving the King with his Minister, who was so nonplussed that it was impossible for him to pronounce a single word.

"Well, Vizier, can you conceive my satisfaction?" Good and Better said to him. "I've finally found the means of returning Ambitious to his duty, and I won't be forced to punish him. What threats and punishments could not have done, the expedient I've found will do."

"Sire," said Zulbach, "It's not for me to contradict the will of my master. Clemency is beautiful, but I fear that your might expose you to a repentance as futile as it will be belated; for, after all, permit me to ask you on what you found that of the criminal prince, and what evidence he has given you of it? You have made it known to him that you were informed of his crime and, without giving him time to reflect, nor to fear your wrath, you have promised him mercy. What am I saying, promised? That's not a strong enough word to describe your procedure, and I'm not saying too much in telling you that you offered it to him with a haste that seemed to beg him to accept it. You even employed the strongest terms to hide from him that you believe that he needs your clemency; it seemed that you took charge of the embarrassment of justifying him, while he has nothing to do but let you act.

"Not content with pardoning him without his appearing to repent," the Vizier went on, "You forestalled him and solicited him to accept the Princess for his son, as a pledge of our good faith. Alas, in heaping him with honors instead of the punishments he merits, you're placing him more comfortably than he was before for piercing your heart. May it please our divinities that the fear in question is without foundation!"

The king responded that he could not have done otherwise, and that it would not have been according a grace to allow him to fear not obtaining it.

"The favors of a King are always favors," said Zulbach. "Only too fortunate are those who obtain them, and even more so are those who are worthy of them; but they ought to be measured to merit, and not lavished on criminals whose crime

142

is certain and their repentance more equivocal. And I beg you to tell me," he continued, "what augmentation you would have put into it if he had rendered you a signal service, or you had done him some injustice, for which remorse urged you to make a reparation?"

The King, who knew that his Vizier was right, but nevertheless did not want to change his manner of acting, interrupted him without wanting to hear any more and sent him away, forbidding him very expressly to reveal the secret to anyone.

While the good King, who judged the hearts of others by his own, was applauding himself for such a generous action, he was doubtless counting on the conquest of the heart of Ambitious. That Prince, who thought differently, withdrawing to his study, summoned the Princess his wife, whose sentiments were no more equitable or more moderate than his own, and who entered joyfully into all his unjust projects.

He told her what had just happened to him, unable, in spite of his passion, to prevent himself praising the King's moderation; it even seemed that that excess of generosity had produced the effect that the monarch desired. He felt almost shaken, and in the resolution to accept such advantageous offers, to renounce his pernicious designs, contenting himself with the grandeur of his son; but the proud Princess opposed that strongly.

"How weak you are," she said to him, disdainfully. "Can you mistake for magnanimity a pusillanimous weakness, which means that you only owe to his timidity the mercy that your blindness represents to you as evidence of affection. Can you doubt that anyone else in your place would have obtained a similar one, and do you not share that good fortune with the least slave? Blood in general horrifies that coward, he fears seeing it shed, and that is all his virtue; however, you have let yourself be taken in to the point that you are ready to accept the frivolous advantages he offers your son, without paying any attention to the unpleasantness that accompanies them, in becoming the subject of the individual that law and nature

143

have rendered yours, and who, without having any obligation to Good and Better, will reign in his turn after you have lived. Would it not be more honorable for that Prince to mount the throne as the son of a King succeeding his father than as a subject who receives the crown by a favor that tarnishes its brilliance?

"You're not making the reflection," said the Prince, "that I'm about to engage myself to a identity that will become indispensable, for I can't refuse to summon my son immediately without rendering myself suspect, and when he's here, he'll be a hostage whose life will answer for anything I might undertake."

"What does it matter?" cries the Princess. "Can you hesitate between the throne and him? Nothing is more commonplace than being a father, and nothing is rarer than being a King. He wouldn't merit our alarm if he were capable of regretting danger, were to be exposed to it in such a beautiful opportunity. But," she added, "all these various interests can be conciliated, since it's easy for you to delay his arrival by means of a feigned illness, and the advantage that is being offered to him is too considerable for anyone to suspect that the that the delay is only a pretext.

"Meanwhile," she went on, "go to the Court, follow the King, and if he perseveres in his foolish confidence, don't hesitate to render him the victim of it. Since he can't fail to be someone's, it's better that he's yours than that someone else might have as much right to the Empire as you have. Above all, hasten the execution as much as you can, and don't give further traitors the time to imitate the first who betrayed you."

Ambitious was delighted to find so much courage in his wife; a residue of virtue had almost made him repent and accept his forgiveness at the price of the generosity that the Prince wanted to show him, but his ambition was reanimated in following the deadly advice of his wife. He sent for the leaders of his conspiracy and, without preamble, he told them that he was obliged to postpone his enterprise and put it off until another day, without declaring the veritable motive.

After having taken that precaution, he waited, not without some emotion for daylight in the King's residence, to which he went, and where the frankness with which he was received finished reassuring him and determining to the treason from which it ought to have distracted him.

Good and Better, greeting him with a gracious smile, asked him whether he had takes measures to summon his son. Ambitious replied, with the most grateful and respectful appearance that was possible for him, that he had given orders as soon as he had received his own, and that he expected to have the honor of introducing him to him the following day.

After having given him a thousand caresses, the King announced the marriage that he had projected, which attracted to the Prince further respects from the courtiers; then he delivered himself fully to the discretion of that treaty, the fortunate success of which, emboldened him the following day to announce to the King with a feigned dolor the pretended illness that would delay his son's arrival for two or three days.

Good and Better's confidence made him content with that excuse, hoping that the delay would not be long. In order that the meeting of his daughter and the young Prince could take place with more liberty, avoiding a certain inconvenient ceremony, he decided that he would go to spend a few days at a house of pleasure that he had, half a day's journey from the city, to which he ordered Ambitious to bring his son.

Nothing could have been more advantageous to that perfidious individual's criminal designs. The château was not fortified, and the King never went there with any other retinue than that of his hunting carriages.

Ambitious did not neglect circumstances so favorable. On the fourth day that the King and the Princess were there, he took the final measures to make the conspiracy burst forth in the middle of the night. He had stayed in the city, where he would render himself master of the palace, and having taken possession of it without effort he would send word promptly to the château where the King was to inform the conspirators who had made the journey, in order that they would take his life without delay and then, seizing Lisimene, they would bring her to him secretly.

But whatever precautions hc took to prevent his plan being discovered, so that those to whom he had given the order would go to the château before anyone could discover what was happening, he could not act cleverly enough to deceive the vigilance of Zulbach, who, desperate to see that his zeal would not be futile with regard to his matter, had taken measures to keep watch on Ambitious. He had done that so cleverly that they would furnish him with the means to escape during the initial tumult and reach the King before the Tyrant's emissaries.

Fortunately for his master, the zealous Minister, more suspicious than him, having been unable to inspire him with his sentiments, had employed all his industry in observing those he mistrusted. Having remarked an extraordinary movement among them, including the fact several of those he knew to be devoted to Ambitious had gone home in a mysterious manner and in small groups, he had no doubt that it was a consequence of the plot against the King that had been revealed so uselessly. He believed that it was very necessary for the wellbeing of Good and Better that he leave home in disguise, in order to discover what was happening, not being able to entrust such an important occupation to anyone else.

The night was very dark, and it was easy for him to instruct himself of everything that he had suspected. He saw Ambitious go into the King's palace with an escort of armed men, whose seizure of the doors told Zulbach that all was lost. He still had time to determine that with certainty, for, thanks to his disguise, slipping among the people, he heard the order of death that the Tyrant gave against his King, and shivered at the evident peril that he knew him to be in. He despaired of not being with him, in order to help him, and to risk his own life in order to conserve one so precious. He was in that perplexity when one of Ambitious' favorites got him out of difficulty by virtue of the advice that he gave the monster.

"Believe me, Sire," he said to him. "Leave the indolent Good and Better in his solitude, and permit him to enjoy life without anxiety for two hours more. He has no suspicion of the fate that is in preparation for him, for it isn't possible for him to receive any information about what is happening here, since the city gates are closed. As you have business here that doesn't permit you to be distant from those whose fidelity ought to be charged with such an important commission, it's necessary to leave that execution to the last.

Zulbach breathed out at that speech, but, not flattering himself that he was strong enough to oppose the violence of the usurper openly, he only thought about means of helping the King and the Princess, thinking that, provided that he could preserve them from the danger by which they were menaced, they would be able to do something.

The city gates were still closed, in accordance with the advice of the rebel, but as the Vizier lived in a old palace that had once been the residence of Kings, predecessors of Good and Better, and it had a tunnel unknown to the public, which, by a route shorter than the ordinary road, went to the house of pleasure where the King was. The generous Vizier flattered himself on the good fortune of saving his master by that means.

Going home promptly, he equipped himself with two sets of clothing of different sex, a purse filled with gold coins and a covered basket, into which he put two pigeons accustomed to playing the role of carrier pigeons and bearing by air the letters with which they were charged.

With that provision he passed diligently into the tunnel and went to the apartment, which was connected to it by a secret stairway. He knocked on the bedroom door of the monarch, who, being too good to suspect that he had enemies, got up without summoning anyone and without taking any precaution, and came to open it himself.

His astonishment was not mediocre at the sight of Zulbach, whose presence at such an hour, by the route that left no doubt that he had very important reasons for taking such a step. The consternated expression that he saw on his face was further confirmation of that thought. He took in at a glance his singular attire, the package under his arm, and the muted lantern in one hand and a basket in the other; everything proved to him that there was something extraordinary in this nocturnal visit.

The Vizier did not give him time to ask questions. "Get dressed promptly, Sire," he said to him, handing him the package he held, "and flee without delay from a place where your august person is no longer safe. The traitor Ambitious, abusing your generosity, has rendered himself master of the city, where he has given orders that crown his perfidy. Someone might come at any moment to murder you and abduct the Princess, and you only have this moment to escape the fury of the conspirators."

The excessive generosity of the King, which prevented him from making violent resolutions against criminal subjects, did not take away any of his courage, and, far from wanting to owe his life to a flight he thought undignified, he only thought of selling his days dearly to the perfidious individual who had dared to attack him.

"I see, my dear Zulbach," he said to the Vizier, "that Heaven has given you more enlightenment than me, and that it was with justice that you mistrusted that scoundrel; but, although the experience teaches me that your sentiment was better than mine, suffer that I still oppose the advice you are giving me. Far from fleeing like a coward, I am returning to my capital, where I intend to appear in the midst of the seditious individuals. The presence of their offended King will certainly recall them to duty, while reanimating the zeal of those who remain my faithful subjects. I shall put myself at their head and I shall punish the rebels, or, if I cannot do that, I shall perish like a King, weapons in hand, without ceding my crown to an unworthy usurper."

That resolution frightened Zulbach extremely. "What do you want to attempt, Sire?" he cried. "I think that you are sufficiently convinced of my fidelity ad my experience not to doubt that, if that means were possible, I would have attempted it, and that if I did not see that everything is lost I would not be advising you to flee. But I know only too well that your loss is indubitable and that the Princess will be exposed to horrors at which I tremble. Oh, Sire, can you think of that without fear, or without such a consideration obliging you to put your person and hers in security, if you will not deign to do so for your own interest?"

That representation touched King to the point of making him shed tears, but without persuading him. Flight seemed to him a course of action so shameful that he could not resolve to take it, and he would never have consented to the desires of that faithful subject if the Princess had not joined the Vizier.

Her apartment was adjacent to the King's. The conversation he was having with his Minister woke her up. She was afraid that the King was in trouble, and got up without calling her women. She threw on a light robe and passed diligently into the room where they were.

One cannot be more surprised than she was to find Zulbach there. "Oh, Princess," he said to her, as soon as he perceived her, "please engage the King to save his own life and yours." Then he told her what he had just said to Good and Better, as well as informing her of the King's reluctance to flee.

Frightened by her father's peril, Lisimene threw herself at her father's feet, imploring him to follow his favorite's advice. "Alas, Sire," she said, "Why do you want to abandon me? What will become of me if you succumb, or rather, how can you conceive the thought of rushing into a danger from which it will be impossible to extract yourself?"

Although the state into which dolor had thrown the Princess touched the King sensibly, he would not have yielded to it if the Vizier had not remonstrated with him, telling him that if he appeared, the small number of those who had remained dutiful would be murdered without obtaining success and without being able to defend themselves, instead of which, if the usurper met no resistance he would not seek to shed blood needlessly, which would only serve to render him odious. He added that if the King would do as he said and withdraw, he could hope for a further change, because the people—who, for love of novelty had just declared in favor of Ambitious—might return with the same lightness to the domination of their original master.

Good and Better finally ceded to the insistence of his daughter and his Minister. It was agreed the Zulbach would return diligently to the city by the same route by which he had come, while the King and the Princess would escape the vigilance of the usurper.

The Vizier helped them dress in the clothes he had brought them and presented the pigeons to the King. "See, Sire," he said, "these faithful messengers. When you have found a refuge, send them to me to inform me of it, and I will make use of the same convenience when I have something to tell you. I flatter myself that my indulgence will find me a means to insinuate myself into the confidence of the Tyrant, and that I will succeed in causing him to perish by his own weapons."

The King and the Princess were ready to depart, and the Vizier was artful enough to enter the stables silently, where he prepared two of the best horses, and took them out without being perceived.

He put the fugitive monarch and his daughter outside the château, and after having seen them go, he gladly went back into the tunnel, having carefully replaced the paneling that concealed the entrance on the side of the apartment, and returned to his palace without anyone having perceived his absence. He was fortunate enough that once he was at home the usurper sent for him, and had no reason to suspect him.

The order to go to Ambitious was given to him at daybreak. He followed those who brought it without resistance and was introduced into the Council Chamber, where all those who ought to compose it were already assembled.

Ambitious made them a long speech which was only intended to disguise his usurpation and make them approve it.

He supported himself on the pretext that he had been given by the weakness of Good and Better, not forgetting to point out the circumstances that made it dangerous, and had rendered the King unworthy to reign over his subjects, whom he could neither defend nor avenge. He added that the impunities that had caused so much disorder under the previous reign would not dishonor his own and that everyone would be secure

That speech, injurious to the legitimate King, having won over the Council, was greeted with great acclamations. The faithful Zulbach, seeing himself alone in his party, thought it appropriate, for the service of his master, to do as the others did. When everyone cried unanimously: "Long live King Ambitious," he joined in with that criminal proclamation, and did so with such good grace that the Tyrant was deceived by it.

The people gathered at the doors of the palace, having heard those cries, joined their own to them, and received a considerable liberality, the new sovereign having a large quantity of gold coins thrown to them. The satisfied expression that Zulbach affected at a ceremony that pierced him to the heart was noticed by Ambitious, who was so pleased with him for testifying such complete satisfaction that he gave him a thousand public marks of esteem and amity, promising him that he would have no less credit under his reign that under that of his predecessor, and that he wanted henceforth only to govern in accordance with his advice, of which he would make better usage than the old King, who had not deserved to have such an enlightened Minister. Far from making a crime of Zulbach's fidelity, he told him obligingly that he held him in higher esteem for it.

Everything being tranquil in the interior of the city, and Ambitious being sure that it was his, he did not want to wait any longer to send men to invest the place where he had no doubt that Good and Better would be found. Those charged with the execution had orders to keep it secret and not to enter the château until nightfall, but to surround it so well that escape would be impossible.

When he took that futile precaution, it was more than four hours since those whom he wanted to doom had gone, and the reason that obliged the Tyrant to wait for nightfall in order to hide his crime in the darkness gave the illustrious fugitives time to distance themselves sufficiently to avoid his fury.

In order not to be charged with the murder of his King, Ambitious had resolved to persuade the public that Good and Better had stabbed himself, and that he had been driven by despair so far as to stab his own daughter. But those to whom he had given such a cruel order against the King and the Princess only learned of their escape much later, since no one had seen them in the château for more than twelve hours after they had gone.

The Vizier having had the good fortune to set them at liberty four hours before daybreak, the officers of the Prince did not know that they were absent until a long time after the sun had passed its zenith, because the King, all of whose personal actions were simple and constant, had the custom of getting up at daybreak to go out into an extremely large park, where it would have been difficult to find him. As he usually went alone, no one was surprised at first not to encounter him, which often happened, and the Princess had the same facility of absenting herself, because she got up very late.

Finally, however, the time of the one's stroll and the other's slumber having passed, people began to get anxious and to look for them. That search having been vain, fear took hold of the little Court. They wanted to send someone to the city to publish the misfortune, or to find out if, by virtue of an unexpected event that they could not imagine, the King and the Princess might have returned there. The troops that the Tyrant had posted to guard the exterior of the château refused to let out those who tried to get through, however, without wanting to listen to them.

The King and his daughter had already been gone for more than twenty-four hours when their flight became known in the city. Ambitious thought he might die of rage, the life of one and the liberty of the other being of such dangerous consequence for him that he had everything to fear so long as they were not in his power.

He sent people after them immediately, but his efforts were futile, and the fugitives had been able to take such good advantage of the time he had left them that it was impossible to find them.

The unfortunate King judged that it would be imprudent to attempt a retreat outside the realm, all the avenues of which were doubtless guarded. As the château he had just abandoned was surrounded by an immense forest, every corner of which he knew for twenty leagues around, he preferred to escape by that route.

It was necessary to have as much courage as Lisimene had not to succumb from fatigue, but fortunately, she had accompanied her father hunting since the most tender age, and that exercise had given her a vigor that she would not have had if she had been brought up more delicately.

They wandered in the forest for six months, carefully avoiding inhabited places, but finally, becoming weary of such a hard life, they hazarded to emerge from the forest, but without daring to approach towns. It was only to enter a deserted region, where they stayed for some time, and where they had difficulty finding the necessary subsistence for themselves, their horses and their pigeons, but where they had every reason to believe that, being more than a hundred leagues from the capital, they were not running any risk.

They finally quit the woods and the wilderness, their assurance having insensibly advanced so far as to allow them to show themselves in the plain. They found one that seemed very pleasant to them; the air there was temperate, sharp cold being as unknown there as extreme heat.

The further they went into that charming region the more beautiful it seemed to them, but at the same time more deserted. There were only a few rustic dwellings, widely spaced, which gave them an extreme extent, being too far apart to limit one another reciprocally. Thus, in one direction they had meadows as far as the eye could see, and in another, fields covered in wheat, which offered the prospect of a rich harvest. A little further away, hills charged with vines were visible. In sum, it seemed that nature had exhausted herself in order to display her magnificence in the region.

The Princess was so worn out by the fatigues caused to her by the length of the journey she had made and the poor nourishment that she had had, which she had often lacked, that she was finally obliged to ask her father whether they might not stop without danger in that place, because she might be able to find a repose and relief there; if not, she was about to succumb.

The King, knowing that he had nothing to fear in such a solitary place so far from the Court, consented with pleasure to his daughter's desire. They turned their steps toward the nearest habitation, which also seemed to them the most apparent, only perceiving others in the distance, and much inferior to it.

Scarcely were they in a courtyard enclosed by a living hedge than they saw a village woman of pleasant appearance emerge from a garden separated from it by a similar hedge. She was no longer young, but had not yet attained old age.

The woman came toward them and asked them what brought them there. Good and Better told her that they were looking for the master of the house in order to request shelter for a few days; to which she responded that there was no master there, and that the house belonged to her.

The King told her then that they were strangers who, after a long journey, had gone astray in the woods, and begged her to give them hospitality for a few days, inventing a story appropriate to authorize the necessity they had had of abandoning their homeland. In order not to render himself suspect, he added that, in time, he would seek information as to whether there was some land for sale, on which he could build a cabin and cultivate enough land to nourish himself and his daughter. Wanting to prove that he had no evil intentions, the disguised King showed her a few gold coins.

The woman listened attentively, while casting an avid gaze over the treasure he showed her. Adopting a milder tone than she had at first, she said that she would take charge of finding what he desired, and that in addition, they could stay in her house and remain there for as long as they wished.

That response satisfied them greatly, especially Lisimene, who was delighted by the hope of no longer having to sleep on the ground, with no other coverlet than the sky, and finding a nourishment more suitable than that to which they had been reduced for such a long time.

They went into a very simple room, but clean enough; several slaves of both sexes appeared there, but left immediately, being called elsewhere by rural occupations. Some were responsible for the care of the livestock, others for preparing nourishment for their companions, who were working in the fields, harvesting the wheat or tending to the vines. In sum, although there were many people in the place, none was wasting time in frivolous amusements.

On entering the room they found, in addition to the slaves, a tall, thin young woman, dark-complexioned, but who had hair redder than the proudest bull. She had rude eyes and a brutal expression, and the rest of her slim figure was so well-matched that nothing was lacking to make her frightful.

She was shouting at a wretched slave who was preparing wool with which to make clothes, often adding strokes of a lash that she was holding in her hand to the insults with which she was heaping her. That monster was the daughter of the mistress of the house, who called her by her name. " *Grippe Mortiboche*," she said to her, "take our guests to prepared rooms; perhaps this young woman needs to put herself to bed."

For from obeying her mother, however, that honest creature, whose name I shall translate as Pigrieche,[6] replied inso-

---

[6] I have left this "translation"—actually a partial anagram—as it appears in the text, save for removing an acute accent from the e, although it is not irrelevant that the French *pie-grièche*

lently that she was very busy and that they would have to wait, because she had other things to do.

At that grim welcome, Lisimene, fearing to give her occasion to become angrier said mildly that it was unnecessary to go to any trouble for her, and that she would wait until it was convenient. In fact, having sat down, she waited patiently for the moment when it might please Pigrieche to do what her mother ordered.

Meanwhile, the woman, after having seen the gold that the King had shown her, and being very desirous of it, asked him straight out whether he was going to pay her. She said that, naturally, she wanted to give him shelter, but had not pretended that it would be for nothing.

Good and Better did not intend that either, and, glad to have found a safe retreat, he gave her to understand that he had no intention of being a burden to her. With that, they agreed the amount he would give her, and for greater surety he paid her for a few days in advance, given that, in spite of the coarseness of the mother and the ill humor of the daughter, they were very glad to have arrived in that retreat, wanting to remain there for as long as their misfortune lasted.

When the King had reason to believe that they could stay there long enough to inform Zulbach of that stroke of good fortune, he released one of his pigeons, and awaited its return with impatience.

Meanwhile, as much to avoid ennui as to instruct himself regarding the situation of the region where they were, Good and Better enquired about his hostesses. The mother told him that her name was *Dorkplindortk*—which is as if to say

---

means a shrike, or, figuratively, an ill-tempered woman. The name supposedly rendered in the original language is also compounded out of French terms, *grippe* meaning influenza or, figuratively, dislike, *mort* meaning death and *boche* being an insulting term for a German.

Richarde,[7] and that is the name I shall give her—and added that she had not always been named thus, but at that present, it that was the fashion in which she named herself. She told the King that she was a widow, and very rich, harvesting abundantly all that was necessary to life for her and for a large number of slaves who cultivated her land; that she had livestock that furnished her with the wool in which she and her people were clad, and that, in sum, she was in a condition to do without the rest of the world—but, somewhat sequestered as she was, she was always very glad to have a few gold and silver coins. For that, she sent the superfluity of her produce to the market in a small town a few leagues away.

"For what do you use that money," the King asked, "since you have all that you need here? I find that nothing is less necessary."

"You're right," she replied, "and I wouldn't care about it if I hadn't taken my daughter to see the market one day and if she hadn't found people there who had clothes made in another fashion than ours, and of more beautiful fabrics, coiffed with trifles that it's impossible to make here. That pleased her, and the chagrin of not having any has caused her an ill humor that I can't prevent, since I don't have enough gold to buy her similar clothes or all those baubles, and it's necessary for her to be content, reluctantly, to be dressed in the cloth we make and coiffed as all the village women hereabouts are. In addition to the dearth of coin, there's the inconvenience of sending a quantity of our fruits for sale large enough to subsidize it. So, to her great displeasure, she does without all those beautiful adornments. I share her pain," she added, "although I don't say anything to her; I admit privately that it's upsetting for a pretty young woman, but as to that, it's necessary to make her decision and console herself for that misfortune, since there's no remedy for it."

---

[7] A *richarde*, in French, is a wealthy woman, but the slang term carries the implication of a resentful sneer.

The King and the Princess had all the difficulty in the world preventing themselves from laughing at the blindness of the mother, who called a prodigy of ugliness a "pretty young woman," but as they were in her house and did not want to risk making her angry, they did not contradict her, having sufficient occasions already for their patience to be necessary without giving rise to new ones.

It was not that they could not have reached an easy accommodation with Richarde if they had only had what was necessary to satisfy her, for her coarseness appeared to be more a result of lack of education than any malice she had in her heart, and she would not have been insupportable if she had not been possessed of such a foolish affection for her daughter Pigrieche that it was impossible to bear. That creature was always discontented, screeching incessantly, and was justly hated by everyone, whom she hated in return.

Her hatred declared itself particularly against Lisimene, whom she had taken in aversion at first sight, and she would have obliged Richarde to send the Princess and her father away if the gold coins she extracted from them had not softened her, destining them privately to buy clothing.

The King's liberalities gave no less pleasure to Richarde than to Pigrieche, but she looked at them from a more advantageous viewpoint, thinking that they would permit her to enlarge her profession and distance herself from neighbors who inconvenienced her. Those ideas encouraged her to render herself mistress of the entire canton; but in order not to be obliged to wait for a considerable time, and to profit immediately from the treasure that was the objective of her desires, she resolved to marry the King.

That Prince was scarcely out of the prime of life and he had conserved sufficient beauty and good countenance to touch a heart more delicate than that woman's. As she was unaware of the condition of the man she wanted to make her husband, she had no doubt that he would find the proposition very advantageous and appropriate, since he would find by that means an establishment ready made, in a region where he appeared to want to spend his life.

The mildness of Good and Better caused Richarde to hope for an infinite pleasure in that marriage, with the consequence that she proposed it to him without hesitation. He was slightly surprised, but his excessive generosity, which did not permit him to contradict anyone, for fear of giving them chagrin, prevented him from refusing entirely, and caused him to speak in an equivocal manner. In the commerce of good society, it would have been equivalent to an honest refusal; but the woman, who did not know very much, took that politeness for a consent, because when she did not want something she said straight out "I don't want that," without taking care to soften the terms. So, judging others by herself, she regarded the matter as settled, redoubling the attentions she had had for him since he had been in her house.

He fell ill at that time, and she cared for him as she would have done if he had been her husband. Far from being content with her attentions, they caused him a veritable pain, because, having no intention of marrying her, he reproached himself for the necessity he had of receiving services from her, which he would repay with ingratitude in resisting her wishes and deceiving her expectation.

His reflections on the injustice of which he accused himself often occupied him, and gradually accustomed him to think that, since he wanted to live in that solitude, he ought to preserve the amity of the woman, which would be very useful to him while he was forced to remain in that estate, and he promised himself to recompense her liberally for the hand that he could not think of giving her, when he had remounted the throne, by heaping her with so much wealth that she could easily find a husband. He flattered himself with the pleasant idea that it would be possible for him to lavish his favors on her without her being able to criticize him, and without fear that he would be reproached for excessive generosity, since he would only be paying a debt that probity would not permit him to forget.

He was nourishing himself on those chimeras when the return of the latest pigeon that he had sent Zulbach destroyed them. The faithful Minister informed him that the usurper was the tranquil possessor of the throne that he had stolen from him, and that it would be necessary for him to be careful not to abandon the refuge he had, which was doubtless unknown, since he was being sought everywhere else with the greatest exactitude, and that a price had been put on his head. Zulbach also told him that Ambitious had made treaties with all his neighbors, by which they were engaged to return the King to his hands if they were able to discover his retreat, and that, in consequence, he had no other resources than that of remaining well hidden and awaiting the time for a favorable revolution.

Zulbach said, in order to give him some consolation, that he had cause for hope, because the Prince, the eldest son of Ambitious, who had as much virtue as his father had wickedness, had proposed that he marry Princess Lisimene in order at least to restore the King's blood to the throne. Ambitious, however, fearing that his son, who would acquire by that marriage a legitimate right to the crown, might steal it from him in his turn, far from consenting to that request, had responded harshly that he thought it quite unnecessary to take so many precautions to assure himself of an Empire that he already possessed, and that he intended to marry him to the heiress of some great kingdom in order to add a new scepter to the one he already had.

The young Prince having insisted on the equity of his proposition, he had been disgraced and banished from the Court, and had been sent to a distant city, but his rare qualities had acquired him the affection of the principal lords of the realm, and he had departed so well accompanied that his Court was as numerous in his exile as his father's was in the capital.

The King was touched by that sad news, more in regard to his daughter's interests than his own. If the misfortune had only concerned himself, he would only have been moderately afflicted, but Lisimene's destiny penetrated him with dolor, all the more so because he did not know what course of action to take.

On the other hand, Richarde was pressing him to marry her or to leave. The gold was running out, and by virtue of the advice he had just received, he could not abandon his refuge without danger. The only consolation he could extract from his present situation was that by staying in that place he had found, as well as security, all the pleasures of a life that suited his humor, for the house only belonged to Richarde by virtue of the gift that the veritable proprietor had made of it when he died to her and her husband, who were then his slaves.

That master had been a philosopher who, disgusted with the world, had retired to that solitude, where he had had a dwelling built in accordance with his taste. His choice, and not necessity, had led him to make that decision; he had established himself there in order to be far from the tumult, and he had put into it everything that might serve to render rural life agreeable. Not content with having transported there what was appropriate to rustic service, having furnished his abode with the necessary agricultural instruments, and slaves to make use of them, as well as all the requisite livestock, he had concluded by making himself a study filled with books, and musical and mathematical instruments. The hunting in the vicinity was agreeable, and the fishing abundant. Finally, as he was the master of choosing his abode, he had settled in a place in which he had nothing to desire in order to spend his life in tranquil and innocent pleasures. He had lived thus for several years, leaving his wealth when he died to Richarde and her husband, who were his favorite slaves.

By virtue of the liberality of their owner, those two individuals, poor slaves as they were, had suddenly become rich and free, and, finding themselves the masters of those who had previously been their companions, had enjoyed all the possessions that were within their custom and range, among those that had been left to them. What they valued least was the study, caring little about the precious things that it contained and whose merit was unknown to them. That was, however, the richest part of the inheritance, although they had neglected it out of ignorance. Fortunately, their house was so vast that the space in question was unnecessary to them, for they were so unaware of the value of what it contained, that if they had the slightest need to accommodate livestock therein they would have had no scruple about converting a scholar's study into a pen, in which they would have placed the vilest animals.

Good and Better, not regarding it with the same indifference, spent the first days cleaning it and restoring to a state in which pleasure could be obtained from a place that the ignorance and stupidity of its owners had caused them to neglect. It was in that fashion that he became determined, and ended up vanquishing his repugnance for the engagement into which Richarde wanted to force him.

The proposition that he had initially regarded as something ridiculous, appeared to him to be the unique resource that he could encounter in his misfortune, and the only one by which he would find security, it being almost impossible that anyone would think of searching for a great King under the appearance of a peasant woman's husband. He therefore said to himself that since it was absolutely impossible for him to recover an authority about which he cared so little, and that nothing was lacking him in this solitude, it would be as unjust to himself to refuse a happiness that sited his temperament so well as it would be to Richarde to scorn the tenderness of a wife who could procure him that wellbeing. His decision being made in consequence, he announced his intentions to the Princess, who could not hold back her tears at such disagreeable news, having no doubt that the marriage would render her miserable.

Good and Better, touched by her trouble, would have liked both to marry Richards for fear of causing her chagrin and not to marry her in order to spare his daughter the displeasure it would cause her; however, as necessity prevailed and tipped the balance in Richarde's favor, he tried to console the Princess, explaining the reasons that determined him. She had no good ones to oppose to his, so, being unable to prevent the misfortune, she yielded to it with a good grace, and by her father's order, it was her who went to inform the peasant woman that she would be Good and Better's wife whenever she wished, begging her to accord her amity.

Transported with joy, the woman embraced her and promised to love her, provided that she was submissive and fulfilled her duty relative to her. Lisimene's dolor at such a rustic response can be imagined, but she hid it carefully.

Pigrieche, whom that alliance pleased no more than the Princess, being less well brought up, was also less politic; without deigning to constrain herself she screeched, moaned, wept and uttered insults against the King and his daughter, as if she had been the one who had plotted the affair, and finally demanded of her mother what use she was counting on making of two idlers who only spent their time singing or amusing themselves in the room of trifles—that was what they called the study, whose value was unknown to them.

All the purchase that she normally had on Richarde's mind, however, failed on this occasion; her rage had no more effect on her mother than Lisimene's mute dolor had produced on Good and Better. The woman appeased Pigrieche somewhat by representing to her that the husband she was about to take was very rich, and that it was only in relation to her and her interests that she wanted to make sure of the gold coins that she presumed to be still in great number, although in fact very few remained.

The marriage was finally concluded, and when it was made, the King, believing himself to be in a tranquil situation, imagined that ill fortune had abandoned him. He found with Richarde all the commodities of life, and in his study that which could satisfy his inclination.

The communication he maintained with the Vizier by way of his pigeons still left him the hope of a fortunate change, in favor of which he hoped to be able to extract his daughter from that desert and place her on the throne that he renounced with all his heart for himself.

For her part, Richarde had everything for which she could wish. She had the husband she wanted, and his extreme mildness left her the absolute mistress of governing him at her whim, which she had not done in the time of Good and Better's predecessor. That first husband had been as brutal as their daughter Pigrieche, and he had made them feel his tyrannical authority like a man who is aware of the coarseness of his state.

Thus, the commencements of that second union passed with reciprocal satisfaction, the King not permitting himself to be wary of a wife who gave evidence of such a tender amity. He eventually ceased to hide his condition, without making the reflection that there are secrets that it is dangerous to reveal even to the persons who are dearest to us.

That indiscretion initially had a good effect. Richarde was delighted to discover that she was the wife of a King. Her imagination represented to her in a charming fashion the happiness of being a Queen, although she scarcely knew what that was; but an ambition of her sort caused her to conceive a thousand pleasures in being mistress of everything she saw and possessing a hundred times more land and slaves than she had. Her rusticity only allowed her to envisage the pleasures of a throne according to her limited understanding, which she projected as little more than being able to send her slaves to guard their herds on horseback and giving them golden cattle-prods to take the cows to pasture.

After having thus commenced in her mind the establishment of her imaginary grandeur, she entered into it as an important article the advantage of being able to put the crown on Pigrieche's head, for she had no doubt that the King would give preference to that monster, to the prejudice of his own daughter, founding that certainty and her hopes on the docility of her husband—which rendered her for some time more obliging than she had ever been.

However, that illusion of grandeur, which was foreign to her, did not stifle her natural cupidity, and did not make her forsake the design of appropriating, in the meantime, the quantity of gold coins that she still believed her husband to possess. On learning that there were none left, however, she felt more anger than she had had joy in the elevation that she believed she had achieved.

It was then that her tenderness ceased.

The continual reproaches that her daughter made her embittered her against her spouse and the Princess, and made her change her conduct toward him and to make him pay dearly for the little happiness that she had allowed him to enjoy for a while. It was worse when she lost the hope of being Queen, seeing after six months had gone by that there was no more hope of the King's restoration than on the first day; and the overly sincere Prince had also said that even if the usurper perished, or the crown was restored to him, he would not have the injustice to deprive Lisimene of her rights in order to transfer them to Pigrieche.

That admission not finding in Richarde a heart sufficiently equitable, nor a mind sufficiently sensate, to approve its justice, it became the source of all the torments that Good and Better and Lisimene endured from those Furies. Richarde acquired a frightful aversion for the father and daughter, incessantly reproaching them because she had the generosity of nourishing them without them being any use to her, and finally declaring to them that she could not tolerate the fact that while her own daughter worked, "that idler"—meaning Lisimene—only occupied herself with singing or trifling with her father.

When the storms burst, in which the mother and daughter delivered themselves conjointly to their fury, Good and Better escaped to his study, but the unfortunate Princess remained exposed to the rage without aid.

One of Richarde's slaves died in the meantime; it was the one that guided the sheep. Pigrieche prevented her from buying another, saying that that employment was not so difficult that Lisimene could not exercise it, and making a stupid and coarse joke about that. "It's perhaps," she said, "because she'd be afraid of spoiling the delicacy of her name that she's reluctant to do what I propose; but it's easy to find an expedient; she has only to keep it until she's Queen, and in the meantime, she can be perfectly content to be called Liron."[8]

Such an audacious proposal made the father and daughter indignant. The King opposed it strongly; but he no longer had time to commence to make himself the master, if he had any desire to be. Richarde, who knew no other household than her own and who was accustomed to the tyranny of her first husband, would have submitted without difficulty to a yoke she believed inevitable, and to which she had been habituated by lashes of a whip, but she had sensed the pleasure of commanding her sovereign and he had degraded himself of that character by allowing Richarde the facility of taking possession of the Empire, which rendered the King's opposition futile, and she imposed silence on him arrogantly in telling him what she wanted.

Pigrieche overbid in blackness what her mother said. When the Princess declared that unless her father commanded her to do it, there was no extremity to which she would not expose herself rather than lower herself to take such an employment, she told her in a tone full of fury that since she had no intention of being useful for anything, and that, far from constraining her to do her duty, her father authorized her idleness, she knew the means of preventing them from living any longer at their expense without doing anything. For a long time she had been playing the idler, and to compensate herself for the wrong she had suffered therefrom, she had resolved to inform Ambitious without delay where to find the head on which he had put a price, because the recompense that he had promised to those who delivered it would indemnify her mother and herself sufficiently for what they had cost them.

---

[8] The notional storyteller intrudes at this point to allege that the name in question is a trivial insult that implies someone dirty. An inhabitant of the south of France, however, would know *liron* as a term borrowed from the Spanish word for dormouse, used colloquially to apply to someone who sleeps a lot—i.e. an idler.

She concluded that speech by announcing her intention to go to the nearby town in order to reveal the terrible secret; and, far from being horrified by such a criminal projected, Richarde was malevolent enough to applaud the idea.

Pigrieche's threat made Lisimene tremble. "Oh," she cried, terrified, "spare yourself such a frightful crime. I won't resist any longer, and rather than give you a pretext to commit it, not only will I guard the sheep, but I'll also clean out the animal pens, and submit to everything that there is of the most base and degrading. Alas, what shall I not have to do in order to avoid the misfortune with which you are threatening me?"

"You'll have to do better," Pigrieche told her, insolently, "for you can depend on it that if you fail to acquit the things that are your duty, you'll both see the Court again before very long, and there you'll be the Princess entirely at your ease, without my preventing you from putting on airs; but assuredly, for as long as you remain here, you'll only be the shepherdess Liron and you'll begin work right now. Go, without delay," she cried, angrily, "or you'll regret it."

The King was in despair; he would have preferred the misfortune of falling into the hands of Ambitious to the shame of suffering so many indignities, but his daughter's interest stopped him. The life of the Princess was at stake as well as his own; it would indubitably be sacrificed if it were delivered to the Tyrant. The hope that never abandons the desperate allowed him to retain the hope that a better time might arrive, when she would be compensated for all that she would suffer. It was that hope that determined him to patience, and without opposing it any further he saw her put on clogs, after having donned a coarse dress that was the apparel of the dead slave, and she was also given a shepherd's crook.

She went to take the sheep from their fold and take them to the meadow, with a spindle by her side, after having received the order regarding the quantity of hanks of thread that she had to bring back in the evening.

The Princess could not see herself reduced to such a humiliating condition without shedding many tears, and perhaps she would not have hesitated to kill herself in order to abridge such an unhappy life if she had not been afraid that Richarde and Pigrieche, enraged to see her delivered from their tyranny, might avenge themselves for it on her father, and even if she had not feared that final shot of the malevolence she would not have been able to resolve herself to abandoning him in that abominable house alone and without consolation.

She therefore took her part courageously, and after having placed her flock in a convenient place she started to spin. Although she was little versed in that work, she was diligent and dexterous, and she completed the number of skeins in less time that her persecutors thought. Her services were not simply limited to guarding the sheep, and when she had returned she was forced to clean out the animal pens.

In sum, the pitiless Furies, abusing her mildness and the fear caused by the danger that her father was in, did not spare her, employing her for the lowest and most punishing tasks.

Her only consolation, when she no longer had anything else to do, was to go and find the King in his study; it was there that they both deplored their misfortune and had the sad resource of weeping together. They would have made the decision to flee if they had known where to go, but that hope was forbidden to them; the King would not have dared to appear anywhere without running the risk of being recognized. The small town neighboring their solitude was strictly guarded; the orders that had been given to observe all strangers encountered there were so absolute that it would not have been possible to avoid the vigilance of the guards.

Nor could they return whence they had come; they had had horses when they arrived, but Richarde had appropriated them. They could not hope to take them away without the woman, her daughter or some of her slaves perceiving it. That failed attempt would be capable of advancing their misfortune. On the other hand, they could not attempt to go on foot because it would be impossible for them to cover much distance, and those wicked creatures would easily have time to alert the governor of the town and to have them overtaken in their flight, all the more surely because the King had forgotten the route by which he had come as far as this desert. He had only ever taken the route once and it was already more than three years ago.

Even if it had been possible to overcome all those difficulties and escape their enemies' pursuit, they still would not have known where to go in order to reach safety. Thus being constrained in every fashion to remain, they encouraged one another reciprocally to be patient; each of them tried to hide their dolor from the other.

Lisimene, now Liron, whose courage was infinitely above her sex, assured her father, to console him, that she was beginning to get used to that way of life, and that, hard as it was, she found herself much less sensible to it than she had been at first.

By virtue of making these assertions, they turned into the truth, and it came to pass as she said; the habit of dissimulating her trouble diminished it gradually, with the consequence that that way of life no longer seemed so harsh to her. Gradually, her mind became more tranquil and she went so far as seeking to make herself agreeable amusements when she had finished her task. She took her lute or viol, which she had brought secretly from the house, and she hid herself in the hollows of trees, which offered niches where she could shelter from the insults of the weather.

The place that she cherished the most was a green expanse of grass surrounded by a circle of hollow trees, which seemed to have been made expressly for shade, with a fountain in the middle. Its lively and clear waters ran into a white marble basin, and were excellent. The grass, more beautiful and fresher in that place than anywhere else, was infinitely better there, with the consequence that Liron's flock became stronger and healthier every day. When the weather was good she sat down on the marble steps of the fountain, and there she sang, accompanying herself on the instrument she had brought. That little concert was so delightful that she charmed herself, and it had the power to suspend her sad thoughts.

It seemed that the sheep were sensitive to the sweetness of that harmony, for as soon as they heard it, they stopped eating in order to gather around her and to gaze at her attentively. A thousand things repeated the soft sounds of her voice, and the water of the fountain, agitating slightly, seemed to form a murmur in order to play its part too.

In sum, in spite of the harshness of her barbaric mistresses, Lisimene had found a means of rendering herself content. The haste she had to reach that charming place obliged her to redouble her diligence, and she almost no longer felt other anxieties, except that the malign Pigrieche might perceive that innocent pleasure and deprive her of it. In order to avoid that misfortune, she carefully refrained from taking pride in the possession of such a precious gift.

One morning, she was on the edge of that dear fountain, where she ordinarily made her toilette, and where she washed her face and hands, for Pigrieche and her mother, far from giving her time for that, took delight when she was in occupying her with the dirtiest and most disgusting employments.

After having rubbed her hands in the water and having removed all the dirt to which her vile occupations rendered her subject, she tried to bend over in order to refresh her cheeks. In leaning over too far, however, she lost her balance and slipped into the fountain.

She believed that she was about to drown. The fear occasioned by the fall caused her to lose consciousness, and as she was not in a condition to make any effort to pull herself out, she was in extreme danger, and doubtless would have drowned if she had been delayed in receiving help that she did not believe that she ought to expect; for when she recovered from her faint, she found herself in a cool place.

She was no longer in the water, although she was surrounded by it, as if she were in a crystal box. She saw crayfish passing by in that mobile crystal, and little fish coming and going tranquilly, being in their element.

That singular spectacle was not what caused her the most astonishment, and she felt more on finding herself in the arms

of three beautiful female individuals who appeared to be hastening to bring her round, with a charming kindness; they were
making efforts to soothe her and giving her fortifying essences
to smell.

Their attire, different from anything that she had seen in
her life, was a partial cause of her admiration; they were clad
in silvery gauze, tinted with different soft colors, which faded
into one another in imperceptible waves.

The Princess was so astonished by what she saw that it
was impossible for her to speak, but one of the beautiful
young women, perceiving her perplexity, smiling graciously,
said to her: "Don't worry, charming Lisimene; there is nothing
for you to fear here, since you're among friends." And without
giving her time to respond, she added: "We are the naiads of
the fountain,[9] who are very glad to see you, in order to make
your acquaintance and express our gratitude to you for the
pleasure that the agreeable symphony with which you regale
us gives us so frequently. We know your misfortunes, and
perhaps you might not find our amity useless in order to interrupt their course."

Liron had difficulty believing that she was really awake
and that what she could see was real, having always treated as
chimerical, and also told for pleasure, what she had heard re-
ported of the inhabitants of the waters, unable to persuade

---

[9] The four kinds of supposed elemental spirits are normally
rendered in English as gnomes [earth], sylphs [air], salaman-
ders [fire] and undines [water], following terminology popu-
larized by a sixteenth-century Latin document falsely attributed to Paracelsus. French, unlike English or German, splits the
terms into masculine and feminine forms: *gnome/gnomide*;
sylphe/sylphide; *salamandre/salamandrine* and *ondin/ondine*.
Although the present text retains *gnomide* and *sylphe*, it con-
flates elemental spirits, in an idiosyncratic fashion, with the
nymphs of ancient Greek mythology, substituting *nayade*
[naiad] for *ondine*, and also adding *hamadryade* [a tree spirit]
to the schema.

herself that there were creatures in human form anywhere but on land. However, as the vision lasted too long for her to be able to doubt that what was happening was actual, she was about to respond with her usual modesty and the gratitude that the promises that had been made to her merited, when another naiad intervened.

"You're forgetting, my sister," she said to the one who had spoken, "that the garments of this Princess are wet, and the interest we're taking in her health ought to make us postpone this conversation until another time. The most urgent thing is to rid her immediately of a costume that is so inappropriate, from every point of view."

Then, without replying to her, her two companions joined her, and all three of them hastened to strip the Princess of her coarse dress and all of her horrible accoutrement. They gave her another in a white and delicate fabric, seductively garnished with the most beautiful lace, intermingled with flowers, of which the mixture of colors and their pleasant odor had an effect that charmed sight and the sense of smell simultaneously.

When Liron was thus adorned, one of the aquatic divinities said to her: "We know that is giving you attire covered in gems we would not be dressing you in a fashion above your condition, but, in addition to the embarrassment that such apparel would cause you in the fields and in the occupations to which you find yourself reduced, we have another reason, which is that it would be useless to you in the disagreeable situation you are in at present, and you could not conserve it, because it would become the prey of Richarde and her daughter without you being able to obtain any more benefit from it."

Lisimene, who had not been nonplussed for long, and was already reassured by the kindness of the nymphs, expressed to them very respectfully how sensible she was to the honor of knowing them and the protection that they had promised her with such good grace. In sum, soon becoming free with her benefactresses, she allowed her curious gaze to wander without constraint over everything that seemed to merit her attention. The fish that were coming and going through the water without falling were what rejoiced her the most; she approached one of them with the intention of seizing one of them playfully, but she was disappointed, the resistance that she encountered having informed her that they were separated from her by a wall that was crystal, like the vault.

After she had amused herself for a few moments with that innocent play and the naiads had laughed at her surprise, they took her into a grotto that served them for communication with the river. There she found all that was necessary for a fine meal, in accordance with the location—which is to say that it was mainly composed of fish and shellfish. Aquatic birds and animals also appeared there, in all sorts of sauces and in all kinds of fashions. She saw animal species she did not know, which are only common in the glacial seas or those of the Orient. But the naiads did not limit their commerce to the fountain; it extended to all fluid places, and the productions of the sea were as common to them as those of their domicile. They also offered Lisimene the most beautiful and rarest fruits that could be picked in all the continents of the world.

They served her eagerly, and invited her to eat with such good grace that she sampled everything without giving preference to one dish over another, because they were all perfect.

When the meal was over, they told her that they wanted to hear from her the story of the unworthy behavior of her unworthy stepmother and Pigrieche. The Princess did so in such a touching manner that her hostesses could not retain their teas, and did not limit the effect of their compassion to that.

"You are not destined to be unhappy forever," one of them told her, "but although we are perfectly certain that your misfortune will cease, we cannot tell you exactly when that time will arrive, nor raise any entire obstacle to the troubles that you might perhaps experience. It is not possible for us at present to do anything more for your service than keep you here for as long as it pleases you to remain, if you want to flee the malign influences that surround you; you would be perfectly safe, and you would be beyond their reach."

"What about my father?" exclaimed Lisimene. "What would become of him in my absence? No, Goddess," she added, "I cannot profit from your kindness, unless Your Divinities deign to take the excess of their benefits so far as to grant to him the favor of enjoying the same refuge that they are so generously offering to me."

"That cannot be," said the smiling *Cristisie*—which means Crystalline—who was the most beautiful of the naiads and the one who appeared to have some authority over the others. "Our grottoes and our retreats are not made to be inhabited by a sex different from ours. Although the example of the nereids could serve to relieve us of those scruples, we do not follow their maxims, and, far from receiving men among us, we only give them entry here to the rivers, with which we only have communication via the streams, our mothers, whose presence alone authorizes us to that license. Thus, we can do nothing for Good and Better, whom your absence would expose, as you must suspect, to the brutality of his wife and Pigrieche.

"Since it is thus, whatever pleasure I find in being among you," said the Princess, getting to her feet, "I confess to you that I am very impatient to return to the land and to return to my father. Alas, perhaps the moments passed so agreeably will be dearly bought. I fear that those Furies might take it into their heads to search for me, and, not finding me, might avenge themselves on the King for my supposed flight by executing the detestable project of delivering him to the traitor Ambitious."

"That apprehension is vain, although well placed," said Crystalline. "No one has yet perceived your absence. Have no fear, we are so distant from the time when you must return to the house with your flock that you will not experience any unfortunate consequences of an adventure that will remain unknown unless you reveal it yourself, and if we are giving

174

you as much pleasure as you say, it will be permissible for you to spend another two hours here without danger."

That proposition would have been too much to the liking of the Princess not to be accepted if the tenderness she had for her father had not raised an obstacle to it; but her urgency and the motive she had for seeing him again were too pressing for her to remain any longer in a place where, but for that reason, she would have liked to spend the rest of her life.

However, she could not help considering the naiads and gazing at them with admiration. Their beauty enchanted her and their attire was so seductive that she could not weary of looking at them. Above all, what gave her the most pleasure, and what she found the most charming, was their coiffure, and their blonde tresses tied up in large curls with ropes of flowers. She could not understand how, only appearing to be retained by such bonds, they could be held on their heads and not fall at the slightest movement; those flowers had so much grace that there was not one of them that did not give a new splendor to their complexion.

Crystalline, noticing Lisimene's attention, said to her: "What do you think of the manner in which we are coiffed? Do you find it to your liking?"

"Oh, beautiful Naiad," said the Princess, "the gleam of the most brilliant gems could never produce such an advantageous effect."

"Well, if you wish," the naiad continued, "we can teach you to coif yourself in the same manner."

"Alas, what use would that science be to me?" said Lisimene, sighing. "Would an unfortunate shepherdess, destined to fulfill the lowest rural employments, have the time required to arrange all those flowers? Even if I could have it, where would I find them? None grow in Richarde's farm, and those I see on you are the rarest—there are even many of species unknown to me. That talent would be all the more useless to me because, in addition to my not having the flowers with which to exercise it, it would only be for myself that I could take that trouble, without hoping that those ornaments would

175

be seen by anyone but my father, whose tenderness is independent of apparel. I ought only think of pleasing him, and employing the moments of liberty that I can steal in profiting from the lessons he wants to give me, rather than occupying myself with an adornment which would be entirely futile."

"I don't think as you do," relied the naiad, "and even though your beauty has no need of foreign aid to appear with splendor, I imagine that when care for oneself does not pass the bounds of reason, far from being reprehensible in a young woman, it is, on the contrary, a necessary quality at her age— especially for you, Princess, who will not always be unknown in the world, and are made to hold a high rank and be an ornament of it. Thus, I invite you to follow your inclination, if only to teach you to do your hair; but since you have no time to lose, we shall act in such a way as to render that science facile and prompt, in order that you will not attract any nasty comment on the part of Richarde and her daughter. Only come into my dressing-room," the naiad continued. "By combing me yourself you will easily see the fashion in which the flowers are arranged in my hair."

So saying, she approached a crystal table, and, placing herself in a chair of the same substance, she simply touched the cordon that held her tresses, which fell freely, thus causing the fall of all the flowers with which they were covered, and which perfumed the place with a charming odor.

The naiad having been bare-headed momentarily, in order to give Lisimene time to take out a few flowers from her hair that had remained entangled there, her beautiful tresses stretched out as if to repose. After a brief space of time, however, she shook her head and they curled again more rapidly than they had extended, forming ringlets again and covering themselves with new flowers in a taste quite different from the preceding one, which was no less seductive.

"Well, beautiful Lisimene," she said to the shepherdess, "what do you think of my diligence? Do you think I waste much time in my toilette? And would not Pigrieche, with her natural contrariety, be obliged to keep quiet?

"You see," she went on, "that the time one spends in coifing oneself in that fashion is not considerable, and if that is the only pleasure that adornment will give you, it ought to determine you to coif yourself in the same fashion. So look at our fashions; do they please you?"

The Princess replied that they would please the most difficult individuals, and that she was enchanted by them.

"Since that is the case," the divinity of the waters went on, "it will be soon done; it is only a matter of speaking." Immediately, she added: "Bright flowers, be born on the head of this Beauty, and be as docile for her in the future as you are for us."

Scarcely had she pronounced those words that Lisimene saw their virtue immediately, and by casting her eyes upon the mirrors that the waters formed on all sides, she found that she was coifed like Crystalline, and that if there was any difference, it was entirely to her advantage.

Although the Princess did not expect to give herself the honor of her adornment, especially in the place that had to be her habitation, she could not be insensible to the pleasure of seeing herself so beautiful, and she rendered to her own charms the homage that others owed to her.

The sun, whose ardors she experienced only too forcefully had, to some extent, damaged the freshness and delicacy of her complexion, but the fountain whose waters she had just traversed had rendered her all her beauty; the joy that she felt gradually reanimated the eyes whose gleam had been extinguished by chagrins and tears, and her charms were so fully reestablished by that new adornment that she was almost unrecognizable.

So many advantages at once, the beauty of the place as well as the caresses of the naiads, all rendered those divinities even dearer to her and made her envisage the moment of quitting them with great regret. It was, however, approaching, and although Crystalline had offered to keep her in her home, she had approved of the motive for her refusal. It was her who told the Princess that it was finally time to withdraw.

"Go, virtuous Lisimene," she said to her, embracing the child. "Go console your father, and merit our esteem even more, but come back to see us or to inform us of our troubles, and we'll assist you with our advice. No longer have any fear that an accident will happen to you without you entering the fountain," she continued, smiling. "You can penetrate all the way to this place easily, simply by pronouncing the name of Crystalline and her sisters; the waters will open their bosom to you and you'll discover the crystal stairway by which we transported you here, which your faint prevented you from noticing."

She added to all these bounties the present of a crook that only seemed to be made of reeds, but whose wood was stronger than the hardest oak, the iron of it being brilliant crystal without having the fragility. In order to teach her the usage of it, the naiad told her that when she wanted to occupy herself with something other than the care of her flock, she had only to plant the crook in their midst. With that precaution she could be certain that her sheep would all be in abundance and that neither wolves nor thieves would dare to approach them.

The second naiad, also wanting to give the Princess a present, presented her with a spinning-wheel and spindle, telling her that she only had to charge it with fiber and place it on the wheel, and that it would spin of its own accord, so well and so diligently that she would not have to fear the reproaches of her malevolent hostesses.

The third, however, outdid the others with the utility of her present. Seeking to rid Lisimene once and for all of the overwhelming difficulty she had in cleaning the animal pens and the sheepfold, she gave her a domesticated beaver, which surpassed its fellows in skill, since, in addition to the natural instinct that renders its species so admirable, the education it had received from the naiads had given it all the talents necessary to be well above its companions.

She told Lisimene that she only had to present the beaver with the work that had been demanded of her in such a dastardly manner, and it would aid her with its teeth, its feet and

178

its tail, and would do everything that there was to do. She learned that it was named *ou Longouy*, which can be more conveniently rendered as Diligent. She only had to summon it to her by that name and recommend it to do its duty.

After having heaped the young shepherdess with caresses and assurances of amity, the nymphs of the fountain put her at the foot of the crystal stairway. Without having to take the trouble to climb it, Lisimene was at the top in an instant. She found her flock assembled, ready to march at the first sign she gave it.

Although the naiads had notified her that the time to withdraw had come, and by the refusal she had made to remain with them she had testified that she was resolved to return to Richarde's house, the moments—which fly quickly when one is enjoying oneself—had passed without her perceiving it. She could not believe that it was so late, and was surprised to see from a distance that her father was waiting for her at the door of the house; by his sad expression she easily deduced that he was troubled by her overly long absence.

She approached him without being recognized, although she was very close; his anxious gaze testified clearly enough that he did not believe that it was her. The fashion in which she was dressed had caused his error, and it was only Lisimene's voice that extracted him from it.

Richarde and Pigrieche appeared at that moment and were deceived as Good and Better had been, but, seeing that he was talking to a stranger, their curiosity led them to advance in order to find out what the person wanted, not being accustomed to see strangers in that place, especially strangers so elegant. Their astonishment was extreme when they found that the object of their curiosity was only their shepherdess Liron.

"Oh, Mother," cried Pigrieche, "it's Liron. Where has she got those beautiful clothes? Who has given them to her? But what am I saying, given? There isn't anyone in this place who can give such presents. It's absolutely necessary that she's had them bought in the town by people who have gone to the market."

"It must be that," said Richarde, "but to have had the money, she must have stolen it from me, or her imbecile of a father, concealing the truth, has saved some gold coins, although he pretended to have given them all to me."

Then, without giving Lisimene time to explain, they heaped her with insults, and said no fewer to the King. Finally, both of them had exhausted their lungs, and as their voices failed, they were obliged to shut up.

Liron, who had listened to them without making futile efforts to make herself heard, began to reply to them, and told Richarde, with a kind of disdain that was manifest without her being aware of it, that to be sure of her facts she only had to count her money, none of which would be missing.

"As for you presuming," she added, still in the same tone, "that my father has given me anything, you're wrong and you have presumed too much. As to what you have supposed in my case, do you not know who you have sent to the town? Ask them whether I have spoken to them, and pay attention for a moment to what common sense tells you, without imagining that I can have gone to the town of which you speak myself, given that I know nothing of this locality but the surroundings of your house."

"Well, wretch," said Pigrieche, stamping her foot, and without wasting time uselessly in false reasoning, "tell us, then, where you got clothes that are so unsuited to your condition."

"And such a coquettish coiffure," added her mother. "You would do better to think about the care you owe to a flock that I have had the goodness to confide to you rather than amusing yourself picking flowers. Where did you get them?"

Pigrieche wanted to add to that speech and, screeching in competition with her mother, they both became so hoarse that they were obliged to shut up again.

Liron, taking her time, told them at her ease and without hurrying about the luck that she had had by virtue of the fortunate adventure of falling into the water. She hid the principal circumstances from them, however, and made a mystery of the happiness that the naiads had predicted for her. She contented herself with telling them that she had fallen into the fountain, where she had fainted, and that when she recovered consciousness she had found herself in the arms of three beautiful young women, who had given her a thousand testimonies of good will and had taken away her poor dress, soaked by the water into which she had fallen; that nothing equaled the welcome she received from them; and that, one of them, whose coiffure was similar to her own, had asked her to comb it, and afterwards, as a recompense, had given her all the flowers that were then ornamenting her head; and that they had only sent her home after making her a present of the beaver and the crook.

No surprise was ever so great as that of the listeners to whom Lisimene told that story. Good and Better was charmed by it, while Richarde and her daughter were dying of chagrin, particularly the latter, in whom it went as far as fury. What embittered her even more was not being able to doubt what Lisimene said, because it was obvious that there was a supernatural cause, one of those that it is impossible to suppose. They could not help rendering justice to Liron's sincerity, knowing that since they had been together, she had never been caught in the slightest lie. Thus, the mother and daughter were in despair at not being able to impute anything.

In the end, however, to please Pigrieche, Richarde said rudely to Liron that although it was not possible for them to penetrate her trickery, she did not intend that her shepherdess should be so elegant, and that she had only to take the trouble to put her ordinary clothes on the next day. In the meantime, with her curls and her fancy clothes, she had to put the flock in the fold.

Lisimene having obeyed without reply, her beaver began to enter into service, working with so much diligence and skill that the work was soon finished, without her being able to involve herself.

When there was nothing more to do she went to rejoin the family, where, throughout the meal, the mother and daughter never ceased to grumble and to say that they did not intend that she remain coifed in that fashion.

Good and Better represented to them in vain that the flowers had not cost them anything, and that they should allow it, since it was an innocent amusement, and that it hardly mattered whether his daughter did her hair in one fashion or another.

That was enough to bring down the storm on him, and, seeing from the tone that the harpies took that they would not finish soon, he made the decision to run away to his study, the only refuge he had in such circumstances.

That infernal carillon lasted until daybreak, when, without giving the sad Liron time to take a moment's rest, she was obliged to take food to the slaves and to the least of the animals under their roof. But the worthy beaver did his duty and she had no other difficulty than that of telling him what she desired him to do; employing his tail instead of a broom or a shovel, everything was done in a moment, and Liron was going to bring her flock outside in order to take the road to the marvelous fountain, where she had arranged to meet her father to tell him what she had omitted from her story, when her stepmother and Pigrieche stopped her by the arm.

"Where do you intend to go dressed like that?" they said to her.

She replied with moderation that she was going to her usual occupation.

"That's very good," said Richarde's insolent daughter, "But it's not necessary to be thus equipped to follow sheep; it's necessary beforehand to take away that pompous outfit, which doesn't suit you at all." At the same time she shoved her rudely in the direction of their room, which they forced her to enter, for fear that if they let her go into her own she might hide flowers there to use another time, and they obliged her to comb her hair in front of them in order to cause the flowers and the arrangement to fall.

The Princess, unable not avoid obeying, removed the cordon of flowers as she had seen Crystalline do, and as her head was more abundantly covered by them than the naiad's, her falling hair dropped a prodigious quantity on to the floor. She combed the hair to extend its curls, and at every stroke of the comb she made, a thousand flowers that they had not perceived fell everywhere—by which the mother and daughter were satisfied, saying continually that Liron had hidden them expressly, but that they were as clever as she was.

Finally, seeing that the flowers had ceased to fall and that the flattened hair could no longer conceal or preserve the slightest curl, they ordered her to put up her hair, not in the same fashion that it had been a moment before, but as when she had left the house the previous day. Having received that permission, Liron hastened to take advantage of it, but scarcely had she passed her fingers through her hair than the curls resumed their place and she found them arranged as they had been when she emerged from the fountain. New flowers emerged everywhere, coifing her in an even more advantageous fashion than when she had been forced to destroy those ornaments.

It would be difficult to describe the surprise and rage of the spectators; they imagined that they had been deceived by the skill of their shepherdess and that she had not thrown down all those accursed flowers. They commanded her again to recommence her coiffure, but when by that second experiment, to which they paid even more attention, they were convinced that no flowers remained and saw them born again, Pigrieche cried that Liron was a witch, that nothing could be more certain, and that she merited the fire, inviting her mother to burn her without delay—for fear, she said, that the wretch would cast evil spells on them or their livestock.

Richarde, who was not as credulous or as wrathful as her daughter, and who would not even have been so malevolent without the ascendancy that maternal love had allowed

Pigrieche to obtain over her, did not hasten to satisfy her, and, as much by virtue of a residue of generosity as the motive of self-interest, which did not permit her to think of depriving herself of a slave, she paid no attention to that extravagant and inhuman proposition; but she wanted absolutely to know whence the prodigy of the flowers came.

"I think that my daughter is right," she said to the Princess, "and your life is in great danger if you do not instruct us of the secret of this affair."

"I have told you everything," said Liron. "If you want to take my life you can, I'm in your power, but there's no need to seek a vain pretext. You can ask me the same question a hundred times, but I won't respond in any other way than I've already done. I tell you, therefore, that it's a present the naiads gave me, and apparently, they have given it the virtue of renewal."

The firmness with which she pronounced that speech, making the truth shine within it, convinced the mother and daughter, reluctantly. Judging that it was impossible to deprive Liron of her coiffure, they wanted at least to profit from her dress, which they forced her to hand over to them, but they were unable to conserve the flowers with which it was decorated, which fell of their own accord once it was no longer on Liron, and were not replaced. Those detached from the dress became entirely useless to them, for they faded so rapidly that they fell into dust.

Finally, the Furies sent Liron away, who, clad as a peasant and coiffed as a goddess, hastened to go and met her father. Pigrieche had given her the worst of her dresses, but the pleasure of being rid of the Megaeras prevented her from having as much regret as she would have had if the dress had not been the price of her liberty, incessantly apprehending that the conversation might end in imprisonment.

She finally set off with her flock and her beaver. The King, who had not foreseen the contretemps that had interrupted her, had gone on ahead and had waited for a long time at the edge of the fountain, where, impatient at her lateness and not knowing to what to attribute it, he was ready to return to the house when she appeared.

He was delighted with everything that she told him. When she had nothing more to tell, she promptly prepared her spindle, having put it in a state to do its duty, and left the wheel to spin. Seeking to pay court to her benefactresses, she played them the same symphony that they seemed to like so much, accompanying it with her voice, and it did not take long for her to know by tremor of the waters, which became agitated, that her gallantry had been agreeably received.

While gratitude occupied Lisimene thus, Richarde and her daughter were no less occupied, but it was in a very different manner.

"Who would have believed," said Pigrieche, weeping, "that that little creature would enjoy such great fortune? No, there's none for those who merit it, and I can see that it's necessary to be unworthy to obtain it. In truth," she continued, on reflection, "these naiads are very prodigal with their favors, and it necessary that they scarcely know what they're doing to heap them on someone like Liron." She added: "See, Mother, how those trivia adorn her, and although she's very ugly, one might take her for the image of spring. And the means, too, by which they embellished her! Who wouldn't be, with such an ornament?"

Pigrieche was so outraged that she would not have stopped talking about it if dolor and anger had not stifled her voice. "Alas," she said, having recovered her breath, "She's always been lucky, and there's only me who was born unlucky. It's your fault, though," she said to Richarde. "If you were less unnatural, if you gave me beautiful ornaments, I'd be more beautiful than her, and I wouldn't have the distress of seeing her efface me."

To console her daughter, whose tears and reproaches afflicted her almost as much as herself, Richarde tried several times to coif her with the flowers that were strewn in profusion on the floor and the table, but it was impossible, for they fell, or the stems of others that broke, remaining on her head,

185

made a grotesque figure that bore a certain resemblance to a hedgehog. Others withered and turned into putrid straw, from which a very bad odor emerged.

The obstacles that she found in embellishing that daughter, so dear to her, put the hairdresser in despair, for although she adored Pigrieche, she was no less passionate about her money; she had hoped to be able satisfy her without it costing her anything, and everything was opposed to such tender hopes. Finally, however, affection and interest acting in unison inspired an expedient that she thought admirable to satisfy both of them.

"Well, my dear Pigrieche," she said, "what prevents you from going to seek as much? The naiad has not given her preference over you. She has only seen Liron, and we can believe that the generosity she has shown her only comes from a lack of opportunity to exercise it with regard to subjects more worthy of it. When she knows you, you'll see that she won't be able to help loving you and giving you presents a hundred times more beautiful and in better taste than those she has given our shepherdess, or that I could buy. Go find these divinities; you have more wit than Liron, and you'll please them more."

That proposal was not entirely to Pigrieche's taste; the fashion of entering the fountain did not please her at all. She could not help being suspicious of the confidence that had been recommended to Liron, and she was quite uncertain of what she ought to do; but the desire to see herself ornamented like the shepherdess was stronger and prevailed over the fear of danger.

She was convinced that there was no beauty that could stand comparison with hers, and that nothing was lacking but apparel to bring out all its splendor, not doubting that if she could obtain it, her fortune would soon be made, and that the least rank to which she could aspire would be that of Queen or the wife of an admiral. She promised herself that if she obtained what she desired, she would abandon the primitive rustic dwelling in order to go and be an object of admiration in the largest city she could find, where, she was convinced, she would not fail to encounter the establishments for which she could not hope in this abandoned land.

That hope fixing her determination, she went to guard the sheep the next day, and did not forget to put on the beautiful dress of which she had deprived Liron.

Thus equipped, she went to the fountain, but at the sight of it, fear took hold of her again and she did not dare to throw herself in the water. Not wanting to return without attempting the adventure, however, she tried to enter the fountain gradually, and, sitting on the edge, she extended a foot, hoping to slide into it gently.

Scarcely had she touched the water, however, than she sank into it completely, not gently, as she had intended, but so heavily that she thought she would kill herself in falling to the bottom of the basin, where the marble was so rough that it gave her as many wounds as it had asperities.

She had time to repent of a project that had not succeeded as she had hoped. She stayed there for a long time, struggling in the water, without it being possible for her to reach the edge, which was too high for her to be able to attain. The water that she drank involuntarily and the fear caused by the danger in which she found herself having finally caused her to faint, she would have died if the naiads, who were rejoicing at her expense, had not rescued her.

She did not see them and only perceived that she had escaped a danger that she had believed to be inevitable when she recovered from her faint and found herself on a table, head down. She had been placed thus in order to enable her to rid herself the mud that was choking her.

When consciousness had fully returned she made efforts to vomit up that noxious mud, which were a further torture for her, and made her curse a thousand times over the indiscreet desire she had had to come to the fountain. In addition, far from having in her misfortune at least the meager consolation of seeing that she was in a beautiful apartment and on a good bed, she found herself in a vile muddy grotto, more reminiscent of a lair of toads than a palace inhabited by divinities of the waters, and in which there was only just enough light to distinguish all the horror of the place.

On opening her eyes she found herself in the hands of three creatures almost as ugly as her, who, in order to bring her round, were tugging and pinching her unsparingly. Far from those supposed naiads resembling the description that Liron had given of them, they were so hideous, and their attire as so frightful, that Pigrieche shut her eyes to free herself from that disagreeable sight, and was almost as frightened to find herself in their company as she had been of the death that she had thought inevitable. Their coiffures were not garnished with flowers but reed-heads mingled with the great, thick, dark green leaves that appear on the surface of marshy waters; some stood up on their heads like a forest of horns, while the leaves that fell over the visage completed the most ridiculous and frightful headwear that it is possible to imagine.

"What have you come to do here, charming Pigrieche?" said one of the nymphs pawing her, in a voice like a frog. "By what good fortune do we have the honor of having you among us?"

"By my extreme stupidity," said Pigrieche, angrily. "I had the weakness to trust that wretch Liron, who gave me to understand that it was nice here and that you received honorably those who did you the honor of coming here."

"Well," said the supposed naiad, "What are you complaining about? Haven't we received you well?"

"You're dreaming, I think," said Pigrieche, raising her voice, "if you call the reception you've given me receiving someone well. Apparently, you give the strappado to those you receive poorly. It seems to me that one can only treat someone worse by letting them drown."

"That's true," replied the muddy naiad, coldly. "But that ought to prove to you that you're complaining inappropriately, for you're not dead."

"How much is that worth?" screeched Richarde's daughter, her petulance excited by the indolence of those reedy faces. "You've rescued me, traitors that you are, but when did you rescue me? When you saw me about to choke, and then, how have you relieved me? By shaking me with such force that my bones are so dislocated that I don't know whether I might die of your accursed rescue."

"That would be unfortunate," the naiad continued in a tranquil tone that, far from being disturbed by Pigrieche's violence, was augmented with every word. "But permit me to tell you, beautiful Pigrieche, that it is to some extent your own fault. We were unprepared for the joy of seeing you; if we had been aware of your intention, we would have received you in our arms at the edge of the fountain. But in sum, it's done now, let's not talk about it anymore. We shall try, by the honors that we are going to render you, to merit that you forget the past. Someone has gone to inform the great naiad Crystalline of your arrival. She is our sovereign, who will doubtless, to express the satisfaction she will have in your arrival, order the great fête of the waters. You'll have the pleasure of seeing them rise up to the sky and fall back in great splashes, forming a thousand figures."

"How I hate you," Pigrieche interrupted, "you and your accursed waters, pitiless and phlegmatic talker. Enough of your ridiculous detail! Would one not think, to hear you, that you have the ocean at your disposal, while your power scarcely extends over four bucketfuls of water?"

"That being so, you ought to agree that you're complaining unjustly about having thought you might perish in it," the talking frog interrupted in her turn, "for a large individual like you cannot drown in such a feeble volume of water. But as you're annoyed, I prefer to yield, for fear of abusing your natural mildness. To amuse you, while awaiting our sovereign, I will, if you wish, cause to pass in review all the beauties of this Empire—but perhaps, being only too accustomed, as you must be, to looking in your mirror, and little flattered by the sight of beautiful individuals, who can never be as beautiful as you, you'd prefer to see our big fish. Speak freely, which would you like better?"

"To break your nose," said the impatient Pigrieche, raising her hand and making a movement to strike her. "Can't you see that I'm soaked to the skin? Has one ever proposed spectacles to someone half-drowned? It's necessary to be very stupid to make such proposals to me."

"Forgive the joy I have in seeing you," said the muddy goddess. "It transports me to such an extent that my zeal..."

"Again," Pigrieche interrupted, "your endless compliments aren't exhausted. I tell you, then," she added, shouting with all her might, "that there's only one thing to do and without delay. I want to change clothes and get out of here."

She was finally obeyed, and without arguing any longer, her wet dress was taken away and she was given another; but she did not obtain such a great advantage from that exchange as she had hoped, since she was clad in the dress of coarse fabric that Liron had left in the naiads' abode previously, in exchange for the one that Pigrieche had taken from her. She had been in such a hurry to change clothes that she did not notice that the dress that had been presented to her was the one she had given Liron when imposing that name on her. In addition, the light illuminating the place was too poor for her to be discern the beauty of the present that had been given to her; when she was satisfied in that regard, she began to feel hungry.

"Do you think," she said to them, with her usual arrogance, "that the advantage of seeing you is considerable enough to satisfy my appetite, and ought you not to be ashamed to wait for me to ask you for something to eat?"

"We shall do whatever you wish," said the naiad. "I haven't offered because I thought you would prefer the pleasure of a stroll to that of the table, but since you prefer the latter, you shall be served."

Immediately, several divinities appeared in the uniform of the one who was doing the honors of her home so well, and hastened to lay a table, which she approached avidly, but from which she drew away with even more precipitation and with as little satisfaction as she had had from everything that had preceded the repast, unable to resist the horror caused by the sight of a basin of toads *à la crapaudine*,[10] another of lizards in mud sauce, accompanied by a roasted baby crocodile and larded with aspics. It was so expertly prepared that it seemed almost alive, as did as its dressing, and they darted such fiery gazes at Pigrieche that they convinced her that she was about to be devoured.

She could not withstand the terror that she felt, and drew away hurriedly from that dangerous table. "Oh, wretched Liron," she cried, "you'll pay dearly for this perfidious trick!" Then addressing the nymph, she said, furiously: "Well, demon of the waters, don't flatter yourself that this will remain secret; I guarantee that I'll publish it, and disabuse the world of the error that it has made in your favor." She did not stop there, and voiced all the insults that her rage suggested to her.

The cold expression with which the nymph listened to her, far from calming Pigrieche, made her even more heated. She would have been satisfied to some degree if she had at least been able to flatter herself that her insults were causing offense, but she was even deprived of that feeble pleasure, and the cold goddess was insensible to the most outrageous discourse.

In spite of Pigrieche's anger and the screams she uttered, loud enough to make the place tremble, she did not make the slightest movement to leave. Unable to resolve herself to going away without the flattering coiffeur that had been the unique objective of her journey, she was in that perplexity when Crystalline appeared, with all the charm and all the apparel imaginable.

Pigrieche's rage died away at the sight of her. The hope of having similar adornments to those she saw on the goddess,

---

[10] The original, naturally, has *crapauds à la crapaudine*, the culinary expression referring to items split in two and roasted. "Lardé des aspics" [larded with aspics] is also a pun, linking the conventional culinary meaning of aspic with another, which refers to vipers.

entering her heart, calmed her bile, and she became as reasonable as she was accustomed to be—which is to say that instead of the howls with which she accompanied her fury, she restricted herself to the simple expressions of a malevolent woman. The consequence of that was that she gave the naiad an account of the insults she had received, for which she demanded justice, swearing that, if it was refused, she would exact it herself, threatening nothing less than filling in the fountain and pouring quicksilver into its spring.

"Don't be annoyed," said Crystalline. "Nothing is lost; everything can be easily repaired. Apparently, you haven't come here without a purpose; provided that your desires are satisfied, I believe that you'll have no reason to complain."

"What you say is true," said Pigrieche, softened by such flattering hopes, "and if this green monsters had been as reasonable as you, I wouldn't be annoyed. Well," she added, "I've been here a long time, and only came here in order to take away a coiffure and a dress like those you gave Liron yesterday, but if you want to please me entirely, you'll take hers away in order to give her in its stead the ridiculous accoutrement in which that vile muddy individual is clad. In exchange for that I'll be content and I'll forgive you the past. But above all, let Liron lose the power to adorn herself thus, for I absolutely don't want the two of us to have anything in common in our adornment; that wouldn't be just, since a slave ought not to be dressed like her mistress."

"You're right," said Crystalline, with a soft smile, "only to ask for that. Speak, there's nothing easier than to satisfy you; your request is so just that I grant it to you and I should certainly like to distinguish you from Liron and her fellows."

Immediately, she ordered the nymph to undo her coiffure, and told Pigrieche, offering her a comb, to examine what there was on her head.

As she had heard Liron say that it was by combing Crystalline's hair that she had acquired her coiffure, she did not refuse to do as much, not without insisting on the generosity that she was showing in consenting to take that trouble.

"It is indeed great for a young woman like you," said the naiad, "but be assured that it will not remain without recompense."

Pigrieche had a great deal of trouble completing the task that she had undertaken, for the nymph's tresses were so clotted with mud and slime that they almost formed a mortar by their mixture with the foliage, the reeds and the ridiculous down that accompanied them. In addition to that, an insupportable odor emerged therefrom, and stubborn reeds that stood up in spite of her efforts caused her an unparalleled embarrassment. She removed them one after another with infinite trouble, and as soon as she had finished that fine work, the nymph was recoiffed. Scarcely had the tresses been replaced, however, than the detestable reeds resumed their position.

"Well," said Crystalline to Pigrieche, "are you content with what you see?"

"Oh, extremely," cried Pigrieche, with a surge of joy. "That's exactly how I desire Liron to be. Grant me that favor; I prefer it to obtaining anything for myself."

"You're too disinterested," said the sovereign of the waters, sarcastically, "and you deserve better than that. It's to you that I make a present of this beautiful coiffure; it suits you marvelously and it would be a pity for it to ornament another face." She added: "Naïve tender reeds, be born promptly on the head of the incomparable Pigrieche; you are worthy of her, and that place is worthy of you."

The naiad had no sooner finished speaking than that marshy forest, by which the head of the nymph was shadowed, flew on to Pigrieche's. The latter was shoved abruptly into the room where Lisimene had been received the previous day and where, in the clarity of the waters, which presented her portrait to her everywhere, she frightened herself.

Her fury, which the hope that had been abused had suspended, was reanimated in the blink of an eye, and, seeking to avenge herself for such a cruel outrage, she tried to hurl herself upon Crystalline; but two kicks that she received simultaneously from two nymphs that were behind her, and to whom she had paid no attention, presented the effect of her ill-will.

Those kicks were so vigorous that they caused her to leap, with a single bound, over the edge of the fountain, and spared her the trouble of going up the crystal stairway. By that means she found herself at the end of her journey, very weary, very wet, very muddy and dying of hunger, having one rib almost caved in by the leap she had made, which had caused her to fall on to stones.

To complete her woes, she was wearing Liron's coarse dress, as dirty as it was ugly, and a coiffure appropriate to make those who had sufficient courage not to die of fright die laughing. Instead of having gained by that excursion, she had even lost the dress that she had stolen from Liron and the magnificent lace with which it was covered.

Fortunately, she was not exposed to appearing before many people in the apparel she had, and before arriving at her mother's house she only encountered a few herdsmen, some of whom fled, crying that the evil spirit as after them. The rest, more assured, thinking that it was a disguise made expressly to render someone ridiculous, thought that those who had imagined it had succeeded perfectly; without recognizing her, they gave her applause, with loud bursts of laughter and infinite jeers.

Pigrieche arrived home to the sound of those agreeable acclamations, and as such music augmented the ill humor that she had not been able to contain, she compensated herself for it by means of a thousand loud imprecations against the fountain, its inhabitants and Liron, without sparing her own mother, by virtue of whose advice she had exposed herself to the misfortune that had overtaken her.

The latter, having recognized her daughter's voice through the racket that the spectators were making, promptly ordered a few female slaves to go to meet her. They ran to her, not because of the affection they had for her, for she was as beloved as she was lovable, but uniquely to avoid the ill-treatment with which she overwhelmed them at the slightest subject of complaint that she imagined that she had.

Those unfortunate woman fled on seeing her and, coming back precipitately, they told Richarde that they were being pursued by a frightful specter. The woman, who was only moderately fearful, did not believe what they were saying to her about a specter, but, wanting to see what had caused the general alarm, she went out in her turn, and thought about fleeing, as the slaves had; but, finally recognizing that it was her own daughter, she waited.

No consternation has ever been greater than Richarde's at the sight of Pigrieche thus bedecked. The latter was so exhausted by the violence of her screeching that she lost consciousness as she reached her mother, who immediately had her put to bed by the slaves. Doing her best to warm her up, she tried to remove the horrible mud that covered her, waiting with impatience for her to be in a condition to talk, in order to be informed of the circumstances of the disagreeable adventure.

She finally learned them; but, not believing it to be as unfortunate as it was, she hoped that by dint of combing her daughter's hair and washing her head she would cause the reeds and their vile foliage to disappear. They did indeed fall off, but only to make way for others, which reappeared instantly and in greater quantity than those of which she had just rid her.

That mother, whose affection for the unworthy Pigrieche was extreme, swore in her first fit of rage the doom of the innocent Liron, but the demon of self-interest, which never abandoned her, immediately represented to her that it would be a loss for her, since she treated her as a slave, from whom she extracted the same service, and that the service in question was all the more considerable because the flocks had never been in better condition than since they had been confided to her guard. That consideration was powerful enough to save her life, and Richarde restricted her vengeance to the pleasure of tormenting her, planning to render her so unhappy that she would desire death.

Meanwhile, Liron, who had seen what had happened from a distance, had prudently absented herself, taking her flock away from the house in order to avoid the first outburst of Richarde's anger. She ran to the fountain, which she entered without any obstacle, and told the naiads about her stepmother's fury, and the dread she had of the consequences of that adventure.

"It's not for me that I fear them," she told them, "it's in regard to the danger to my father. Those people, who have no honor or humanity, are capable of dooming him to avenge themselves."

Crystalline and her sisters reassured her, and to render her necessary to those evil creatures, they gave her the power to remove the marsh from Pigrieche's head, for twenty-four hours only, every time it was her who let down her hair. That necessity of preserving her life would be sufficient to make the mother and daughter respect the King's days and her own.

"So, my dear Lisimene," the naiad went on, "you have only to return tranquilly to your habitation. "Here is the shell of a river mussel; take it to your father and let him tell those monsters that having found it on the edge of the fountain, what you read in it caused you to return promptly to bring them the relief of the power that the shell attributes to you."

The Princess returned as quickly as possible and, slipping into the King's study, from which he had not emerged since he disorder had commenced, she showed him the shell and the oracle of sorts that it contained.

Good and Better, who feared that before his daughter had had time to make herself heard she would be maltreated by the Furies, approved the naiads' precaution and took the shell to them himself. It was necessary, as he had foreseen, to endure all kinds of insults before being able to explain, but having finally succeeded in making himself heard, he calmed them down somewhat by means of the hope that he gave them.

"Let the wretched slave come," said Pigrieche, "since she has an understanding with the witches of the fountain, and she can soothe the evils that she has attracted to me."

Liron appeared, trembling, and when she went to work they saw with joy that in fact, she succeeded in causing the frightful adornment that covered an even more frightful head to disappear; but such an important service, which would have excited gratitude in benevolent souls, was not capable of engaging Richarde or her daughter to love Liron anymore. On the contrary, the necessity that she had acquired rendered her even more odious to them.

However, as they could not make any attempt on her life without losing a great deal, they allowed her to pass a few days in relative tranquility, sometimes guarding the sheep, as usual, and sometimes playing a symphony for the naiads.

Everything comes to an end, however, and one day, as Liron was setting forth as usual, Richarde called her back, saying that she wanted to employ her for another occupation: that of picking pears of perfect beauty in order to take them to the town to sell them.

A single tree planted in the middle of a meadow bore those marvelous pears. It was covered with them, but it was not easy to reach the branches, which were tufted like those of a palm tree, placed at the top of an extremely smooth trunk more than three hundred and sixty feet high, which was so prodigiously thick that it was not possible to embrace it.

Liron remonstrated with her in vain that the branches of the tree, all high, could not be used to climb it, and that, having no ladder that could even extend over a tenth part of the trunk, she was being ordered to do the impossible.

Richarde was not unaware of anything that Liron told her, and, the disastrous experiments that she had made, having already cost the lives of several slaves who have attempted to climb the dangerous pear tree, testified clearly enough that it was sending someone to their death. It was precisely that terrible danger that determined Richarde to send Liron to pick the fatal pears, for, vanquished by the perpetual insistences of

Pigrieche, she finally ceded interest to the fear of her daughter's death, who threatened incessantly to kill herself if she delayed any longer in killing the odious Liron.

The utility that she had to Pigrieche, which had protected her from their initial fury, no longer counted for anything, because the furious young woman had dreamed that it was Liron's life that constituted the charm that rendered her frightful every twenty-four hours, and that she would become as beautiful as before as soon as Liron was no more. Although, on waking up, she had known that it was only a dream, she had treated it as a mysterious revelation, because it flattered her hatred against the unfortunate Lisimene.

Pigrieche was not the only person sufficiently unjust or unenlightened to commit a crime on the basis of the harmful of favorable objects rendered to us by the vapors of slumber. That reason, which can only be one for a person abandoned to her chimeras or her fury, determined the mother and daughter—which meant that poor Liron, in spite of all her representations of the impossibility of what was demanded of her, was not even heard, and received an absolute order to go to the pear tree.

Pigrieche said to her disdainfully that she could not see that there was any more danger for her in collecting pears than in traversing the waters, and that everything ought to be easy for her. "If you're refusing the employment that is given to you," she added, "it's because you have no hope of finding a new manner of coiffure, and it's solely a matter of your particular advantage."

Liron protested in vain that the tree was so high that no one had ever been able to collect an entire pear, since they only had those that fell. The fruit were so large and heavy that the pears were crushed when they fell, and they were only known to be excellent by virtue of a few pieces that had fallen on to grass softer than the ground after exploding. But Richarde, who did not like to be contradicted, put a stop to the conversation instantly.

"If you don't have a basket of pears from the great tree today and don't take them to the town, you can count on my going there tomorrow and that your father won't be long in following me." As she spoke, she threw a basket outside, and taking her by the arm, she put her outside as well, shutting the door on her.

There never was an embarrassment equal to the one in which the sad Liron found herself; the threat, which was only too intelligible, frightened her extremely, but the impossibility discouraged her, and made her envisage her father's doom as certain. Without the hope of succeeding, however, and solely not to have to reproach herself for having neglected an interest so dear to her, she went to fetch a ladder, dragged it away with difficulty, and still had to set it up, running the risk of being crushed by its fall twenty times over.

Finally, after a labor as difficult as it was dangerous, she succeeded in securing the ladder. She climbed up it, but she had not yet reached the middle when it began to tremble in its entirety and, the great height having caused her head to spin, she would have fallen if she had not dropped her basket in order to grip the ladder with both hands.

When her dizziness had passed she went down to pick up the basket, and, attaching it to her waist, she climbed up again, and reached the top of the ladder; but the effort was wasted, since the ladder would have had to have been much longer to reach the branches. Seeing that it was futile to make further efforts, she came down a second time.

When she was at the bottom, half-dead from the fear and fatigue she had endured, she began weeping over her father's death, which she regarded as inevitable, although she paid no attention to her own, which would indubitably follow, occupying herself uniquely with the danger that the King was in. She knew the dastardly peasants well enough not to hope that she might soften them with the story of the futile attempt she had made.

She was abandoning herself to her just despair when her beaver, who was looking for her, presented himself to her gaze. On casting her eyes upon him, she recalled the hand from which she had received him; which caused her to remember that Crystalline had recommended that she come to see her whenever she found herself in some difficulty. As she had already found a great deal of help there, she had no hesitation in returning, and, the crystal stairway having appeared at the first movement that she had imparted to the water by putting her foot in the fountain, she was in the naiad's palace in a trice.

"What brings you to this place, beautiful Princess," the naiad said, embracing her. "Why are you weeping? Has some misfortune arrived so considerable as to allow you to believe that we cannot bring any remedy to it?"

"Alas, my august protectress," said Liron, still in tears, "it's all over, I'm doomed; for my stepmother, who is only looking for a pretext to make us perish, is attaching my father's life and my own to the execution of impossible tasks. She wants me to collect pears from the great tree, although she is not unaware that no one has ever been able to do it, and that they're so high that they break on falling, so that none has ever been seen entire."

She told her about all the dangers and difficulties to which she had exposed herself in the futile attempt that she had made to obey Pigrieche's cruel order, and ended up by imploring her to protect her father, in such a way that she alone would remain exposed to the fury of the two Megaeras that were tormenting her.

The naiad, wiping her eyes tenderly with her hand, told her with a kind expression that what she had learned appeared to be troubling, but that those difficulties, great as they were, were not entirely insurmountable.

"It requires," she said, "friends to make themselves known. Come, my dear Lisimene, console yourself. I promise you that your father won't die and that you shall have the pears.

"It's necessary to tell you," she went on, "that there is no tree that does not serve as the abode of a hamadryad; she is, in a sense, its soul, and when it dies naturally, or by virtue of some accident that might occur, she remains adrift until she is able to grasp another and combine herself with it. The one who is the soul of the great pear tree is a friend of ours, and she is the most reasonable of all the rural divinities. As they only emerge from their bark by night, she is certainly in her pear tree now; take your lute and go and give her a little serenade. If you know any songs in praise of arbors and beautiful trees, don't fail to make them heard. She isn't proud, and, soon realizing that you're taking that step to please her, she won't take long to give you a sign of her satisfaction; then, talk to her as if you could see her in person. Tell her about your misfortunes and, above all, tell her that we love you. I'm convinced that, out of consideration for us, she will give you as much fruit as you wish.

"Go, lovable Princess, don't waste any time; it's a long way from the great tree to the town. By the way," she added, "in spite of the diligence to which I invite you, it's necessary to change your dress; the one you have on is too ugly to appear in society."

Without waiting to be thanked, the naiad had Lisimene undressed by Pigrieche's chambermaids, but they did so more honestly. They dressed her again in a white robe like the first, which was even more elegant and neat. She also gave her suitable shoes, because her clogs were not appropriate. To the rest of the outfit she added a large gauze veil embroidered with flowers, which covered her entirely—for fear, she said that she might be recognized; but actually in order to protect her from the ardor of the sun.

She added to that present a pair of otter-skin sabots that seemed so gross and ill-made that they appeared to weigh a hundred pounds, although they were no more inconvenient than a pair of gloves; they imitated so perfectly those that Richarde forced her to drag around that it would have been impossible to distinguish them; she told her to hide them in some hollow, from which to take them when she returned, so that they might serve her stepmother's gaze without her thinking that she was rid of the difficulty the others gave her. Finally, for a last present, she made her take a basket made of rushes interlaced with flowers, after which, having given her a light snack, she sent her away.

"Go boldly," she said to her, "where the piety that you owe to your father summons you; go, Princess, I predict that the success of your journey will surpass your hopes."

Penetrated by gratitude for her benefactress, Lisimene thanked her in the terms most appropriate to express it. "But, Goddess," she said to her, "since your kindness inspires in me the boldness to explain my embarrassment to you, I will take the liberty of remarking to you that the basket you are giving to me is very large."

"It will hold more fruit," said the naiad, smiling at that anxiety, "and your stepmother will be all the more satisfied."

"I agree with the fact," replied Liron, "but as it is so heavy while it is still empty that I have difficulty carrying it, you can judge that it will be impossible for me to move it when it is full."

"Don't let that worry you," said the divinity. "Put it on your head and cover it with your veil; you'll find that you're stronger and that it's lighter than you imagined. Adieu; go promptly."

With those words Lisimene found herself at the top of the crystal stairway, to which the naiad had guided her while talking to her.

Encouraged by what that generous friend had told her, Liron took advantage of her instructions and went to entertain the rural divinity.

She did indeed receive signs of satisfaction; the tree shuddered more or less excitedly, according to whether the cadences of her lute were more or less lively; the hamadryad seemed to be accompanying her visibly, and the earth in which her roots were embedded seemed to be beating time with a tremor that the Princess felt beneath her feet.

When the time that she had destined to the serenade had passed, she made her compliment to the tree as Crystalline had told her to do.

The hope that the nymph had flattered was not deceived, and what gave her as much surprise as joy was seeing that the tree, which was more than fifty feet in circumference, and which seemed to be hard enough to sustain the fall of a house without danger, became so supple that it touched its crown to the ground and she was able to choose the most beautiful pears. It even seemed that the tree, fearing not to have displayed enough of them, invited her to pass without fear into its branches, for they slipped adroitly under Lisimene's feet as if they wanted to indicate to her the pears that most merited being picked. For her part, she was careful not to walk on them, for fear of scraping, or even breaking them.

When the basket was full, the Princess, not wanting to limit the gratitude that she owed the pear tree to her songs, ran to a nearby spring, where she had noticed a pitcher that some of Richarde's slaves had left there, and brought it back full. Lifting the earth slightly with the crystal of the crook, she watered the tree amply.

After she had acquitted that duty, she thought about setting forth for the town, but, having tried to lift her basket, what she had anticipated occurred—which is to say that it was impossible to shift it.

That put her in great difficulty, but, remembering that Crystalline had told her to cover it with her veil and put it on her head, she did not suppose that the naiad would be as unjust as her stepmother and order her to do something impossible. Presuming that the veil must have the property of lightening her basket, she extended it over the top without hesitation.

The confidence with which she followed the advice was favorable to her, for she lifted the basket once the veil was over it with as much facility as she would have lifted a leaf, and she walked with a lightness that surprised her. Having turned her head, however, she perceived by her sides two young winged men, who were sustaining her beneath her arms with one hand, preventing her from touching the ground, which they were not touching themselves; and with the other hand they were lifting up the basket, which was only resting lightly on her head.

Thus aided, she arrived in the town in a short time, where, in spite of her diligence, she still had the mortification of having arrived too late, the market being finished; which caused her a terrible chagrin, not doubting that she would receive a terrible correction. Not knowing any means to avoid that entirely, however, she hoped to avoid at least a part of it by her diligence, putting her unique hope in the consolation that the naiads would give her, and counting on going to visit them before returning to her stepmother.

So, she took the road back to the desert, and in order to abridge it she passed through a forest that was between the town and Richarde's house. The fear of being scolded and the hope of being diligent were stronger than the fear of wild beasts, which rendered the place unsafe and meant that few people went there unless they were armed.

She was thinking about the reception that she would not fail to find when she arrived when she was interrupted by the sound of a hunting horn, and a short time thereafter, she saw a richly-dressed young man appear, followed by many others, who by the respect that they rendered him, made it evident that he was their master—which was even more easily noticeable by his noble and majestic manner than the regard that everyone had for him.

In the three years that Lisimene's exile had lasted she had only seen wretched slaves, even more crushed and brutalized by labor than by their condition. They bore more resemblance to animals than men, which caused her to look at the Lord with a pleasure that reminded her of happier times, when all those who surrounded her had equaled that young man in magnificence, if not in his fine bearing.

She sensed at that sight the suspension, for a time, of the dolorous idea of her present condition, and, forgetting her cruel situation, she imagined that she was still at Good and Better's Court. But that agreeable error did not last long, and the sentiment of her actual woes soon resumed its place.

The unknown man, who also had his chagrins, although they were much less violent than Lisimene's, was extraordinarily surprised to find in that desert, and so simply dressed, a person with such a noble stride; for the veil that covered her prevented him from judging her beauty, he could only judge her condition by her apparel, which, in spite of its neatness, only presented to his eyes a villager. He approached her unceremoniously, but with all the honesty that he had in general for the fair sex.

"What are you carrying in that huge basket, beautiful child?" he said to her. "It seems to me that you're well-laden; don't you fear succumbing under that heavy burden?"

He spoke thus because the sylphs that were aiding her were invisible for him and his retinue.

"Milord," replied the Princess, "I had gone to the town in the hope of selling this basket of fruit, but unfortunately, I arrived too late and I'm going back."

"Perhaps you live a long way from here," said he hunter. "It's hot and we can find an opportunity to oblige you and relieve you of an importune weight of which we can take advantage. We'll take your fruit; it will refresh us and you'll be rid of it."

So saying, he made a sign to those who were following to take the basket from Lisimene's head, and as that could not be done without removing her veil, which served as a cover for the fruit as well as her, she dazzled the Lord, who gazed at her at that moment and was surprised by the splendor of her beauty.

Her charms gave a further merit to the pears, by favor of the charms of their presenter; he proclaimed their extreme magnificence. He tasted one and found it admirable. They were, in fact, but perhaps they would not have attracted as much attention if the seller had been less beautiful. He distributed them to his courtiers, who, in his imitation, as much to pay their court as to render justice to the truth, could not weary of praising them.

The natural generosity of the young Lord, animated by the sight of the young woman who was then its object, did not permit him to limit himself to the highest price for which a basket of fruit could be sold. He took a large quantity of gold coins from his pocket; and after having put them in Lisimene's basket, fearing that they were insufficient, he asked all those accompanying him whether they had gold on them, and to give him more, in order that, after having run the risk of being overburdened by the fruit as she went, she would have been no less on going back with the gold that had been put in the place of the pears, if she had not had the aid of the sylphs.

After having paid so liberally for the fruits, the young Lord thought it would at least be permissible for him to ask the name of the seller and where she lived.

"You don't appear to be born for the employment in which you are," he said to her. "Will you refuse me the pleasure of learning your name, your condition, and how it is possible that, since I hunt in these woods, I haven't had the good fortune of meeting you before. In what remote place can you have hidden from my gaze?"

"Milord," she said, modestly, "my name is Liron. At present I'm a shepherdess, and my stepmother, in whose house I live, ordered me to go sell fruit in the town. Her habitation is not far from here, but the rocks between which it's necessary to pass and the turnings that separate them from the forest have doubtless prevented you from conceiving the desire to go hunting in a place whose appearances promise nothing but wilderness."

"Since we're separated by such a short distance," the young man said to her, "I hope, charming Liron, "that if you have pears to take to the town again, you'll give me the preference, and spare yourself half the distance as well. If you want to sell me as many as these tomorrow, I'll pay you dearly enough for you not to regret having given me the preference."

Enchanted by the generous and polite manners of the hunter, Liron promised him not to fail in what he asked of her, provided that she had the permission of her stepmother, and departed quite content with her journey, hoping that the profit she was bringing back would take away from Richarde's desire any pretext for maltreating her.

Meanwhile, the young man, who was sorry to see her leave, would have liked to have a reason to delay her departure.

Liron knew her stepmother's avarice too well to be mistaken in the judgment she had made, and the satisfaction that Richarde manifested at the sight of the sum that she presented to her—her eyes were dazzled by it and her heart was bathed in joy—gave her a cheerful and affable expression that she had not had for Liron for a long time.

She asked her how she had been able to make such a considerable sale; the shepherdess made no secret of her adventure, adding that the hunter had asked for more the following day, and had promised to pay for them as generously.

Pigrieche, who was listening, and who was less affected by the profit that she had made than the jealousy that Liron caused her, commenced complaining against her mother for applauding such a little thing.

"See how you spoil her" she said. "It seems, to see your admiration, that she has done something quite marvelous in selling a basket of pears, as if anyone couldn't have done as much."

Richard tried to represent to her that, in truth, although anyone could sell pears, not everyone could obtain such a large sum for them.

"That's exactly," her daughter went on, bitterly, "what ought to prove to you that it isn't to the sale of your fruit that you owe it, but rather to the price of the flirtatious manner and simpering of that stuck-up slut, who, as you see, hasn't failed to return to the sabbat in search of a new dress; the one she had wasn't beautiful enough to go chasing men. Go on, Mother," she continued, "far from being so charmed by the booty that she's bringing you, you ought to have scruples about taking it, and even more about sending her in search of more."

"Well, then," said Richarde, whom the weakness she had for her daughter always led her to think as she wished, "go in her place; it's not far, since he'll come half way along the road. You're good, and you won't do anything that isn't reasonable."

Pigrieche had never seen people of the Court, and Liron's story had given her an extreme desire to see such a handsome, magnificent and well-accompanied lord. That prevented her from balking at that proposition, as it was her custom to do with everything. She rendered herself such scant justice that she was convinced that if she had never had lovers, it was not to her lack of beauty that she ought to attribute it, but to the solitude in which her mother retained her, which forced her to live unknown, preventing the success that she might have hoped of her charms. Only seeking an opportunity to make up for lost time, she accepted joyfully one that appeared so favorable to establish her charms in the eyes of connoisseurs.

She was, however, slightly opposed by the apprehension that her success might not conform to her merit. The adventure of the naiads was still present in her imagination and proved to her sensibly that Liron's good fortune did not decide her own. She made her mother party to that uncertainty, but Richarde reassured her, remonstrating that this occasion was quite different, and that it was not a matter of throwing herself into a fountain.

Finally, curiosity and the desire to make conquests prevailed over Pigrieche's fear, more vanquished by that reason than those that her mother had represented to her. She declared to her that she had resolved to go and sell the pears.

That conversation and Pigrieche's resolution had not been witnessed by Liron, it had all passed between themselves, while she had been forced, on her return from the market, without even being given time to have a bite to eat, to resume her usual occupations. Thus the shepherdess Princess, who expected to see the unknown man, was very astonished the next day when she wanted to take the basket, that the women ordered imperiously to leave it, and to go with the sheep.

She had almost not slept in her impatience to see that day arrive; the unknown man had occupied her involuntarily, without it being possible for her to drive the idea away; the new caprices that destroyed the hope with which she had flattered herself and which had made the night seem so long, were more sensible to her than all the previous woes has been.

As you can imagine, she could not explain what it was that she felt, but, adopting the pretext of her stepmother's interest, she tried to represent to her the loss she would suffer if she neglected such a good opportunity to sell her pears. Her zeal was poorly recompensed; far from being heeded, she attracted a torrent of insults, and was shoved outside by the shoulders, with a reiterated order to go without any further argument to guard the sheep.

Pigrieche, whose ill-humor and jealousy against Liron was ever alert, disdained to take any instruction on the fashion of gathering the pears, because the day before, having learned on waking up where Liron had gone, she had been curious enough to follow her at a distance, perhaps in the hope of seeing her take a tumble and kill herself falling from such a height.

As she only got up when it pleased her, while she was still in bed Liron had had time to go to the fountain, and she had arrived at the pear tree just at the moment when Pigrieche was slipping from bush to bush, and was close enough to hear what she said and to see the facility with which she had picked the fruit.

Thus, she believed that she had no need of more ample instruction, and did not imagine that she had any need to entertain a tree that belonged to her as politely as Liron had done—politeness of which she was incapable.

She approached it brutally, as she did everything. "Come on, quickly," she said to it. "I don't have the time or the desire to amuse myself paying you compliments; I need pears, lower your branches promptly."

At those tender words, pronounced by such a beautiful mouth, the pear tree remained motionless.

After having waited for a moment, Pigrieche continued, in an even shriller voice: "Well, then, who is it that I'm talking to? Wouldn't one think that this accursed pear tree is made of wood and can't hear me? See, then, how it will work out; if you make me go to the house to fetch arms and axes, I can assure you that I'll teach you to obey."

The hamadryad that inhabited the pear tree, discontented by that threat and wanting to avenge herself for it, lowered all her branches at once, with so much vigor that they fell like a hundred thousand blows of a stick on to the shoulders of the rustic orator.

A salvo so unexpected and so violent knocked the unfortunate Pigrieche down. Before she was able to get up she received at least one more blow from each branch; there was not one, down to the smallest, that had not wanted to have that pastime.

After that expedition, they rose up again, and so did the virago, but she was not finished yet, for she needed pears, and the pear tree, which could not honestly refuse them after the agreeable speech that she had made, did not wait for her to ask again. Shaking her tree rudely, the hamadryad caused fruit to fall on Pigrieche's head and shoulders in such great quantity that she thought she was being crushed. One of them squashed her nose, and another staved in three teeth.

When that storm had passed, although Pigrieche was in a horrible fit of wrath and in a state to spread fear, the ardor that she had to go and obtain a lover was so strong that, swearing that when she returned, Liron and the pear tree would pay for the trick they had played on her, she started picking up the pears that she thought the least damaged. There were very few entire, but there were some that were only bruised. She was not tranquil while she picked them up, for the great movement that the tree had made had shaken those that remained so strongly that some of them were detached from time to time, and always fell on her, giving her further blows.

In spite of all these inconveniences, however, having arranged them as best she could, and supposing that her charms would make up for the dilapidation of the pears, she consoled herself for the poor beginning of the adventure by means of the hope that the end would be more agreeable, and wanted to put on the flowers that were around the basket; but Pigrieche found them as recalcitrant as those with which she had tried to ornament her head at Liron's expense.

Finally, discouraged by such futile effort, she took up her burden, with was thoroughly unappetizing and took the road to the town. The burden was so heavy that—not having, like Liron, the aid of sylphs—she succumbed to the weight, which obliged her to rest frequently, and delayed her considerably. The day was almost over when she arrived at the place where the handsome hunter was waiting for Liron.

Already, in the excess of his impatience, the hunter, unused to waiting, had explored all the paths in the forest and had ordered several of his servants to climb trees in order to see into the distance and inform him whether anyone was coming, but to no avail.

Finally, after much disquiet, he began to savor the joy given by the hope of soon seeing the person or whom he was waiting with so much impatience; one of his men had shouted to him that he could see the shepherdess.

To spare her a part of the journey and to bring such a sweet pleasure forward by a few moments, the young hunter spurted his horse and hastened toward her. Pigrieche had also deprived Liron of her second dress and had taken the veil she had received from the naiads, which deceived the unknown man and left him in no doubt that it was, in fact, the desired individual. He offered her a hand to relieve her of the burden by whose weight she was curbed.

"How impatient I was to see you, beautiful Liron," he said to her. "I feared for a long time that you would break your promise. Alas, you must be very weary from carrying that enormous basket."

So saying, he hastened to liberate her from it. In his imitation, all his men did likewise, and it was soon done. As her veil covered the basket, as it had done Liron's, however, the beautiful Pigrieche appeared uncovered, with all her charms, and the obliging unknown, only finding a horrible face, instead of the lovable and so desired shepherdess, recoiled in terror, crying: "Just Heaven! It's not Liron."

"No, in truth," said Pigrieche, in a bitter and angry tone, "it's not Liron, but it's me, who wouldn't change myself for her."

Seeing the confused expression of the hunter, who did not think as obligingly on her account as she thought herself, she flew into a horrible rage. "Look how motionless it is," she said, showing her his hand. "Should one say that because it isn't his coquette, the fruit is less good? Am I not well paid for the trouble I took collecting my best fruit and bringing them hear? I'm mortally weary, and this is the gratitude I get!"

"You could have saved yourself so many cares," retorted the hunter, in a chagrined tone, "and without taking the trouble, you had only to charge the beautiful Liron with it."

The last word augmented Pigrieche's wrath. "The beautiful Liron?" she said, bitterly, in her shrill vice. "What's so beautiful about her, the beautiful Liron? It's necessary that you have very poor taste to find her likeable and not render justice to me, who is worth more than her. But it isn't strange, and that's what happens to girls who amuse themselves coming to find runners of the forest, who have no more discernment than the beasts they hunt. Know, blockhead that you are, that the beautiful Liron is only a little wretch that we nourish out of pity, as well as her father, who is no better than her, and that if the whim takes me, I can deliver both of them to persons who wouldn't make them so many cajoleries."

That torrent of impertinences wearied the hunter and made his retinue laugh. The substitution of Pigrieche for Liron having not put him in a good mood, he wanted to get away, and without responding to her extravagances, he interrupted her, saying: "Let's see your fruit."

Then she got up, with difficulty, from the place where fatigue had obliged her to sit down, and having uncovered the basket, she showed him the pears, which were not similar to those he had seen before. They were in pieces, mingled with the stones and sand that sylphs had maliciously introduced on the way, to make the burden heavier, and were piled one on top of another. That, combined with what trickled from them and mingled with the flowers that had served to ornament Liron's basket the day before, gave the impression of a mass of spread marmalade.

"What's that?" said the hunter, turning his eyes away in horror. "You must have lost your mind, to present me such disgusting fruits. I certainly don't want them. Oh, they're nauseating."

Pigrieche, knowing that her merchandise was having as little effect as her beauty, began raging again and heaping all the insults imaginable upon the hunter.

She was even angrier on seeing that her ranting, far from causing the man she wanted to annoy any chagrin, was not even noticed by him, while it excited a great deal of laughter from the young men accompanying the hunter. They uttered it without any reserve, amusing themselves instead of trying to appease the beautiful fruit-seller, and giving her yet another subject for her anger.

Some of them asked, designing a politeness by which she was not duped, where she had acquired such a noble education, how she came to be so mild-mannered, and who had taught her to adorn fruits with such an appetizing appearance. One suggested to her that she had taken too much trouble in bringing that beautiful jam so far, which had doubtless escaped the neighborhood peasants. Finally, they took their mockeries so far that Pigrieche, whom it did not require as much to move to bile, picked up one of the largest pears and hurled it into the middle of the jeering troop.

That gesture doubled their hilarity and augmented the jeers; but the matter took a more serious turn, and they ceased laughing, when they saw that the pear had struck the handsome hunter full in the face.

"You're very brutal," the young man said to her, with a great deal of moderation, wiping his face calmly. "You certainly merit that I treat you like the insolent peasant that you are."

Without giving him time to continue, however, the men of his retinue who had not taken the matter with as much tranquility as him, indignant against Pigrieche, peppered the impertinent young woman with a storm of slaps and kicks, which were so abundant and so prompt that she thought the heavens had fallen upon her body. Soon recovering, however, from a hail that had only stunned her, she tried to defend herself, and hurled herself upon some of them in order to avenge herself, at least a little for the blows she had received from them all. It was not possible, though, for they pushed her away and sent her from one to another like a balloon.

That pastime, which was very agreeable to those young men, and amused them a great deal, might have ended up becoming deadly for the ridiculous shepherdess if the hunter had not taken her out of their hands. It required no less than all his authority to bring it to an end; and Pigrieche, being unable to avenge herself on the practical jokers with an equally forceful pleasantry, sought compensation in a tongue-lashing, by shouting the crudest insults at them.

The tragicomic scene having finished, the young hunter, as he went away, said to the rustic creature that he was sorry for the treatment that she had received, but that she had merited it thoroughly, and he advised her not to attract similar treatment again; after which he quit her, drawing away as quickly as possible.

Far from profiting from such sage advice, she lavished further abuse on them; although the troop had lost sight of her, they could still hear her cries, which continued for a long time after the disappearance of the hunter, and which she only ceased to screech for want of an adequate voice.

After having eaten a few pears that remained to her, she got up, and, limping badly, took the road to her habitation.

The first person she encountered was her mother, who, in her impatience to see her again had come to meet her dear daughter, and the treasure she was supposed to bring her. Richarde, who was expecting to find her laden with gold, was very surprised to see her covered in mud, her clothing in tatters, uttering frightful cries.

At that cruel vision, the good mother thought she would die of alarm and affliction. She scarcely had the strength to ask her questions, so Pigrieche spared her the trouble and recounted to her, while cursing against Liron, the fatal adventure that had happened to her.

Richarde tried to criticize her for taking the pears, since she admitted that they had been soiled in falling, but her daughter, whose ill humor had not yet found an object to satisfy it sufficiently, was delighted to be furnished with such a plausible pretext. She started vomiting further imprecations, accusing her mother of having sent her into the trap that Liron had extended to doom her, sustaining, as a certain fact, that she had stationed those forest bandits—as she called the hunters, whom she supposed to have tried to murder her—in order to kill her. She wanted absolutely that to avenge her, Richarde should put Liron to death without delay and that the pear tree should be cut down.

The woman, who entered into all her daughter's furies, consented to that at first, but, reason—or rather self-interest and avarice—caused her to reflect that the tree, unique in its species and the rarity of its fruit rendering it precious, might bring her a considerable profit, which she could only receive by means of Liron's hands. That was enough to make her retract the sentence that she had pronounced against the tree and the shepherdess.

Pigrieche who was not satisfied by those reasons, might perhaps have brought her back to her original sentiment if she

215

had not been retained by Richarde representing to her that Liron was more useful to her than anyone else, since, in addition to the services she rendered in the house, and the fatigue of which she was promising to augment by avenging herself, she alone could remove the mud and reeds that grew daily on her head. That was more appropriate to deflect her from her cruel design than all the other arguments that Richarde had employed, and she contented herself for the time being with the promise she made her to render Liron so unhappy that she would desire death.

Pigrieche was content with that hope, and the day passed almost entirely in putting her to bed, washing her wounds, ridding her of mud and giving her all the relief of which she had need. The mother and daughter were so busy with those tasks that they did not even think of mistreating Liron.

At dawn the next day, however, Liron received simultaneously orders to do all the work that there was to be done in the house, the livestock pens and the stables, and to execute those various commands diligently enough to have time to go and gather pears and take them to sell in the town.

The last of those orders rendered all the others facile. Liron was delighted by it, for the charms of the handsome hunter had made an impression on her mind that extended as far as the heart. So she hastened to obey her stepmother; she redoubled the diligence she ordinarily employed, and, assisted by her dear beaver, everything was done in very little time.

Richarde, seeing that she was ready to depart, gave her a basket larger and more cumbersome than the one she had had before, in order to begin causing her chagrin with further mortifications. She was not content with increasing her burden; she wanted to put as much malevolence into it as she could. Instead of her white dress—which, in truth, was no longer wearable—she made her put on a dress of coarse fabric and her clogs, enveloping her head in a dirty rag, which hid her coiffure.

It was in that wretched attire that Liron was sent to the pear tree.

She laughed internally at that futile precaution, convinced that in order to be more appropriately clad she had only to go and find the naiads. Thus, adornment was not what caused her anxiety; she was more apprehensive that the handsome hunter might have been discouraged by the previous day's adventure and would not want to return to the same place. In any case, she judged it appropriate to commence by going to the fountain.

She was received and regaled there as usual, and expressed to the naiads, the pain caused by the vile clothing she was wearing. "As it is only to mortify me," she told them, "that my stepmother wants to oblige me to appear before the young lord thus clad, I confess to you that she ought to be satisfied, for she has succeeded marvelously."

"We could thwart her malicious intention," said Crystalline, "if you desire that. The rag that you have on your head is of no account, and it would be easy for us to change your dress. But my dear Princess, if you trust me, you will keep the one you have and leave your headwear as it is. My science tells me that the handsome young man has taken a liking to you; I'm confident that he renders justice solely to your charms. I would like you to owe the conquest to your beauty alone, and for that it is necessary that the hunter does not suspect that coquetry plays any part in your actions; that would be enough to inspire more scorn than love. If you trust me, you'll present himself to his eyes as you are, contentedly ornamented by your own charms."

Crystalline's sentiment was not that of the Princess; the latter dare not presume sufficiently on her charms to hope that they might prevail over the frightful apparel that Richarde had given her. In addition to her natural docility, however, she had complete confidence in the kindness and prudence of the naiads. Furthermore, the shame of having thought of taking such a step in order to please an unknown man prevented her from insisting.

So, ceding to the advice she had been given, she departed without delay, accompanied by her aerial spirits, who came to relieve her as they had done the first time. To hasten her task, they had collected and gathered the pears, in such a way that they were soon arranged in the basket, which, thanks to the sylphs, only appeared to have a very light weight.

The hunter had been in despair over the previous day's adventure, and, fearing that he might not see the beautiful fruit-seer again, he had made arrangements in advance and posted men on horseback at various distances, with the order to come and inform him if she appeared on the road to the market. Not satisfied with that precaution, he was there himself, asking all those who passed by whether they had seen a young woman dressed in the fashion in which Liron had appeared to his eyes; but no one could give him news of her, and he had almost lost all hope when one of his followers, who had climbed a tree in order to satisfy his anxieties, shouted that he could see a woman in the plain, but that she was too far away for him to discern whether it was Liron, or even how she was dressed.

In spite of the uncertainty in which that advice left him, the hunter was delighted. His heart told him that it was the shepherdess, so he went forward, and found her at the entrance to the wood; but his joy was moderated somewhat when he distinguished objects more clearly, and he had reason to fear that it might not be Liron, whose previous attire was so different from that she was wearing now.

Although unable to recognize her under the obscure veil with which Richarde had covered her, he approached her nevertheless with great honesty, presuming that the woman might be some slave from the same house, from whom he could at least obtain news of Liron.

"Good slave," he said to her, "would you like to sell me your fruits?"

"Milord," replied the pretended slave disguising her voice, "I'm only bringing them with the intention of disposing of them. If you are kind enough to buy them, I will be much obliged to you. My misfortune having caused me to fall into the hands of a cruel mistress, I shall be very sorely mistreated if I don't sell them. On the contrary, if you deign to take them, as that would spare me the trouble of going all the way to the market, I shall be able to return, and avoid by my diligence the ill-treatment that I invariably suffer when I'm too late."

She said those words in a voice so touching that, even though the hunter did not know her, he was touched by the sad condition that she described.

"I'll deliver you from that misfortune," he told her, "And, not limiting my good offices simply to relieving you of your fruit, not only will I pay you for it, but if you can render me a service, I will give you what you need to buy your freedom. For that, you only have to tell me whether you live in the same house as Liron, and if you have news of her. Tell me, promptly, why she no longer comes to sell fruit. It's also necessary for you to tell me the road she normally takes; by that means, you can hope for all my gratitude."

"How would it serve you to be informed of what you are asking of me?" said Liron. "You would be poorly received where she is, and your presence would serve as a pretext for the rigors to which she is subjected. So, Milord," the pretended slave went on, "follow my advice and cease looking for her. Your acquaintance is not sufficiently old for you to have any difficulty in renouncing it."

"Oh, there's no longer time," said the hunter. "I've seen too much of her for my repose; it's necessary that I see her again, or I'll die."

"Since you deign to confide your sentiments to me thus," added Liron, "suffer, Milord that I suggest to you that you are abandoning yourself too much to the violence of a passion that cannot have a fortunate outcome. I am in the same place as that shepherdess, and I know everything that she thinks. I share her misfortunes. Her troubles are mine; but they would be considerably augmented if she thought you were thinking so disobligingly of her, since the idea you seem to have of her is entirely opposed to the one that her virtue ought to inspire in you..."

"Oh, dear slave," said the hunter, precipitately, "since you are her friend, assure her that the love I have for her is not incompatible with the most perfect esteem. I have only seen her for a moment, and her beauty has delighted me, but the tenderness and merit that shine throughout her person have inspired as much respect as love."

"Perhaps," said Liron, "you are attributing the effect that her elegant attire produced in your mind to a love that your heart does not feel, but if you saw her dressed differently, you would be disabused and would be annoyed by your error."

"Those vain adornments," relied the hunter, "could not deceive me. I am accustomed to seeing, without emotion, those of the ladies of the Court. I can tell the difference between natural grace and those that are due to artifice. There are none there that can enter into comparison with the charming Liron...

"But," he continued, in a kindly manner, interrupting himself, "I'm talking and I'm not paying any heed to the fact that you're standing there, crushed by the weight of that enormous basket."

So saying, he made a sign to his servants to take it. It was so heavy that two men could hardly lift it, which touched the hunter with an extreme pity.

Liron would have liked to withdraw without being discovered. What she had heard, in letting her know the young unknown's sentiments entirely, had caused her a certain timidity, which caused her to fear the ensuing conversation if he perceived that she was the same Liron of whom he was amorous. Raising a hand to her veil with that intention, she tried to retain it, but she could not prevent it following the basket and the hunter from recognizing her.

"What! It's you, charming Liron!" he exclaimed, with a transport of joy. He continued; "Alas, it's you! My heart told me so, and without penetrating the reason, I could not resolve to draw away from such a dear slave." Changing, his expression and testifying to as much dolor as he had appeared to experience joy a moment before, he went on: "But by what misfortune have I attracted your hatred? Why do you refuse me the pleasure of knowing you? What am I saying? That isn't all: you've disguised yourself as a slave in order to come and tell me that my love offends you; and in listening to your scruples, you're declaring to me clearly that I have no hope of your heart."

"The condition you see me in is not a disguise," said Liron, "it is my usual costume. Without being a slave by the right of war or the baseness of my birth, I am one to a stepmother, who treats me as if the law authorized her procedures. The clothes I was wearing two days ago were a present that was given to me, but because of a misfortune that befell the daughter of that rigorous stepmother yesterday, of which she imagines that I am the sole cause, she and her daughter have used that pretext to deprive me and to send me here dressed as you see me.

"But that is not what causes my anxiety; on the contrary, I quit that costume joyfully, thinking that by that means I could be less recognizable, and I hoped that in another costume I might avoid speeches to which it is not permitted to me to respond. That precaution has been futile; I have been unable to evade the effects of your politeness and your generosity. But in sum, Milord, since you know my face, I do not believe that I ought to hide my character from you; it only requires a brief word. That is that if you want me to bring your our fruits in future, you must refrain from speaking to me in that fashion; I shall expose myself to any risk rather than listen to you."

Confused by that excess of severity, the hunter tried in vain to engage Liron to relent. Seeing that his efforts were futile, however, he fell back on requesting at least her confidence and her amity, swearing to her not to attempt anything that might make her repent of having granted them to him, and begging her insistently to allow him to share troubles to which, if she would permit him, he might perhaps be able to bring a few remedies, personally or by means of the assistance of his friends. He begged the favor of her, therefore, of informing him of her veritable situation.

The shepherdess had already listened to her penchant too much to resist his solicitations, and she told him that the reason and the propriety that did not permit her to regard him and suffer him as a lover could not prevent her from according him the satisfaction of receiving him as a friend. She refused to tell him her name, that of her father and their place of residence, but she did not disguise anything of the ill-treatment that she received on the part of Richarde and her daughter.

The young man was indignant on learning of the barbaric conduct of those Furies; he could not contain himself, especially in thinking about the audacity they had in maintaining in the clothing and occupations of a slave a free individual whose education announced an illustrious birth.

"If your abject garments shock me, beautiful Liron," he said, "it is not because they take away any of your charms; you are still the most lovable person in the world; but it is horrible that those creatures, who have no right over you, and who are doubtless as inferior by birth as they are in every other fashion, treat you so unworthily. I can punish them, and it's necessary that I avenge you."

With these words he summoned his servants, who, out of respect, had retired to a distance. But Liron, who feared consequences of which she did not want to inform her new friend, stopped him urgently.

"What do you intend to do?" she said to him. "Remember that you can attempt nothing to avenge me without dooming me. It's necessary that I fulfill my destiny, and it isn't permissible for me to make the slightest effort to change it. I've lost all hope. It's only death from which I can expect any rescue."

The hunter, who was not deterred by her arguments, begged her to let him act, or to take him entirely into her confidence, but he could not obtain either of those requests, and she was obstinate in not saying any more, while continuing to demand that he did not take any steps in her favor.

To persuade him to obey her, she needed all the influence over him that her charms gave her. She only succeeded by promising him to come back and see him as often as she could; and in spite of that promise, it was not without difficulty that she prevented him from following her. It was necessary for her to add to the pleas she had already made the threat of withdrawing to some unknown location where she would be sheltered from his persecutions.

He finally left her, for fear of displeasing her.

She had been paid this time with great profusion than the first, and she returned laden with gold, which pleased Richarde greatly, and would almost have made her forget her anger, as well as her daughter's accident, if Pigrieche had been as easy to satisfy. Far from calming her, that great success only served to redouble her fury, by comparing it with her own. It was necessary for Richarde to like wealth as much as she did for her to hold firm against her daughter's solicitations. But the sight of the gold coins and their abundance were such a powerful protection for Liron that the miserly Richarde could not resolve to harm her while the pears lasted.

Liron went to carry them every morning, and the hunter, punctual at the rendezvous, often spared her half the road. He would have come further with great pleasure if she had permitted him to do so. He always found a new pleasure in seeing her. She shared it, and they never separated without an extreme regret, while Richarde only saw her returning with an infinite joy.

On her return from the market, Liron went to guard the sheep in the vicinity of the fountain, paying her ordinary court to the naiads by means of her songs and her lute, while the hunter, on whom those frequent conversations with the shepherdess had completed casting a spell, thought about nothing but the happy moment that would bring her back to him. Liron, who was only too sensible to the pleasure of seeing the lovable unknown again, was no less impatient to find him at the rendezvous.

However, when the fruit ran out, the lovers, who were accustomed to the pleasure of seeing one another every day, found much to lament, even though their conversations had lasted no longer than an hour and the scrupulous Liron had always forbidden her lover the liberty of talking about amour. But for want of the tongue, the hunter made his eyes talk, and he had little doubt that they were understood, since they even received a involuntary and unwitting response occasionally. That was an extreme consolation for him, which suddenly ceased with the sale of the fruit.

The privation of the pleasure that Liron found in going to sell her pears was not the only misfortune to which she was exposed. As soon as she was no longer bringing a profit, the fury of the daughter found access to the heart of the mother. They searched conjointly for new opportunities to torment Liron and do her more harm than ever. For that, Pigrieche imagined a means that she believed to be infallible.

A league from their dwelling, in an extremely deserted spot, there was a windmill that was known as the Mill of Misfortune. It had been named thus because, for many years, no one had been able to go there without suffering some nasty accident. Many people had not returned, without it being possible to discover what had happened to them, and the less unfortunate were those who came back with a few dislocated limbs, or having been bitten by venomous or ferocious creatures. The inevitable dangers that surrounded the deadly mill had driven everyone away, and no one ever went there, although, in spite of the misfortunes that were experienced in its vicinity, the flour that came from it was invariably excellent, and always worth twice as much as that made elsewhere. Even so, it had been renounced absolutely, which meant that no one went there.

All the accidents that occurred for a league around were imputed to the miller and his wife, who, it was said, had made an alliance with evil spirits to cause all those who approached their abode to perish. What gave the most force to these suspicions was their solitary humor. The land surrounding the mill belonged to them, and without emerging from that enclosure or ever having commerce with anyone, they lived in seclusion, in which it was impossible to know what they were doing.

That singular life and the peril that there was in going to visit them rendered them so redoubtable that they had given rise to a malediction. When anyone was angered by his enemies, he wished that they might be obliged to go fetch flour from the Mill of Misfortune.

It was to that terrible mill that Richards ordered Liron to take her wheat. That proposition made her tremble, but the sentences pronounced upon her were without appeal, and it was not permissible for her to make the slightest protest. On the contrary, the reluctance that she expressed only served to fill her enemies with joy, with the result that it was necessary to depart without delay.

Fortunately, they had not taken it into their heads to deprive her of her crook and her beaver. She was given an old, lame donkey laden with two sacks of wheat, and forbidden above all to abandon it. She was ordered to bring it back just as she had taken it.

There was a malicious motive for that prohibition, as well as giving her a mount so lame, because they hoped that the accident that was inevitable on the road on which they were sending her would not fail to befall her while she was occupied in looking after her donkey, or even defending it.

She set forth, therefore, dragging her gross clogs—or, rather, the light footwear that she owed to the naiads, which resembled them externally.

Her stepmother said to Liron when she left that it required a great deal for her to trust her, because she knew how idle she was, and was convinced that in order to avoid the trouble of making the journey, she was capable of pretending to take the road of misfortune without going there. She intended to have authentic proof that she had been there, and for that it was necessary that she bring back flowers: not those that were ordinarily found in flower-beds but gems that were rumored to grow in profusion in the garden of the Mill of Misfortune. She ordered Liron to bring back an ample bouquet; if not, she would deliver Good and Better to the cruel Ambitious.

Liron knew all the dangers of that journey, having no doubt of the motive that had obliged her stepmother to order her to make it, but the threat that accompanied the order did not permit her to make the slightest reflection; thus, without taking the trouble of making futile representations, she set forth, not to go directly to the mill, as Richarde imagined, but to go to see the naiads, counting on the fact that she would not emerge from their abode without having received salutary advice.

She went there with all possible diligence, and, leaving her flock in the care of the faithful Diligent, penetrated into their palace, where she explained hr new commission and the fear she had of succumbing in its execution.

"Have no fear, beautiful Liron," Crystalline said to her. "However dangerous this occasion might be, you will get out of it gloriously, and far from being fatal to you, good fortune will emerge from the persecutions of your cowardly enemies. So, carry out all the orders they have given you tranquilly. To begin with, it is simply a question of limiting yourself to three things: prudence, exactitude and kindness. This is the explanation.

"Firstly, avoid the high road; it is the shortest route but the least safe. Listen attentively to everything I am going to tell you. You will find a path to the right, it is that one you must follow, without being deterred by its length. You will undoubtedly hear voices on the road, from which you will only be separated by a hedge, but whatever sounds you hear, or whatever is said to you, refrain from turning round either to see or to hear. Resist courageously the curiosity of learning what does not concern you. Prudence and discretion will defend you; your security requires that, and is dependent on it.

"It is here," the naiad continued, "that exactitude is necessary, for you to rest the fear that ferocious beasts might cause you, which you will not fail to encounter. Remember that not only do I forbid you to flee from them, but that I order you to wait for them while standing firm. The confidence that you have in our amity will augment your courage and ought to convince you that I would not expose you to that danger if I could not give you a means of preserving you from it. That is to touch them with your crook. As for venomous beasts, you will not have the trouble of defending yourself from then; it will be the affair of your beaver to protect you from their fury without your deigning to flee or to combat them.

"If, on the way, you find an opportunity to render a service to someone, do not resist your benevolent humor, and if you encounter brutal individuals who speak to you uncivilly, only combat them by the mildness of your responses, without neglecting to oblige them for that, remembering that it is necessary to do all the good that one can, and not to pay attention to whether those who receive it seem worthy of it. It often happens that a good deed received by someone that one believes to be wicked or worthless is recompensed a hundredfold, and acquires the person who has rendered it faithful friends, who have as much power as gratitude.

"That isn't all," continued Crystalline. "When you arrive at the mill, you will find aggressive dogs, which will try to hurl themselves upon you, but by presenting them with this cake, you will appease them; throw it to them and it will render them mild and submissive. That is the last danger that you will find on the route, if you behave prudently. There is another one that awaits you at the door of the mill, which it will be easy for you to avoid by not taking the knocker in your hand; refrain from touching it, and content yourself with picking up a stone with which to knock.

"If the miller and his wife receive you poorly, appease them with your mildness and your politeness. Provided that you act in that way, their ill humor will dissipate easily. I know them, and I'm not unaware of the reasons they have for acting in that way. I can assure you that you will not be sorry to know them, nor to have made the journey. Go, my dear Lisimene; depart without further delay; before the end of the day you will have experienced the utility of my advice and your stepmother will be the dupe of her malice. Above all, don't forget to ask for the bouquet of gems that she ordered you to bring back. The miller or his wife will give you permission to pick them yourself, but don't do that, and if they are obstinate, come back without the bouquet rather than doing so. Adieu, Princess; you have no time to lose."

After having listened very attentively to all that her protector had said to her, Lisimene departed, firmly resolved to comply with it.

She had scarcely gone two hundred paces, following the route that the naiad had told her to take, when she heard two women on the road, who were arguing bitterly on the subject of some clothes that they had agreed to make together, but it would have taken a great deal for them to agree as to what they share of the returns should be. They were reproaching one another for their lack of probity in terms so amusing, and recalling circumstances so singular that Liron could not help laughing.

What increased her desire to do so was that she believed that she recognized the voices of two of Richarde's favorite slaves, and the only ones that she trusted. She made a movement to part the hedge, but, remembering the advice she had been given, she reproached herself for her indiscreet curiosity, and went on her way, increasing her pace.

She was going extremely quickly when her march was slowed down by the sweet sound of a flute, the excellence of which was sustained by that of a woman's voice, which was singing words whose meaning was that the efforts one can make and the obstacles with which one can attempt to oppose amour, far from destroying it, only serve to render it stronger and more confident.

After having stopped singing, the woman pronounced these words, very distinctly: "Alas," she said, "it's only too true that one exposes oneself to everything when one is in love, and prudence speaks in vain. I am experiencing that at this moment. I find myself here—why did I come here?—entertaining a lover hated by my family, and whom they have forbidden me to see. Oh, Shepherd, to what are you exposing me? If this step is taken, I am lost without resources. What would people say if they knew that we were alone in this deserted spot? No, I cannot draw away too promptly to repair the imprudence and to flee the dangers that surround it."

"Why do you want to deprive me of your presence, charming Shepherdess," said a man, who was doubtless the one who had been playing the flute so delicately. "There was no danger in emerging from your house and setting forth, since you were not perceived on the way, and it's impossible at present for anyone to suspect where you are. Please leave me the pleasure of playing for you without poisoning it with these cruel reflections. These moments are so rare, alas; why trouble them in that fashion? It seems to me that my amour merits a more favorable fate. And since your flock is secure, you can give me a few more of these precious moments, the only ones capable of making all the happiness of my life. Don't refuse them to me."

That speech surprised Lisimene all the more because she had not seen any gallant shepherds in the locale, nor elsewhere, having always imagined that herdsmen of the species to which he and his shepherdess must belong only existed in books, and were known in no other realm than that of fiction. She had been convinced until that moment that all the sheepfolds in the world only played host to coarse pastors, who are everywhere that there are sheep.

That novelty inspired in her a violent desire to see the pastoral couple, and but for Crystalline's warning she would have gone down into the road through a gap in the fence near to where those voices where coming from; to encounter the objects of her curiosity she only needed to draw away from the path she was on by two steps at the most. Just as she was about to succumb to that indiscreet desire, however, her beaver, which as marching on her heels drew level with her and nudged her in passing, which reminded her of the strict instruction she had received not to stray from her route.

She was ashamed of having been so curious, and continued on her way, promising herself to be more wary in future of such seductive occupations, for it would not have taken much to make her yield to it. She was still occupied by that thought, and had no doubt that it was a continuation of the naiads' generosity that had made the beaver draw closer to her so appositely, when she heard a noise from the nearby undergrowth, as of some animal traversing it.

The noise made her turn her head, and she saw a horrible wolf emerge from a dense thicket, its fur bristling, its eyes fiery and its mouth agape, which came toward her to devour her. She shivered at the sight, but without making any movement to flee. On the contrary, having allowed the wolf to approach, she dealt it a blow it in the mouth with her crook, which laid it dead at her feet.

The facility with which she had escaped that danger inspiring a new courage in her, she was not frightened to find venomous creatures much larger than the ordinary on her heels, to the right and the left. Diligent, who had perceived them at the same time as his mistress, hurled himself upon them, and drove them away in a trice with thrusts of his paws and his teeth. Marching in front of Liron, he finished ensuring her route.

She was not far from the mill when the dolorous cries of a child, attracting her attention, caused her to run to the place from which they were coming. She no longer feared contravening the advice of the naiad, because she had abandoned both the main road and the path, a turning having taken her away from the former entirely, and the path had subsequently faded away in a meadow that remained for her to cross, the mill being on the far side of it. The cries she heard were not very distant and could only be coming from a spring close, to which it was necessary to pass in order to arrive at the place she wanted to go. Far from going there at a walk, guiding her lame donkey, she abandoned it to the care of the beaver and ran toward the place where her help was needed.

Nothing covered the spring, which only had bushes for its borders; she was frightened on arriving there to see a child who appeared to be no more than five years old. She feared not being able to save him, because his soaked garments were dragging him down by their weight and had sapped the strength required to reach the bank, with the result that he could hardly keep his mouth out of the water, and without the assistance of a small branch to which he was clinging, which was ready to break, Lisimene's good will would have been futile.

Although she did not hope to find naiads in the spring, and the cold was excessive, she did not hesitate as to what she had to do. The generous Princess descended into the spring, where she had water up to her stomach, and it was not without risk to her life that she saved the child's. She finally seized him; but, not being able to get out of the spring holding him in her arms, she was obliged to throw him on to the bank.

It was not while playing that the little boy had fallen into danger, but by virtue of the fear he had of a she-bear that was chasing him eagerly. He had been obliged to jump into the water, having no other means to avoid the fury of the cruel beast, which had been prowling around the spring for some time; that was what had made the child utter the screams that Lisimene had heard. At the sight of her, the she-bear had hidden in a big bush, but it emerged as soon as its prey was out of the water and rushed upon him.

The little boy would have been carried away if Lisimene, who had finished emerging from the water, had not flown to the child's aid with as much agility as if her clothes had not been wet. She ran so quickly that she reached the bear and killed it before it had time to do its prey any harm.

Although the child was not injured, he had fainted from fear or fatigue, so that Liron was obliged to carry him in her arms as far as the mill, where, on her arrival, she endured the attack of four furious dogs that tried to throw themselves upon her; but she appeased them by throwing each of them a piece of the cake that Crystalline had given her, which immediately rendered them as meek as sheep.

Having not forgotten the naiad's instruction, Liron carefully refrained from touching the knocker; she picked up a stone and threw it against the door of the mill, which opened immediately.

"What's this fashion of knocking?" said the miller, angrily. "Isn't there a knocker on the door, without you making use of stones to break it down? Don't do it again, for if it happens a second time, I'll make you repent of it."

Liron did not find the man any less brutal than he had been described to her, but she wanted to appease him. "I beg your pardon, Milord," she said, softy, "I had no intention of offending you; if you knew my reasons I'm sure that you'd receive my apologies..."

"Good, good, reasons and apologies, there's no lack of them; but if you come back, you'll see that I don't intend to be mocked. However," he added, "since you're here, I'll overlook it this time. Come in, and let's see what it's about."

Liron, whose clothes were dripping wet, took advantage of the permission he had given her and approached the fire tremulously, next to which the miller's wife, who appeared no less sullen than her husband, was sitting.

Their ugliness, and a certain roguish attitude with which it was seasoned, had taken away the confidence of the shepherdess in the matter of asking for help for the child she had saved from the water; she held him enveloped in the front of her dress, without daring to show him.

"What do you have there?" said the miller's wife, brusquely.

"Alas, Madame," said Liron, "it's an unfortunate child who is half-dead from cold. I pulled him out of the water, where he was drowning, and if I've committed an impoliteness in knocking on your door in an unconventional fashion, I only did it because of the haste I was in to see myself in a state to soothe this poor child, who has an extreme need of warming up."

"What do I see?" the woman cried, taking him in her arms. "It's my son! Oh, beautiful shepherdess, where did you find him?"

The miller came running at these cries. Liron naturally told them what had happened, and what she had done to save their son, without knowing him. As she spoke, the brutal faces of the miller and his wife cleared, to give way to a gentle and affectionate physiognomy.

When Liron had finished talking, the miller's wife embraced her, unable to weary of praising the generosity with which she had risked her life in order to help a child she did not know.

Meanwhile, the child, whose mother had stripped him of his wet clothes and given him dry ones, having warmed up and recovered his spirits, recounted himself all that Liron had done for him. The miller, who went out, returned a short time afterwards dragging the she-bear after him,

"Courageous Princess," he said, "beautiful Lisimene, a good deed is never wasted; you have rendered me he greatest service that I could receive, and it is only just that in your turn you have reason to be content with my gratitude.

"You were sent to this place to doom you," he continued, "but the evil intention of your enemies, far from succeeding as they hoped, will turn to your glory and their confusion, and you will always remember with pleasure having come to the Mill of Misfortune, since it is only here that you will find the help that will save your life."

The joy that the father and mother felt in seeing their son escape two great dangers had prevented them at first from perceiving that Liron had no less need of a change of apparel than the child; having finally noticed it, however, they gave her one promptly, far richer than that of the naiads; it was in a fabric embroidered with as much magnificence as good taste. The miler then invited her to take a stroll, while he had her wheat ground.

After having shown her the magnificent gardens he took her into a grotto, in which she found another, the most extraordinary she had ever seen. The grotto was formed of seashells and pebbles of sculpted gold, mingled with precious stones; it was surrounded by a golden trellis, which sustained similar trees laden with all kind of fruits formed by diamonds, rubies and emeralds. The bottom was a flower-bed where all the flowers, from the violet to the cinnamon were made in the same fashion. The sun did not illuminate that superb garden at all, but the lack of its light was compensated by that of four torches made of carbuncles, placed in the four corners, which threw out a hundred thousand times more fire than the day star could have done.

It was in that place that the miler terminated the Princess's stroll. He obliged her go sit down, and, judging that she had need of something to eat, he simply raised his voice, taking no other trouble, saying: "Let us be served."

Immediately, Lisimene saw the face of a woman appear between the trellises, who was no more than a foot tall, very ugly, and with a head larger than the rest of her body. That monster of sorts hastened to execute the order she had just received, and presented Lisimene, with the most delicious dishes, which her hosts invited her to eat. Whatever need she had for nourishment, she did not know what to do, the naiad having omitted to inform her in that regard, which embarrassed her a little.

The miller, remarking her perplexity, said, smiling: "I'm not offended by that suspicion, which is only too well founded, and I can't complain, since it's by my own cares that I've give myself the terrible reputation of being the wickedest man on earth—but I've never merited that of traitor. Since I assure you that I'm one of your friends, my word and the service you have rendered me ought to be a guarantee for you of the sincerity of my promises"

Ceasing to hesitate then, even though she was not entirely reassured, Liron did not refuse to eat a little, but gradually. Her hosts showed such a sincere affection for her that her timidity disappeared, and she showed them as much confidence as she had in the naiads.

As her apprehension calmed down, she recovered the noble boldness so natural to persons of her rank, no longer remembering the character that befitted the slave Liron, she spoke with the assurance and liberty of a king's daughter.

"Milord," she said to the miller, "for in spite of the simplicity of our occupation, I believe that title is your due, all the more so as what I see here does not permit me to doubt that there is a mystery in your condition, although I shall not seek to penetrate it indiscreetly. I shall restrict myself to asking you for permission to seek information as to the reason you have or rendering yourself the terror of the land, and why everyone is unaware of your generosity. For myself, who has received marks of it so obliging. I have a veritable impatience to return to my father in order to tell him and to publish it..."

"It's not necessary," the miller interrupted. "If you want to oblige me, I beg you to do nothing of the sort. Whatever evidence you receive here of my gratitude, I only demand of yours not to divulge what has happened here. On the contrary, I ask you to do me the favor of keeping my secret; by revealing it you would only cause me a great deal of chagrin, not without exposing me to finding myself the butt of the curiosity of fools or the cupidity of scoundrels. But to except you from the general rule and prove my esteem for you, I want to confide to you what I hide from everyone else; I shall even tell you without demanding your oath, presuming that the slightest word that you give me will be sacred. So, I shall simply beg you to keep my secret. I count so firmly on your discretion that, without waiting for your response, I shall, in order to satisfy you, tell you whom I am and what the reason is for my living in such a singular manner.

"My father was of the same profession as me, my grandfather too, and since there have been windmills on the earth my ancestors have always made them turn. It is to my forefathers that an invention so useful to humankind is due.

"That métier does not seem very illustrious to the vainglorious, but as my ancestors began to exercise it before vanity had corrupted the simplicity of mores, they have thought it more honorable to continue in the hereditary employment of their fathers than if they had gained a crown by illicit means.

They did not grow rich, but by laboring they raised themselves above poverty and, content with their estate, they limited themselves to it entirely, especially my father, who would not have wanted to exchange his mill for the palace of the greatest King.

"He was in the best years of his youth when he perceived that his money, far from diminishing, was visibly augmented, whatever sum he drew out of it, and that what his métier produced for him increased in a fashion so visible that he often thought that he was mistaken in his calculation. Finally, that became so marked that it was no longer possible for him to be mistaken. However, although he had paid enough attention to it to be convinced that there was something extraordinary in that augmentation, in order to be even more certain, he counted his cash exactly and made a note of it. A few days later, having counted his money again, there was no more doubt about that singular increase, especially in finding that his copper or silver coins were not only converted into gold, but that there were a hundred times more than his note had recorded.

"That advantage was indubitable, but my father did not know to what to attribute it, and whatever care he took to clarify the obliging mystery, it still remained impenetrable, without it being possible for him to suspect any mortal of that liberality and being unable to doubt that it was to some supreme intelligence that he had the obligation of so much wealth.

"His presumption was just. One day, when the fortunate miller was in a little garden that he cultivated in his hours of leisure, as he was thinking about his luck in a sort of reverie, he could not help talking to himself aloud: 'Is it possible,' he said, leaning on his spade, 'that the fortune that accompanies me might render me unhappy, whereas it would make the happiness of any other? I am heaped with wealth, but I don't know from what hand I obtain it; that ignorance forces me to be ingrate, and prevents me from testifying to my benefactor the gratitude that I have. Oh, generous intelligence, do not give me so much, and show yourself!'

"He fell silent, and was continuing his reverie when he perceived that the place to which his gaze was attached was moving gradually and rising up, as if a mole were laboring underneath. He advanced slowly toward the moving spot, in order to deceive the delicate ear of the animal that was shifting it, and when he was within range he lifted his spade with the design of striking it from above the moment he perceived it on the surface of the ground. The iron was already in the air, ready to fall on the supposed mole, when, instead of one of those animals, he saw a tiny woman appear with a form similar to the one who served us.

"She approached him, with a rather tender expression. 'I'm granting your wish,' she said to him. 'You desire to know the author of the favors you receive every day; it's me. I've come to show myself to you, since you wish it. I'm a gnomide, and mistress of an immense treasure. I have done you good, but that is nothing in comparison with what I can do for you.

"'Your happiness depends on you; it's merely a matter of marrying me, and then I shall have nothing more to give you, for you will be as much master of all I possess as myself. A considerable part of the treasures that the earth contains will be yours. You will only have to wish to see them to possess them.

"'I confess,' she continued, 'that I am not charming, and I render myself enough justice not to find it strange that you are not enchanted by my face, but I am not afflicted by the agile sentiments of Milords the Sylphs and Miladies the Sylphides; my sole assets consist of a good heart and a mind as tender, which is solid and constant. If you accept my proposition, and want to unite yourself with my good and bad qualities, I will communicate my power to you; everything that depends on me will be subordinate to you; but if the repugnance that I inspire prevails over your true interests, I will say adieu forever.

"'Make your reflections, and have no fear regarding your inclination, for your refusal will lead me to abandon you and discontinue doing you good, but it will never excite me to do you harm, nor to deprive you of what I have already given you. I know that taste is free, and that it does not depend on us to love or hate out of complaisance, so respond to me without constraint.'

"The question was sharp and the vision astonishing. My father, who was not accustomed to the conversation of subterranean beings, did not know what to reply to his interlocutor. The gnomide was short, stout, ugly and dark-hued; however, whether her benefits prejudiced my father in her favor or, having the intention of pleasing her, the design was embellished by it, he did not find her as displeasing as she might have appeared, with features as deformed as those I have just described to you.

"As she did not give evidence of having much self-esteem, my father thought there was no risk in agreeing that she was not beautiful, but he added that he was touched by the generosity that had preceded her visit, and even more so by the moderation she was showing, in not trying to engage him by threats to feign an amour that he did not have. He assured her that he would not be long in making his decision, and only asked for a brief delay in order that they might have the time to get to know one another reciprocally.

"She granted him that gladly, and came to visit him often, never without heaping him with new benefits. Gold and precious stones became common in his hands; she anticipated everything that might give him pleasure. If he wanted to sow his field, he no longer had the trouble of preparing the ground, and four or five hundred thousand moles rendered him that good office in less than two hours; after withdrawing, they carefully refrained from returning until after the harvest. The grain he had sown brought him a crop so abundant that it was impossible to doubt that he had the obligation of it to his lover. In sum, he was fortunate in everything, and he could not wish for anything without his desires being satisfied.

"Such generous manners gradually effaced from my father's heart the idea of the subterranean nymph's ugliness; in any case, she had as much tenderness in her character as unpleasantness in her face. One gets accustomed to anything; he ceased to think her so ugly, telling himself that she was not the first small person that he had found lovable; that, in truth, she was a trifle substantial, but that was advantageous for a husband who loved his wife, since plumpness denoted good health; and if the lady was a trifle dark-hued, that tint had its merit in the country, where it would not suffer from the insults of the atmosphere.

"In sum, Princess, he sought all the reasons that might serve to diminish the faults of the gnomide, and told himself so many things in favor of her character and good manners, always preferable to beauty, that he married her with pleasure.

"What is astonishing is that, in spite of her deformity, he always loved her; that for her part, she did not adopt with him the arrogant fashions that are only too common in women when they have a spouse of a nobility inferior to their own, or whose fortune they have made. Something equally singular is that the immense riches of which that marriage had rendered him the possessor did not inspire in him a single impulse of ambition; he only engaged himself to the gnomide after she had promised him not constrain him to change his condition, and also that she would leave him the liberty to keep his fortune secret.

"He wanted absolutely to remain a miller, and wealth could not make him lose his taste for a profession that had been that of his ancestors. That was not all; he also demanded that if he had children, they would be obliged to follow the same métier, and that in the case that they wanted to leave it, he made her promise to deprive them of all the advantages that they obtained from a gnomide mother.

"The gnomide, who was only marrying my father because he pleased her, easily granted his demands; if she had loved grandeur she could easily have chosen among those who were the most illustrious and most elevated on earth, even among Kings; but what would she have gained? There are none as powerful as she was, and the least of subterranean lairs far surpass the magnificence of the most celebrated palaces. In addition, the taste that her husband had for rural life was for her a sure guarantee against the inconstancies of a man in opulence. How could a woman so ugly not fear the distaste and deviation of a husband if the most beautiful individuals are continually exposed to him?

"Thus the gnomide, finding security and repose in her husband's proposition, gladly allowed him the choice of doing whatever he wanted. I was the sole fruit of their marriage.

"My father, satisfied with his lot, cared little for appearing in society, and fearing, on the contrary, exciting envy, he took as much precaution to hide his good fortune as another would have employed in making an exhibition of it. He continued his métier tranquilly and enjoyed a fortune all the sweeter because it was not even suspected.

"However, although my father lived with such scant ostentation, I was nevertheless brought up like a child that it was desired to render perfect. Scarcely was I born than my mother confided me to the care of a gnome whose long experience and natural genius set him far above those petty speculative philosophers who mistake their chimeras for realities, although they have never even touched upon the knowledge of the slightest operations of nature. By the cares of that excellent master, all the secrets there are were revealed to me, and when I was sufficiently advanced no longer to need my tutor's help, my mother recalled me to the surface and made me travel the world.

"I simply passed for a man among men, but with the elementary peoples, for whom my mother had not made a mystery of my birth, I passed for what I was. They treated me as their equal and I received a thousand evidences of generosity; they are often at war with one another, but their various interests do not conflict with the common wealth of nature; they are so attached to it and have such affection for it that they do not hesitate to come together every time that it is a question of serving it.

"I profited attentively from the times that they came to the earth and what they were able to give me, to converse with them and to learn their customs, their temperament and their laws—in sum, all their good and bad qualities—which instructed me and diverted me, and contributed more to my education than the formal lessons that had amused my youth. Finally, beautiful Lisimene, after having spent several years like that, I came back to my father's mill.

"The occupations that I had had since my birth were too different from the métier to which he destined me for them to have inspired a taste for it in me, and when he wanted me to employ myself in it I found it so disagreeable that I could not hide my sentiments from him. I did my best to inspire in him the desire to renounce it. I was no more ambitious than him, but I was more philosophical, and I was in despair when I thought that it would be necessary for me to quit study in order to grind wheat. In addition to that, being accustomed to the magnificence of the subterranean world, it was impossible for me to please myself in this cottage.

"I made every effort to persuade my father not to force me to follow his métier and not to deprive me of the liberty to savor in this solitude the sweetness of repose, but he was inflexible, and he had sworn an oath on his own behalf and that of his descendants never to abandon the profession, adding that if there was ever someone who wanted to contravene it he would be deprived of his succession.

"To remove all means of disobeying him, he obliged my mother to swear that she would withdraw to the empire of the gnomes and would never protect the first violator of the paternal law; that, on the contrary, she would deprive him of all his rights—with the consequence that it was necessary for me to resolve to follow the estate to which my father's obstinacy had condemned me.

"The alliance that he had made did not dispense him from paying the tribute to nature; he finally died, and I remained by virtue of his death the master of my conduct, apart from the matter of my profession, for I had not been able to dispense myself from renewing the oath that he had made, which obliged me to do likewise. It was not fear of losing his

241

wealth that forced me to submit to that law, but in addition to the riches, about which I care little, I would also have lost the knowledge that I had acquired with the amity and familiarity of the elementary peoples, which was the sole reason for my distaste.

"Thus, although I was no longer dependent on anyone, I was not free to quit the mill; on the contrary, I found myself more tightly bound to it that when my father was alive, since, while my father was alive I at least had the liberty to study and the time to entertain my friends the elementals, whose affairs, or the amity that they had for me, had attracted them to the surface. But once he was dead I was overwhelmed by his work, and, unfortunately for me, the flour that my mill made being better than that made anywhere else, the crowd did not abandon me. I was obliged to occupy myself relentlessly with a métier that I did not like and which did not leave me a moment of liberty.

"My mother tried in vain to soften my ennui, at least by satisfying the penchant for magnificence that I had received from my first occupation, building me palaces such as those I had seen—of which you can see a specimen in this garden. Nothing could console me for the constraint that I was under, and I fell into a depression that made the elementary peoples, in concert with her, redouble their efforts to ease my trouble. That was exactly what augmented my chagrin, however, because I could not profit from their good will, nor give them more than a few moments, cruelly interrupted, finding myself forced to quit the most agreeable conversation to listen to the coarse remarks of a peasant, or the importunate crowd of old women who trooped to the mill bringing their wheat.

"That inconvenience was pushed to such an excess that I finally lost patience and applied myself to finding a means to extract myself from that cruel slavery without contravening my oath. I could not imagine one more suitable than rendering the road to my habitation so difficult and dangerous that no one would be bold enough even to look at it. Nothing was easier for me, and my power had soon executed it, which leaves me at present to breathe in peace.

"I don't refuse service to anyone, and I grind the wheat of those who are fortunate enough to get as far as here, but it's rare for anyone to be able to approach, and the number is so small that I have all the liberty I wish. The elementary peoples have seconded me with all their power, raising storms, causing floods, fires and earthquakes, and finally making specters or malevolent phantoms appear—which, not being content to frighten the importune with their horrible faces, do not spare them the blows that their obstinacy merits. Sometimes, in the form of wild or venomous beasts, they correct their determination to come my mill.

"At first, the accidents that happened to those who dared to take the road were regarded as a pure effect of chance, but subsequently, everyone having perceived that only the obstinate who could not cure themselves of the whim to bring their grain to be milled here had anything to fear, and that those who went on their way without any design to come to the mill did not suffer any accident, they did not doubt that I was responsible. They finally gave up the mania of making such a dangerous journey; it is more than ten years since I have had to practice, enjoying my immense riches in peace, and the rarities that the bosom of the earth contains, as well as the possession of a demignomide, whom I married as soon as I was delivered from the importunity of my clients, by whom I no longer fear being surprised.

"Your arrival here tells me," the miller continued, "that you know some of my friends, who have doubtless informed you of the means of avoiding the perils that one runs in coming to my home, and the sole route that I am obliged to leave free in order not to contravene my oath—but I soon found a means to make those who dare to take that favored route repent, by making objects of curiosity appear on the high road, which attract them and punish them immediately, giving them more desire to return home than continue their journey.

243

"You had the strength to resist all the traps that were set for you, and to triumph by virtue of your prudence. I'm delighted by that, Princess, and I want to give you such solid evidence of my amity that you will never repent of having made our acquaintance.

"I know what your fate is, charming Liron," he said, looking at her fixedly, "and I also have the satisfaction of being able to announce to you that it will be fortunate; but all your troubles are not over. Misfortunes and perils still remain for you to endure, under which you would have succumbed had you not made this journey. Have courage, you will have nothing for the present but annoyance, but you ought not to have any fear of consequences; I shall make it my business to preserve you. However, not limiting to that unique concern the good will I want to express to you, you can ask me anything you please in the meantime."

Touched by so much generosity, Lisimene was so satisfied that she would not have desired anything more, but her stepmother's absolute order was so precise, that the threat she had made in case she failed to bring her a bouquet, did not permit her to neglect his offer. She naturally told the generous miller, therefore, of the necessity she was in to abuse his complaisance, and the reluctance she had in so doing.

"You're wrong, Princess," he said. "The treasure that seems to you so precious is too small a thing for me to oblige you to make apologies. So, you may choose boldly the flowers that appear to you to be the most beautiful, and make the bouquet demanded of you."

Lisimene, however, who had not forgotten Crystalline's lessons, started to smile and looked at the miller with a subtle expression. "I thank you, Milord," she said, shaking her head, "but I won't, if you please, push temerity so far as to choose between so many beautiful things. Who knows," she added adroitly, "whether I would not be sufficiently maladroit to pick some of the flowers that you want to let to go to seed?"

The miler smiled at that speech and understood her thought. "You have nothing to fear," he told her. "I don't take the trouble to keep the seed, the nursery of these flowers being inexhaustible, but since your suspicion or your discretion prevents you from choosing, I'll do so for you, and you won't lose by it, for I'm convinced that you wouldn't have taken as many as I shall give you."

He did, in fact, make up two large bouquets. "This one is for your stepmother," he told her. "It's the larger. And this one is for you. Now, lovable Lisimene," he added, "listen to me and pay great attention to what I'm going to tell you. Take note of the one that I destine for you, and be careful to visit it several times a day.

"As long as you find brilliant and stable stones there, you can live in repose without having any fear of the ill will of your persecutors; but as soon as you see them tarnish, don't fail to stay on your guard, it won't take long for some of them to fall. Then you will have no time to lose in employing the key that I am giving you. To begin with, put your bouquet in the milk, that will give it the virtue of putting everyone in the house to sleep and you will have the liberty to open the coffers and cupboards with this key. Search everywhere until you encounter a candle whose end is mixed with black and bloody red; take it and replace it with this one, which is exactly similar; for fear that it might escape your hands and, by some misfortune, Richarde or her daughter might encounter it and take possession of it. Take it promptly to your friends the naiads.

"That exchange will enable you to live tranquilly, and be assured that all the efforts of those who want to doom you will be futile, no matter what misfortunes might overtake you; in whatever danger you find yourself, await its end constantly, and be sure that it will not be deadly. On the contrary, after a short duration, it will give way to the most perfect happiness.

"But," he continued, "I repeat, everything depends on removing the fatal candle from their possession and replacing it with the one I am giving you."

After having instructed Lisimene, the miller took her for a stroll in his subterranean palace. His wife the gnomide, who was, like him, part-human and was not as small or as dark as unmixed gnomides are, also made the Princess a thousand amities—after which, her wheat having been ground, she took her leave of her hosts, who sent her away laden with treasures and heaped with caresses.

More impatient to see her unknown man again than satisfied with her success, she had not dared to ask the savant miller for news of him, presuming that since he had not touched upon that article, he was unaware of it, or had his reasons for not saying anything about it. She feared that, after having refused to tell that exceedingly charming mortal where she lived, she might never see him again, and was even beginning to repent of her excessive restraint.

What consoled her was the reflection she made that the miller had promised her that she would be happy. Well, the only way that she could never be happy was if her lover had changed and no longer responded to the sentiments she had for him.

Let's wait a while, she said to herself. *Since I'm to be happy, I'll surely see again the only man that can make my happiness.*

Entertaining such flattering thoughts, she went back to Richarde's house. The latter was terribly astonished not to see her crippled, or at least bruised by blows, as everyone else had been who had made the journey to the mill, but finding her, on the contrary, in perfect health. Seeing her clad in a dress much richer than the one she had received from the naiads, she was as surprised as she was afflicted. Over the flowers with which her dress was embroidered, the bouquet of gems that she had received from the miler was visible, and her hand was ornamented with the one he had destined for her stepmother.

"What do I see?" screeched Pigrieche. "Where has Liron obtained that magnificence? Does that befit her, truly?" Addressing her, she said, insolently: "By what right, little creature, do you wear clothes of that beauty?"

"I fell in the water," said Liron, "and these were given to me to change into. How could I have refused them, in the state I was in?"

"Who is it that gave them to you?" Richarde continued.

"The miller at the Mill of Misfortune," said the shepherdess, tranquilly.

"Aha!" cried the wicked woman, "the miller of the Mill of Misfortune makes such presents, and yet people decry him. Look, I pray you, see the injustice that has been done to that stuck-up individual. To hear her father talk, one would have thought that all was lost, but she comes back adorned like a Queen."

She summoned her spouse. "Look," she said to him, bitterly, "here's your daughter in charming attire. Have I done her so much harm in sending her to the Mill of Misfortune, for you to shed so many tears?"

Good and Better, who had only learned of the malign intention of the evil creatures after Liron's departure, had been in despair because of it, because he had not doubted the loss of his daughter. He was agreeably surprised to see her return in such good condition. He did not reply to Richarde but, running to embrace Liron, he shed as many tears of joy as he had shed of sadness, and the Princess, giving her stepmother the bouquet destined for her, followed her father back to his study. It was there that she gave him an account of her adventures.

Meanwhile, Richarde, who had been delighted with her bouquet, after having admired it at her leisure, put it in her cupboard, but the following day, having wanted to enjoy the pleasure of considering it again, she no longer found it, and was greatly astonished that a bundle of thistles had been put in its place.

She was very angry, and throwing it at Liron's head, she declared to her that she had to take it for herself and surrender hers in exchange. Whatever regret the young woman had and however valuable the item of jewelry had—less by virtue of the consequence of the gems than the warning she expected from them—it was not possible for her to dispense with that exchange, and she abandoned the precious bouquet. No sooner had it left her hands, however, than it augmented the number of thistles that Richarde had, while the one she had given to

Liron in place of her own became as many gems as soon as she touched them.

A marvel so contrary to that interested woman's desires surprised her as much as it displeased her. When she demanded of Liron what that signified, Liron replied that she had no more idea than she had, but that she presumed that it was evidence that the miller intended his presents to remain in the hands of those to whom he had given them.

"If that's so," said Richarde to her daughter, returning the other bouquet of thistles to Liron, "I advise you, my dear Pigrieche, to go to the mill in your turn. There will be no more danger for you than for the guardian of our flocks."

Whatever temptation those rare gems offered to Pigrieche, she had no desire to purchase them so dearly. One unfortunate experience had taught her that Liron, luckier than her, returned triumphant from ventures from which she only emerged disagreeably. She also had the adventure of the fountain present in her mind, as well that of the pear tree and the hunter, and represented that ardently to her mother.

That miserly woman, however, dying of the desire to have gems like Liron's, and, seeing that she had deprived her of that treasure without any profit for her, since the jewels became thistles in any other hand than that of the shepherdess, made so many representations to Pigrieche that she finally persuaded her to attempt the adventure. Richarde recommended her, above all, to be milder, telling her that it was her rudeness that had always caused her misfortunes.

That advice, the soundest that had ever emerge from Richarde, was received by her daughter in the fashion in which she was accustomed to take everything that did not please her. Far from profiting from it, it only served to make her say all the nasty things she could think of; but finally, the avidity to possess diamonds as beautiful as Liron's put a limit on her fury, and, putting off until she returned the rest of what she had to say, she departed with a cargo of wheat similar to the one that Liron had taken to the mill. Instead of the wretched mount that the Princess had been given, though, Pigrieche took the finest mule in the stable.

Although the greatest good fortune that could have befallen Liron would have been to see her principal enemy perish on that journey, the kindness of her heart would not permit her to let her depart without instructing her as to the fashion in which she could avoid the dangers to which she was about to be exposed. Still having a piece of the cake that had appeased the dogs, she gave it to her, telling her that it was the sole means of stopping them.

Pigrieche listened to her without any sentiment of gratitude, and almost without paying attention to what she said. However important it was for her to have what was necessary to soothe the terrible dogs, the cake appeared to her to be so good that she ate it, in spite of the opposition that Liron tried to put up, saying that was more natural that she ate the fine treat than give it to the mill's wretched dogs, her greed prevailing over her security.

However, she took the route preferable to the high road, because Liron took generosity to the point of going to show it to her. And as the symphony commenced, as soon as she quit her, Pigrieche would not have gone far without suffering some accident if she had had more liking for music; but its charms were so indifferent to her that, far from running any risk by listening to it, she did not even pay attention to it, and went on her way without finding any obstacle.

It was not the same with the second encounter for, having perceived a furious tiger that was coming straight toward her, fear made her lose the memory of the merit of the crook, which Liron had had the charity to lend her. She fled as fast as she could, running through the fields without knowing where she was going, until, finally exhausted by weariness and sensing that the monster on her heels was about to reach her, she found a stout tree into which, in spite of her fear, she still had the strength to climb.

It was not without a great many scratches that she reached the crown, but the tiger, which was alert and at least as agile as Pigrieche, climbed the tree as rapidly as her and was about to devour her when, by virtue of a final effort, which was the work of instinct rather than reasoning—of which she was no longer capable—Pigrieche repelled it with the crook, which, being attached to her dress had, so to speak, accompanied her involuntarily.

The terrible beast had scarcely felt the touch of the marvelous crook than it expired and fell out of the tree. Pigrieche thought of doing the same, and descended, with even more difficulty than she had climbed up. She was not even in that embarrassment for the entire length of the tree, for she was still twenty feet from the bottom when she could not help slipping, and fell so heavily that she sprained her wrist. The pain she felt made her utter horrible screams, but it was pointless, the placed being too deserted for her to be able to expect any help.

She was constrained to get up by herself and to bandage her wrist herself, cursing Liron—which was her usual resource—after which she went back to her cart, and, spurring her mule, she continued the journey, having reason to believe that she no longer had any accident to fear, since there was only the meadow to cross, at the far end of which the mill was visible.

That meadow was covered in sheep. The shepherd who was guarding them, lying down in the shade of a bush, had enveloped his head in one of the flaps of his coat in order to protect himself from flies. On seeing him thus, Pigrieche was tempted to beat him, not because his negligence might be prejudicial to the advantage of the owners of the livestock, because she did not care enough about the advantage of anyone but herself, but solely because the repose that she saw him enjoying excited her ill humor.

She restrained herself, however, making the reflection that the man was not her slave and that he might not suffer the correction she wanted to give him passively, and, being alone in this remote place might well return the blows she dared to give him freely. The apprehension that he might be the stronger was the only motive that held her back, but she had not gone far before she encountered an opportunity to compensate herself for that forced moderation and avenge herself very agreeably on the repose than the pastor was enjoying.

Thieves having arrived, one of them said to the others: "Here's a fine opportunity to enrich ourselves; let's take away the miller's flocks while their guardian's sleep—but let's hurry, because I can see a young woman who isn't asleep and might wake the man up. If she does that we'll be doomed, because he'll call the four dogs that are in the shade in the nearby ditch. They're so furious that we won't escape death; they'll kill us without difficulty, so let's be quiet, but hurry."

So saying, they took the sheep away diligently.

Far from their having anything to fear on the part of Pigrieche, her natural malice made her imagine a veritable pleasure in the chagrin that the loss would cause those who would suffer it and the ill-treatment that the shepherd would probably receive. It only depended on her to spare them that, since she would only have had to wake him up, as the thieves had feared; but instead of having that thought, she drew away expressly from the path she was on, in order not to deter them from such a good deed. After having seen from a distance that their project had succeeded, without the shepherd having woken up, she advanced joyfully toward the mill, to which she was close, and where she would easily have been able to heard if she had cried for help when the sheep were being stolen, which she could not believe were owned anyone but the miller, since she had heard the thieves say so.

As she thought that she could enter the mill without any obstacle, the dogs, which perceived her, came to receive her, and, as she had eaten the cake herself, it was not without difficulty, nor without having received numerous bites, that she reached the door, where they finally let her breathe.

Although they had moved away from her, she feared that they might come back, so she picked up a stone as quickly as possible to knock, and to make even more noise, she thought she ought to aid herself with the knocker; but she let it go more promptly than she had taken it, although it was not soon enough not to have her hand burned. She uttered frightful screams, which made the miller emerge.

"What's the matter, beautiful young woman?" he said to her, in a mild tone. "Has someone caused you some displeasure?"

"May all maledictions fall upon you," she replied, shouting with all her might. "Accursed man that you are, you make your door-knocker red hot to cripple your clients. I'm not astonished that people shun your house like the plague. I believe that the Devil has engendered you."

It was thus that she exhaled her fury, while the miller listened with prefect tranquility, without making the slightest effort to interrupt her. Finally, seeing that she was exhausted, with a kind of malice that tended to reanimate her wrath, he said to her coldly: "It's very annoying, I admit, that the knocker is a trifle warm. I'm careful always to keep it like that in order to stop the flies attacking and soiling it. But you don't believe that," he continued. "Doubtless it should be for you that I take care to maintain the knocker at a slightly sharp degree of heat, for you're so beautiful, so tender and so honest that one always ought esteem oneself fortunate to receive you.

"Anyway, my lovable young woman," he went on, "that's a mere bagatelle, and it's necessary to forget the little accident..."

"What! Little accident! Bagatelle!" cried Pigrieche, furiously. "What! I have a burned hand, wretch, and I might be crippled by it, but you have the effrontery to tell me that it's a mere bagatelle!"

With that she recommenced screeching more loudly.

"But, charming Pigrieche," the man said to her with a phlegm that put her into a horrible wrath, "don't you think that you ought to preserve a little more delicacy in your bosom, and that you're exhausting yourself in vain, since whatever you might say, you could have had less trouble today, and you're even fortunate that you haven't had more."

Although the miller had spoken those words without raising his voice, Pigrieche regarded them as a kind of threat, which caused her to fear angering him and cease insulting him. She entered the mill, saying in a milder tone that she had wheat to grind.

"So much the better," replied the miller. "Sit down. Your job will be done in less than half an hour, and you can go home early."

That response, which did not mention the bouquet, the unique objective of her dangerous journey, caused her to lose patience and forget the pain she felt in both arms, only remembering the extreme desire to possess a treasure like Liron's. That desire obliged her to demand brusquely of the miller whether he thought that she had come to see him for his beautiful eyes, and whether she was to go back without seeing the garden where her shepherdess had seen so many rarities.

"Oh, no, in truth," he replied. "Forgive me if I haven't offered it to you; that's because I thought you were too tired and ill to stroll; but since you command it I'll take you there immediately."

With those words he marched in the direction of the grotto, and the beauty followed him without making any response—a rare thing, which might never have happened to her before.

As is easily imaginable, Pigrieche was enchanted by the beauty of a place whose magnificence had surprised a King's daughter, and without making him a longer compliment, she said: "Milord Miller, it seems to me that you ought to give me a bouquet to console me for the bad turns you've done me. I don't believe that you'd be stupid enough to require to be begged, for you must love to lavish those bouquets, and not know what to do with them, since you give them to the likes of Liron. On that basis, I don't expect you to refuse me one, and I believe without too much vanity that I merit being treated at least as well as our shepherdess, although there's no comparison to be made between us."

253

"I'm glad to see that you render yourself justice," he said, "and you need have no fear that I'll make a comparison that would, indeed, be odious. I'm too well aware of the difference that ought to be put between the two of you. And to convince you of that," he continued, "know that I picked the flowers of which I made her a present, and that I was careful not to leave her alone here; but in your regard, beautiful Pigrieche, I won't act in the same way. You'll have discretion, and I'll leave you to go and see whether your flour is made. However, I beg you only to take one bouquet; it wouldn't be appropriate to strip my flower-bed."

So saying, the miller withdrew.

As soon as Pigrieche was along, she not only collected, without consideration, an enormous bouquet, but, stripping the flowers in order that her theft would seem less, she filled her pockets with the gems that she detached.

After having crammed them with as much as she could get in, as she was not yet satisfied, she had recourse to the sacks that she had left on her mule, and took the largest, which she filled with as little discretion as if it were a tiny purse, or if she was only putting flour therein. The timidity that she had had at first having gradually dissipated, she collected everything that came to hand. Not content with stripping the flower-bed, she broke the branches on the espaliers, carrying away the leaves and fruits. When the sack was so full that she could hardly drag it, she put it back whence she had taken it, and returned tranquilly as if she had performed the finest action in the world.

As she went back into the mill, the shepherd arrived, greatly alarmed, crying that thieves had taken away the entire flock."You were greatly mistaken not to call for help," said the miller, "since you can see very well that from any part of the meadow, if you had shouted or blown your horn, we could easily have heard you."

"Yes, if he hadn't been asleep," said the malevolent Pigrieche, in a mocking tone, "but the darling was in a tranquil slumber, not thinking about you or your interests. He's so delicate," she continued, "that for fear of spoiling his complexion, he had taken care to cover his face... I saw the whole scene," she added, "which amused me greatly."

"What!" retorted the miller, astonished. "You saw this theft taking place, and you didn't wake the poor fellow up?"

"I carefully refrained from doing so," she said, bursting into laughter. "His idleness merited that punishment, and you merited it too, for being foolish enough to confide your property to such a bad servant."

"What, lovable Pigrieche," replied the miller, smiling, "you, who are so generous, disdained to render us a service that would have cost you so little, at a time when you have come to ask us for a favor? And you find it strange that the door-knocker spared you the trouble of blowing on your fingers? Go, you only have what you merit. The beautiful Liron conducted herself very differently in our regard, since she risked her life to give us evidence of her good will. It would not have been that lovable young woman," he continued, "who would have allowed our sheep to be stolen; she would have been killed first, so we showed her that we know how to recognize a service."

Instead of making apologies, delighted to have succeeded in doing him harm and finally seeing that he appeared sensible to it, Pigrieche replied with a thousand nasty remarks. "Am I made to serve you and guard your flocks?" she said to him. "That's all right for Liron, who is a shepherdess and who would have been following her métier, but me...! I think you're raving; I find you amusing, in truth."

She was in full flow, and would not have finished for a long time if the miller, weary of listening to her, had not loaded the flour on to the mule himself, as he was obliged to do by his profession. That being done, he put Pigrieche outside by the shoulders. "Go," he said, shoving her. "Go away, and remember that I'm not as wicked as people like to believe, since you're returning home with your flour and my jewels, although you've merited perishing here only too well."

That speech, which testified to a certain anger and gave the impression of being a threat of sorts, frightened Pigrieche, who, judging that she was risking too much by remaining any longer in that place, departed without reply, consoling herself for so many misfortunes by the possession of so many riches, not to mention the joy she had had in seeing that the miller had not appeared to pay any attention to the bag of gems, next to which he had placed the bag of flour that he had ground, without showing any curiosity with regard to the sack that was already on the mule and what there was inside it.

Pigrieche had been very frightened on seeing that it was him who loaded the mount; she had not expected that. As there was no one who had not complained about the miller's pride, she had not had the slightest suspicion that he would lower himself to that. When she saw her sack on his shoulders she had trembled for the one that contained the treasure she had acquired so unjustly, and which became all the dearer to her by virtue of the danger she had run of losing it.

She thought with an inexpressible delight that she possessed more jewels than she needed to ornament the reeds that grew on her frightful head, and that the singular mixture in question, far from being disagreeable, would be something very elegant. She arranged them in her imagination, and decorated her garments with them, counting on the fact that in that condition, she would enchant everyone, and would have as many lovers as there were men to whom the sight of her would be exposed.

She was entertaining herself with that pleasant idea when she heard someone talking on the road, from which she was only separated by a hedge. It was the voice of a man, who was saying to another: "It's necessary to admit, my brother, that we're fortunate to have found these six gold coins; it seems that Heaven has sent them to us expressly to get us out of the difficulty in which the injustice and inhumanity of a creditor has put us, In spite of his wealth and our poverty, not content with taking possession of our wretched cottage, he would have made us slaves for the four gold pieces we owe him, if we hadn't had the industry to thwart his cruelty by running away. It's lucky that we took this road, since the treasure we've encountered so fortunately will give us the means to pay our enemy, recover our cabin from his hands and enjoy our liberty, making with the rest of this money a petty commerce in fruits and vegetables, which will aid us to subsist, and to rescue our wives and small children, who are in such great necessity."

The music had not been capable of attracting Pigrieche's attention, but having heard that there was question of a treasure as considerable as six gold coins, the desire to split them with those wretches, who had so much need of them, and whose situation and poverty would have moved anyone but Pigrieche to give them a share of her opulence rather than wanting to attain theirs, drove her without hesitation to pass through the hedge and go straight toward them.

The two men, seeing her coming, got up to flee, but she retained the one who had been less prompt to rise to his feet, because he was occupied in putting his gold in his pocket.

"Don't think," she said, seizing him, "that I'll let you go like that. I intend to have my share of what you've found. I know you," she added, "and if you don't give me two gold pieces immediately, I'll denounce you to the man on whose land you found the treasure, and I'll have you deprived of all of it."

The men were very annoyed at having been overheard, and even more so at seeing themselves deprived of a third of what they had obtained from fortune. Intimidated by her threat, however, the one who had custody of it was about to give her what she asked when his companion opposed it, saying that he did not intend to share a wealth of which hazard had made him a present.

Giving his brother a sign to follow him, he set off to leave her alone, but Pigrieche, to whom the hope of gain gave strength, opposed the departure of the one who was carrying the gold coins, seizing him by the throat and swearing not to let him go until he had given her what she claimed belonged to her.

That violence was inopportune, having made the man she was holding in that fashion veritably angry. Far from giving the beauty what she demanded so insolently, and wanting to get rid of her at any cost, he suddenly landed two furious punches on her simultaneously, which made her let go and also knocked her unconscious—after which he and his companion ran away, leaving Pigrieche not only in no condition to follow them, but even to take note of the direction they had taken.

Scarcely had the unworthy creature recovered consciousness than all her dolors were reawakened by that new accident. She tried to get up, but as her two crippled hands, to whom the desire to take had given agility, then refused her their service, she found that it was impossible for her to move. To complete her embarrassment, darkness, rain and violent wind coming to assail her, she was reduce to rolling in the mud without being able to get out of it, dreading in addition being battered by hail or eaten by wolves, and—something more touching for her—apprehending that thieves might come to steal the booty that she had taken from the mill.

Her embarrassment is easily imaginable. The unique consolation that remained to her was to heap insults on the beautiful Lisimene, on whom that inconsiderate individual always took out everything that happened to her. As you might think, she did not spare her mother, who had inspired her with the desire to make that journey; and the miller, who, she said, had sent the two men after her in order to murder her, also had his share.

In that extreme disorder, at the moment when she was no longer hoping to get out of it, some of Richarde's slaves went by, who were going to fetch their livestock, grazing in the distant marshes. Pigrieche called to them, and the slaves, having recognized her voice, ran to help her. One of them, having dismounted, put her in his place, with the aid of his companions, but not without causing her a thousand pains and receiving insults and threats instead of the thanks that such a good deed merited. In spite of that, they did not leave her to go home on her own, a part of the company being sufficient to go and gather the scattered livestock.

The movement of the horse, which augmented the pains that Pigrieche was suffering, caused her to utter such loud screams from time to time that they could be heard a long way off. Richarde, who, on seeing night considerably advanced without her daughter having returned, had left the house in order to come and meet her, on hearing her crying out in that fashion, no longer doubted that some disastrous adventure had befallen her.

She was only too convinced of that when she was brought down from the horse. The tender mother asked her immediately what had put her in such a terrible state, but Pigrieche, whose ill humor was augmented by her injuries, howled even louder at the question.

"Isn't that a misplaced curiosity," she said, "and when you ought only to be thinking of helping me, is it any time to be asking me such a stupid question? As if you didn't know that I've come from that accursed mill, where you had the fury to send me; see what great pleasure awaited me there!"

The injuries she had suffered authorizing, in a sense, her ill humor, Richarde made no response, and hastened to give her aid. A surgeon was absolutely necessary, but where could one be found? It was night; they were a long way from the town, there was none there anyway, and the gate, which was closed, would not be opened again until morning.

Good and Better, who had come running with all the rest, and whose excellent nature never had to be asked, tried to soothe the invalid. As the different studies to which he had applied himself in his room had furnished him with the means to learn medicine, it was to that with which he had been most occupied, that science appearing to him to be very necessary in a deserted place, where one could not hope for any help from a town that was some distance away. The good King did not disdain to make use of medicine on the subjects from which he ought perhaps have liberated himself, if he had recognized the fact. The overly generous monarch, touched by his stepdaughter's cries, began by resetting her wrist, which he did with all possible dexterity.

As the operation was painful, the impatient Pigrieche lavished all the insults she could think of on the royal surgeon, threatening to punish his awkwardness, but without that unworthy behavior putting him off. He applied balm to her wound; although it was excellent, that did not prevent the hand from remaining slightly disabled, but that would soon heal.

Given the slightest reflection on the tenderness that Richarde had for her daughter, it will easily be presumed that she was extremely angry with the miller, the mil and all those who had inhabited it since it had existed, or would inhabit it in the future. After that fury had calmed down slightly, however, Pigrieche's wounds had been bandaged, she had been cleaned of mud and had had something to eat, Richarde, who rarely lost sight of her interests, thought about visiting the flour that her daughter had been to have ground through so many dangers, fearing that it might have been soiled by the storm.

She was confirmed in that thought on finding the sacks soaked and seeing that her mule was so lame that it could hardly walk, for the men who had beaten Pigrieche had pushed vengeance so far as to throw stones at the animal, innocent of its rider's faults. Fortunately for Pigrieche, they had not touched her treasure, not suspecting that not all the sacks were filled with flour, which they had not thought of carrying away because its weight would have slowed down their precipitate flight.

Richarde hastened to empty out the flour in order to give it air, but her efforts were wasted; it was no longer anything but dough mixed with muddy water, which smelled so bad that the infection that emerged therefrom inspired the thought that there was plague in the house.

That was not the only inconvenience that the accident caused, for scarcely had such a horrible broth been exposed to the air than it started moving, and one part becoming worms, another became weevils, a species of vermin that live in wheat, and the third took on the form of a swarm of gnats, which spread out through the room and flew in such large numbers that they extinguished the lights. Then they threw themselves furiously upon everyone, with the exception of Liron and her father, with the result that there was no one who was not obliged to flee, abandoning the unfortunate Pigrieche, who screamed for help in vain, but who, not being able make use of her hands to protect her from so many assassins, was exposed to torments that it is easy to imagine but not easy to describe.

Her blood ran in all directions, and as if that pain were not enough, the weevils, wanting to do their part, climbed on to the bed, buried themselves within it and surrounded Pigrieche in such a fashion that was no less inconvenient than the gnats that were devouring her, for she could not move without crushing thousands of them, the insupportable odor of which suffocated her.

She had never been in a more manifest danger of losing her life, and might not have escaped it if Good and Better, who never panicked, had not run to light a lantern and, pushing courageously through that noxious cloud, had not reached the bed of the lovable invalid. Taking her in his arms in order to snatch her away from the torture that she had merited only too well, he carried her into the next room, where he tried to remove of the torturers that were working under her skin; but as the majority had already burrowed too deeply, it was necessary to plunge her into hot water, and in spite of that expedient it was very difficult to rid her of them.

They finally brought it to a conclusion, and then put her into another bed, where she continued to utter frightful screams. Her entire body was nothing more than a wound; it was not possible to touch her without causing her frightful pain. To complete the good work, the evil odor of the crushed weevils adhered to her body so strongly that no one could bear to go near her. Her own mother was unable to stand it, and Pigrieche would have perished for lack of help if the King had not overcome the repugnance that it caused everyone and given her the relief for which she could only have hoped from such a good Prince.

The cares that he gave her enabled to pass the night well enough; finally, the pains having diminished, the beauty opened her eyes—which is to say, she opened one of them, for the gnats had punctured the other; imagine, if you please, her despair when she perceived that new beauty spot. Nothing equaled her fury, however, when, instead of the consolations she should have expected from her mother she saw her lamenting the loss of the flour and only occupying herself with the disorder that the worms had caused, as well as the state in which her mule had come back, without even thinking about her daughter and without giving her any thanks for the treasures she had brought back, which ought to have been amply sufficient to compensated her for a few miserable bushels of wheat, whereas nothing could repair what Pigrieche had lost.

As you might think, she voiced her sentiment without restraint. There were no reproaches that she did not make her mother, and in terms so harsh and offensive that they would have deafened her if the riches she had brought had not muffled the noise.

However angry Richarde was, it was impossible to maintain it at the sight of so many beautiful things, by which she was dazzled. After having sufficiently satisfied her sight with all the precious stones, she was about to take them in hand, but Pigrieche, who still had her one and only eye attached to her treasures in spite of her woes, alarmed by her mother's design, uttered terrible screams.

"What are you doing?" she cried, furiously. "Are you still determined to deprive me of my wealth? Hasn't it cost me dearly enough? You want to rob me of the fruit of so many difficulties? Rather than steal from me riches so well acquired, can't you go and search for as many?

"No, no," she continued, "I know you, you wouldn't have any difficulty sending me back there; what I've suffered wouldn't be capable of putting you off; but the idea and the fear of the slightest harm that might happen to you is enough to hold you back; you're too delicate and too idle when it's a matter of yourself, although you count the most painful labors of others for nothing."

The anger into which she flew obliged Richarde to protest that she was mistaken in the judgments she had made of her intentions, assuring her of the contrary, and that, far from seeking to appropriate them, she had only been thinking of locking the gems away to prevent any of the spectators from stealing them. However, as she believed that she could take her share without scruple, she resolved to appropriate as many as she could covertly.

Commencing by putting her hand on a jewel that represented a blooming rose, so perfectly worked that one might have mistaken it or a real rose, she hoped to profit from it. That precious rose was composed of thirty or forty gens, as many diamonds as rubies, emeralds and garnets, and it was a masterpiece of art by virtue of the delicacy with which it was mounted. Having grasped it with a firm hand, Richarde was trying to slip into her pocket when, no longer able to resist the unexpected pain of a cruel pricking imparted by a few imperceptible thorns hidden under the leaves of the rose, she was obliged to relax her hand and drop the prickly treasure, with less precaution than she had taken in stealing it.

That involuntary action, having revealed her intention, exposed her to all the reproaches that Pigrieche could find. She spoke of her bad faith in terms so insulting, in an access of fury so long and terrible, that she wore out her mother's patience, already worn too thin by the pricking. She was getting ready to beat her daughter when, the pain finally diminishing, Richarde's natural petulance diminished too. She thought she ought to suffer anything in the hope of carrying out a more fortunate theft by taking more time.

That is why she did what she could to appease her daughter, trying to persuade her that she had only done it as a joke, solely to find out whether she knew how many flowers there were, and whether she would perceive the absence of the rose, which was remarkable in its singular beauty. To finish calming her anger, she made her hope that with such great treasures and jewels so well worked, she would be rich enough and sufficiently adorned not to cede anything in beauty or power to the greatest Princesses, that there would be no sovereigns in the world who would not desire her, and even reckon it a great honor to marry her.

That pleasant hope rendered Pigrieche all her good humor and made her gaze at her treasure with an even more favorable eye, regretting the loss of her other eye all the more because that misfortune deprived her of the satisfaction of seeing so much wealth with two good eyes.

After having considered it for a long time, however, it was necessary to call a truce to such a pleasant spectacle. What had happened having inspired strange suspicions against her mother's probity. Pigrieche was absolutely insistent that someone should bring her a large casket, the key of which, having locked her treasure away herself, she suspended around her neck, very impatient to be cured in order to have the pleasure of heightening her charms with such a brilliant adornment.

Although Liron was innocent of the catastrophe that had just occurred, and Pigrieche had merited it too much to be able to complain about it, the timid Liron had not dared to present herself before her mother and daughter, knowing that they were sufficiently unjust for her to have every reason to fear that they would punish her for their own fault. That was what obliged her to go out earlier than usual and come back later.

She took her flock to the fountain, but whatever care she took not to become bored, and although she had recourse to music, reading and her other ordinary amusements, that was a feeble resource for her. The tender Lisimene, always occupied with the handsome hunter, no longer had any taste for the innocent pleasures that had once been her dearest delights.

Without any hope of seeing again a lover from whom she had kept her dwelling secret, and without repenting of that virtue, her heart and mind were only filled by the idea of the charming young man. It was impossible for her to think about anything else; but she dared not go in search of the naiads, dreading that they might divine her secret and that, unaware of its true quality, they would criticize the tender sentiments to which she had abandoned herself for a unknown man who, in spite of the magnificence in which he appeared to her and the simplicity of her present condition, might perhaps be unworthy of the daughter of a great King, albeit dethroned and unfortunate.

It was already been four days since the fruit had finished. Having nothing more to sell, she had stopped going to market, and then she had gone to the Mill of Misfortune. It had been another four since she had returned. Those eight days, in full, had seemed eight centuries to her.

She was lying on a patch of grass, leaning her head against a tree, with a book in her hand that she had already tried in vain to read several times, in order to dissipate her ennui, without being about to succeed in that. She had cast many gazes upon it, but she fixed them there in a reverie, without remembering the book, when the sound of someone walking nearby caused her to turn her eyes in the direction from which it was coming.

They were agreeably struck on seeing recognizing the same hunter with whom she was occupied. He had had more difficulty finding Liron than he had in recognizing her; he approached her with an urgency that clearly expressed the satisfaction that he obtained from the fortunate encounter, for which he had wished with all his heart, but without expecting to find her.

In despair at no longer seeing his shepherdess, he had repented more than once of having observed too scrupulously the prohibitions that she had imposed forbidding him to follow her.

The transport that he exhibited was so sharp that there was no room to doubt that his love was extreme. What Lisimene had suffered herself since she had last seen him was even more appropriate to convince her of the pains that her absence had made him endure; that conformity of sentiments rendered her so sensible to the pleasure of seeing him again that she abandoned herself to it without reserve. She no longer thought about disguising it from him or trying to persuade him that he was indifferent to her.

The handsome hunter threw himself to his knees and said everything of the most tender that he could imagine to her. To all that speech, Liron only replied with her eyes, but that language, which is ordinarily the most sincere, has no need of an interpreter for a lover.

Liron, recovering herself slightly, tried to criticize him for the fact that, in spite of her prohibition, he had taken steps to find her, but she did it so weakly that he had no reason to be alarmed, and he savored the pleasure of the fortunate encounter no less. He had never spent moments so agreeable.

Seeing that she was surrounded by instruments, the hunter understood that she could play, and, delighted with that new perfection, he immediately begged her to give him the satisfaction of hearing a voice that could not be other than charming. Liron did not have to be pressed, and the joy of seeing her lover augmented the delicacy of her throat as well as that of her fingers. She enchanted the hunter, who had no need to discover that new charm in order to be the most amorous of men.

The naiads, astonished by the perfection of what they heard, which was so far above the serenades that Lisimene usually gave them, had difficulty believing that it was coming from the same person. They were attentive under the water, not daring to breathe or fear of stirring it with their breath, in order not to lose a single note of the music.

Liron would certainly not have been sorry that they were profiting from it, but to speak naturally, that was not what preoccupied her then; she was no longer thinking, at that moment, that there was anyone in the world except her hunter— and between us, that forgetfulness was quite forgivable. since it is scarcely possible that at the sight of a lover, burning with the same fires whose effect one feels, one could take it into one's head to think that that there are freshwater nymphs in the world, whatever obligations one might have to them.

The moments spent with the person one loves flow past so rapidly that the time of separation was already well advanced without our two lovers having perceived it; they believed that they had scarcely been together for three minutes when it was necessary to think of parting. That was not without regrets, and not without the promise of seeing one another in the same place the next day.

The joy of seeing the handsome hunter again had stunned Liron with regard to the consequences of such conduct, and the promise she had made him to return every day; but when she was alone, reason, resuming an empire that amour had weakened, represented to her sharply the harm that step would do her in society, in spite of the appearances that made her hope to keep it secret. Thinking of something more essential, she also made the reflection that even if the hunter maintained an eternal silence about the adventure, it would always be something at which she would have to blush inwardly, since it is that of what veritable shame consists, when one is sensible to honor and duty.

That reason determined the Princess not to expose herself any longer to the danger of seeing a man who pleased her too much. Far from listening to what a flattering penchant might tell her in favor of the unknown, to whom she had promised too much, too lightly, her virtue regained the upper hand and she no longer hesitated over breaking her word, and whatever pain she felt, she took a different route the following day, sighing, from the one to which her heart beckoned her.

How long that day seemed! She had never endured such ennui. Her sheep, which were accustomed to go to the edge of the fountain, continually tried to take that route, as well as Diligent. It was a double difficulty for her to resist her flock and her own desires. She spent the day in that perplexity; night finally came to extract her from it, and take her back to Richarde's house in an excessive sadness.

It was impossible for her to obtain a moment's rest. The chagrin that she did not doubt that the hunter would have felt, in not seeing her arrive, penetrated her with dolor. In that anxiety, and without knowing why, daylight seemed to be very long in appearing. She had scarcely perceived it than she got up, and after her ordinary work, having taken her sheep out with the intention of doing what she had done the previous day, she followed them in a dream.

Her reverie was so intense that she paid no attention to the fact that her flock took the route that she wanted to avoid, and she only realized it when she was beside the trees, her usual shelter.

She did not hesitate about the course of action she had to follow, drawing away abruptly; but, coming to consider that, as it was still early, she had time to wash her face and hands and go and salute the naiads before the hunter had arrived, she slowed down, and retraced her steps.

In spite of the resolution she had formed never to see her lover again, and, on the contrary, to avoid him carefully, she found pleasure in thinking that he loved her, that he would search for her, and that he would be afflicted by her withdrawal. She even feared that he might be inconsolable, and although she had a veritable pity for the chagrin into which she believed him to be plunged, she did not allow herself to apprehend that he might not be so sensible.

Such opposite sentiments were confounded within her to such an extent that she could not reconcile them; she feared the presence of the handsome hunter and simultaneously dreaded not encountering him; but in the meantime she apprehended no less that that step, to which virtue forced her, extinguishing his amour, might deter him sufficiently to make him abandon the locale and return to the town without thinking of her again.

It was thus that she was suspended, without being able to bring those various strands of thought into accord; but her unknown was very far from the sentiments that she seemed to fear; he had been very exact at the rendezvous the day before, and, not content with waiting all day, he had waited all night.

Although in despair at not having seen his shepherdess, however, and tormented by the dread that some unfortunate accident had befallen her, he had nonetheless allowed himself to succumb to the drowsiness that was overwhelming him. In order to avoid the gazes of the curious, for fear that the sight of him might causes difficulties for the lovable Liron, he had taken refuge in an old tree-trunk, where he had scarcely been savoring the sweetness of repose for an hour when a sheep, having entered it by chance, was prompted by fear to exit again promptly, and the noise it made woke the sleeper.

The sight of that dear sheep caused him a joy mingled with dread and hope. He got up precipitately, to see whether he was hoping in vain. He was not mistaken in his expectation; perceiving Liron washing herself in the fountain, he was transported by joy and ran to her.

"So I see you again, my beautiful shepherdess," he said to her, "but alas, what your absence has cost me! By what misfortune did I not see you all day yesterday? What a day I spent waiting for you! Just Heaven, how long it seemed! No, I would not have been able, without dying, to support another like it. Tell me, please, the cruel reason that deprived me of a benefit that is as dear to me as my life, and which obliged you to break your word to a lover whose amour is sufficiently known to you for you to be able to judge his impatience...

"You're not replying to me," he went on, after having waited for a few moments. You seem nonplussed. You're turning away; it seems that my presence embarrasses you. Weren't you looking for me? Is it possible that it was your own cruelty that deprived me of the pleasure of conversing with you yesterday?"

Liron did not know what to reply. She did not have the strength to flee a lover in whom her heart as so tenderly interested, and the reason that had triumphed over amour when the object was distant, only had sufficient force in its presence to heap the poor shepherdess with reproaches and to make her know that she was acting against propriety and against her duty, without that same reason having the power to have the laws that it was dictating executed.

She hesitated for some time; in the end, listening to the voice that is so powerful in virtuous hearts, she no longer disputed with duty a victory that covers the vanquished in glory. She declared to her lover that she wanted absolutely for him to cease coming to find her; but, seeing that he went pale, and believing that she ought to soften the extreme rigor of that sentence, she said to him in a low voice that, at least, he should not come so frequently, assuring him firmly that if he did not promise what she demanded, or did not keep his promise, she would never come to the fountain again for as long as she lived, which would deprive her of the sole pleasure she had in her misfortune.

The hunter—whom I ought to longer to call thus, since it was no longer in that garb that he showed himself to her eyes, having taken that of a shepherd in order to conform to the condition to which he believed the object of his desires had been born—the hunter, or rather the shepherd was crushed by that speech.

"You want my death, then," he said, in a tremulous voice. "Well," he continued, "be content; it will cost me my life, but I shall not regret it, since it is odious to you." On saying those words, his spirits abandoned him; he let himself fall on to the grass, devoid of strength and consciousness. The pallor of death spread over his face, to the extent of making Liron fear that he might die.

All the woes of which she had felt the afflictions previously no longer seemed to merit that name, when she compared them to the one by which she was threatened. She ran to the fountain and brought back water, which she threw over that cherished face, accompanied by the most tender speeches and cares, and the most touching regrets.

Those urgencies finally succeeded, and the new shepherd, having recovered his senses, said to her in a voice punctuated by sobs: "Alas, cruel Liron, why do you not let me die?

I would be happier to expire at your feet than to drag out, far from you, that deplorable life that you are conserving for me. Yes, inhuman woman," he added, "since you want to deprive me of the pleasure of seeing you, don't expect me to survive that cruelty. I shall deliver myself, in spite of you, from the distress to which you're condemning me."

Liron was in a state no less deplorable than the one in which she saw her dear shepherd. She wept, and could not speak. Finally making an effort, however, she said to him: "The state in which you see me, and the tears I cannot retain, ought to prove to you that you are unjust in the reproaches you make to me. You are not so lacking in clear sight not to know the regret I have in giving you displeasure. But in sum, Milord, do I not have a duty to myself? Is it permissible for me to injure the rules of propriety in receiving you here and giving you a rendezvous? Oh, far from finding the propositions I am making to you strange, if you loved me as I ought to be loved, you would be the first to give me lessons in my duty."

"As our conversations and my sentiments have nothing by which virtue can be offended," said the shepherd, "I cannot conceive for what reason you make a scruple of them. But, beautiful Liron, there is a means of banishing it. I offer you my hand and my heart; deign to accept them. Emerge from an unworthy slavery; follow a husband, who will make it his joy to please you."

"That offer is very generous," replied the shepherdess, whose embarrassment was redoubled by that speech, "but Milord," she added, "we do not know one another well enough to make such a serious engagement; we do not know what we can be to one another. Perhaps, if we knew one another better, we would find the certainty of an obstacle that I fear, and which, if I dared to explain myself, would only serve to reveal to you that Liron, shepherdess as she appears you to be, perhaps cannot be united with you."

"What are these obstacles that I cannot vanquish?" cried the unfortunate hunter. "Are you engaged under the laws of hymen? Is another the possessor of the happiness to which I aspire?"

"No," she said, "I have no other engagements than those of obeying my father and reason; but the inequality of our conditions is more than sufficient..."

"If that is the only reason that is stopping you," the lover interrupted, "it's an obstacle so slight that it ought not to retain you. What does the state in which I see you matter to me? That chimerical difference, which human pride puts between humans, ought to be entirely in favor of virtue. Yours is worthy of the throne. It is Destiny, and not you, that it is necessary to criticize, if it has not placed you at the rank where you ought to be. But as I only love you, and I am charmed to have the opportunity of testifying to you a love detached from any other interest that than its own, I am not embarrassed by the condition in which blind fortune has caused you to be born. On the contrary, it is a joy for me to be in a condition to deliver you from the humiliating employments of which dastardly individuals have charged you, and which are so unworthy of your merit, as well as your beauty.

"There, beautiful Liron," he continued, "those are my sentiments, and they always will be. Their purity reassures me with regard to the obstacles that I could dread on the part of your father, because I believe him to be too reasonable to raise any by caprice."

The more that tender lover spoke, the more he caused his generosity to burst forth and the more Lisimene was afflicted by it. She had not been able to help loving him at first sight, without knowing whether the qualities of his soul responded to those of his face. Thus, one can hardly think that a lover who made visible sentiments capable of rendering him as estimable as he was charming would not make great progress in the heart of the Princess. Unfortunately, that love, those virtues and those charms, which spoke in favor of the handsome shepherd, could not efface in her mind the fact that she was the daughter of King Good and Better.

She dared not reveal her secret to him, thinking that he would only make use of it to afflict them further, and that they would be less unfortunate if she spared him that despairing confidence. Thus, they separated without having a fuller explanation, and, her heart so filled with love that, in spite of the necessity she had imposed on herself of telling the shepherd that it was necessary for the separation to be eternal, not only did she not think of talking to him about it but she even forgot to tell him that he must leave at least a few days without coming to look for her. She only remembered that when he was too far away to call him back; which made her think that that was an indispensable reason for returning to the same place tomorrow, in order to repair the fault that her memory had just made her commit.

Although she believed herself to be firmly resolved not to see her lover any longer, and everything appeared to oblige that sacrifice to duty and virtue, although she did not think for a moment of denying their authority, she was nonetheless agitated by it. She told herself in vain that the crook she was carrying for the moment made no difference to her owing her life to a great King, who, by virtue of a revolution, of which examples are not rare in history, might recover his throne and dispose of his daughter in favor of a man who was in a position to help him triumph over the usurper.

Those invincible reasons did not diminish her amour. However powerful they were, they were too feeble to extract her heart from a passion so tender; the sad memory of her ancestors caused her to blush in vain to love an unknown; although she had as much shame in it as if the dishonor had been public, she did find the maxims of the century any less unjust and barbaric.

How extravagant prejudices are! she said to herself. *Why must I blush to love a good and generous man, who believes me to be a simple village girl but does not hesitate in the design of raising me as far as him?* She sighed. *But that charming man is not a king, and all his attractions, any more than his generosity, would not prevent me from being dishonored if*

I united his destiny with mine, which, unfortunately, has made me born to marry a king, or never to accept an engagement. Perhaps the man who is reserved for me will have all the qualities that render a man despicable, but it will not matter if he reigns, and I would be less dishonored by the vices of a spouse than I would be by an inequality of conditions.

Let us sacrifice love to glory, then, she added, shedding a few tears. *That will perhaps be fortunate for my lover, since I have nothing to bring him as a dowry but misfortune; his own interest demands that I make every imaginable effort to extract my heart from a futile passion, which would be deadly to the man I love. I must therefore engage him to make his decision, as I have made mine.*

Having formed that resolution, the only question remaining was deciding whether it was more appropriate to inform the shepherd vocally or to cease coming to the place where she was certain to encounter him. Both seemed equally dangerous. In exposing herself to explaining the reason that was making her act she feared his despair and dreaded not having the strength to resist it. But in avoiding that inconvenience by her absence she saw another that seemed to her to be no less great; even discounting the harshness there would be in letting him believe that she scorned him, she also had to fear that, only consulting his dolor, he might come to Richarde's house in search of her.

Those two alternatives appearing to her to be equally dangerous, she was examining the question of which she ought to prefer when a third came to mind that appeared more suitable. That was to confide in her father and to be governed by his advice. She knew the King's prudence and could not doubt his tenderness for her. Thus, everything bearing her to address herself to him, she determined to do it, and hat firm resolution rendered her a little more tranquil as she waited impatiently for the return of Good and Better, who had gone hunting.

The Princess posted herself on his route and, having seen him appear she went to meet him and asked him to sit down for a moment to listen to her. She was so emotional and tremulous that the King had no doubt that she had endured some new chagrins on the part of Pigrieche or her mother. He stopped to console her. But after he had employed everything that seemed appropriate to do that, seeing that instead of calming her down, her tears were augmented, without her having the strength to say a word, he took her in his arms and hugged her tenderly.

"What is the new misfortune that has brought you to this excess of affliction?" he said to her. "Call a truce to your dolors, my dear daughter, and tell me what is causing them. I cannot doubt that the subject is important, since it has triumphed over your constancy. I have seen it too severely tried and admired it too much not to be convinced that your despair is not founded on slight chagrins. Alas, I know that the firmness so far above your age, which consoled me for all the displeasures we have found with the unworthy creatures with whom we are forced to live, is finally at an end. Since it is exhausted, nothing remains for us but to die. I am prepared for that, without seeking further means to conserve a life so unfortunate that I can only regard as a happy moment the one that will terminate it."

"No, my dear Father," said the Princess, making an effort to stop sobbing, "I hope that the Heaven that has saved you from the hands of the Tyrant will not abandon you and will protect your virtue. There is nothing new on the part of your wife or her daughter; they are not the cause of the difficulty I have. In spite of that, however, I have never felt one more forcefully; I find myself on the edge of a precipice, into which you alone can prevent me from falling. It is from you that I expect my only aid, and yet I tremble to tell you my woe, since I cannot tell you without making you ashamed of my weakness."

That speech, which the King did not understand at all, surprised him to the highest degree. In order to reassure his daughter, and to engage her not to hide anything from him, he protested to her that whatever the nature was of the secret she was about to reveal to him, she could speak in full assurance that she would only find in him an extreme indulgence, accompanied by the aid that she ought to expect from a faithful friend, without encountering the severity of a father.

Reassured by the further expressions of tenderness that she received from Good and Better, Lisimene did not hesitate any longer to tell him about the mutual inclination that the handsome hunter and she had acquired for one another, confessing to him naively everything that had happened between them, including the internal conflicts that she had had, without disguising from him what it had cost her to make the resolution no longer to see him, and finally, the uncertainty she had as to whether she ought to return to where her lover would undoubtedly to be waiting for her the next day, or whether she ought to cease going in that direction, where she was certain to find him. She represented to the King the inconveniences she saw everywhere, and begged him again to guide her in that dangerous occasion.

The King listened, maintaining a profound silence; he allowed her to talk without interruption. But, seeing that she was no longer saying anything, and that she was waiting for his response, he invited her to be tranquil, praising her extremely for having made a decision as wise as confiding herself to him.

"It's too late," he added, "to stay here any longer; that would attract harsh words on the part of our harpies. So, my dear child, let us go back in as promptly as possible. I will go out tomorrow, under the pretext of going hunting, and I will follow you closely. When we're at liberty, we'll search together for the means of terminating your anxieties."

After having made that arrangement, they separated, and took care to go back to the house by different routes.

Although Liron could not think of any other means that her father might propose to her except that they would send the handsome hunter away, she still encountered a great relief in that, in thinking that she would not be obliged to acquit that disagreeable task herself. In spite of the affliction that she felt, she spent that night more peacefully than the previous one and the day that had followed it.

As soon as the one when she was to converse with her father dawned, she got up, and after having fulfilled her ordinary occupations, she took her flock out, stopping a short distance from the house to wait for the King, who did not take long to follow her. She was resolved to carrying out his orders, but she did not expect him to tell her to take the sheep in the direction of the fountain. She would have obeyed him without a murmur if he had ordered her to avoid it. With all the more reason, she submitted to a command that flattered her dearest desires.

The new shepherd, who had not yet arrived, leaving them time to converse, gave the King the opportunity to explain to the Princess the measures he intended to take to ensure their repose. She dared not repeat to her father the urgent request she had made him the day before to prescribe the conduct she ought to take. Although she was determined to obey, she was afraid that what he prescribed would not be to her liking; she was even sure of it. But she gave no evidence of it, and was awaiting in silence whatever she had to dread or hope from the step she had taken when Good and Better, looking at her with an affectionate expression that reassured her, although it was accompanied by a sort of gravity that was not usual to him, finally said:

"You ought not to doubt the tenderness that I have for you, my dear daughter, nor the joy that I would feel in seeing you on my throne; I destined it for you, and I had resolved to abdicate when you were married; I would assuredly have done so with great pleasure, if fortune and my enemy had given me time. I have done what I can to conserve for you the rank into which you were born, but I am finally beginning to doubt that my wishes can ever be fulfilled.

"Ambitious is enjoying his usurpation placidly; his cruelties have assured his power; he is at peace with his neighbors and my subjects no longer remember the generosity that I had for them, or, if there are some who have not absolutely lost the memory, they are without credit and cam only lament without daring to undertake anything for my service.

"So, my dear daughter, I no longer hope to see you become Queen, although your youth can permit you to hope that a fortunate revolution might render you the grandeurs that I have lost. But if you are at the age of hope, I no longer am, and the advantage that you can expect of the spring of your days cannot protect me from death. My old age, or rather my chagrins, perhaps render that event closer than we think.

"If that accident happens to you, what will be your resource? Alas, unfortunate Princess, I shiver at the fate to which you would be exposed. My death would leave you prey to the fury of an implacable stepmother, and to please her Pigrieche, you ought not to doubt that she would deliver you without hesitation to the tyrant, who would not fail to take your life immediately, or render it even more frightful than death.

"So, my dear Lisimene," he continued, taking a familiar tone, "if you believe me, you will renounce the ambition that opposes your happiness. Thus, for your safety, and following the movements of your heart that your virtue cannot oppose, you should resolve to live in a deprived condition in which you will be happy, with a young man who loves you and who is loved by you. I cannot doubt that he is virtuous. The generosity of his conduct makes that evident enough—which obliges me to advise you as a friend, as I promised to do, to fix your fortune to your lover and forget a vain grandeur that, to all appearances, is lost to you without resource.

"It is not the case," he added, "that if this young man has birth and credit, that he might not be able one day to render value to your rights to the crown, which are neither obscure nor equivocal. But unless an opportunity presents itself that is as sure as it is favorable, I exhort you to deflect him away from risking the success of an uncertain event that, if he failed, instead of raising you to the throne, would precipitate him into the tomb."

This discourse, for which Liron had not dared to hope, caused her an inexpressible joy, and inspired an increase in her infinite tenderness for a father whose complaisance was able to flatter his daughter's taste so agreeably. Penetrated with gratitude, she kissed his hands several times, ecstatically, assuring him that she was resolved to conform to his advice, having never had and not wanting to have any other will than his.

A conversation so interesting would, to all appearances, have continued for a long time if the individual who was its subject had not emerged abruptly from a nearby wood, whose thickness had hidden them mutually from one another, and they encountered one another at such close range that they could not have avoided one another if they had had the intention of doing so.

The shepherd, finding a man with Liron, did not doubt for a moment that it was her father and, fearing that he was only there to forbid him ever to see his daughter again, he appeared so emotional that Good and Better, touched by the state in which he saw a young man whose physiognomy was extremely attractive, begged him to come nearer in a voice that reassured him somewhat.

"Milord," he said to him, "You seem surprised to see me with my daughter, but if your intentions are such as she has represented them to me, and as you have tried to persuade her yourself, my presence ought not to displease you, since I am only here with the design of rendering you both happy, and I shall do so with all the more pleasure because I see nothing in your person that does not give me a very advantageous opinion of you."

The handsome shepherd, who had been so alarmed at the sight of Liron's father, was greatly encouraged by a welcome that he had not dared to expect, and by which he as delighted.

"My Father," he said to him, with a great deal of respect, "I can only express to you feebly the satisfaction I feel in being able to protest to you that my tenderness for your lovable daughter in infinite. I have offered her my hand, and begged her to accept it, but although it was with as much sincerity as love, offers that she merits so greatly have not been able to prejudice her in my favor. She only speaks of insurmountable obstacles that she has never wanted to reveal to me. Is it possible that you have had enough generosity toward me to deign to smooth them out?"

"My daughter was right," the King said. "She told you the truth in saying that there are obstacles opposed to your happiness; but however strong they might be, they are not absolutely invincible. Merit can substitute for a difference in conditions. So, Milord, commence, if you please, by telling us who you are; that point is essential, since you will agree what we cannot make any engagements or take any measures with you without knowing you.

"I am entirely disposed in your favor, "Good and Better went on, "But to confirm me in that disposition, it is necessary to prove on your part that you have an entire confidence in me."

"You would be entirely able to inspire it in me if I had less frankness than I have naturally," the young man replied, "and I protest to you, my Father, that I shall never have any secrets from you. But before telling you who I am, permit me to demand a promise from you. The first time that I saw the charming Liron, I only consulted her charms in order to give her my heart, and not her birth; permit me then, also to be accepted for your son such as I am, without asking me for an account of my ancestors. In whatever rank I was born, however, I also ask you not to constrain your daughter, for I only want to obtain it from you after having obtained it from her. So, venerable old man, without offending you by my delay, allow me to beg the beautiful Liron to explain herself regarding my destiny."

"What you ask," said the King, smiling," is not without some difficulty; well-born young woman rarely explain themselves on that article. But Milord, Liron's eyes seem to respond to that question as favorably as you could desire, and you ought to be content with that. However, since doubts remain to you, as I am informed of my daughter's sentiments more as a friend than a father, I believe I can assure you that you have nothing to fear in the direction of ambition, and that it is not the hope of a more elevated rank than her own that determines her in your favor."

In spite of the assurance that response gave him, the shepherd persisted in wanting Liron to explain herself by means of her own mouth. That beauty, seeing herself pressed and knowing what Good and Better thought, became bolder, and told her lover that she had nothing to add to what her father had just said, and that she could only be very happy with a husband whom he accepted.

"That is enough, charming Liron," cried the unknown, transported with joy. "I know the full price of my happiness, and I sense it redoubled by the pleasure that I have in telling you that I can give you a rank worthy of you, and admitting to you at the same time that I am not a slave of mine, since I am sacrificing it without regret and without effort to my tenderness, even though I am the elder son and the heir presumptive of Prince Ambitious, presently master of the realm that belongs to King Good and Better. The people, who ordinarily impose names on their Princes in accidence with their caprice, call me *Chemzem*"—which is to say, Perfect—"a name that I would like to merit, and I confess, to my shame, only owing to a favorable prejudice."

The confession of Perfect's birth astonished both the father and the daughter. "What, Prince!" said the monarch, in surprise. "You're the son of Ambitious? How and by what hazard does the heir to a great Empire find himself in this remote place, detached, so to speak, from the rest of the land?"

"The reason is simple," said Perfect. "Although it seems that I ought to have seen with joy the usurpation that my father had carried out of his King's estates, since success has enabled him change his name, and instead of the odious title of usurper he has given himself that of conqueror, I was not able approve of it, nor disguise my sentiments sufficiently to prevent Prince Ambitious and his wife being informed of them, as well as all their Court. I was born too sincere to betray my thought in such a criminal occasion.

"In addition to my natural frankness, another movement was also opposed to my rejoicing in seeing my father placed in the supreme rank, to the scorn of his honor, law and justice, in sum, at the expense of the best King on earth, for whom I have always felt an inclination and a respect that attached me more strongly to his interests than those of the people from whom I received the light of day. For I must confess to my shame that the sentiments I have for them do not resemble those that nature imprints in the hearts of children, and I have often needed all my reason to submit to what the sacred names of father and mother impose on us.

"I was nourished until the age of seven in Good and Better's Court, and that generous Prince did not seem to put any difference between his inclination for Princess Lisimene, his only daughter, and that which he had for me. He had me brought up with her. That Princess was then four years old, and at an age so tender, one could already perceive in her the hope of an admirable beauty; her intelligence, her inclinations, everything responded to the charms of her person and announced a prodigy.

"The King often told me to strive to merit that he might give her to me as a wife, and often called me his son-in-law. I was so flattered, in spite of my infancy, by his promises and his kindness, that I redoubled my efforts to render myself worthy of them. Far from resenting the lessons I was being given then, I forced my masters to give me extra ones; I would have liked to anticipate, so to speak, an education that seemed to me to be too slow. I believed that everything that I did not know was a fault capable of rendering me unworthy of the King's generosity.

"But among the cares that my father took for my education, that of inspiring great ambition in me was the keenest, and it was to that end that my masters were ordered to apply themselves most. I recognized only too well subsequently how odious the motive was for that, but in those days I received those impressions avidly. It is not difficult for a passion that is ordinarily masked by the specious exterior of a fine glory to take possession of a young heart that has insufficient discernment to recognize the difference. I rendered assiduous cares to the Princess, and my father also facilitated them, but they were too insistent not to be dictated by politics alone. That was a subtlety of which I would have incapable at the age I was, if inclination, in accord with my other motives, had not made me act; my urgency came from the heart. The fashion in which the Princess responded seemed to be born of a similar source, which was often a diversion for the King.

"The season in which my extreme youth permitted me to remain with her having gradually elapsed, I was separated from her; I was afflicted by that, but as I was made to understand that the objective of that distancing was to put me in a state to merit her, I consoled myself more easily. On leaving the Court I was taken by my father's order to a rather distant location, inhabited by solitary scholars whose virtue served their reputation even more than the rumor of their science.

"I stayed with them for eight years without emerging and without seeing my family again. The indifference I experienced on the part of my father and my mother inspired an equal one in me for them. It is to that reciprocal drawing apart that I attribute the scant enthusiasm that I feel in their regard.

"I was fifteen when I saw men other than my solitary hosts for the first time. There was an officer in my father's guards who made a celebration out of announcing news to me to which he had no doubt that I would be very sensible. He told me that I only had to spend one more day in that desert. The King had declared publicly that he wanted to give me as a husband to Princess Lisimene, which would render me incontestably the heir to his throne. The officer told me that the monarch had ordered my father to summon me immediately, and he did not doubt that I would be more amply informed of my happiness the next day at the latest, presuming that it would be by Prince Ambitious himself.

"'The respectful affection that I have for you,' the officer added, engaged me to advance by twelve hours the pleasure that such fortunate news ought to cause you, and to inform you at the same time that the King's resolution makes the joy of public hopes. The certainty of seeing him with such a worthy successor has caused it to burst forth everywhere and attracted further praise to him and further blessings from his people.'

"The officer had thought that it was prudent to inform me in private of the glorious fate that was in preparation for me; no one else was informed of it, and he left again immediately, not wanting to be found by Ambitious, or those that he did not doubt would come on his behalf, fearing that the Prince might be offended by that excess of zeal, which might reveal too soon a secret that the King or he might have wanted to tell me in person. He recommended to me as he left to maintain a silence that I could not break without dooming him.

"I thought, as he did, that the King might want the pleasure of informing me of the happiness he destined for me himself. So, without having confidence in anyone, I abandoned myself to the sweetest hopes. I confess to you that on that occasion I was only flattered by the motive of ambition. For, in spite of what I have told you about the initial movements of sympathy that had been remarked between us in our childhood, Lisimene and I were so young when we were separated that, never having heard mention of her since, I had entirely lost the idea of her, only remembering that when I was with her, people had said that she was beautiful. But then I recalled that memory, and I was touched by the praise that had been given to her excellent character, which flattered me more, not representing to me any of the features of the young Princess. Even if my memory had been faithful enough to retrace those of a four-year-old child, I would not have been able to obtain much assistance therefrom to depict her present beauty.

"That did not prevent me from spending the night in a very agreeable idea and awaiting the day impatiently. It finally came, that day so desired, but it seemed to me much longer than the night that had preceded it, and my joy was extremely inhibited when I saw it end without receiving the charming news, which in the fashion in which the officer had spoken of it was too sure for me not to suspect some snag appropriate to change the nature of things. However, I not only spent that day without seeing anyone, but a further fortnight went by before I saw the effect of the promises that had been made to me.

"The zeal of the man who believed that he had announced such a great good fortune to me had a success very different from his intentions. For, before having learned anything of the King's designs, if I had ambition, at least it was limited and did not exceed the rules of moderation; it was not the same when the hope that I had just acquired was revealed.

"The transports that it caused me were so vivid that the anxiety alone made me fall ill, and I was only cured when I finally received the order so much desired and impatiently awaited. It was accompanied by a royal pomp, which delivered me from the dread that the annoying delay was an effect of a change in the King's intention.

"Reassured by that appearance, I was not surprised by all the honors that were rendered to me on the roads, attributing them to the consequence of Good and Better's favorable designs.

"I arrived at the palace, and I did not doubt, on seeing my father, that he was disposed to introduce me to the monarch to whom we had so many obligations. But my surprise was extreme when, instead of acquitting that just duty, he declared to me that there was no other King but him. 'You see him in me, Prince.' he said to me. 'I have worked for you, and I have acquired a throne, which will infallibly be yours, unless you act in a fashion that renders you unworthy of it, as Good and Better did, whose incapacity has led his people to dethrone him and put me in his place.'

"I was so surprised by that unexpected news that I could not find terms in which to reply. I contented myself with rendering him my homage by putting a knee on the ground and kissing his hand. But my Father, dare I tell you that, far from sensing in the speech of that Prince any impulse of gratitude for what was advantageous to me, I felt a horror that I had difficulty in suppressing, and I never made any effort that cost me more than kissing that hand, which, although it was my father's, appeared to me no less criminal toward its King and benefactor.

"The violent effort I made to hide my repugnance was so strong that I fainted. That accident was attributed to a residue of the illness by which I had been afflicted a few days before, and without seeking other reasons, I was carried to my apartment, where I quickly recovered consciousness. Taking advantage of that sudden illness, I used it as a pretext for sending everyone away, wanting to remain alone, and pretending to need repose, although in truth, it was only to have the liberty to think about that unfortunate event, and to prepare myself to compose my expression and hide my sentiments. For if ambition had opened my heart to joy, when I believed myself to be the legitimate heir to a great kingdom, that heart had not been accessible to it while I was only able to aspire to that glory with the aid of a crime, and I detested grandeur at the price at which it was offered to me.

"The solitary individuals to whom I owed my education had never tried to give me a distaste for the pleasure of reigning, but they had painted a frightful picture for me of a state that had a King that only owed that title to an unjust usurpation, incessantly repeating to me that in wearing a crown, or in leading a private life, it was equally necessary to conserve a virtuous heart and to be at peace with oneself, without having any reproach to make oneself.

"Following their principles, which had only served to cultivate my taste for equity, the title of usurper appeared odious to me and very far from their instructions. But in the end, being unable to bring any remedy to that misfortune, I resolved to pretend, so long as I could do nothing in favor of my veritable sovereign, to whom I promised privately to restore his property if ever I found myself the master of so doing.

"After having put some order into my thoughts, and feeling certain of my resolutions, I presented myself at the Court of the new King, where, with all the precautions I could imagine to avoid becoming suspect, I sought information with as much discretion as I could regarding the man whose place he occupied and the destiny of his daughter, the deplorable Princess.

"As I had no experience of the Court as yet, and I had always heard it said that it was very important to be wary of the character of those to whom one entrusts one's confidence, I did not know to whom to address myself. Judging my father's sentiments by those I felt for him, I feared, justly, arousing his suspicion. I was extracted from that embarrassment by the same officer who had me to announce my new grandeur to me. I was not risking as much with him as with any other, since it was at least as important for him as it was for me to keep the secret.

"He told me, therefore, that the unfortunate King had fled, as well as Lisimene, which was the best course of action for them to take and the greatest good fortune that could have happened to them, since they were proscribed and a price had been put on their heads. He said that if they were alive, they only owed their life to the diligence they had employed and to the universal ignorance of the route that they had taken, not having taken anyone with them. He added that he could not understand by what good fortune they had been informed of the criminal revolution soon enough to reach safety, nor to what place they could have withdrawn.

"I was more sensible to their sad fate than to the brilliant destiny that seemed to await me. I deplored the misfortune of a great King and that of a beautiful Princess, both reduced to wandering through the world as vagabonds, lacking the things most necessary to life. That dolorous spectacle, which I imagined as vividly as if my eyes had been witness to it, drew sincere tears from me, rendering me almost insensible to the honors and pleasures by which I was surrounded.

"King Ambitious paid no attention to that; he was only concerned with whatever could affirm his usurpation, and in any case, the indifference he had for me naturally did not permit him to observe my sentiments. All his tenderness was determined in favor of my brother, who had only just been born when he sent me to the solitaries. But the preference that the Prince gave him over me was nothing in comparison with the passion that his wife had for that cherished son.

"When I appeared at Court after the detestable enterprise that had put the crown into our family, that affection was so considerably augmented that I surely only owe to that predilection the hatred that my mother has for me. Even though the people said loudly that the preference in question was unjust, I was not very afflicted by it. There was no one who did not treat as blind the mad passion that the Queen had for a child whose eyes, even at the age of nine, seemed already to be devouring the throne, without considering that by right of birth it would belong to me one day, being, in addition, as cruel as he was superb and only being loved by a blind mother.

"My brother, prey to his ambition, not only saw me with a jealous eye, but would not have hesitated to snatch the crown from his father's head if he had been able to do so, to set it on his own. I lived in the midst of the Court almost as a hermit; the only courtier with whom I had some conversation, because he was the only one that seemed worthy of my esteem, was the principal Vizier, Zulbach. The attachment he had always testified to Good and Better rendered him dear to me; and although it seemed that his master was effaced from the number of the living, by virtue of the care he had taken to render his retreat impenetrable, that generous Vizier nevertheless made an attempt in favor of the fugitive King by proposing to the reigning King to render himself the placid possessor of the crown he had usurped by marring me to Lisimene. The Vizier added boldly that there was no other means of appeasing celestial justice, the murmurs of the people and giving me a legitimate right to the rank that he destined for me.

"When I learned of that proposition, it appeared so advantageous that, not doubting that King Ambitious would accept it joyfully, I obtained an extreme satisfaction from it. It was of short duration, however, since I learned almost at the same time that, far from consenting to it, my father had audaciously refused it; that it had only served to renew his fury and make him offer a higher price to any scoundrel who was capable of bring him Good and Better's head.

"It was then that, indignant at his barbarity, I could not help testifying to him what I thought of it; but I was very poorly received. He replied to me proudly that he was in no humor to yield, or to possess by title of grace a property that he had already acquired; that far from wanting to share his fortune with a daughter without any establishment other than what she owed to his own generosity, he intended that my hand should serve him to make an alliance as useful as honorable by having me marry a Princess who would bring me a sovereignty as a dowry, not a wretched fugitive devoid of wealth and refuge.

"Indignant at his unjust sentiments, I dared to reply to him that in spite of the deplorable situation to which Princess Lisimene was reduced, I placed more value on her rights than the fortunate situation in which I found myself. But that frankness, far from softening my father, attracted a very harsh response, which my mother outdid, adding everything she could imagine of the most scornful, and, seizing that pretext to punish me for what she called a lack of respect and sentiment, she always affected thereafter to treat me with the utmost coldness.

"I was less sensitive to that scornful behavior that I ought to have been; conforming without regret to the fashions of acting that she had with me, I continued to live alone and not to mingle in anything. It is true that my youth authorized to some extent the scant confidence that the King and Queen testified toward me, but they should have thought in my regard as one naturally thinks of a son who is to succeed his father. Instead of distancing me from affairs of state, they ought to have given me a place in their Council to instruct me gradually in the art of reigning. Entirely to the contrary, the Queen only sought opportunities to mortify me, having entry to them refused to me by her husband.

"However, a war that the King undertook against a neighboring Prince drew me out of the inaction in which the distaste I suffered retained me. I asked to serve; the King granted me that, in spite of the Queen's opposition, who, being unable to prevent it entirely, restricted herself to demanding that at least I should not command the army. But she wasted her effort in that, and contrary to her desires, I found myself at the head of a hundred thousand men.

"I was fortunate in my expedition; without giving you an account of the war now, it is sufficient for me to tell you that in less than two years I reduced our enemy to requesting peace, which he only obtained on very deleterious conditions.

"After having made sure of my conquests I returned to my father the King, who, satisfied with my conduct, received me in a sufficiently obliging fashion. But the Queen could not bring herself to look upon me favorably; on the contrary, I found that her coldness increased in proportion to the praise I received; and the evidence of affection that the Court and the people gave me caused her a pain that she did not try to hide.

"I was hardly touched by the evidence she continued to give me of her ill will. I confess to you that her indifference did not surpass mine, and I had need of all my virtue to limit my sentiments to that. I was in despair at owing to her the life that I respired, regarding the duty that attached me to her as the most painful thing to which it could subject me. And I reproached myself in vain for not being able to feel in respect of the King either the tender impulses that nature inspires in well-born hearts. I have nothing for which to reproach myself, for having been lacking in their regard in that which depended on me, nor of having lent a criminal ear to those who, remarking the displeasure that the Queen showed me incessantly, or attracted to me on the part of the King, offered to form a party in my favor and to put the crown on my head.

"Far from listening to such culpable propositions, I only kept the secret of those who made them to me on the promise that I demanded from them that they renounce that odious project, being disposed, if the occasion presented itself, to give my life without hesitation in order to preserve that of Ambitious and his wife, in spite of the scant affection they had for me and the distance I felt for them. Alas, far from cherishing them, as it seems that nature demands, and as the recognition of the continual promises that King gave me of soon placing me on the throne—which, he said, he had only conquered for me, and that he was only seeking to render more powerful in the design of making me one more glorious—ought to have engaged me, I never approached them without sensing the spontaneous movement of an involuntary horror, whose foundations were entirely unknown to me, although I felt their agitations.

"In spite of the promises so frequently reiterated by Ambitious, I regretted a thousand times not being rather of the blood of the unfortunate Good and Better; I would have shared his flight and disgrace with more satisfaction and tranquility than I had in enjoying a fortune so unjustly acquired, and I would have preferred the advantage of living unknown with him to the misfortune of reigning with the man to whom cruel destiny had caused me to be born.

"Shortly after my expedition, the King I had vanquished died, and my father judged it appropriate to marry me to the Princess, the daughter of the deceased King. He arranged that matter without consulting me, without even having deigned to mention it to me, and when everything was settled he rendered it public. But he was astonished to find in me a resistance had had not had any reason to expect.

"I told him that naturally, since he reigned, I could hope without any crime to succeed him one day, and that the throne ought also to be mine because I knew positively that the intention of his predecessor was in conformity with that hope, but that that I could only accept it innocently by fulfilling the condition that he had attached to it. For as long as Princess

Lisimene lived, it was only by that marriage that it was permissible for me to believe that I had a legitimate right to a throne that belonged to the father of that Princess. I added, without departing from the respect I owed him that I had always hoped that he would enter himself into such just reasoning, and that honor and equity made it an inviolable law for me.

"A response so opposite to the King's intentions put him into an extreme anger, soon redoubled by the care that the Queen, informed of my refusal, put into embittering him against me.

"To punish my resistance, which she treated as rebellion, she urged him to do nothing less than arrest me; but the King dared not do that; the people were too blindly attached to me, and it was, in any case, easy for him to determine that the troops would never suffer an attempt on my liberty, since on the mere suspicion that they had had of that, on the basis of a few threats uttered by the Queen, in immediate reaction there had been a kind of uprising, which had only require me to render it dangerous, and could have made me master of the realm if I had wished. Far from profiting from the opportunity, though, I had made everyone return to duty, without that moderation earning me any merit on the eyes of the King or the Queen. Quite the contrary; my mother's hatred only increased further.

"In order to remove from her sight an object so disagreeable to her, I begged the King to assign me a province to which I could retire, and from which I swore on the holiest oaths not to emerge without his orders.

"That proposition might perhaps have had some difficulty with Ambitious had he only consulted himself. There are many fathers who, without being very tender, have more affection for their sons than mine had for me, but he did not hate me absolutely, and his politics would perhaps have engaged him to treat me more gently if the Queen had been in the same sentiments; but hers were unequivocal, the evidence of hatred to frequently manifest to offer any doubt.

"As she had a considerable ascendancy over the mind of her husband, she bore him to receive with joy a means of distancing me from the Court and obliged him to send me without delay the order I requested to retire to this desert, which I call by that name although it is a province where there are several towns; but it is so far from the Court and even from the other Provinces composing our estates that there are no other ways of communicating with it than a long sea voyage. One might say that it is entirely separated from our continent, to which it is, in fact, only linked by immense forests and inaccessible mountains. In any case, the people who inhabit it are so primitive that it can be regarded as a new world.

"That was precisely what determined the Queen to give preference to it as my place of exile. I paid scant attention to that because, limiting my wishes to getting away from the Court, anything that distanced me from it was equally agreeable to me, all the more so as the Queen did not push her hatred so far as to remove all my means of rendering my solitude as tolerable as I could. I was permitted to transport here everything that I imagined to be capable of preserving me from tedium without her raising any obstacle to it. The sentiments that she had for me not permitting me to flatter myself that it was to give me pleasure, I attributed that indulgence of sorts to the desire she had to put me in a state not to regret the Court, and to have to reason to want to return to it, having more trust in the wellbeing I had in my distant abode to keep me away than to oaths.. She did not render me enough justice to believe that they were sufficient to retain me.

"But if those secret reasons were appropriate to make her see without difficulty the measures I took to make my retreat agreeable, it was not the same when she saw the escort that as preparing to accompany me; for I was followed, to her great regret, and without her being able to oppose it, by the larger part of the youth of the Court, who abandoned it without hesitation in order to follow my destiny. That brilliant nobility, which was without contradiction the elite of the realm, was imitated by a large number of soldiers and brave officers who had served under me, whose esteem and amity I had been able to win.

"The Queen was outraged; the evidence of attachment that I received, visibly, from so many young noble and the cream of the troops, informed her clearly that hearts had more affection for me than for my brother. She dared not, however, oppose that torrent of good will; it would have been dangerous for her not to maintain any reserve in that matter. In any case, although the affection of the aristocracy and the people seemed to reproach her for her lack of affection for me and her injustice toward a son who was judged worthy of a better fate, on the other hand, that cruel mother found a great deal of facility in consummating the project she had forced in favor of my brother, since, in allowing those who were attached to me to go away, only those who remained entirely attached to her remained, who, far from supporting my interests, would all take the side of her beloved son if the King were to die. Thus, she let me depart tranquilly.

"I have, therefore, been in this deserted place for a year. I have built a château here, which, although it is not as magnificent as those I have abandoned, is not without its pleasant features and has all the necessary comforts. Moreover, although my Court is not as numerous as my father's, I have the satisfaction of seeing that it is surely better composed.

"Since I have been in this region, my principal occupation has been to civilize the people, who are extremely primitive. I make it an amusement, which has succeeded and to which I am attached. I find myself more content here than when I arrived, which has inspired in me a sincere resolution not to emerge from it for as long as the King lives. But when he has paid his tribute to nature, there will be no difficulty that is capable of stopping me. I shall search everywhere for Good and Better, having no other ambition than reestablishing on his throne a King who was expelled from it so unjustly, and if, to the misfortune of his people, that great monarch is, according to all appearances, unable to enjoy the fruits of my goodwill, turning them entirely to his daughter, I will do for that Princess what I could not do for her father.

"Before having seeing the charming Liron," Perfect continued, "I had resolved, if I could find that unfortunate Prince, to throw myself at his feet, and perhaps, instead of punishing me for the outrages he has received from my family, and confounding me with the culpable, he would have been generous enough to accord me the hand of Princess Lisimene; but amour has ordered otherwise. Thus, without varying the duty prescribed to me of the restitution of a usurped property, content to lead a private life with my dear Liron, I will renounce a rank that I could only conserve at the expense of my love or my innocence."

"I would like," the young Prince went on, "all these various interests to be in accord, and legitimately to have a crown to put on a head so beautiful, but my shepherdess has too much virtue not to have the same scruple as me; thus, I am only offering her that which I believe she can accept without remorse."

Good and Better and his daughter had listened with as much attention as surprise to what had to interest them so powerfully. The King could not weary of admiring Perfect's equity and generosity. The moderation of which he gave evidence toward such an unjust father, from which he had received such a dangerous example of usurpation, was no less a subject of admiration for him than the piety of the Prince toward his sovereign. The wicked behavior that he had endured on the part of his parents was more than sufficient to stir a young heart.

"Generous Perfect," the monarch said to him, "your inclinations are too virtuous for you to be able to fear that Heaven will refuse you its protection, and you are too worthy of the scepter for it not to fall into your hands.

"Without having sought by a criminal curiosity to penetrate the secret of the gods, I can boast of having some knowledge of their supreme will. It is by virtue of that since that I believe I can assure you of their part, that you will reign legitimately, that you will marry Lisimene, and that Good and Better, who has always cherished you, will be delighted to see you reign with her. As I know both of them particularly well," he went on, smiling, "I believe I can assure you of their consent."

"There is no longer time, my Father," Perfect interrupted. "I have already said that I renounce the honor of their alliance; but I am agreeably flattered by the hope that you give me of being able to render my homage to them; nothing can perhaps be sweeter to me than that pleasure. Please," he added, urgently, "since you know their retreat, do not delay that glad satisfaction for me: I imagine one sensible to their sensible to their maintenance and I dare to flatter myself that the part I take in their misfortune might soften its cruelty. I can even, while awaiting the time when I can render them more essential service, procure them many comforts, which they doubtless lack. Finally, by means of the help of my friends, I can give them better protection than they have, and I can take away all fear of their falling into the hands of Ambitious; but that will be, if you please, without claiming any other recompense than the glory of doing my duty."

"But," said Good and Better, "does not that detachment from the throne come from the scorn in which you hold it, or some movement of hatred for Lisimene?"

"What are you saying, my Father!" cried Perfect. "Me, hate Lisimene, of whom all the world speaks as the most touching beauty? What heart could be so ferocious, far from having hatred for her, as not to be touched by her virtue, her attractions and her misfortunes? No, assuredly, I don't hate her; my sentiments are very far from those you attribute to me. I would no longer have been insensible to the desire to reign and simultaneously to be united with an illustrious person, for whom I have had throughout my life as much esteem as respect, but to possess two such great advantages it would have been necessary for me to be able to enjoy them without crime, which is henceforth impossible, since, not being able to be the husband of Lisimene, it would be necessary in order for me to

296

reign that, in imitation of my father, I continue to maintain myself in his usurpation, or, sacrificing my amour and that Princess to my unjust ambition, I married her solely in view of my interest, without my heart being able to follow the gift of my hand.

"No, no!" he cried. "Lisimene does not merit such insulting treatment; and the man who will be fortunate enough to become her spouse ought not to be animated be any other passion that that of pleasing her."

"I have however, resolved," said Good and Better, "to enable you to receive Lisimene for a wife; I even flatter myself that you will not refuse her from my hand, and that I shall have enough power over your mind to remove all the difficulties that you have formed in regard to that alliance."

In saying those words, he took his daughter by the hand. "Behold," he said to him, "that unfortunate Princess, whose fate is no longer deplorable. Since you love her, receive her from me, dear Prince, and with her, receive also her rights and mine to a throne that belongs to me, which I cede to you joyfully, and of which you will be able to make full value when the time comes."

"What, Sire," cried Perfect, throwing himself to his knees, "you are the virtuous King Good and Better, whose misfortunes have moved me so greatly! My adorable Liron is the august and excessively unfortunate Princess Lisimene! Oh, great King," he went on, with a transport of dolor and tenderness, "how can you see at your feet without horror the son of a rebel subject, whose ingratitude and perfidy have caused all your misfortunes?"

"Let us not talk any more about our common misfortunes, my son," said the generous monarch, embracing him. "I find that you have more to lament in having, with so much merit, a father so unworthy of you, than I have had in the state to which his perfidy has reduced me." He turned to the Princess. "But my Daughter, for being the son of an unworthy father, this Prince ought not to appear any less estimable to you. On the contrary, it is necessary to agree that he has more virtue than another, for not having succumbed to bad examples and the pernicious education that he was given to begin with. Thus, I order you to love him, or rather," he continued, agreeably, "I permit you to do so, and I approve of your sentiments; for I know that you have not waited for my consent to surrender to your penchant.

"Don't blush, Princess," he said to her. "That inclination has nothing that that could offend the most austere duty. You have been able to give it limits so narrow that severity itself could not have prescribed others. I also know that if virtue had been ordered to you, you would not have hesitated to sacrifice that inclination to it. But nothing can be encountered more fortunate than the innocent sympathy that I find between you, to which I tried to give birth in your early infancy.

"So, Prince," he went on, addressing Perfect, "I give you my daughter, and I do not believe that it would be possible for me to do anything more advantageous for her. But at present, it is a question of knowing what you are going to do to conserve that gift, without exposing all of us to almost inevitable dangers."

Good and Better had picked a bad time to put Perfect's prudence to the proof. That lover was so enchanted by his happiness that it was impossible for him to think of anything but testifying to his dear Princess the joy by which he was penetrated. Emboldened by the King's approval, he kissed his mistress's hands with a transport that took away any other concern than that of tenderness.

"Charming Lisimene," the Prince said to her, "is it permissible for me to flatter myself that you will confirm by a voluntary confession the generosity of your father, and that you will suffer without difficulty that he disposes of your hand in my favor? Whatever joy a present so precious ought to give me, I confess that it could only make my felicity, and that it would, on the contrary, only serve to cast me into despair, if you refused to confirm the gift with that of your heart. Speak freely, beautiful Princess, and do not constrain yourself; my efforts to place you back on the throne are independent of my amour. I know my duty, and if I were unfortunate enough not to please you, that misfortune could not disengage me from the cares of a subject. I would believe myself no less obliged to work to render you a property that belongs to you so legitimately."

"Milord," said Lisimene, smiling graciously, but with a hint of embarrassment, "why do you want to force me to express my sentiments in your regard? I could have some reason to complain of that violence. Has what I have done thus far proved to you that I have any hatred or scorn for you? Oh, Prince, without wanting me to employ terms that are so new to me, ought you not say to yourself that when you have talked to me about your amour, and that I have informed the King of it, I have admitted that you are not indifferent to me; that I have even added that, in wanting to deprive himself of the quality of father, he has only wanted to act with me in that of friend and confidant. Thus, you ought to be convinced that in what he has said to you, he has sought as much to favor my inclination as to content yours and his own.

"Is it the sacrifices that you were disposed to make for me," she went on, tenderly, "that should make you apprehensive that I have changed my sentiment? No, my dear Perfect, you ought not to have that anxiety, and the King, in permitting me to love you, has given me a further testimony of his generosity."

A response so obliging gave so much satisfaction to the Prince that he was only able to express a small fraction of it; his eyes said more than his mouth, and the shepherdess responded to them with all the urgency that modesty could permit.

The King knew that Perfect was not sufficiently himself to concert in planning the measures necessary to their security, and, thinking that they were not pressed for the moment, put off taking them until the next day, when, prudence being in a state to operate, they would be more accurate and surer. Thus, he thought that he ought to let the lovers enjoy the pleasure that two young hearts savor in the liberty of a first conversation, and, drawing away on the pretext of having some reading to do, which he seized with great pleasure, he left them alone.

After having read for a time considerable enough to give his daughter and Perfect the opportunity to say many things to one another, Good and Better returned to them, in order to remark that it might been appropriate to have a light meal.

It would, in fact, have been very light, for Richarde, accustomed to not giving any others to the shepherdess, did not put her in a state to invite two people to eat provisions so meager that they were scarcely sufficient for one alone. The joy that accompanied the guests, however, would have made them find the insipid dishes of which the feast consisted excellent, and they had already extended themselves on the grass when, a movement in the fountain having caused them to turn their heads in that direction, they saw the great naiad emerge, followed by many others, who immediately set up their crystal table, and served with as much diligence as propriety a repast that bore no resemblance to those that the father and daughter ate in their rustic cabin.

Although the King knew from the Princess's story that the fountain was inhabited, he was nevertheless struck by astonishment and respect, while the Prince, who was not informed, thought for a few moments that there was an enchantment; but the aquatic divinity soon dispelled that error.

"Great King, and generous Perfect," she said to them, "how can I express sufficiently the satisfaction that we have in seeing you assembled at our edge, and the pleasure I feel on my own part in being able to tell you that this happy event ought to be for you a favorable augury, which doubtless announces the imminent end of your misfortunes, and the commencement of all your prosperities."

The King and the Prince testified to Crystalline by a profound reverence the respect that she inspired in them. The naiad went on, addressing Lisimene: "You have mistrusted us, Princess, but I pardon you that mistrust, for the motive that caused it. You could not bring yourself to reveal to us a penchant to which you feared to yield; that discretion, or rather,

300

that timidity, has cost you difficulties that we would have spared you by informing you of the name and fate of your unknown.

"But that error is in the past, and you have savored the pleasure of the recognition all the more. At present, therefore, it is merely a matter, to ensure your happiness, of being attentive to the moment that will render your stepmother mistress of the fatal candle, and of not failing to seize it. When it is my hands, you can be sure, whatever obstacles might appear, that you will overcome them all."

Before speaking to them thus, Crystalline had invited them to eat, and she had served them in the interim. Seeing that their meal had finished, however, she had the table cleared, and bade them farewell, advising them to return without delay, in order not to arouse their enemies' suspicion.

After giving them that advice, she plunged under the water with her retinue, leaving all three of them extremely satisfied with that visit, as well as having the approval of such a benevolent deity and being sure of her amity.

Although they did not separate without difficulty, they did not hesitate to follow the advice of the obliging naiad, and the King, followed by his daughter, went back to their disagreeable abode, while Perfect went to rejoin his squire, who was waiting for him at a sufficient distance to have seen nothing of what had occurred. The Prince changed his clothes and remounted his horse, while Lisimene, the shepherdess Liron again, took her sheep back to the house, and her father, taking a different route, came back to it by another path.

The fortunate events of that day had given the lovable Princess a joy that shone in her eyes in spite of herself. That excess of contentment did not escape the gaze of the two Megaeras whom she was forced to join. Pigrieche, who was beginning to quit her bed, was the first to perceive it, and she pointed it out to her mother.

"Why is Liron joyful, then?" she said to her, loudly. "Apparently, she has some new mischief to inflict on me."

Liron replied mildly that it was unjust to accuse her of the woes she had suffered, and that she ought to remember that it was not her who had invited her to expose herself to them, since, on the contrary, after having experienced the same hazards first, she had given her all the advice she had appropriate to ward off the dangers she had run, and that that advice would have protected her if she had wanted to follow it.

Everything that Liron said was true; Pigrieche could not dispute it, but the shame of being obliged to confess that she was right was sufficient to excite her ill humor. She shouted, grumbled, and said all the harsh things that it was possible to imagine, without having the pleasure for that of causing any emotion to the shepherdess, whose heart and mind were too agreeably occupied with her lover that she did not pay the slightest attention to those screeches. When the time to go to sleep arrived she went tranquilly to lie upon her meager bed, leaving Pigrieche in despair at seeing her insensible to so much harshness, which augmented her rage and caused it to last all night.

She finally ceased grumbling, but that silence was not the work of slumber; on the contrary, she had never been so awake; so, without knowing the reason, Liron's joy gave her no rest. She wanted to penetrate its cause, at whatever price. That is why, having got up before daybreak, she slipped out of the house silently and went to hide a short distance from the fountain, in a clump of bushes that hid her from everyone's view.

Scarcely had she placed herself in that ambush when she saw the handsome Perfect appear, in the costume of a shepherd. She recognized him instantly as the same hunter to whom she had tried to sell pears, and who, in spite of the disagreeable scene that he had attracted upon her, she had not been able to help finding charming. She also remembered with pleasure that he had not contributed to her disagreeable adventure. Although her unworthy character brought her to complain about everyone and to hate the entire world, amour had the power to make the Prince an exception to the general rule; he appeared to her to be even more lovable than the first time, and she conceived for him at that moment a tenderness that was not made for such a surly heart.

But the ardor that Perfect inspired in her, and the jealousy that she had against Liron, rendering her clairvoyant, did not permit her to doubt that it was her of whom he had come in search in that solitude, and that the joy that she had seen shining in her face the previous evening could only come from their having spent the day together.

She was occupied with these conjectures when, to confirm them, the shepherdess appeared with her sheep.

As soon as Perfect saw her he ran to meet her, and Pigrieche had the mortification of seeing him at her feet, where he covered her with caresses, which the permission that her father had given for them enabled the agreeable reception.

Pigrieche would have liked to hear what they were saying, but she was too far away. She simply knew, from their movements, that they were not talking about indifferent things, without her being able to penetrate any further.

Seeing that she was making a futile effort in listening, not being able to hear the sound of their voices, she had all the more impatience to inform her mother of all that she had seen, and to consult her as to what she ought to do in order to obstruct the lovers. So, waiting for a moment when their backs were turned as they strolled, she slipped away adroitly enough not to be perceived.

The anger and jealousy that possessed her obsessed her so forcefully that she could hardly speak when she returned to her mother.

"What's the matter, my dear Pigrieche?" the latter said, on seeing her so emotional. "Has that miserable Liron given you some new subject for anger?"

"Ah," said Pigrieche, almost beside herself, "she's cleverer than us, and I'm no longer astonished that she goes to guard her sheep with so much submission and docility. She had her reasons, the sly chit; someone was aiding her to guide her flock; a handsome shepherd came to keep her company, in order that she didn't get bored alone. I've just seen them together without them seeing me, and I can assure you that they're very intimate with one another."

"Oh, the hussy!" cried Richarde. "I'd like to see what that imbecile father might say on learning that good news...but who is he?" she continued. "Do you know him? I swear by my head that if he's one of my slaves, I'll make him pay dearly with lashes of the whip for the pleasure he takes in wasting his time and robbing me of his work to go amuse himself with that little wretch."

"Good, good," said Pigrieche, "he's not afraid of you. Know that, far from being your slave, he's the hunter, her pear-merchant and the captain of those brigands who thought about murdering me out of spite because I took the place of that wicked Liron."

"Oh, I'll wait for Good and Better to tell him about her game," cried Richarde. "We'll see what he has to say to justify such conduct.

"What he can say!" say the furious Pigrieche. "Can you doubt it? Doesn't he always think that she's right?" She shed tears of rage, and went on: "But is it possible, then, that I'll only ever find men with no taste, and that I'll spend my entire life sadly in this frightful solitude, while that insolent child pleases everyone who sees her, and everyone incessantly gives her an unjust preference over me? For I can see only too clearly that if our pastors or our slaves dared to lack respect for me without fear of the whip, I'm certain that they'd serve her before me. It's necessary to admit that I'm very unfortunate."

At that reflection the tears were redoubled, and to console her, her mother told her that it ought not to seem strange to her that people as coarse as their pastors found Liron more agreeable than her, because people ordinarily love their peers.

"But with regard to the handsome shepherd," Richarde continued, "he only saw you for a moment, and perhaps if he saw you again, you'd triumph over that ugly little thing, for you're surely much prettier."

"I think like you," said Pigrieche, calming down, "and I'm convinced that the shepherd is only amusing himself with her out of pure idleness, and for want of anything better, or enticed by the advances that she's stupid enough to have made him."

"Well, if you believe me," said the mother, "you'll take the flock out tomorrow and make the acquaintance of the shepherd."

Pigrieche was dying to do that, but past events had made her apprehensive. "I'm unlucky," she said, "and I fear that some catastrophe might overtake me."

"What are you afraid of?" Richarde replied. "What danger is there in guiding sheep? It's not a matter of going to the witches' mill or looking for devils in the water. It's only one man, who won't be brutal enough to beat you, and if he doesn't welcome you as he ought, you can simply leave him there and come back."

"All right," said Pigrieche, encouraged by what her mother said. "I want to, and I'll do it, since you advise me to. But guarding sheep is only a vain pretext. Am I not the mistress of strolling where I live without asking permission from anyone or rendering an account to anyone? I intend to make him know the difference that there is between me and the shepherdess. Besides which, I'll never find a more appropriate opportunity to do myself honor and adorn myself with the beautiful gems that I brought back from that accursed Mill of Misfortune."

Richarde applauded that plan. She had several good reasons for that, for, in addition to the fact that she knew that it was not safe to contradict the gentle Pigrieche, she also expected that her daughter would be so greatly embellished by her adornment that the shepherd would not be able to resist such victorious attractions, sustained by the brilliant gleam of the jewels. She hoped to obtain another profit, too, and resolved to drop as many stones of the side of Pigrieche's bad eye as she could appropriate unknown to her daughter. Furthermore, she had no doubt that when the shepherd saw her so magnificently clad, he would take her for a Princess, or at least the daughter of a financier, and would be very honored to be loved by and to marry a person so beautiful and so rich.

Thus, Richarde concluded that it was unnecessary to suffer any longer that Liron should take the flock to the fountain, because it would be much more comfortable in a park near the house, and, no longer giving her that pretext to leave the house, she would forbid her to stray from their dwelling, thus removing all the means she had of seeing her shepherd. He, no longer finding her and only seeing the beautiful Pigrieche, would soon forget his first amour in order to devote himself entirely to his new one.

Things were thus arranged between Richarde and her daughter. The impatience that Pigrieche had to see herself adorned did not permit her to wait for daylight; she wanted to work on her attire before the night was half passed. She had neglected the day before to have her hair let down by Liron, who had presented herself at the unusual time, but unnecessarily, because Pigrieche wanted to go and hide in the bushes. In consequence, the reeds had not failed to reappear at the appointed hour.

She could have got Liron out of bed to suppress them, but, not wanting to give her any indication of her design, she preferred to keep them. As those flowers and reeds had become a part of herself, the excess of her self-esteem had enabled her to become accustomed to them, and she took her folly so far as to imagine that the singularity had a kind of elegance that suited her marvelously. In consequence, far from waking Liron to rid her of them, she repented of not having paid more attention to the graces that the verdure gave her, promising herself not to remove them again.

She got out of bed, therefore, and, when she looked at herself in the mirror, it confirmed her in the idea of the charms that the strange coiffure lent her.

She took the dress that the miller had given Liron, combined with it a decoration of gemstones intended to heighten its beauty and bring it out perfectly, casting an unparalleled gleam. As she had a prodigious quantity of them, she put them everywhere, unsparingly, only consulting her fantasy in so doing.

When she had attached so many that there was no more room, she thought about her coiffure. But as she could not put up her hair on her own she engaged her mother to get up as well, and in spite of the suspicion she had been given of her probity, Pigrieche was forced to make use of her to aid her.

Richarde rendered her that office joyfully, reckoning that it was the surest means of appropriating a few jewels. Forming strings with all the gems that could be enlaced together, she made use of them to knot to reeds into tufts. The result was somewhat reminiscent of an accumulation of glittering horns, which, mingled with a few more diamonds, make the beauty's russet hair sparkle. That last feature put the finishing touch to her allures. When she had as many as she could carry on her head and her dress, she made a few bands of them around her neck and arms.

In that state, brilliant ant ridiculous, she might have been mistaken for one of the idols, as precious as they are frightful, with which the temples of China are ornamented.

Having finally made the last adjustment to her attire, and believing herself then to be at least as beautiful as she was rich, she wanted to go out in order to experience the power of her charms. But the daylight did not second her impatience; it had not yet appeared, with the result that, fearful of wolves, she was obliged to suspend her excursion. Having nothing left to do for her beauty, she threw herself on her bed to wait for dawn.

In spite of the desire she had not to remain there for long, she became drowsy, while her mother, who had no intention of accompanying her on her stroll, went back to bed and fell profoundly asleep.

Scarcely had she savored the first pleasures of slumber, however, than Pigrieche's repose was cruelly interrupted by the pain of numerous insupportable stings, which all made themselves felt simultaneously.

She leapt to the floor, only half awake, but the pain, which was augmented from one moment to the next, soon succeeded in rendering her the usage of her senses. Imagine her terror when, on opening her unique eye, she saw that she was covered with wasps and hornets, which occupied the places of the gemstones that she had taken the trouble to position with as much pleasure as profusion. Every diamond had been converted into one of those insects, which were working hard to make her suffer a thousand torments.

At the screams she uttered, Richarde leapt out of bed, without any precautions, ran half-naked, and thought she would die of dolor on seeing her dear daughter, whom she could scarcely recognize, in the midst of the cloud of insects by which she was surrounded. As time was pressing, and it was necessary not to waste any, she had recourse to a broom that she found close to hand, with which she started driving the cruel beasts away.

Her charitable intention as followed by an unfortunate success, for a corps of five or six thousand enemies, having been detached from the bulk of the army without weakening it overmuch, hurled itself on Dame Richarde and put her in a state of no longer being able to think about anything but her own peril, which, in a moment, was no less than that of her daughter.

She was not the only one to whom Pigrieche's misfortune became common. Several slaves were enveloped by the same disaster. And far from employing themselves to one another's relief, they only managed to get in one another's way. Some threw themselves against the walls and risked breaking their heads in order to crush the wretched insects. Others burrowed under the beds. Yet others, more courageous and more prudent, ran to jump in the water, at the risk of drowning, and all of them, in unison, uttered such frightful howls that the place bore more resemblance to a wild beasts' lair than a human habitation.

That frightful racket, which the tranquility of the night and its darkness rendered even more evident, finally woke the

King and the Princess, and frightened them greatly without them being able to divine what they had to fear. They got up, however, and ran to where they heard the most noise.

The surprise caused to them by the horrible spectacle was unparalleled, and in spite of the grounds for complaint that they received continually from the mother and the daughter, without reflecting on the danger there was of sharing their torment in trying to help them, they courageously set about driving away the wasps. The pain that was rendering the mother and daughter furious, however, almost took away the desire to relieve them, especially Pigrieche, who was, so to speak, embroidered by the insects. The King found no other expedient to deliver her from the torture she was enduring than to take her in his arms and carry her outside, where he did everything he could to rid her of those enraged squadrons, at the risk of being devoured himself. But although he exposed himself, as Liron did, without taking any precautions, they did not receive the slightest sting.

Finally, after having had a great deal of difficulty undressing Pigrieche and her mother—whom dolor and lassitude had caused to lose consciousness—they plunged them into vats full of water. It was there that, finding a little relief, Pigrieche gave Liron time to rid her of all the dangerous ornaments that she had strewn over her head. She also removed the charming reeds by the same means, decorations henceforth useless, on which Richarde's daughter had founded the hope of so many conquests.

When the mother and daughter were delivered from that furious quantity of torturers, the King, aided by the Princess and some of the slaves who had had the good fortune not to arrive soon enough to share in their mistresses' torture, carried them elsewhere and put them, half-dead, in beds, where the wasps could not reach them.

Pigrieche, who had been more difficult to strip than her mother, because she was fully-dressed, had also been more maltreated, and her head was so swollen that it was monstrous. Although she had a mouth of enormous natural grandeur, the swelling had shrunk it to a point that it was only with a great deal of difficulty that a few aliments could be trickled into it. In spite of that frightful state, however, she made an effort to ask, in a language that was almost unintelligible where there were any of her gems left. Her dolor was augmented by half when she learned that not a single one remained and that they had all been changed into wasps.

At that fatal news she cursed, mumbling, the miller, the mill, her mother, who has sent her there, and above all Liron, to whom she attributed that event, in spite of the cares that the amiable Princess took to relieve the monster, which she perceived without being touched by any sentiment of gratitude, having similarly forgotten that she had given her all the advice necessary to avoid accidents, to which she had only succumbed by her obstinacy in not doing what she had been recommended to do and the greed that had exposed her to ill-treatment by the dogs.

As the advice by which the mother and the daughter had determined that Liron would cease to guard the sheep had been kept between themselves, the shepherdess had no knowledge of it. She went out at the usual hour, her enemies not being in any state to pay attention to it. And while the King, whose kindness was inexhaustible, hastened to seek remedies for the domestic furies, the daughter occupied herself more agreeably in conversation with her lover.

The help that Good and Better had the generosity to give the unworthy invalids had as much effect as one could have wished, and they were extremely relieved by it. After three days, they were beginning to see clearly, and were in a state to get up. It would take time before they were fully cured, but in proportion to what they might have suffered, and what they had had to fear, they were very glad to have got out of it at that price.

As soon as they could converse with one another, Pigrieche, in whose heart ingratitude seemed to crown all the other vices, only employed the health that she owed to her stepfather to inspire in her mother the intention she had to undo the innocent Liron. The amour that she had conceived for Perfect, and the jealousy that the dangerous competition caused her, redoubled once again the desire she had to doom her.

"You can see," she said to her, "without being able to deny it, that I have no hope of having anything in this world while that pernicious creature lives; she spreads a visible misfortune over my slightest actions, while everything succeeds as desired for her. It's absolutely necessary that she dies, in order to put an end to the evil spells that she's put on me."

Richarde tried to represent to her that she had an interest in conserving her life, since she was a slave who had cost her nothing but who was nevertheless very useful, bringing a considerable profit with very little expense. Pigrieche, however, who was not accustomed to seeing obstacles raised to her will, told her resolutely that if she did not give her a just satisfaction, she would be able to obtain it herself, and that, without paying any heed to the danger to which she would expose herself, she had resolved to plunge her knife into the odious Liron's heart.

Such a threat frightened Richarde. She loved her daughter, and did not doubt that she was violent enough to carry out her threat. Knowing, moreover, that she was in love with the handsome shepherd, she understood that the amour in question further augmented Pigrieche's fury against her overly fortunate rival.

Those considerations might have prevented her from hesitating to sacrifice her, for she did not hate Liron any less than her daughter could hate her. That interest being sufficient to destroy all the advantages she obtained from Liron, she would have ceded to the pleasure of satisfying her dear daughter if a more pressing motive had not retained her, which was the fear of consequences.

Although the habitation was far removed from any human commerce, it was not far enough away for it to be easy to put Liron to death with impunity. If that action were discovered, she would be exposed to inevitable execution, violence of that nature being published very severely by the law of the town, which made continual rounds in the vicinity of the most solitary places. In any case, how could one hope to stab the Princess fatally without her father raising an obstacle to it? In addition, Richarde was certain that none of her slaves would be bold enough to lend her their ministry, even less so because the kindness they experienced on a daily basis from the father and the daughter had won their affection to the extent that they were all entirely devoted to them, and far from wanting to harm them, they would have been the first to denounce their employers if they dared to attempt the life of Good and Better or his daughter.

Thus, in order to content Pigrieche, nothing remained to Richarde but the aid of poison. But she and Pigrieche, while knowing the name and having heard mention of its effects, did not know where to obtain it or how it was composed.

She strove to persuade her daughter that her arguments were just, and in the end she would have made her to yield to the impossibility of satisfying her, if the daughter's inexhaustible malice had not inspired a means that she believed to be infallible and against which her mother had no reply.

There was in the region a famous witch who lodged in the rocks scarcely two leagues from Richarde's house. The heart of that witch was more inclined to do evil that good; there was no one who could boast of having obtained any advantage from her amity, but there were many who had felt the effects of her hatred. When she took against someone, she caused their livestock to die and hail to fall on their crops, and those were the least of the evils that one had to fear on her part, for she often turned her fury in the direction of people, causing them to fall into a languor that was only terminated by death.

The various experiences that the inhabitants of the region had endured, and all the evils that happened to them coming from that direction, had finally obliged them to seize her. They would have drowned her if she had not had the industry to frighten them, by threatening them with an infinity of woes that, if she was to we believed, would not fail to fall upon them as soon as they had killed her, promising them, on the contrary, to heap them with benefits if they saved her life.

Interest on the one hand, and fear on the other, had preserved the wicked woman from the death that she had so thoroughly deserved. But the inhabitants of the desert only let her go after having demanded an oath that magicians cannot infringe, by which she promised not to pass the limits that were prescribed for her abode and never to do any harm to the inhabitants of the canton, either to those who had been born there or those who were to be born there in future, nor to their slaves, or even their livestock.

It was by means of that witch that the perfidious Pigrieche hoped to content her fury. Her mother, to whom she imparted the design she had to address herself to that dangerous woman, confirmed it with pleasure, adding that it was necessary to send Liron there, because the journey could not fail to cost her dear. But that was not Pigrieche's intention; she sensed only too forcefully, albeit to her great regret, that Liron's virtue, always enabling her to triumph, would not fail to get her out of trouble. Thus, not wanting to give her material for further triumphs, she entered into fury at that proposal.

"What are you thinking, speaking in that fashion?" she said to her mother. "You apparently intend that that unworthy little creature should come back laden with yet more treasure to cause me more pains and make me experience catastrophes even more cruel than the first ones. Are you forgetting that we've never attempted to put her in danger without enduring the displeasure of seeing everything that becomes a subject of joy for her converted into bitterness for me?

"No, no," she added, "I don't intend her to go to see the witch; this time, it's necessary that you make the journey yourself, for the sly Liron would certainly seduce her if she tried, and by means of her hypocritical expression she'd make the effects of the just anger we have against her fall back upon us. So, mother, go find that woman, and above all, describe Liron's malevolence to her, and her dangerous skill."

Richarde, who had initially approved that idea, suddenly remembered that such a step would be futile, since the witch, bound by her own oaths, no longer had the power to do evil. She represented that to Pigrieche, but the objection threw her into a fury.

"It doesn't matter," she cried. "Go anyway. I can see clearly that you're only seeking vain pretexts to protect your shepherdess, and pretending not to know that practitioners of the black sciences always have equivocations ready to get themselves out of difficulty."

Seeing that her daughter was getting carried away, Richarde dared not contradict her any longer, and departed without delay. After having seen her set forth, Pigrieche went out herself in order to go and hide in some hollow tree near the fountain, in order to be within range to overhear the discourse of our two lovers.

As the distance between Richarde's dwelling at that of the witch was not considerable, she did not take long to arrive there, and that dangerous individual, informed by her art of the visit she was about to receive, came to meet Richarde at the edge of her limits. She was mounted on a large black stag, and having set Richarde on its rump, it only took her three minutes to return to her lair.

It had been so long since the witch had done any harm that, on seeing an opportunity reborn that was so much to her taste, it seemed to her that she was reborn with it.

"King's wife," she said, to the woman who was so little worthy of that name, "I know what brings you here, and I can satisfy your desires, although it will not be without difficulty, for the divinities of the waters, those of the earth and even those of the air have granted their protection to your enemy, and will not suffer her to be unfortunate for long. But if I cannot attack her happiness, I can put limits on her life and render you mistress of it, in spite of all the powers that are interested in her favor and in spite of the engagements I have made not to do certain things."

"Powerful and marvelous woman," Richarde said, "your promises flatter my dearest desires, but I fear that the zeal you express to render me service might surpass your power, since you are engaged by oath not to harm anyone..."

"It's true," the witch interrupted, "that I'm limited not to undertake anything against those who were born or will be born in the canton, but fortunately for us," the Megaera added, with an overflowing of joy, "Lisimene is excepted from that rule, since she is not from the region and only has an accidental domicile here, which prevents her from enjoying the constraint I'm in, and excluding her from my engagements Furthermore, it won't be me who will attempt her days, but you.

"Look, King's wife," she continued, "it will be by means of this candle that your will and the fate of your enemy will be decided. Lock this treasure away preciously, and only make use of it when you want to terminate the life of the Princess. For this candle is made in such a fashion that your stepdaughter will cease to see daylight at the moment when its light is extinguished. But for the charm to have its entire effect, and for that action not to have any danger for you, it's necessary that when it is no more than a stub, you throw it on the ground and you say, stamping on it in order to snuff it out: 'Finish with you the one against whom you were formed.'

"Those words will have the power to take away Lisimene's life. Adieu. Go home, but above all, refrain from too much precipitation, and don't forget that if you choose your time badly, not only will the candle cause someone's death but it will take away everything that is dear to you in your loss."

After these words she put the fatal candle in her hands, and gave her a light tap on the shoulder, which had the power of putting her to sleep. Richarde only woke up again when she was outside the limits of the witch's domain.

Good and Better's wife delighted to find herself the arbiter of Liron's days, returned home triumphant. However, she could not savor that satisfaction with a perfect tranquility; the last words that the old Fury had spoken to her gave her some anxiety. She thought that, since she had not disdained to enter into her sentiments and her designs for vengeance, she might have explained more clearly, to prevent her by means of her advice from falling into the accidents that she made her apprehend, it being almost impossible to protect herself against dangers that were unknown.

She was in that uncertainty when Pigrieche appeared; her presence expelled from her mother's mind all the reflections that had been tormenting it a moment before.

The young woman, impatient to be instructed as to the success of the abominable journey that Richarde had made at her solicitation, came to meet her with great urgency. She was delighted to see the candle, and having learned its usage, she wanted to put it into practice without delay. But her mother, retained by two powerful reasons, refused to satisfy her impatience.

The first reason was that it was necessary to buy a slave to replace Liron before getting rid of her, and the other, which was of no less consequence, came from the dread of choosing her time badly and falling by virtue of too much precipitation into the inconvenience by which she had been threatened.

"Why so much hurry?" she said to her. "Since Liron's life is entirely at our disposal, we will always be the masters of taking it away from her whenever we wish, and we run the risk of doming ourselves by an imprudent precipitation. We are threatened with death if we light that candle at the wrong time, and it would be to expose ourselves visibly, for that simpleton of a King, desperate at the loss of his daughter, would doubtless kill us to avenge himself; and if that misfortune happened to us, what would we have to say about it?"

Waiting for a surer occasion was not at all to Pigrieche's taste, the ardor to rid herself of her rival overriding the fear of the accidents of which her mother seemed apprehensive, without being able to give her good reasons to combat her own. She would have prevailed by her screeching and her importunities if Richarde, as a last resource, had not taken it into her head to tell her that when Liron was dead, no one would be able to take away the clumps of reeds and gladioli by which her head was shaded.

"You can be sure," she told her, "that the verdure in question will not fall without returning incessantly; you'll be permanently crushed by that disagreeable weight. So, before depriving ourselves of Liron, who is the only one capable of removing it, it's at least necessary that we have engaged her to obtain from her friends that they undo their fine work."

It required no less that such a consideration to make Pigrieche consent to the delay on which Richarde insisted. She was disabused of the hope that the marsh would fall off if Liron died, or rather, had never had it, and had ceased to feign it. Nor did she persist in the idea that it was an ornament for her; the weight with which she was charged was augmented every day, as well as the infection that accompanied the burden, which made her desire to be rid of it.

On the other hand, the conversation she had overheard animated her more than ever to Liron's doom. Hazard had served her curiosity only too well in guiding the shepherdess and her lover toward the tree in which she was hidden. They had scarcely begun to greet one another that Good and Better had arrived, who, on reaching them, had said, graciously: "Well, my children, are you not sufficiently convinced of your mutual tenderness? And is it not time to take serious measures to render you happy without difficulty?"

"My Father," Perfect replied, kissing his hand respectfully, "permit me only to occupy myself in the pleasure of admiring the charming Lisimene, while entrusting myself to your prudence, in swearing to you to follow blindly what you deign to prescribe to me."

"Nothing is better said," said the King, "but it's impossible for me to execute our projects alone. If I were still on my throne, I would only charge you with the care of loving her and that of uniting you would occupy me uniquely, but Prince, you can see that I cannot give you a tranquil happiness if your father does not approve it. Thus, it is necessary to deliberate on the means we shall employ to engage him to consent to it. I can only imagine one, which is that you write to him and offer him, on my part, an entire abdication of my rights in his favor, while you oblige yourself to let him enjoy them, and never emerge from the respect and obedience that you owe him. It's necessary that you also write to the Prime Minister and charge him with representing to Ambitious that nothing is more convenient to his interests, since my daughter, not being in his power, might marry some Prince who would make use of her just rights and bring into his Estates a war whose outcome would be dubious. The Vizier has virtue and credit, and I'm certain that he will do his best to satisfy you.

"However," the monarch went on, "as, in spite of his eloquence and the merit of his reasons, your father might not yield to them, and might have the intention of punishing you for your attachment to his enemy, it's prudent that you put yourself in a condition not to fear his wrath, and that you fortify yourself in this country. It is easy to defend, since it's impossible to reach it other than through deserts and immense forests, or by sea, which is dangerous on these coasts because of the rocks by which they're surrounded.

"The brave young men who have followed you will be delighted to distinguish themselves in your service, and the old soldiers who have followed their example and preferred to follow you in your exile rather than remain with the usurper will give those young heroes lessons capable of rendering their zeal profitable. In addition, the local people, whose valor surpasses the ordinary limits, and who are not enfeebled by the delights of a voluptuous Court, love you dearly and would be able to defend you alone. Furthermore, the climate seems to contribute further to your security, since this land furnishes everything necessary to life and is not without pleasures.

"So, Prince, my advice is that, without delay, you put everything to work that might contribute to your defense, in having the ancient fortifications renewed and adding new ones to them.

"It is not, my dear Perfect," Good and Better continued, "that I am inviting you to fail in your duty; on the contrary, I am advising you to leave Ambitious the throne that he had bought too dearly, since it cost him his virtue. And whatever advantage the strength of arms might give you over him, I urge you never to pass beyond the limits of this province to pursue him. Let those limits be those of your ambition. Whatever injustice your father does, do not forget that he bears a name sacred to you; but although the title of son forbids you to attempt anything against him, it does not oblige you to allow yourself to be immolated by an unjust sentiment. Without fear of offending honor and nature, you can defend yourself in a place that does not even seem to be of this world, and only merits being regarded as a part of my daughter's rights.

"That is what I think," he continued. "Tell me now whether your sentiments are in conformity with mine."

"Whoever could think otherwise," exclaimed Perfect, "would not be worthy of belonging to you and being Lisimene's husband. But Sire, I find in your sentiments all the generosity and virtue imaginable, without seeing what I desire the most. You speak to me of the conduct I ought to have with my father, but you have not explained the assurance of my happiness. You have not told me whether, if he is unjust enough to refuse his consent to my marriage with the Princess, that obstacle is sufficient to prevent me from seeing an end to my troubles. Can I not hope to possess your charming daughter without being obliged to wish for my father's death? Oh, Sire, don't expose my virtue to such a dangerous proof; although I admire the generosity of your advice and I am happy to submit to it, my reason cannot sustain that uncertainty if it endures, and it might be capable of taking my life."

Good and Better was surprised by the agitation in which he saw Perfect. He made no reply, and fell into a profound reverie. But the young Prince brought him out of it by beginning him with the most forceful insistence to explain himself.

"If you don't decide in my favor, Sire," he said to him, "permit me only to follow your advice in part, after having endured the unjust refusal, of which I am almost certain in advance. I shall abandon myself to the despair that offers me no other way out than that of renouncing life or of raising our Estates against the usurper and obliging him, by force of arms, to accept the conditions that would have ensured his felicity had he listened to virtue.

"I know that Prince," Perfect added. "He is implacable. Judging my heart by his own, he will not believe that he can reign in safety if he sees me in possession of the legitimate rights that I will have received from the Princess. Thus, I have no other course to take, apart from the one I propose, except to put myself in his hands, and leave my mother's hatred free to act; she would be delighted that her husband will have a plausible pretext for depriving me of the throne, which her predilection destines for my brother, and will not spare my life, in order to destroy all the obstacles that she can find to her designs."

"Heaven preserve you from executing a design so cruel, my dear child," exclaimed the King, "and, without becoming criminal toward your father, it is necessary to hope that the gods with soften the heart of Ambitious and that our common happiness will not cost you a crime.

"I have given my advice," the good King added, "and you have approved it; instead of abandoning yourself to despair, tell me yours, and be persuaded that you will always find me disposed to do everything in your favor that is possible to me."

"Since you render me hope," said Perfect, "and you permit me to respond, I beg you, Sire, to tell me what inconvenience you see in granting me the hand of the Princess now, without awaiting an assured refusal. You cannot be unaware that it is not ambition that engages me to seek your alliance. The design that I expressed to renounce the throne in order to possess the shepherdess Liron is a sure guarantee that I am only seeking in Lisimene the happiness of being hers, and I beg you to consider that if our marriage were made, my father would be forced to approve it. At the worst, I would defend our refuge with a more legitimate right, as the son-in-law of the veritable King, rather than a son in revolt, whose steps might always have an appearance of rebellion, which would detach all virtuous hearts from my party.

"Furthermore, Sire," he added, "in the proposition that I am making, you ought to see two real advantages: firstly, that of not being separated from a daughter who is dear to you, and secondly, of seeing yourself at the head of your subjects, whose courage has need of the presence of a master capable of defending them against a tyrant who oppresses them. It is the only means of rendering them the happiness they had before.

"Finally," the Prince continued, my father might perhaps be constrained to leave us in repose in this province almost unknown to the rest of the realm—which is more appropriate to serve as a retreat for wild beasts than to excite the desire of humans—if you appear here in a fashion worthy of you and if I have the honor of belonging to you by virtue of such tender bonds.

"I confess," he added, "that I envisage in that tranquil life a happiness that makes me desire it ardently, and that my joy would be unequaled, since I would see you sheltered from the caprices, and perhaps the perfidies of the terrible creature with whom fate forced you to seek refuge. Forgive me that term, but the unworthy conduct of the person of whom I speak is so undeserving of the honor you have done her that I would think myself the happiest of men if I were able to remove you one day from the cruelty and persecutions of that Megaera."

Perfect's arguments had nothing in them that was not plausible, and made visible a tenderness for the King by which that good Prince was touched. In spite of their force, however, and all the advantages they had for his security, he was very reluctant to give his daughter without the consent of Ambitious, being good enough to believe that the agreement of the tyrant was necessary and that in its absence, it would be forming a criminal alliance. But Perfect was able to represent to him so vividly the unfortunate situation he was in and the perpetual danger that he and Lisimene were running that he could not resist any longer.

Lisimene, who had not mingled in the conversation, awaited her father's orders with lowered eyes, but the King discerned through her discretion that the Princess shared Perfect's anxiety

"Since you both want it," the monarch said, "it's necessary to satisfy you. I consent to it, but let us at least put Ambitious in the wrong by exposing ourselves to his refusal. As we would then have nothing more for which to reproach ourselves, I will lend my hand without reluctance to a marriage that I projected even when I was the master of my estates."

Delighted with that assent, Perfect could not find terms to express his joy and gratitude. But Good and Better spared him the trouble by leaving him with his daughter, under the pretext of continuing a hunt with which he had colored his excursion, and Pigrieche, from her hiding place, had not missed a word of that conversation.

It is easy to judge the effect that it had in her heart. She thought she would suffocate with rage, and could not be soothed by the absence of the King, who only went away to allow the young lovers the liberty to congratulate one another reciprocally on such a happy success.

That conversation, more charming for them than for the desolate Pigrieche, lasted a long time, and the Prince would have taken it further if Lisimene, making an effort on herself, had not represented to Perfect that it was time to separate. Seeing that he could not retain her, he said, tenderly: "So you're leaving, my charming Princess, and quitting a lover who adores you to go find implacable Furies who take a barbaric joy in tormenting you...

"How I hate them," he exclaimed, "and how happy I shall be when a sweet marriage has delivered you from them." He went on, carried away: "I don't know whether I have enough power over my just resentment not to avenge you on those unworthy enemies."

"I ask you, on the contrary, as a favor," the Princess said, "for the only vengeance befitting us, which is merely a sovereign scorn, more not being permissible for me to bring down upon my father's wife... But my dear shepherd," she added, "Are we not avenged sufficiently by all the misfortunes that Pigrieche's brutality has attracted?"

Those words reminded Lisimene of the adventure of the naiads, that of the Mill of Misfortune and, most recently, that of the gems transformed into wasps. She could not help telling the whole story to Perfect.

The Prince, whose mind was satisfied, laughed wholeheartedly. The scene of the precious stones, especially, which she described to him, made him utter bursts of laughter that bore a thousand dagger-thrusts to the heart of Pigrieche, and those thrusts seemed all the more painful to her because the more she saw of Perfect, the more she was smitten with him. The stings she had suffered had not caused her as much pain as those she suffered from the Prince's joy at the story Lisimene told him.

That torment finally ceased by virtue of Perfect's retreat, forced by the Princess. Scarcely had he gone than she gathered her flock and went back to the house, while the furious Pigrieche emerged from the tree. What she had heard brought her rage to its peak. But in her unhappiness however, she had a malign joy in being informed of the most secret affairs of the young lovers, and promised herself to make advantageous usage of them.

That evil creature was agitated by all those impulses when she encountered her mother, who was arriving from the witch's abode, and it was then that, Richarde having shown her the candle, she learned its terrible virtue. Her excitement was so violent that, without amusing herself with the wicked woman's threats, she wanted absolutely not to postpone the use of the present until another time, only agreeing to the delay that prudence should have prescribed to her, because there was only Liron who could rid her of the marsh that was incessantly renewed on her head.

To put an end to all the representations that her mother made to her regarding such an important article, she said that she knew a very simple means of removing at a stroke the obstacle that was opposed to her enemy's death, since it was only necessary to summon her immediately and tell her that her father's life would be over if the reeds reappeared again.

Richarde, obliged to cede to her daughter's petulance, summoned he unfortunate Lisimene, and declared to her without preamble that if Pigrieche was not delivered forever from her ridiculous coiffure before the end of the night, Good and Better would be taken to the town the next day and surrendered to the tyrant.

That threat frightened the Princess so much that, without opposing the two malevolent woman, giving no thought to the impossibility there was of satisfying them, and the fact that the day had just given way to an exceedingly dark night, she ran to the fountain.

Although the location was quite a long way from Richarde's house, the sad Lisimene traveled the route with a diligence that would have exhausted her strength if the generous Crystalline, touched by the troubles and the piety of the virtuous daughter, had not come to meet her.

"Time is precious for you," the benevolent divinity said to her, when they met. "Turn back, and redouble your vigilance, or you are doomed. Although your enemies do not merit the mercy that they have sent you to ask of me, I shall grant it to them. But that mercy will only last as long as I need to make you safe and to work for your happiness."

With those words, she left her, and Liron, from whom the dread of the peril that threatened her father had taken away all memory of herself while she had had that anxiety, found herself overwhelmed by such weariness that she could hardly sustain herself once she no longer had anything to fear for him, and in spite of the diligence that the naiad had recommended to her for her own interests, it was impossible for her to return other than at a slow pace, leaning on her crook.

During her absence, the naiad's orders had been carried out, and without anyone being involved, the reeds had detached themselves from Pigrieche's had of their own accord, leaving to reign in their place her old, ugly red hair, with which the beauty was delighted. Self-esteem had always made her regard it as the most charming ornament that could ornament a head.

On seeing the verdure fall, she uttered a cry of joy, which departed less from the pleasure of seeing herself free from that odious burden than from the eternal remonstrations of Richarde, who was still opposing her daughter's fury on the pretext of the reeds.

"There's nothing more to stop us," she cried, "and that wretched Liron no longer being useful to us, it's absolutely necessary to light the fatal candle." Upon which, seeing that Richarde was still hesitant, she repeated everything that she had overheard. But although she succeeded in passing all her anger into her mother's heart, that woman, alarmed by the witch's menaces, still feared picking the wrong time.

"My dear Pigrieche," she said to her, "you're right to be irritated, I'm no less so than you are; but let's avenge ourselves more surely, and above all let's not render ourselves the victims of our own fury. To avenge ourselves successfully, let's act in a fashion that can have no fatal consequences. Let's deliver the father and daughter to King Ambitious, who will doubtless kill them, and that monarch, very glad to see himself delivered by our means, will reward us liberally..."

"Very good," Pigrieche interrupted, impatiently, "but if the politics of that Prince oblige him to let Liron reign, we'll be the dupes of those fine hopes."

Richarde pointed out to her that, in that case, nothing would be lost, because they could light the fatal candle then, which would cause her rival to fall at the first step she took to approach the throne.

As it mattered little to Pigrieche in what fashion she made the object of her hatred perish, she finally consented to the proposition made by her mother. But a very embarrassing difficulty presented itself: they did not know to whom it was necessary to address themselves in order to inform the tyrant of what it was so important for him to know, not believing that there was safety in giving that advice to the governor of the town, who as apparently devoted to Perfect, and who would doubtless inform that Prince of their intention. In that case, they had everything to fear on his part, and even that of Good and Better, it being not improbable that his mildness, great as it was, would be embittered by such a stroke of black malevolence.

Pigrieche's fury, however, inspired all sorts of expedients. "Is it so difficult," she said to Richarde, "to go to the royal city? You have only to embark and you can go there in a short time. It isn't as dangerous to go as it as to come back, because the fishermen in the region know the sandbanks and reefs that make these shores redoubtable to the most famous pilots when they aren't familiar with them.

"You can talk to the King yourself," she added, "and after having informed him of the evil intentions of those three criminals, you have only to ask, as a recompense for that signal service, that he enables me to marry his son. As he has no reason to fear the rights that I will bring to Perfect, whom he does not like, from what I overheard, there won't be any difficulty to raise, and there will also be a considerable advantage for you in the affair, since, being extremely rich and allied with Ambitious, you can't fail to find another husband."

Although it had been Richarde herself who had first made the proposal to denounce the father and daughter, she had not had a very strong determination, and, malevolent as she was, she could not form without horror the design of delivering to certain death a husband who had never given her any cause for discontentment, whose generosity, on the contrary had always prejudiced him. But the fear of a just resentment that Pigrieche made her envisage made up her mind, and finally caused her to resolve to depart in two days' time, in order to go and commit the most frightful of crimes, in betraying her husband and her King.

After they were both firm in that resolution, they stopped talking about it, because Good and Better appeared at that moment and Liron was not far behind him. To disguise their evil intentions, they constrained themselves not to quarrel with the father and daughter.

They were surprised by that; that mildness, so untypical of two such malevolent women would have been capable of raising many suspicions, if the King and the Princess had not been persuaded that the fall of Pigrieche's reeds and the joy that Richarde had in seeing the charms of the dear object of her wishes shining was the sole motive for such extraordinary good will.

However, as Liron hardly ever went to bed without visiting her bouquet, and the naiad had renewed the advice to be attentive to it, weary as she was, she did not fail to consult it, and not only did she find the gemstones tarnished, but one of them had even fallen off.

That warning left her in no doubt that it was time to search for the candle on which her security depended, and having taken her bouquet, she put it adroitly in a jug full of milk.

Scarcely was it there than everyone in the house fell asleep, nor excepting the slaves who were lodged in the most remote places, and even the dogs. The charm attached to the bouquet had spread a lethargy, rather than a slumber, over all the inhabitants.

Lisimene found herself free to do whatever she wanted in the midst of the sleepers, and immediately made use of the key that the miller had given her. Seizing the candle whose conservation was so important to her, she substituted for it the one she had brought from the Mill of Misfortune, about which Crystalline had just reminded her. Then she closed the cupboard, and after having taken her bouquet from the jug into which she had put it, she retired swiftly to the place where she slept, where, before going to sleep, she had the pleasure of seeing that the gemstones had become more brilliant than ever.

She was so agitated by the joy of having succeeded, and by the impatience to see daylight arrive in order to go and deposit the candle, so fatal and so precious for her, in the hands of her protectors, that she could hardly sleep a wink. No night had ever appeared so long to her; one might easily believe that the desire to see her lover again played the greater part in that impatience, but whatever it was, she departed as soon as the first light began to appear.

Running to the humid palace, she descended into it and gave Crystalline the candle on which the fate of so many people depended. The naiad received it with an obliging joy, by which Lisimene was delighted.

"Now we're sure of your happiness, beautiful Princess," said the nymph, graciously, "and we'll have the satisfaction before long of avenging you on your enemies by their own hands. They're going to fall into the trap that they've set themselves. I can now promise you with certainty that you shall be as happy as you are beautiful, always provided that you're prudent.

Lisimene was accustomed to enjoying herself extremely with the naiads, but at that moment she would have liked to be elsewhere, for she did not doubt that her lover was waiting for her.

Crystalline, who perceived her impatience, and was not unaware of what was happening in her soul, did not want to retain her any longer.

"Go, my dear Princess," she said, smiling. "Take advantage of your present happiness; the pleasure of seeing your lover will be even more touching for you than everything I have just predicted for you."

Lisimene blushed on seeing that the nymph had penetrated her sentiments thus, and she replied that she did not find any moments sweeter than the ones she had the good fortune to spent with her.

But Crystalline, with a playful and tender expression, said: "Be more sincere, and believe that we don't hold the preference that you don't accord us against you. Adieu, beautiful Liron," she added. "When you have some misfortune to dread, come to find us; we will do everything in our power to help you."

As she said those words, the nymphs took the Princess back to the edge of the fountain. She had scarcely emerged before Perfect appeared.

He begged her pardon a thousand times over for being the later to arrive, and had no difficulty in obtaining it; they said a thousand tender things to one another about what their separation had made them suffer, although it had only lasted for the space of a fairly short night.

The beautiful shepherdess, to whom the pleasure of seeing her lover again and the fortunate situation of their affairs gave a great deal of gaiety, remembering the obligations she had to the generous naiads, had an extreme desire to express her gratitude to them, and, knowing that it was not in her power to display it in a more agreeable fashion than playing a serenade, she took up her theorbo, and sang several songs in harmony with it. By the tremor of the waters, which began to agitate, on might have thought that they wanted to accompany the Princess's voice with their murmur, and the movement they made in the fountain announced the nymphs' satisfaction.

While Lisimene fulfilled the duties of gratitude in that manner and her lover shared the pleasure of it, Richarde was making preparations for her journey. Good and Better observed her without anxiety, believing, as she told him, that she was only going to the town where Perfect was resident and that the journey concerned the affairs of her commerce, in which he had never mingled, having no suspicion of her because he did not know that the secret had been discovered.

The envoy charged with Perfect's interests in regard to his father had already departed, and the Prince had also taken measures for his security. Following the advice of Good and Better, he had charged the old warriors to discipline their young soldiers, as well as the inhabitants of the cantons. In spite of the violence of his amour, he was no less occupied in taking the precautions necessary for his defense and for the safety of the King and his daughter. But while acquitting those cares, those he gave to his tenderness were no less keen.

On departure, Richarde, who did not trust Pigrieche, took with her the candle that she took to be the same one that the witch had given her. Either because she feared that her daughter might make use of it inappropriately, or because she wanted to be mistress of the Princess's life herself in case, contrary to her hope, Ambitious consented to ally himself with Good and Better, she did not want to leave it behind.

While she was occupied with the criminal concern of executing her abominable design without danger, the Prince and his lover were only thinking of enjoying the pleasure of loving one another and telling one another so without constraint. The King shared their happiness, and the naiads were often witness to the young lovers' transports.

In order not to trouble them in the pleasure they were enjoying, Good and Better took charge of planning in his study, in secret, the works that they wanted to carry out. Perfect had brought him a map of the locale, and everything that could be fortified in the province. Good and Better, who understood fortifications perfectly, traced all the works that he thought necessary, which were executed precisely by engineers who admired the talent of their Prince, for Perfect, not wanting to confide the King's secret to anyone, let them believe that the plans he gave them were of his own composition.

As the journey of the Prince's envoy could not be made as promptly as he would have desired, everything was in a state of defense long before Ambitious's response could arrive; the proposition with which the envoy was charged was of too great an importance not to be examined maturely, and unfortunately, there was too long a delay, for a few days before the response was made, Richarde arrived, when, in a secret audience that the usurper granted her, she informed him of the measures that her son was taking conjointly with Lisimene's father, in order not to be troubled or surprised in the execution of their design. Carefully refraining from talking to about him about what might have been able to justify it, she suppressed

330

what Pigrieche had overheard that was good and generous while they held council, saying, on the contrary, everything that might augment the anger and alarm of the tyrant, who was already very irritated by the propositions that Perfect had made.

As it was important for Ambitious to prevent such a dangerous secret from leaking out, however, he had Richarde imprisoned in an impenetrable place, and, having taken all the measures appropriate to such a delicate situation, he sent away his son's ambassador, only responding to his propositions with a formal refusal, without allowing it to be perceived that he had the slightest knowledge of the intimate liaison that there was between the King and the Prince, pretending only to see in the propositions political reasons dictated by the desire to reign.

Perfect was not astonished by a lack of success that he had expected, and instantly asked Good and Better to carry out the promises he had made him. The King did not hesitate to satisfy him; they resolved that all three of them would immediately and go very secretly to a little rustic temple that was not far away from the abode of the naiads. The high priest, altered by the Prince was ready for the ceremony, which as to take place without ostentation.

But Pigrieche, who spied on them incessantly, and who, by means of the bush in which she hid every day was informed of all their plans by their own mouths, seeing that the union so cruel for her was close to its conclusion, fell into an inexpressible despair. It was all the more violent because she did not know what to do in order to thwart the projects of the happy lovers. She cursed her mother's negligence a thousand times over, and the precaution she had taken in carrying away the candle, by means of which she would have administered justice at a stroke if it had been in her power.

That expedient lacking, her amour caused her to imagine another, which, although very extravagant, was not absolutely impossible. She flattered herself that it might succeed. That was to deceive Perfect and engage him to marry her instead of

Lisimene. Pigrieche knew of a herb whose virtue was to put to sleep for twelve hours anyone who lay on top of it, taking away all their sentiments. She went to collect a handful and put the under the King's bed, where the herb had its usual effect, putting the monarch to sleep so completely that he resembled a dead man rather than a man plunged in slumber.

Lisimene, finding her father in that state, tried in vain to wake him up, and, seeing him cold and motionless, did not doubt that he was dead, or on the brink of extinction. Then she abandoned herself to cries and tears, appealing for help to the gods and humans. She implored that of Pigrieche with the most humble supplications, but that Fury, far from being touched by a distress of which she as the cause and allowing herself to be softened by the dolor of the Princess, only thought of profiting from the state in which she had put the father and daughter. Putting on Liron's clothes, and covering herself with a great veil, she went to the place where her rival was awaited.

She was, in fact, awaited there with all the impatience of which amour is capable of causing in a veritably smitten heart. The Prince, who believed that he was within reach of the happiest moment of his life, had preceded the daylight by more than two hours, and there was only a very faint light when the surly Pigrieche appeared, under a resemblance that she was hardly cable of sustaining.

The Prince, deceived by the clothing, not failing to be mistaken, ran toward the feigned Lisimene with an urgency worthy of the one she was representing. "Finally, beautiful Princess," he said, utterly transported, "this is the happy moment that will unite us forever. How I have wished for the sweet moment of this charming union, which alone can make my happiness. No obstacles can delay it. But," he added, on seeing that the false Princess as alone, "where is your august Father? What can have retained him elsewhere, at a time when his presence is so necessary? Just Heaven!" he cried, "can the King have changed his sentiment?"

Pigrieche dared not reply for fear that her voice might betray her.

"What does this silence signify?" he continued, with a great deal of vivacity. "You are silent, my dear Lisimene, and at the moment when you ought not to fear saying too much! Oh, please, speak to me, tell me what has become of the King. Don't leave me in the trouble I'm in. Alas, why deprive me of the pleasure of your beautiful eyes? Lift that importunate veil, which you can resume when we're at the foot of the altar; we are in a solitude where that ceremony need not be observed as rigorously as at Court or in cities. But alas, are you not covering yourself to hide the reluctance you have to render me happy? Just Heaven, am I unfortunate enough that my love displeases you?

"If you still love me, my beautiful Princess," he went on, falling to his knees, "let me know that you share my happiness and extract me from such a cruel doubt."

With those words, the impatient Prince was about to lift the deceptive veil, whatever efforts the monster who was covered by it made to forbid him—but he did not have time.

Four men, who were immediately followed by thirty, emerged from between the trees, and seized him without him having a moment to collect himself let alone to defend himself. At the same time, several of their companions threw themselves on to Pigrieche, and they carried both of them off to the sea shore, where two ships were waiting for them. They put the Prince aboard one and Pigrieche, in spite of her screams, was put on the other.

But who could describe the dolor of the Prince when he saw Good and Better carried aboard, and by virtue of that cruel contretemps lost the hope of possessing Lisimene. What imprecations did he not utter against destiny, which he accused of a misfortune of which the execrable Richarde was the sole author, the abduction of the King, and his own being the fruit of the advice that that malevolent woman had given Ambitious, who had thought that he ought not to employ overt force against his son, nor commit to fortune a success that the valor of Perfect rendered very doubtful.

The tyrant had dispatched faithful men who were devoted to him and guided by one of his confidants, who, under the pretext of fleeing his cruelty, had pretended to be coming to seek refuge with his son. Because that happened quite often, they succeeded in deceiving Perfect, with all the more facility because Richarde had informed them precisely of all the Prince's steps, and above all the frequent journeys he had the custom of making to the places where Liron took her sheep to pasture, to which he went alone and without defense.

They had orders to abduct the lover and his mistress, but, deceived as he had been by Pigrieche's attire, they had seized her instead of the Princess, believing themselves very fortunate to have encountered her so fortunately.

Their commission was not limited to the abduction of the Prince and the object of is amour; they had been ordered above all to seize Good and Better.

To execute that order, while one party of the soldiers took away the lovers, the other went to Richarde's habitation, where they found the King. The sleep that Pigrieche's artifice caused him had just ended, but the monarch was still so dazed by it that he had a consciousness no more distinct than that of a man emerging from a long drunkenness. It was in that state that he was carried into Perfect's presence, and as the tyrant's satellites believed themselves to be in possession of all those they had been commanded to arrest, they departed immediately.

Lisimene, desperate at seeing her father abducted at the moment when she as beginning to recover from the apprehension into which his apparent death had thrown her, and seeing him fall into an even greater danger than the one from which he had just emerged, without any hope of being able to extract him from it, threw herself at the knees of the barbaric kidnappers, but she begged them in vain at least to grant her the sad favor of taking her with him.

They were deaf to her pleas and tears, and as they did not know the Princess, far from believing that her abduction was of any import to Ambitious, they took her for an affectionate slave, whom, in spite of their ferocity, they esteemed sufficiently not to mistreat, even though she threw herself in front of them and did everything she could to liberate her father from their hands.

In spite of all she could do, her efforts being insufficient, and her strength unequal to her good will, she had he dolor of seeing the King carried off by men who cared little enough about her person to refuse to charge themselves with her. But the fidelity she showed to Good and Better, whom they believed to be her master, touched them with a kind of compassion that did not permit them to think of doing her the slightest outrage, and, leaving her to utter futile cries, they fled with their prey, marching with such diligence that they had reached the vessel that as waiting for them and had left the shore before Lisimene could arrive there, even though she ran after them with all her might.

She only saw the vessel closely enough to know that Perfect had had the same destiny as the King. The dolor of the unfortunate Princess was redoubled, and, losing all hope, she ran for a long time without knowing where she was going. Finally, overwhelmed by dolor and lassitude, she let herself fall on to the grass, devoid of strength and almost unconscious, and only came round from that frightful state to envisage all the horror of her misfortune.

"Miserable creature that I am," she cried, in a voice almost stifled by sobs, "what will become of me, and what ought I to do after such a great catastrophe? My father and my husband will doubtless perish, and I am the cause of their misfortune. If Perfect had not been seized by the deadly amour that has doomed him, our common tyrant would have let him enjoy in peace the liberty he had in this desert. He would be living here tranquilly, and my father would have continued to support his ill fortune constantly. Only the desire that I had to get out of the deplorable situation I was in has precipitated them both into an abyss from which I cannot hope to see them emerge.

"Thus," she added, "I no longer have any resource but death. Well then, let's die."

With those words, she fell unconscious, which would have spared her the trouble of abridging her days, the state in which the Princess was in being more than sufficient to grant her that fatal aid. She would doubtless have expired if, by a fortunate hazard, she had not happened to be underneath the marvelous pear tree, which was on the path that the kidnappers had taken; it was near to that tree that Lisimene's strength had abandoned her.

There, her despair having reached its peak, she was finally ready to render her last sigh, when an extraordinary event recalled her to life, obliging her to make a diversion from her dolor.

The pear tree suddenly shifted, without it being agitated by any wind, and a voice that had nothing frightful about it, although it resembled the noise that a saw makes on wood, pronounced these words distinctly:

"What are you thinking, sad lover and unfortunate daughter? Is it by surrendering to dolor that you think to triumph over your misfortunes? Have you lost the memory of the nymphs of the fountain? How is it possible that you are scorning their aid?"

That reproach, which, without having any bitterness, was so appropriate to recall the Princess to herself, reanimated her courage and her strength. She stood up diligently and thanked the hamadryad that had given her such salutary advice, reminding the afflicted Princess of the protection of the naiads, which the dejection with which her unhappiness had overwhelmed her had completely effaced from her memory.

She ran to the fountain and threw herself into it with so much precipitation that she did not even think of calling the nymphs. She was well received nevertheless, even though those divinities might have had some reason to be offended by the lack of confidence she had had in them; Lisimene's dolor inspired too much pity to leave room for the slightest resentment and he naiads loved her too much to heap her with reproaches on such a pressing occasion. For a long time, tears were the only interpreter of her troubles, but Crystalline finally interrupted that sad silence with her kisses.

"I know your new misfortunes," she said to her, "and I cannot hide it from you, my dear child, that you will have need of all your constancy to support them."

"Alas, Sovereign of the Waters," cried the Princess, sobbing, "Is this the happiness you promised me, then, and is it only be founded on a virtue that does honor to a heart without soothing it? Have you forgotten what you said to me when I brought you the mysterious candle to which my days are attached?"

"I did not promise you that no more misfortunes would overtake you," said the naiad. "That exceeded my power, and I did not say anything else to you except that you would triumph over the evil intentions that were aimed at your life. I exhorted you to be patent; that is, in fact, the only resource you have today. But in spite of your present woes, you would be wrong to abandon yourself to despair, since that would raise an invincible obstacle to the remedies that they might yet have."

Those final words restored a little calm to the heart of the afflicted beauty, and rendered her a ray of hope. She thanked her benefactress, and begged her to add to all her kindnesses that of giving her a means to join her father.

"No, my dear Lisimene," replied the divinity, "I have ideas about that very different from yours, for I have resolved that you will remain with us until the moment that Good and Better and your lover are delivered from the hands of the usurper."

The Princess dared not resist, whatever regret she had in being distanced from her father the King, and perhaps from Perfect.

Meanwhile, Good and Better, Perfect and Pigrieche, having sailed for some time, arrived in Ambitious' court.

Pigrieche had become furious; she had made a thousand efforts to hurl herself on the sailors, whose eyes she wanted to scratch out, at the least. Her gross rages had been pushed so far that they were constrained to tie her up. She was very lucky that the error of those who were guarding her had persuaded them that they were charged with conducting a Princess, for if they had not been retained by the respect that the title in question imposed, they would have acted a little more familiarly with that beautiful prey. Convinced, however, that Pigrieche was Lisimene, they respected her in spite of her extravagances, although she told them a thousand times that they were mistaken, and that she was not the person they had been ordered to arrest.

They listened to that discourse as if it were a pretence; the only fruit she obtained from it for some time was to attract further considerations as the price of her rudeness, although they regarded her as a Princes unworthy of the high rank at which destiny had placed her. In the end, however, her redoubled rants, her ridiculous threats and the insults with which she seasoned them attracted the scorn and indignation of all those who were exposed to the torrent of her impertinence.

The rages of the supposed Princess diminished to some extent because the voice of the surly creature had lowered involuntarily, and she was weakened by the fatigue her cries had caused her. The sailors began to listen when she told them again in a softer tone that they were mistaken and that she was Richarde's daughter. But that clarification came too late to be favorably received and to be of any use to her; on the contrary, it nearly proved deadly, since the abductors, in despair of their mistake, deliberated as to whether they ought not to throw her into the sea. They were only retained because they hoped to justify themselves more easily by presenting her dressed in Lisimene's clothes and taking her as a witness as to the place from which they had abducted her.

If it had only been a question of returning to the desert in order to leave her there and capture the veritable Princess in her place, they would not have hesitated; but how could they hope to do that? It was not natural that the shepherdess Princess would have waited for them after the uproar that the three previous abductions that had caused in the locale, and above all in Richarde's house.

Another motive, caused by a sentiment of humanity, also prolonged Pigrieche's days. The man in command of the troop was not unaware of the fate that was in preparation for Lisimene, and although the fidelity that his officers had sworn to Ambitious, whom they regarded as their sovereign, had led them to acquit exactly the commission with which they had been charged, they could not think without pity that the death of the Princess had been decided. But as they presumed that she would be put to death when they arrived with a great deal of mystery, in order not to run the risk of a sedition in her favor and that of her father, they hoped that it might be done soon enough and secretly enough not to give their master time to penetrate the error that they had made. Thus, Pigrieche's death would produce two events equally advantageous for them and for Lisimene, since, while saving the life of the Princess, it would prevent their blunder from being discovered. The man to whom that thought had occurred communicated it to his companions, who all approved it.

The torment to which Richarde's daughter had subjected herself since her detention had been so violent that not only had she ceased to speak, but weakness had also obliged her to close her eyes, and she seemed to be buried in a profound slumber. That deceived her guardians, inhibiting their constraint and the precaution of moving away from her in order to discuss a matter that was so important to them; but Pigrieche did not miss a word of it.

The horror of the destiny that was prepared for her having rendered her strength, she recommenced uttering cries that went as far as howls. "What!" she screeched, struggling and making efforts to break the bonds that retained her. "You intend, scoundrels that you are, to save the life of a criminal Princess, at the expense of mine! Neither my innocence nor your duty being able to retain you, it's necessary that I perish

339

for the security of the unworthy Lisimene, that culpable Liron, who has seduced the son of the King, rendering him a rebel against his father's will, and took audacity so far as wanting to make him her husband!

"What fate has determined," she continued, "that my attempts to prevent that crime, far from doing any harm to a person as culpable, have turned to her glory, and become fatal for me? If she had gone to the assignation, it would have contrived prodigies for her conservation, whereas it has worked them for my doom.

"It's necessary to admit that virtue is severely persecuted at present," she added, "but, cowards and traitors that you are, don't expect that I shall suffer your attempt tranquilly and allow you thus to abuse the confidence that your King had in you. I shall alert him to that infidelity, and you will be punished as it merits."

Although Pigrieche said to them everything that she thought most appropriate to make them change their design, it was in vain that she deployed her petulant eloquence, and she was speaking to the deaf. Although the fear of death, and a death that would assure the life of her rival, had given her back the strength and the rage that her weakness had suspended, the men who were listening to her did not change their plan for that, and only laughed at the frantic woman's fury.

However, as her clamors troubled everyone's repose, and they prevented the sailors hearing the orders that were given to them for the maneuvers, the commander of the vessel, after having threatened several times to hasten the end of her life by throwing her into the sea, settled on another expedient to make her shut up, which was to put a stick in her mouth and attach it firmly behind her head, connecting it to the bonds that held her. That caused her mouth to remain open without her being able to proffer a word or utter a cry; and to prevent her from freeing herself from the stick they took the precaution of tying her hands.

That was not all, and Pigrieche's misfortunes were not at an end, for the reeds from which Liron had delivered her by soliciting the naiads in her favor came back with greater abundance than ever as they were getting ready to disembark.

That prodigy frightened everyone on the ship, and they no longer doubted that Pigrieche was a witch; which obliged the crew to watch her more closely in the dread that she might escape them.

The first concern of her guards, on arrival, was to put her in a profound and obscure cell, separated from Good and Better and very distant from Perfect's prison.

Ambitious, delighted to have his most redoubtable enemies in his power, judging that only a prompt execution could guarantee him against their vengeance and assured him tranquility, swore their death.

In vain the voice of blood tried to raise itself in favor of his son. The sentence of the Prince was pronounced like that of the others. It was enough that he was linked by affection and interest with Good and Better for him to be judged unworthy of pardon. In any case, the tyrant could not see any other means of uprooting all the seeds of rebellion than to sacrifice that unfortunate son and to make an example of him appropriate to intimidate those who might form the desire in future to conspire against him.

The Queen, even more barbaric than her husband, and who idolized Perfect's brother, fomented the King's fury by her most vehement discourse, and excited him to a double parricide.

Having assembled his Council, purely for form's sake, Ambitious caused the unfortunate Princes to appear there, reproaching his son for his pretended revolt, to which he gave the most odious and most criminal colors. Also imputing to Good and Better having seduced Perfect and having armed him against his father in order to topple the throne, he pushed calumny to the extent of saying that he had excited the Prince to kill him.

The captive King, whose courage and virtue, as well as the misfortunes that had overwhelmed him for such a long time, had, so to speak, disgusted him with life, made no effort to preserve his days. He employed his concern uniquely to justify Perfect, preferring to charge himself alone with everything that was imputed to him than to commit the Prince for his own justification, which would in any case have debased that unfortunate King too much. But as he was speaking to a prejudiced man and Ambitious wanted to doom his son, everything that Good and Better could say was futile.

Perfect and his companion were unanimously condemned to perish by fire. And the usurper, not yet being satisfied with those two victims that his tyranny sought to immolate, ordered that Lisimene also be brought, in order that he could reunite her by death with her father and her lover.

The two illustrious prisoners has sustained with an admirable constancy the sentence that had just been pronounced on them, each of them only appearing to be touched by the loss of his friend, but when they heard the Princess, whom they believed to be in the tyrant's hands, condemned to the same kind of death, their firmness abandoned them.

"Cruel Ambitious," cried Good and Better, "What do you have to fear now? Is my doom not sufficient to assure you of the crown you stole from me? Why soil yourself with the blood of an innocent Princess, devoid of support and aid, who ought not to pose any challenge to you. If your political barbarity obliges you to take my life, think that you cannot deprive my daughter of hers without blackening yourself with the most frightful of crimes.

"Remember, you ingrate," the monarch continued, softening, "all the affection that I have had for you, that I have been the master of putting you to death, that I should have done, and that, far from doing it, I heaped you with graces. I do not remind you of that memory in the design of engaging you to revoke the cruel sentence you have pronounced against me. I shall die without regret, and even without hating you, provided that you do not attempt the days of my dear Lisimene."

The King spoke in a tone capable of softening the most inflexible hearts; only that of the perfidious Ambitious was capable of resisting it. Insensible to such touching plaints, far from deigning to respond to them, he did not even listen to them.

If the dolor of Good and Better was excessive, that of Perfect was no less so. "Cruel Father," he said to the usurper, "ought you not to be content with taking my life, without attempting that of your master? And can it be without trembling that you also dare to immolate Lisimene? Is it not enough that you have despoiled them of everything that belonged to them so legitimately, without pushing rage so far as to causing a generous King and an innocent Princess to perish? At least respect her beauty and her virtue. Remember that if she is culpable, it is only of having fled a Court where her tears and her presence would doubtless have roused resentment against you. Far from seeking to avenge her father and avenge herself, she sought a refuge in the most savage place, where her hand was only armed with the crook of a shepherdess, while she abandoned her father's scepter to your criminal ambition."

Perfect spoke with so much vehemence and he was so penetrated by the sad fate of his mistress that he did not think of sparing his terms, believing that they could not be too strong in expressing the sentiments inspired in him by the peril of the Princess. But, reflecting on what he was saying, and finally thinking that in lacking the respect owed by a son to his father, far from softening the tyrant, he was, on the contrary working to drive him to greater extremities, he changed his tone and prostrated himself at the feet of Ambitious.

"Pardon me, Sire," he said to him. "I was innocent when I appeared before you. I have never conspired, nor even taken the slightest step that ought to attract your anger to me. But the excess to which I have just been transported renders me absolutely culpable. I merit death, and I desire it as a justice that is due to me. Redouble, if it is possible, the torments you are preparing for me; I shall suffer them without murmuring against your rigor. The only mercy I ask of you is not to deliver me to the cruel despair of seeing enveloped in my misfortune a person who is dearer to me than life, and who has never offended you."

The affliction and groans of the Prince had excited such compassion in the hearts of the assembly that everyone was weeping. There was only Ambitious who conserved his harshness, and looked at Perfect proudly.

"Infidel and perfidious son," he replied, "I am delighted to see your cowardice revealed to me and furnishing such a fortunate opportunity to punish you as your crimes deserve. Do not expect any mercy from your irritated king; you shall die, and to make the torture proportionate to the crime, you shall see before dying the fatal Princess who made you forget your duty expire before your eyes. Your death will become a formidable example to those of my subjects who might be tempted to resemble you. To commence your punishment, you will be shown your lover charged with chains; you shall see her expire under torture, and you shall hear soon afterwards your own sentence pronounced."

That inhuman response chilled the senses of the Prince and put him in a state where he did not have the strength to reply.

He was in that disastrous situation, and Good and Better, who was at least as consternated as Perfect, was ready to die of dolor, when the pretended Lisimene appeared.

Her cries announced her a long time before she was seen. The liberty of speech had been returned to her, but she was in a humor so violent that, having been informed by her guards that the tyrant was only asking to see her in order to take away her life, they had been obliged to enchain her arms for fear that she might strange those who were accompanying her. Thus, she was crushed by the weight of irons, having the burden of three people, at least.

While she had languished in her cell, her tears and her blood, which was trickling in several places by virtue of the blows that she had inflicted on herself in her despair, combining with the mud that had stuck to her face, made a kind of paste there, which, being confounded with the reeds by which she was shaded, augmented the horror that she inspired naturally, with the consequence that nothing in nature had ever been so hideous.

Her presence struck terror into the hearts of all the spectators, and fear made them think of fleeing. Ambitious himself was not exempt from the general terror, imagining that what he was seeing was a specter that had taken on the form of Lisimene to punish him for so many crimes. But the fury to reign that was the sole principle of all his actions, stifled the remorse and fear that the sight excited in his culpable soul.

He was the first to pull himself together and, recalling those who were fleeing, he shouted that he did not require any other evidence against Good and Better, or against his daughter, than what he saw. It was obvious that both of them had commerce with infernal spirits, which could only be with the intention of dooming him and perhaps causing the whole kingdom to perish. That criminal design was doubtless the only reason that had engaged Lisimene to disguise herself in that fashion.

Pigrieche, who heard that speech, could not remain mute on such a fine occasion to speak, and having preceded it with a torrent of insults said what she had to say for her justification. She replied to Ambitious that it was false that she was an infernal spirit, since, far from it, she was an innocent and unfortunate young woman...

At that assertion, without hearing any more, Ambitious, convinced that, in fact Pigrieche was only what she said—which is to say, an unfortunate young woman, since she was in his hands and that he still took her for the Princess—asked those who were holding her whether it was possible that the person he was seeing was Lisimene. They replied that it was, at least, definitely her that was about to marry the Prince, having been arrested with him as they were about to go into the temple.

"What," said Ambitious, scornfully, "this is the beauty so perfect, and the worthy object of the passion of a reckless youth? It's surely necessary that Heaven has struck him with blindness, or that it is to punish him for his revolt that his mistress has been changed into a monster."

A general murmur went up in the assembly, caused by astonishment at the Prince's bad taste, while the amorous Perfect, who had been almost dead of dolor a moment before, who realized the mistake instantly, passed from the funereal state in which he had previously been to a mild tranquility. Without embarrassing the conclusion of the event excessively, he maintained a profound silence.

As for Pigrieche, she was talking incessantly, without being any better heard for it. The fear of death troubled her so strongly that she was gibbering, without being able to articulate a single word.

Ambitious was having difficulty convincing himself that that monster was the Princess that he had seen so frequently in her infancy, and in order to clarify the matter, addressing Good and Better, he commanded him arrogantly to declare whether that frightful creature was his daughter.

That demand made Pigrieche shiver, and the peril that she saw attached to it rendered liberty to her tongue.

"Oh, don't believe him," she cried. "He'll have the malice to say that he's my father in order to have the pleasure of seeing me die, but it's a great lie."

Good and Better, whom Pigrieche's presence had reassured as much as Perfect with regard to the fate of Lisimene, could not help smiling at that speech. "I ought to justify your fear, and admit you for my daughter," he said to her. "You would merit my taking advantage of that opportunity to avenging myself for all the chagrins you have given us, and to punish you for the ill humor you have inspired in your mother. But, Heaven having preserved my dear Lisimene from the evils that Ambitious prepared for her, it would render me unworthy of that mercy to offend it by a lie. Thus, since the truth is favorable to save your life, I shall not refuse to be its voice, No, Ambitious," he added, addressing the tyrant, "this is not the Princess you seek; she has escaped your pursuit. You are right not to be misled, since she is as beautiful as the one who appears to your eyes is frightful."

"Who is she, then?" asked Ambitious.

"She's Pigrieche," the King continued, "the daughter of Richarde, a former slave and presently the wife that your cruelties forced me to take in order to shield myself from your pursuits and to find a meager subsistence during the course of my misfortunes."

Without the King's response touching the usurper with pity or remorse, he had no difficulty believing what he said, and he was veritable chagrined by it; nevertheless, he addressed Pigrieche and asked her by what hazard it had been possible to mistake her for a Princess that she resembled so little.

In spite of her stupidity, the surly individual did not allow herself to take offense at that speech, although she sensed no less what was disobliging therein; but the person who was speaking of her beauty with such irreverence was the King, and malevolent. So Pigrieche, seeing her life at the discretion of that terrible master, without daring to repeat the nasty things she had said to him, told him the truth, not even daring to disguise the crime she had premeditated, in wanting to honor herself with her alliance by means of that unworthy trick.

She could not have chosen better terms to reveal herself, for the wrath into which the intentions of Good and Better and Perfect had put Ambitious did not permit that Prince to pay any attention to the insolent desire that Pigrieche had had to be his daughter-in-law. Without making her any reproach, he sent her to find her mother.

Richarde was extremely surprised to see her arrive. The tenderness she had for that daughter caused her to listen to the story of the dangers she had run with as much fright as if she had seen her exposed to them again. She put her to bed in order to relieve her. That was not unnecessary, for never had anyone suffered as much as that unfortunate young woman had since she had been kidnapped; and if her torments had lasted another two days, she would infallibly have succumbed to them.

Meanwhile, while waiting for Lisimene to be found, Ambitious, to prevent the accidents that might occur and snatch away his prisoners, thought he ought to hasten their doom, and ordered that they be placed on a pyre that same day on the bank of the river that traversed the city. His design was to throw their ashes into it after the execution.

While those deplorable Princes had been at liberty, the entire kingdom had testified to a penchant to revolt in their favor, but in the present fatal occurrence, as it did not appear that they could ever find themselves in a state to put themselves at the head of their party, no one dared to do anything more for them than lament them, and even that was only done in secret. In consequence, the tyrant found no obstacle to his designs. The unfortunates were bound together and taken to the place designated for their execution.

The people flocked there in crowds, but it was only to solemnize their loss by tears. Ambitious' troops were too numerous to leave the friends that remained to the King and Perfect any hope of rescuing them.

The executors of the tyrant's fury, only awaiting his orders, and in order not to cause any delay, had already put their victims of the pyre when a frightful noise, emanating from the river, caused a general panic. That noise was accompanied by the flooding of the river, which in less than four minutes inundated the place where the most abominable of executions was to take place.

The water rose with so much promptitude that the crowd barely had time to flee and reach the roofs of houses. Ambitious, who had come to witness the barbaric spectacle, was obliged, like the others, to flee to his palace, where he scarcely saved himself, with his family and a few of his courtiers.

That general flight was so sudden that no one gave a thought to the security of the prisoners; they remained alone on the pyre, but so laden with chains that if anyone had been touched by the concern of preserving their lives, it would have been impossible to save them from the danger that threatened them. In consequence, they disdained to make futile efforts, and allowed themselves to be dragged away tranquilly by the rapidity of the flood, which resembled the waves of a furious sea.

The people, who saw those sad victims thus carried away by the waters from a distance, mourned their destiny and, soon losing sight of them, had no doubt that they had found in that element the fate that they had been condemned to find in that of fire.

As soon as they had disappeared, the river became calm again and returned to its bed, leaving no other evidence of its passage than a frightful mud. However, the people cried prodigy, saying that their god had wanted to spare the King and the Prince the shame of perishing at the hands of executioners.

Ambitious, who was not embarrassed by those assertions, and to whom it was indifferent whether it was by the aid of water or fire that he was rid of his enemies, was triumphant at that adventure. The only thing that his joy lacked was that Lisimene had not yet been enveloped in the doom of her father and her lover. He had magnificent obsequies given to those he no longer feared, and prepared to savor the sweetness of that fortunate success.

All his subjects had been extremely surprised to see the harshness with which he had wanted his son to die, without it seeming that nature had rendered the slightest combat in his heart in favor of such a likeable Prince. But if that insensibility was astonishing, the sentiments of the Queen were even more so, for she did not hide the joy that she felt at that fatal catastrophe.

Those who sought to hope that their King still had some humanity regarded the tranquility that he had manifested in giving his barbaric orders as a certain proof that, without the accident that had deprived those Princes of the light, they would have got away with a fright, not doubting that they had been carried away from a pyre to which he was in no hurry to order that it be set alight.

As it did not matter to Ambitious that people had that thought, he made no effort to destroy it; on the contrary, having perceived that it pleased the population and that did him honor in crediting him with a sensibility of which he was incapable, but which might conciliate hearts to him, he erected a vain tomb to the Princes and rendered all sorts of funeral duties to their memory.

That ceremony produced an effect very advantageous for him, for it caused his preceding cruelties to be forgotten, and the people, forgetful in everything, gave him a thousand praises for his piety.

The tomb of Good and Better and Perfect was erected in the same place where the pyre had been, and, everything was ready for that lugubrious fête, Ambitious, followed by his Court, went to the place destined for the ceremony, preceded by a large number of victims, who, before immolating them, the high priests would offer to the divinities of the waters, begging them humbly to render their Princes to them, dead or alive.

Those prayers were scarcely finished when they were granted; the river was suddenly covered with a dazzling light, and in the midst of that sparkling light a chariot even more brilliant surged on to the bank; it was covered with seashells that ceded nothing in beauty even to precious stones A prodigious quantity of naiads clad in silver gauze, mingled with the most vivid colors, accompanied that brilliant chariot, where everyone was astonished to see the King, Lisimene and Perfect.

Finally, while a celestial music caused the shore to resound, and combined with the noise of the acclamations of the people, whom that event had seized with admiration and filled with joy, the Princes and the Princess were seen to emerge from the marvelous chariot.

At the sight of them Ambitious remained motionless, but fury soon prevailed over surprise and he advanced proudly toward the King, crying that the pompous spectacle as only an illusion and an enchantment that his enemies were employing

Perfect, encourag
the King to grant him
and release the culpab
more difficulty in obta
all the others. On the c
praises for the exceller
could go where filial
Perfect, delighted by th

"Permit me, Sire,"
fully and detaching his
the King, to render you
from the hand of a son,
of being odious to you
owes you."

"You are generou;
as you are working fo
touched by an action in
deur of soul, and since I
to make your magnanin
On the contrary, the se
that which I am receivin

Meanwhile, Zulba
master, was speaking to

"I am convinced, g
tunes will not have alte
that it is still as incline
that Ambitious had used
granted him; the abuse
stopping the course of a
deadly to you as your c
you ought not to hope t
as your faithful subjects,
will plunge a dagger int
who, in the time your m
ruin and that of all your f

"My dear Vizier,"
am grateful for the zeal t

to doom him, but that whose spell it was easy to destroy by arresting the authors of those vain tricks.

The tyrant ordered in vain that it should be done; no one dared obey him, fear and respect retaining everyone, which caused him to judge that the presence of Good and Better at that conjuncture was capable of toppling him in his turn from the throne from which he had expelled his King. That meant that he no longer hesitated to attack him, and, finding no other resource for his security than to kill his enemy, he drew his sword, which he would have plunged into his breast if Perfect had not thrown himself forward and retained his father's hand.

While the furious Ambitious struggled in the arms of the Prince, whom he called an unnatural son and reproached for joining his enemies in order to doom him, he did not stop making every effort to pierce the King, and might perhaps have succeeded if Crystalline, who was at the head of the cortege had not cried out, in a loud and touching voice:

"People, here are your Sovereign and your Princess; merit without delay pardon for the cowardice with which you abandoned them to the fury of a usurper; return to your duty and deliver the tyrant to your master, and help your Prince, or you are doomed."

Those words and the threat with which they were accompanied had such an effect on the hearts of all the spectators that Ambitious' own guards seized him, in spite of his resistance, in order to take him to prison, while the rest of the warriors who were under arms to prevent the tumult that almost always accompanies public fêtes, ran to do the same for the wife and son of the perfidious individual.

The voice of the naiad had moved the populace to such a pitch of fury against Ambitious and his family that they would have torn them apart if Perfect had not forbidden them—especially Ambitious, against whom the people were so enraged that the Prince, his son, only preserved him from that first movement by taking him in his arms and carrying him into the palace, where Good and Better and his daughter followed him.

The Vizier Zulba
Prince and Pigrieche
all those events had
paying attention to it.
er, because he had be
proposition that Perf
Lisimene's marriage. '
needed no more to eng

Scarcely had Go
he perceived the abse
concern was to ask fo
was in irons, he went t
a liberty that he had or

While the good F
generous subject, Perf
difficulty, from the fu
himself at the feet of
mercy to Ambitious.

"I know that he i
portant to your security
your natural clemency
life; I beg you to think

The King, listeni
that had been so poorly
my dear son," he said,
not know you and the
clemency, can you fear
Lisimene, I could reso
world believe that you
generous Prince, do no
the bloody head of Ar
will not see the hands c
that is so precious to yo
ject as he was a father,
name of Good and Bett
that it was given to m
pompous titles."

see with pleasure that your fidelity and your attachment are
not belied; this fervor for my interests proves to me that it is
not my fortune that you have loved, but me alone. Thus, without pausing on the maxims of Kings and Ministers, let us
speak with open hearts like true friends.

"Tell me naturally, then, what you want me to do. Is it
permissible for me to have the harshness of bloodying this fine
day by overwhelming the heart of a young Prince, whom I
want to make my son and the support of my throne, with the
sharpest dolor? Do you want me, at the same time as I give
him my daughter, to soil myself with his father's blood—that
of a man, in sum, linked to me by the tightest bonds, who
would have been my legitimate heir if Lisimene's rights had
not raised an obstacle to it?

"Can I only protect myself from the traps and attempts of
Ambitious by his death? Is it not better to send him to the fortress that Perfect has constructed in the town in the desert than
to expose myself to the reproaches that I could not prevent
myself making to myself for having been too cruel? The town
to which I shall relegate him is henceforth beyond insult; a
strong garrison with answer to me for him."

They were at that point in their conversation, and the Vizier, who could not approve of a means so subject to many
problems, was still arguing, representing to the King the inconveniences that might result from it, while the Prince was
making him know that the decision was made and that he was
absolutely determined not to use more violent means, when
Perfect appeared. He had just been harshly dismissed by his
father.

He came in and asked the King respectfully what destiny
he reserved for Ambitious after having granted him the mercy
of his life. Good and Better told him that he would limit his
vengeance to exiling the culpable Prince and sending him to
the same place from which they had arrived.

Although Perfect could only praise such moderation, he
sighed on thinking of what a severe duty demanded of him in
that circumstance. Making his decision without hesitation, he

Perfect, encouraged by that obliging response, begged the King to grant him entire mercy by permitting him to go and release the culpable Prince from his irons. He found no more difficulty in obtaining that favor than he had found for all the others. On the contrary, the King gave him a thousand praises for the excellence of his nature, and told him that he could go where filial duty summoned him. At those words, Perfect, delighted by that permission, ran to make use of it.

"Permit me, Sire," he said to Ambitious, bowing respectfully and detaching his irons, "profiting from the good will of the King, to render you this service, and I beg you to receive it from the hand of a son, who, in spite of the misfortune he has of being odious to you, will never forget the respect that he owes you."

"You are generous, Prince," said Ambitious, dryly, "but as you are working for your own glory, I ought not to be touched by an action in which there is more vanity than grandeur of soul, and since I am giving you such a fine opportunity to make your magnanimity manifest, I owe you no gratitude. On the contrary, the service I am rendering you is far above that which I am receiving from you."

Meanwhile, Zulbach, who had been left alone with his master, was speaking to him with his usual frankness.

"I am convinced, great King," he said, "that our misfortunes will not have altered the generosity of your heart, and that it is still as inclined to forgiveness as ever. It is in vain that Ambitious had used against you the mercy that you have granted him; the abuse that he has made of it is incapable of stopping the course of a generosity that has always been as deadly to you as your clemency; you will continue in it. For you ought not to hope to correct Ambitious. I shiver, as well as your faithful subjects, in seeing you spare a scoundrel, who will plunge a dagger into your breast tomorrow if he can, and who, in the time your mercy accords him, will meditate your ruin and that of all your family, once again."

"My dear Vizier," said the King, "I protest to you that I am grateful for the zeal that makes you speak thus, and that I see with pleasure that your fidelity and your attachment are not belied; this fervor for my interests proves to me that it is not my fortune that you have loved, but me alone. Thus, without pausing on the maxims of Kings and Ministers, let us speak with open hearts like true friends.

"Tell me naturally, then, what you want me to do. Is it permissible for me to have the harshness of bloodying this fine day by overwhelming the heart of a young Prince, whom I want to make my son and the support of my throne, with the sharpest dolor? Do you want me, at the same time as I give him my daughter, to soil myself with his father's blood—that of a man, in sum, linked to me by the tightest bonds, who would have been my legitimate heir if Lisimene's rights had not raised an obstacle to it?

"Can I only protect myself from the traps and attempts of Ambitious by his death? Is it not better to send him to the fortress that Perfect has constructed in the town in the desert than to expose myself to the reproaches that I could not prevent myself making to myself for having been too cruel? The town to which I shall relegate him is henceforth beyond insult; a strong garrison with answer to me for him."

They were at that point in their conversation, and the Vizier, who could not approve of a means so subject to many problems, was still arguing, representing to the King the inconveniences that might result from it, while the Prince was making him know that the decision was made and that he was absolutely determined not to use more violent means, when Perfect appeared. He had just been harshly dismissed by his father.

He came in and asked the King respectfully what destiny he reserved for Ambitious after having granted him the mercy of his life. Good and Better told him that he would limit his vengeance to exiling the culpable Prince and sending him to the same place from which they had arrived.

Although Perfect could only praise such moderation, he sighed on thinking of what a severe duty demanded of him in that circumstance. Making his decision without hesitation, he begged the King to complete all the favors that he had obtained by permitting him to accompany his father in his exile.

"For in the end, Sire," he said, sadly, "although I cannot hope for any return or sensibility on the part of Prince Ambitious, I owe it to him nevertheless to share his disgrace and try to console him in his captivity."

Surprised by the Prince's resolution, the King, without responding positively, told him to reflect on that proposition, and that he could not hide from him that it would cause him a mortal chagrin if he persisted in it.

Lisimene, who came in at that moment, having learned that Perfect wanted to leave the Court, asked him tenderly whether he had thought hard about it, and if he had paid attention to the fact that she would remain while he went away.

In saying that, her beautiful eyes filled with tears, which were soon accompanied by those of her lover and the King, who, also moved, offered his hand to the Prince and asked him whether he disdained his daughter and his throne sufficiently to have no regret in abandoning them, or whether he no longer loved Lisimene?

"Sire," sad Perfect, sighing, "when I aspired to be united with the Princess and I solicited you with so much ardor to grant me that favor, I adored her, and yet I had no more love for her than I have today, but at the time when I attached myself to the Princess, my father was fortunate. He is unfortunate now, and I owe to his disgrace all the cares that I gave previously to a passion that is not permitted to prevail in my heart over the duties of nature.

"It is not appropriate for me to establish myself as a judge between my King and my Father; if Ambitious were even more culpable, he ought not to be anything but unfortunate for me, and an eternal object of my cares and attentions. It is not in the state that he is in that I ought to think of taking advantage of your generosity, and what would you think of me, Sire, if you saw me only occupied with the cares of a marriage that would put me on the throne, while my father as groaning in irons?"

While Perfect was speaking thus, the Vizier observed the King, and, knowing by the movement of his eyes the dangerous compassion that that speech introduced into his heart, feared its deadly consequences. That obliged him to speak with precipitation.

"Oh, Sire," he said to Perfect, "to what does his speech tend? You know the Prince your father, and you're not unaware that he is not of a character to be vanquished by the force of generosity. To satisfy the duty that the name of son imposes upon you, do you want to expose the King again, his Estate, the Princess and yourself to become the victims once again of a fatal indulgence that has already caused so many woes. The ties of blood ought not to have any more credit in the heart of the King than they have in that of Ambitious; nature has its rights, Sire, and if you owe much to your father, you owe more to your sovereign, who is the father of all families in general. It is to that sacred interest that any other interest ought to yield."

"You're right, virtuous Zulbach," said the Prince. "I can only admire the wisdom of your advice; so believe that I am not reckless enough to ask anything of the King that might be against the interests of his Estate or is person, to which the strongest reasons render a thousand times dearer to me than to all is subjects put together. That is what is making me sacrifice myself to my ill fortune; I am renouncing the wealth that he offers me in order to deliver myself entirely to a cruel duty, which is tearing me way from my King, my Princess and, in sum, everything in the world that I love, in order to accompany a father who hates me and from whom I have no hope of milder sentiments."

"What, my dear Prince!" said Good and Better. "Is there no alternative, and can we not find a means to conciliate our various interests? I will admit to you naturally that I cannot resolve to accord you what you are asking of me, and that there is nothing that my amity is not ready to risk in order to retain you with me. See what I can do," he said to the Prince, tenderly, "I make you judge between Ambitious and me, and consent generally to anything that can keep you here without wounding your honor and your duty."

The Prince, confused by his master's generosity, did not know what to decide; he was aware of the excess of injustice there would be in prevailing, as well as the danger that that would follow that abuse and the usage that his father would make of it, having no doubt that the proud Prince would not neglect the first opportunity to abuse the King's clemency in the same fashion that he had before, knowing that that would expose the monarch to new criminal attempts and to deliver him, bound hand and foot, so to speak, to the fury of a man incapable of remorse.

In that perplexity, Perfect, torn between the dread of exposing the King again or not fulfilling sufficiently the duties that nature prescribed for him, dared not resolve the dilemma, and had abandoned himself to a torrent of thoughts without being able to settle his irresolution, when an earthquake suddenly made itself felt and extracted him from the lethargy into which he seemed to have sunk.

That tremor, which had shaken the palace, only lasted for a moment, and did not produce any other effect that that of opening the earth to give passage to a small, extraordinary ugly woman, wider than she was tall, with a head of enormous volume, of a disagreeable brown color, accompanying in perfection one of the most unpleasant faces imaginable.

Lisimene was the only one not frightened by that apparition, because she had seen gnomes at the Mill of Misfortune, and recognized the little monster as belonging to the gnomide nation.

The gnomide was holding by the hand a lady who, to all appearances, was not a compatriot, for she was tall, blonde, beautiful and shapely, and although she had passed her first youth, it would have been difficult to find a more likeable person. The lady had something so distinguished in her bearing that she inspired both love and respect.

A thousand gems of an admirable beauty glittered on the garments of the newcomers.

"Powerful monarch," said the citizen of the bosom of the earth to Good and Better, "we have come to relieve you in the dilemma in which you find yourself. This beautiful lady and I hope to have the pleasure of removing the difficulties that have arrested you and restoring calm among you...

"However," she added, "we can only explain ourselves more fully in the presence of Prince Ambitious and his wife. Order, if you please, that they be brought here right away. When they are here I will reveal a secret to you that will surprise you, in which they will be very interested, and which will settle everyone's irresolution."

The King having ordered what the gnomide desired, Ambitious and his wife arrived shortly thereafter.

"Do you recognize me, Madame," said the gnomide to the captive Princess, "and do you remember the generous aid that I once gave you?"

"I recognize you only too well," said Ambitious' wife, uttering a sigh of rage, "and I have seen you too much for my liking, for you are the cause of all my misfortunes."

"Speak more truthfully, unjust Princess," replied the gnomide, proudly. "It is your crimes and not my cares that have doomed you." Then, addressing the King and those who were present, she said: "Listen to me, King, and all of you who are here." Speaking to Good and Better she continued: "You have doubtless not forgotten, Sire, the late Prince, your brother; the amity you had for him, and the tender respect that he conserved for you, do not permit me to think that death has effaced him from your memory..."

"Assuredly not," said the King, sighing. "His memory is precious to me, and I regret him all the more because the hope of his posterity was destroyed with him."

The gnomide smiled, and without making any response to that speech she continued the one she had commenced.

"You lost that Prince, she said, "during a war started by a neighbor jealous of your grandeur. As you made the decision to command your army yourself, you left the government of your Estates to you brother, dispensing him from following you for some time because the Princess, his wife, was about to have a child, your ever-attentive generosity wanting to give him the pleasure of remaining with his wife until she had given birth to that fruit of their marriage."

"I agree with all you say," said Good and Better, "but Madame, what is the point of renewing these sad memories, which cannot extract us from the difficulties we are in."

"They are more pertinent than you think," replied the subterranean Princess, "since it is in order to inform you of the fashion in which you lost that Princess and her spouse that I am reminding you of their death, the circumstances of which have never been explained.

"Know, then, that immediately after your departure, this monster"—she indicated Ambitious—"who knew that your brother would succeed you if you had no children, and that while he lived, he would always place an invisible obstacle to his pernicious designs, wanted to remove it promptly, and gave him poison. But he could not have been sufficiently adroit, for the dying Prince had violent suspicions of the truth and asked for help. That was futile, all those surrounding him having been seduced by Ambitious, with the consequence that the Prince was allowed to die without anyone wanting to accord him the slightest relief. There was only the Princess, his wife, who made efforts to give him a remedy, but it was in vain, and the tenderness she showed him only served to hasten her own death; she rendered herself redoubtable by the scant precaution that she took to hide her despair.

"As well as the just suspicions that she had regarding the kind of death that had taken her husband from her, the Princess had had the imprudence to threaten the perfidious individuals who had been the accomplices of the Prince's death with your vengeance; that was her own death-sentence, and in fear that she might talk, Ambitious resolved not to leave her the time to make you hear her complaints, nor to bring into the world a child that he would be obliged to destroy, at the hazard of being discovered.

359

"He had not planned in advance to have her buried alive with her dead husband; it was an unexpected opportunity that presented itself, which determined him by offering him a favorable expedient. The Princess, who had not quit her husband, succumbed to her dolor when she saw him expire and fainted over his body. That unconsciousness was so profound, and accompanied by symptoms so extraordinary, that she was believed to be dead.

"Ambitious, profiting from such a favorable circumstance, first put around the rumor that the Prince and Princess had died of a contagious malady, in order to dispense with exposing them to the eyes of the people, as was customary with persons of their rank. That exhibition might have had a consequence with regard to the cause of the Prince's death, and, not limiting his barbarity there, he went so far as to have the Princess buried in your unfortunate brother's coffin, without even deigning to order that anyone finishing taking the life of the unfortunate woman. Finally, after having rendered great honors to their memory, he had them put in a grave so deep that he had no fear that cries of the Princess would be heard if she recovered from her faint.

"Those cries penetrated nevertheless, but it was not as far as the surface of the earth; they were too distant to be heard there. They only reached me. I flew to her aid and extracted her from that frightful situation at the moment when she was about to choke, and had lost consciousness. As soon as she had recovered her senses I took her to our subterranean palace, and I was too touched by the dire state in which I saw her not to give her all the help that depended on me, as much for her as for the fruit she was carrying. My cares had a success so fortunate that she gave birth without any accident to a charming Prince.

"I would willingly describe him, Sire," the gnomide continued, "if he were not before your eyes; but you know Perfect, and all the good things that I could tell you would not equal those you know yourself. You see, Prince," she said, addressing the person whom that news rendered motionless, "the movements of nature are not deceptive, they are faithful in only inspiring you with horror for a man who not only is not your father but is the murderer of the man to whom you owe the light of day."

That terrible story excited a cry of indignation in the assembly. Ambitious uttered one too, but it was of dolor in seeing his crime discovered. He looked at the Princess his wife with eyes full of wrath, while she lowered her gaze, the remorse of the past and the fear of the future painting on her face a consternation mingled with fury, which testified clearly enough that she was incapable of repentance. But the purest and most vivid joy shone in the eyes of the King, the Princess, Perfect and the Vizier.

"What joy, my dear child," cried the King, hugging the Prince in his arms. "You can now accord your duty with your desires and my interests! Oh, I cannot understand how we were able to be blind for such a long time regarding your birth. Should we not have seen that Heaven, which had formed you so virtuous, could not have made you born to the cruel Ambitious."

Then the monarch, reflecting, bowed to the gnomide and went on: "But joy has transported us to the point of lacking propriety, and we have interrupted our generous protectress. However, as she has given us proofs of the sensibility of her heart, I hope that she will not be offended by seeing that we have given our first reactions to nature."

With those words, the King ran to the Princess, his sister-in-law, whom he had not recognized at first, although he had always loved her tenderly; but he had believed her to be dead and having not seen her for twenty-two years, the excuse was legitimate. He found himself anticipated by the Prince, who embraced his mother with the transports that nature alone is capable of inspiring, and which had made him know at first glance the woman who had given birth to him.

The gnomide was weeping with joy. "You can see," she said to the King, pointing out to him the tears that she was shedding, "that the spectacle is more touching for me than all the ceremonies that you might have practiced in my regard."

"Finish informing us, then," said the King, "of all the obligations we have to you, and tell us how you were able to have my nephew raised by Ambitious, who had so much interest in dooming him?"

"The Princess your sister-in-law having given birth successfully," replied the gnomide, "it would have been easy for me when you returned to return the mother and the child to your hands and to inform you at the same time of the crime that had robbed you of a brother so worthy of your amity. But, knowing by my science that you were on the point of experiencing misfortunes from which I did not have the power to protect you, I judged it appropriate to let that malign influence pass. I feared increasing your woes by augmenting your cares, and I made the decision to have the Prince nourished in secret, where I would take care to raise him in the sentiments appropriate to his birth.

"But as Ambitious' wife had given birth on the same day as Perfect's mother, I resolved to profit from that opportunity to place him advantageously. I caused extraordinary signs to appear to that Princess twenty-four hours later, which seemed to announce that she would not have any more children. That rendered the one she had just had more precious to the father and mother; I had conceived the design of stealing him from them and substituting Perfect in his place.

"Occupied with that project, I no longer abandoned their palace, where fortune soon favored such a generous ambition. Ambitious could not contain the joy he had a seeing that he had an heir, and the wife of the cruel Prince, who was avid to imitate her husband in everything, could no longer let her son out of her sight, and, keeping him constantly in her apartment, she unwittingly put an obstacle to the project I had of stealing him; but it was that excess of tenderness and the accident it caused that allowed me to succeed in the objective of my desires.

"After a dinner that the Princess took in her cabinet, she was surprised by a slight desire to sleep, and, having gone to bed with her son, whom she was holding in her arms, she ordered that she be left alone. Apparently, however, during that slumber, she made a movement that caused the child to slip, and which turned him over on to his face, for, on awakening, she found him in that position; she turned him over immediately, but it was too late, and the young Prince had choked.

"You can imagine, Sire, that her dolor was extreme; the natural penchant that the most ferocious hearts have for their own blood was sufficient to cause that; but to that reason was added another, no less considerable, and the apprehension of the just reproaches that Ambitious might make her did not permit her to take any consolation. She envisaged at a glance that if a legitimate King who has no children is sometimes exposed to unfortunate events, there is all the more reason for a Prince who has no other right to the crown than those furnished by usurpation to need a family that can make his people hope that a numerous posterity will guarantee them for several centuries from the accidents inseparable from revolutions.

"Those considerations exciting the Princess' dolor, she abandoned herself to it without moderation, taking her affliction so far as to lacerate her face and tear out her hair; she bruised herself with blows and was on the point of taking her own life, preparing to throw herself into the river that flows alongside the terrace of her apartment when I appeared.

"The design I had rendered me very assiduous toward her, and as soon as she made the first movement to surrender to her despair I rendered myself visible. 'Have courage, Princess,' I said to her, 'it is unworthy of a heart like yours to abandon yourself in his way to the dolor you possess; is it not better to seek remedies for your woes than succumb to them in such a cowardly fashion?'

"My unexpected presence caused her some fright; however, as she has more firmness than is usual in members of her sex, she pulled herself together promptly and looked at me sadly. 'Whoever you are,' she said, 'who offers me consolation, how can I receive it and how I can I put an end to my misfortune? I have lost my son, and all my hopes with him. What can I have that is sufficient to resuscitate the child whose life I have taken by my imprudence? Furthermore, in addition to the dolor a mother must experience in such a cruel circumstance, how can I remain without alarm in seeing myself exposed to the just resentment of my husband? The slightest effect that I have to fear from his wrath is to be repudiated, in order to put in my place a wife who can give him heirs, of which he sees himself frustrated today by my fault and he impossibility of my hoping for a further pregnancy.'

"'I cannot bring a remedy to your grief, nor make you a mother,' I replied. 'Your son is dead; that is a woe that time alone is capable of softening; but with regard to the unfortunate consequences that might stem from it, I can help you. Cease weeping.' I added, 'continue to feign sleep, in order to prevent anyone perceiving the loss that you have just suffered, and wait for me for a moment'

"On saying that I went back underground, where, taking Perfect, whom I had given to one of the gnomides to nurse, I presented him. 'Here, Madame,' I said to her. 'This will preserve you from the wrath of your husband; the weak features of infancy will prevent anyone from noticing the exchange; have no fear that the deposit I am confiding to you is unworthy of the rank to which your interest summons you; he is of royal blood and will have all the virtues; he is destined to reign; it is for you to cultivate his fine qualities. Adieu, conserve him, and let the fatal experience you have just had keep you on guard against similar accidents.'

"With those words, knowing by her gaze that she was satisfied with the help that I offered her, I picked up the dead child, which I took away, leaving my little Prince in his place, and I disappeared.

"I came back again, invisibly, shortly thereafter, to see how my nursling was being treated, and witnessed that the Princess, calling her women, handed Perfect to them without any of them being able to perceive the difference there was between the first child and the second. I came to see him often, but without showing myself, being very glad to know by means of my own eyes how what provision was made for the education of the little Prince, being extremely apprehensive that he might be inspired with the same sentiments of ambition by which the supposed parents were devoured. To prevent that misfortune, I had disguised gnomes presented, from which he received the various lessons that he needed. Seeing with pleasure the fruit of my cares, I rendered an exact account to the Princess his mother, who had not seen him since he was born.

"I had removed him from her sight in order to prevent the habitude she had of seeing him, by redoubling her tenderness, redoubling her dolor when it was necessary to separate them: an absolutely necessary precaution, as much for the interest of his education as or that of his health, for the abode of the earth's entrails is not healthy for temperaments as delicate as those of new-born infants ordinarily are; and this Princess, worthy of everything I had done for her, was too prudent not to yield to my arguments.

"Eventually, after seven or eight years, during which time we could flatter ourselves that Perfect would always be an only son, and in spite of the signs of my fashioning that had deceived the physicians, the pretended mother became pregnant, contrary to everything that was to be expected after such a long sterility, and gave birth to a second son.

"Ambitious, full of joy, regarded that new scion as a favor of fortune that rendered his rights to the crown surer and seemed to impose a kind of necessity upon him to usurp it. The tenderness that he immediately had for that new child, which the first had never inspired in him, as well as the unexpected birth, appeared to him to be a favorable presage for his designs, but the Princess, his wife, who was not, like him, in pleasant error, sensed a true despair, unable to think without a mortal chagrin that Perfect, an unknown child that she had been given by a kind of monster—for, without vanity, it was thus that she did me the honor of naming me—would forever keep her legitimate son away a throne that she regarded as his due. That gave birth a hundred times over within her the desire to get rid of that supposed child by the secret means of poison; but the surprising and, so to speak, supernatural fashion in which I had confided him to her, was the Prince's surety, because she feared that any murder she might attempt would turn against her.

"That proud Princess regretted a hundred times a day not having preferred the most horrible effects of her husband's wrath to the fatal means that had preserved her from it. She conceived such a powerful hatred for Perfect, and that hatred was so clearly manifest, that it surprised the entire Court by whom the child was adored.

"The same reason that assured her life also assured her secret; that false mother dared not reveal herself for fear of incurring my wrath. But that forced silence did not soften her; on the contrary, she did could not think without transports that went as far as fury that she had given the crown herself to an unknown, to the prejudice of her son; and those movements were redoubled by the knowledge she had, Sire, of the intention you had of marrying Lisimene to that Prince. But if the dread I inspired in her prevented her from the execution of evil intentions, she was not capable of engaging herself to suffer any longer the presence of an object that had become odious to her, and, adopting for a pretext for sending him away that he would be better raised in retirement from the court, where too much dissipation was to be feared, she obtained permission from Ambitious to send him to the solitary scholars, whose mores were entirely appropriate to form those of youth.

"I was delighted by that resolution, and I conjectured that with the dispositions that the Prince had received from nature, the education that he would be given would be a complete success. Besides which, she anticipated me in seeking to distance him from her and her husband. I would not have consented to leave him permanently in the hands of two persons who, by their pernicious maxims, might have damaged his natural goodness.

"If they both had a coldness toward Perfect, a sentiment caused in the heart of Ambitious by movements of which he was not the master, and in that of his wife by the knowledge of the status of that pretended son, it was similarly felt by the young Prince; for he also had a great deal of indifference for both of them. Nature showed him the truth internally.

"When he was of an age to discern that sentiment, he attributed it to the short time he had lived with them and the dry fashion in which he had always been treated by them; but that indifference changed into horror when he saw them again after the culpable action that had taken the crown away from you. It was necessary for him to summon all his virtue to the aid of his duty; it was that alone that prevented him from breaking away and trying to find partisans who could put you back on the throne.

"His return having given a new vigor to the hatred of Ambitious' wife, it redoubled so strongly as the moment of the Prince's elevation approached that in order to rid herself of it she would have overcome the obstacle that retained her and would have exposed herself without hesitation to all my vengeance if she had not been retained by a new incident, which was for her a renewal of fury. That was the general affection that Perfect had acquired, and with might have rendered his loss deadly to anyone who dared to attempt it.

"But that affection only lasted for as long as he was at liberty; the zeal that the entire State testified to him having become mute as soon as he was seen to be a prisoner, gave that cruel woman the facility of abandoning herself to her fury; she abandoned herself to it without hesitation, and when the Prince proposed the treaty of which Lisimene was to be the seal, the fear that Ambitious might consent to it and destroy by that means the fortune of her only son finally bore her to reveal the secret of Perfect's birth, at least so far as she knew it, for she did not know of whose blood he was formed.

"The knowledge that she gave to the tyrant determined him to the Prince's doom, as well as yours, and by virtue of the treason of the infamous Richarde, he would have succeeded in causing you both to perish if you had not been protected by a supernatural power. But all the malign influences are dissipated now, and you no longer have anything to fear that is contrary to your happiness. You are now united; I am rendering Perfect the advantage of his birth, and I am adding to that present that of recovering his mother, as well as enabling you to see again the wife of a brother you cherished. The virtue of this Princess renders her well worthy of the sentiments that you have for her and for that unfortunate brother.

"Adieu, great King," the gnomide continued. "I shall withdraw; but always count on my amity for you and all the persons that are dear to you."

With those words, she disappeared, leaving Good and Better, his family and his Court in an extreme joy.

"Sire," said Zulbach to Perfect then, "after what you have just learned, will you continue to protect a guilty man?"

"No, wise Vizier," replied the Prince shivering, "but the blood that barbarian has shed excites my anger too much to dare to want to be the master of his destiny. The vengeance that would prevail over generosity might perhaps lead me to an excess that, in staining my glory, would scarcely be worthy of the sentiments of my King, and would abandon me to everything that a just fury inspires in me against a disarmed Prince, who, in spite of his laxity, has the honor of being a relative of our sovereign. Thus, it is for that monarch alone to render me justice for my father's death, and it is also from him that I request it."

As he spoke those words, Perfect threw himself at the King's feet.

"Let us be generous to the end, my dear son," said Good and Better, "and not retract the mercy that we have granted. Although the wretch is even more criminal than he appeared to us, let our generosity and the impotence that he has of abusing it henceforth be his torture. Go, wretch," he said to the perfidious individual, "I deliver you to your remorse and I leave you your life.

"Let him be taken with his wife and son to the fortress of the desert," he added. "Let them be served there not according to their merit but according to their birth, and let them lack nothing except the liberty, which my generosity would still accord to them if prudence were not opposed to it. I even promise them not to envelop their son in that disgrace; he is innocent of it and if, in a few years, the young Prince makes it know that he has not inherited their sentiments, I shall recall him to my presence, where he will resume the rank that is due to him. I wish with all my heart that he has virtue enough to make the crimes of those who gave him life forgotten."

The King went out after those words, followed by his sister-in-law, Perfect, Lisimene and the entire Court, leaving Ambitious alone with his wife and son, contenting himself with ordering that they be strictly guarded until the vehicles destined to conduct them to their exile were ready.

Scarcely had he taken a few steps outside the room, however, when frightful cries were uttered. The King came back precipitately, and thought he would lose his life there, for Ambitious, a dagger in his hand, launched himself upon him, and would have plunged it into his bosom if Perfect, who had also come back, had not perceived the movements of the furious individual soon enough to prevent him, by throwing himself between the King and him and retaining his arm.

Although he thus raised an obstacle to the scoundrel's execrable design, he could not prevent him from rendering himself justice by piercing his own breast with the same blade that he had had the audacity to raise against his master.

The screams that had been heard had been uttered by the wife and son of that cruel Prince, whom in the excess of his fury, he had immolated to his despair. He was about to fall beside them, and in spite of that new crime, the King nevertheless ordered with his ordinary generosity that they be helped. It was all over for the Princess and her son, but although he was dying, Ambitious proudly repelled with his dagger those who dared to approach him, and looked at the King with an expression so scornful that while he was held in his irons he said to him:

"Did you think, feeble Good and Better, that I have as little courage as you, and did you suspect me of having an attachment to life so cowardly as to want to conserve it in remaining your subject? No, no, render me justice and don't believe my soul is so base. I was not born to obey you. The throne or death were my only resources; I have lost the hope of reigning, and since, for once in your life you have been prudent enough to avoid the effects of my just fury, I have no other course to take than that of emerging from slavery, and I die content, in not leaving in your power those who belonged to me."

He seemed still to want to exhale his rage by means of further speech as audacious, when he expired.

Although that criminal prince had thoroughly merited his mortal destiny, that spectacle softened the heart of the King, who, unable to sustain it, would have retired almost touched by the fate of the unfortunate family if it had not merited its misfortune. But that impulse of pity having given way to more just concerns, the next day was employed without any delay in preparations for Perfect's happiness.

Meanwhile, Richarde was very anxious about the fashion in which her husband might act toward her after all that she had done against him, but she was reassured by the knowledge she had of his generosity. She was in that uncertainty when she was taken out of it by the order she received to come to see him in his study.

She threw himself at his feet when she went in, and, attempting to justify herself, was trying to deny that she had had any part in the danger to which he had been exposed, when the monarch lifted her up.

"You can hope for anything from my bounty, Madame," he said to her, "but it would be too much to count on my credulity on that point. I would like to pardon you and testify more sensibility for the pleasure you gave me in giving me a refuge in the time when I was unfortunate than I want to at the memory of what you have done against me. That unique motive prevents me from punishing you, or even ceasing to be your husband, although I have no intention of making you Queen...you would be too out of place in a rank so distant from the one to which you were born.

"Don't be offended by my intentions," he added, "I am doing you no wrong, since I shall renounce supreme power myself tomorrow, wanting to live henceforth as a simple individual. You will have no reason to complain of your fate, since I am treating you alike myself, and I shall not conserve a status above yours. Furthermore, you can choose for your habitation whichever of the royal houses pleases you the most; you will be treated with respect there and will not lack anything, nor will your daughter. Go, withdraw, be ready tomorrow and allow yourself to be taken to wherever you decide. And in future, no longer abandon yourself to passions so violent that they would have cost you your life if I were less generous."

Without daring to reply, Richarde returned to her apartment, where she gave Pigrieche an account of what had just happened. Those creatures, who would have regarded it as a great mercy a moment before to be confined to prison perpetually, treated as manifest injustice the mildness with which the King was acting in their regard, and above all they were outraged by his abdication, for they had intended at least to share the honors of the throne with him.

"What," said the impertinent Pigrieche, "you will suffer that a rank that is our due, and which we would fill with so much majesty, is stolen from us? To complete the horror," she continued, "it will be necessary that we see that Liron, previously our slave, enjoying with the ingrate Perfect grandeurs of which we shall be deprived. Furthermore, can you doubt that both of them will not soon obtain from your imbecile husband that we are sent back to our desert, or perhaps lose our lives? Oh, Mother," she screeched, "let us not allow our enemies to triumph thus. Let us have more courage than they would have in our place and prevent them."

"I'm as angry about it as you are," said Richarde, animated by her daughter's fury, "but what can we do about it?"

"You're the mistress if Liron's life," the abominable individual replied, "What are you waiting for? Light her candle, and let that fatal flame, in illuminating the first steps she takes toward the throne, precipitate her into the grave.

"That isn't all," she added. "If you have courage, and if you love me, you're in a position to enable me to reign in her place, since the custom of the kingdom is so favorable to us that we'd be doing ourselves a great wrong not to take advantage of it. Young women who are marrying must, as you know, hide themselves from all eyes on the eve of their wedding, under a veil that it is only permissible to lift on the day after the wedding. Even the husband does not have the privilege of touching that mysterious veil, known as the modesty cap; it is even forbidden to the husband to speak until after having spent the first night together. You can see that it seems that all the articles of that ceremony have been dictated by some intelligence that is protecting us and watching over our designs. I have already taken advantage of those fortunate circumstances in the desert, having been able to profit from the usage of the veil, which would indubitably have rendered me Perfect's wife if I had not been abducted in Liron's clothes just as we were about to enter the temple. But according to all appearances, I have no similar interruption to fear here.

"On the eve of the ceremony," the pernicious creature continued, "you have only to light the candle. I shall introduce myself adroitly into Liron's bedroom, where I shall hide, and when she is dead, I'll carry her body to some hiding-place and put myself in her bed in her place, dressing in her attire in the morning. I'll be taken to the temple by those who mistake me for her. The execution of the project is very easy, since the Princess has to be alone and to dress herself without being aided or seen by any of her maids."

That proposal made Richarde shiver, not out of horror of the action, for she was incapable of remorse when her daughter gave her an order, but fear of the consequences made her hesitate.

"What are you proposing to me?" she said, "Do you want to run to certain death? Can you doubt that when the King and Perfect will discover the crime, along with the deceit that will have accompanied it, that they won't make us perish to avenge the death of Liron? Should not the deadly consequences of that action turn us way from it?"

"Good, the consequences!" said Pigrieche, in a mocking tone. "What can happen? They'll curse Heaven and earth, they'll scream, they'll be in despair, and they'll finally console themselves, while Lisimene will still be dead and I'll be married.

"Don't you know Good and Better?" she added. "Since he was cowardly enough not to punish Ambitious, should you dread that he'll have any more courage to do us harm? As for Perfect, after the thing is done, it will be necessary for him to console himself, and he'll make his decision. I'll tell him, to finish tranquilizing him, that having gone into Lisimene's room by chance and having found her dead I thought that I could take her place, since I am, after her the nearest heir to the throne, and that what determined me to do it wasn't ambition but the love I have for him...he'll surely be very flattered by that proof of my affection, for I'll accompany it with caresses so touching that he'll soon be consoled.

"Oh, what cannot the attentions of a pretty woman achieve over her husband's heart? After all," she said, with a conceited expression, "I don't think I'm doing him any wrong in giving myself to him. Perhaps he'll be compensated more advantageously for what he'll have lost? And aren't I worth more than Lisimene?

"Take note," she continued, "that in addition to the advantage you'll find in establishing me so conveniently, you'll also have worked for your own establishment, for it's to be presumed that the King, having lost his daughter, will no longer think of abdicating, and in that fashion, you'll see yourself on a throne again, which he only wants to take away from you to give it to the odious Liron. Take note, if you please, that whatever charm the crown has in my eyes, I'm consenting, out of consideration for you, only to ornament my head with it after the King's death. Since Perfect is his heir, I can't fail to reign in my turn. And as you're my mother, I want to have the kindness to let you reign first."

Although that project was as ridiculous as it was criminal, Richarde, who could not refuse her daughter anything, and who was also dazzled by the brilliant vision presented to her, consented to everything.

Meanwhile, Zulbach was with the King and the Prince. His joy at seeing them out of any danger was so great that he did not know how to show it; and he was so attached to them that he could not resolve to go away for a moment. His proven fidelity giving him a great liberty with the two Princes, he took advantage of it to ask by what good fortune they had been saved from the flood.

As Lisimene knew more about the circumstances of that prodigy than her father and her lover, it was her who told him about the generosity that the naiads had shown her until the moment when the King had been abducted.

"At the memory of my father dying, as it had appeared to me, and in the hands of those barbarians," she continued, "I abandoned myself to the most frightful despair, and although I was surrounded by naiads who hastened to console me, insensible to all the cares that those nymphs took to reassure me regarding the peril that the King and Perfect were in, I could not obtain a moment of repose.

"In spite of that terrible situation, however, I obeyed without resistance everything they ordered me to do, although that docility was due more to the fact that I had lost my reason than any hope that remained to me. I passed almost without knowing what I was doing through the damp routes where they commanded me to follow them; and from the fountain that the naiads inhabited I suddenly founded myself in the bosom of the river that runs through this city, on the edge of which my father and my lover were to be immolated. I think that in order to reach it we went under the sea, for I heard a frightful noise over my head, which could only have come from the waves.

"Finally, when we were in the river, and at the precise moment when the Princes were about to be delivered to the fury of the flames, Crystalline raised up the waters, which overflowed with so much rapidity that all those who had come to see the fatal spectacle that Ambitious had prepared for the people only found their salvation in a prompt flight, leaving the field free for the effects of our protectors' good will, and the waters the liberty to carry away the illustrious victims that the usurper had devoted to his cruelty.

"I had all the pleasure of surprise, for the generous Crystalline had not informed me of what she wanted to do for the King and the Prince, who were impelled by the waters and transported to the grotto where I was lying on a bed of reeds, sadly occupied in deploring my fate and that of my unfortunate family, without it being possible for me to reassure myself by means of the naiads' promises or the hope they gave me.

"There is no need, sage Vizier," Lisimene continued, "to tell you about the joy that the unexpected arrival of persons so dear to me caused me to feel, and that which they testified to me. It was necessary for me to endure a mild reproach from my hostesses regarding the scant confidence that I had appeared to have in them, but I was hardly sensible of that. I was only affected at that moment by my happiness, and I owed them enough to listen to them with respect.

"Those benevolent divinities, after having kept us for four days, finally placed all three of us in their chariot, which was the same one in which we were seen to arrive, and interrupted the celebration of the vain tomb that Ambitious had prepared for his King."

The Princess finished thus, and Perfect, suffering impatiently everything that delayed his happiness, begged Good and Better to abridge the ceremonies. Zulbach took responsibility for hastening them after the King had fixed the moment for three days hence, the zealous Minister having asked for no more in order to carry out the orders he received.

The next day, Good and Better published the news of that marriage so much desired, and, by virtue of the Vizier's cares, the short time he had been given for the preparations for the great ceremony did not prevent it from being disposed with great magnificence.

Lisimene, whose nature was as inclined to goodness as her father's, forgetting the cruel treatment she had received from Richarde, receiving her with as much mildness and as much regard as if she had not rendered herself unworthy of the honor of being her stepmother and as if she had not combined her insulting conduct with the mot detestable of all treasons.

That impudent woman was, in spite of it, bold enough to present herself at any hour at the Princess's apartment, where she was welcomed in a fashion that would have touched any heart but hers. But that base soul, far from being moved by any kind of repentance, imitating Ambitious in the usage she made of the King's indulgence, only profited from the liberty that had been accorded to her to slip while everyone was occupied in the preparations for the wedding into a little room that communicated with a gallery that was little frequented.

As if everything were favorable to the designs of the Furies, the gallery also had a communication with her daughter's apartment; she opened the connecting door, because it was by that route that the perfidious Pigrieche intended to carry the body of the Princess into her room when she was dead, and to put herself in her bed in her place.

Measures having thus been taken by the mother and daughter, and as they had no doubt of the success of their detestable project, they waited for the evening that was to precede the wedding with an impatience that yielded nothing to Perfect's.

That fatal moment finally arrived, and Richarde, who had retired early, under the pretext of a slight indisposition, shut herself in her dressing-room, where she lit the mysterious candle that ought to put an end to Lisimene's days. After having made that horrible expedition, she went to bed.

However firm she was in her resolution, she had scarcely seen the fatal candle ignited than she sensed a secret horror and a general tremor. Attributing that to the uncertainty of the outcome, however, she did not have the slightest desire to extinguish the murderous light, and the agitation in which she found herself did not prevent her from going to sleep.

But sleep did not calm her anxieties—far from it. A thousand frightful dreams came to increase them. The woman thought she saw her dear Pigrieche expiring, and heard the bloodiest reproaches emerging from her mouth. "It is you, unworthy mother," she said to her, "that is precipitating me into the tomb." It also seemed to Richarde that she felt herself crushed by the weight of her daughter's corpse, which threw itself upon her furiously.

That dream made such an impression on her senses that she woke up and ran to see what state the candle was in, fearing that some unforeseen accident might have extinguished it, but she found that it was burning as well as could be desired, being almost consumed.

Richarde stayed to watch it finish, and when it was completely melted, she threw the residue on the ground, extinguishing the light underfoot, and saying the words that the witch had recommended to her:

"Wretch," cried the abominable woman, with a surge of joy, "I finally have the pleasure of seeing the end of your odious life."

Scarcely was that inhuman action completed that Richarde was struck by a sudden terror; she thought she heard a scream and a frightful voice that said to her "Oh, wretched mother, what have you done?"

At the cry she fled, and went, greatly disturbed, to throw herself into her bed, where it was impossible for her to find a moment's repose. She believed Lisimene to be dead, and the evil was without remedy. But far from considering that action with the complaisant eyes with which she had regarded it thus far, she began to envisage all the consequences that might follow such a frightful crime, which caused her a just terror, without it being accompanied by any remorse.

In spite of that, she was tormented internally nonetheless, and she reproached herself more than once for having listened to her daughter's passion. But those anxieties were suspended from time to time by the joy given to her by the hope of seeing Pigrieche become the wife of Prince Perfect that very day.

The daylight that she desired so ardently finally appeared, and found her in that alternation of fear and satisfaction. But the sound of instruments whose fanfares were inviting the people to a spectacle so generally desired finally determined her heart to joy. She abandoned herself to it entirely in thinking that all those preparations would soon complete the glory of her daughter and herself.

As Richarde was not Queen and had no other rank, and her crimes were public knowledge, she was excluded from the honor of going to the temple to witness the august ceremony that would unite the two lovers. It was not that she had not had the audacity to request permission, but it had been refused. However, as the King suffered more when he was forced not to grant what was asked of him than those who endured his refusals, he permitted, in order to console her, that a niche be fabricated, in which, from behind a blind, she and Pigrieche could see the ceremony without consequence and without being seen.

Richarde took advantage of that condescension and went to place herself in the location prepared for her at the moment when the happy couple entered the hall where the high priests were waiting for them. The men who escorted the King's wife to the place destined for her had received very precise orders from their master not to lack respect for her, believed that it would give her pleasure to hasten to offer to fetch Pigrieche, in order that she could share with her the pleasure that the pompous spectacle was giving the entire State, but Richarde, who knew the reasons that would prevent her daughter from showing herself, responded that the offer was futile and that Pigrieche, who was indisposed, had no wish to see it.

As they were slightly embarrassed, they did not persist and did not mention it again. Richarde went alone to see a celebration that caused her so much impatience and anxiety and had cost her so many crimes.

The joy that was shining on Perfect's face and the assured stride of his spouse appeared to Richarde to be certain proof that Pigrieche had not been surprised or interrupted in the execution of her project.

The King, who had arrived first, was sitting on a throne glittering with gold and precious stones, and when his daughter came in, accompanied by her lover and covered in her white veil, he gave them a sign to approach, standing up to make room for them.

It was at that moment that Richarde surrendered herself entirely to the pleasure of seeing Pigrieche where she had wanted so ardently to be, regarding that day as the happiest of her life. She saw the ceremony finish with delight in conformity with the tenderness that she had for her daughter.

My dear Pigrieche is Queen, then, she said to herself, *and nothing can trouble our happiness henceforth. Even though this marriage is the fruit of a deception, I know the probity of the King too well not to be convinced that he will make it a duty to maintain my daughter in the honors to which her industry has just elevated her.*

In the midst of her transports, however, Richarde could not help making herself a few reproaches with regard to what it had cost her; far from stopping her, however, she rejected those anxieties regarding the pain that the cruel surprise was about to cause the entire State, the King and Perfect, for whom she had the goodness to feel slightly sorry, admiring the generosity of her own heart, which made her compassionate to the chagrins of her enemies, to her own prejudice.

When everyone had left the temple, Richarde, all her wishes granted, went back to her apartment to await the denouement of the affair tranquilly.

The day passed without her hearing any tumult that could inform her that the crime had been discovered; the cries of joy that resounded everywhere were sure guarantees for her that everything was going well, which reassured her entirely.

The evening having arrived, the bride, following the custom of the land, retired and went to bed without the aid of her maidservants and without taking off her veil. Perfect also went into the nuptial chamber without any retinue or ceremony. To satisfy the laws of their nation, the lovers would not summon any other witness to such a charming occasion than Amour, who compensated them with interest for all the troubles they had suffered before arriving at such a happy moment.

That delightful night having finished, the mystery of the veil also ended, and with the return of daylight, Lisimene, dispensed of the obligation to hide, received the King with her face uncovered, as well as all the women destined to serve her, who hastened to fulfill their ministry.

The Princess finding herself in a state to appear, her first concern was to go and salute Richarde, thinking that she owed that respect to her father's wife.

The noise that ordinarily accompanies similar visits having announced to the King's wife the person she was about to receive, and not doubting that it would be Pigrieche, she ran to meet Lisimene. But imagine her surprise when, instead of her daughter, whom she believed to be still veiled, she saw the Princess appear, whom a vivid joy rendered more beautiful and more brilliant than she had ever been.

Lisimene, no longer considering in Richarde the baseness of her origin or that of her soul, and only seeing her as a mother-in-law—a title that rendered her respectable in spite of the frightful vices of which she had given abundant proof—advanced toward her respectfully, expecting to receive the embraces that she ought to have expected in the circumstances. Although she was convinced that the woman hated her no less than before, she believed that, constrained to disguise her hatred, she would receive at least with an exterior gratitude a step that honored her so much. Thus, she was extremely surprised when Richarde, having considered her, instead of the reception that she should naturally have given such a great Princess, recoiled with horror, uttering a frightful scream.

"What do I see?" she cried. "My dear Pigrieche, where are you?"

With those words, pushing Lisimene away furiously, she ran to her daughter's room and opened the curtains that surrounded her bed precipitately, calling to her in a voice that her agitation rendered frightful. But imagine her dolor on finding the one whom she sought lifeless and metamorphosed into a charcoal statue, her body being at least as dry and as black.

"Oh, wretch that I am!" cried the mother, desolate at the sight of such a terrible spectacle. "My dear daughter! I should have suspected it; it's me who has derived you of life.... Perfidious witch!" she added, "you have doomed me." As she finished speaking, she threw herself on to the frightful remains of Pigrieche, and, rage suffocating her, lost the power of speech along with consciousness.

Lisimene, surprised by the abrupt and extravagant reception of her mother-in-law, had nonetheless followed her, with all the Court what was accompanying her, unable to understand whence came a fit that appeared to contain madness. Wanting to see the end of it, she found Richarde motionless, holding her unfortunate daughter in her arms.

The Princess did not understand at first what she saw, and it did not even enter her mind that the black and burned corpse that was offered to her eyes was that of her most mortal enemy, even though she recognized all its features. Finally, however, she remembered what the mother and daughter, as malevolent as one another, had attempted in order to destroy her, and especially the visit the old Megaera had made to the witch of the desert, from which she had brought back the fatal candle. She understood then that Richarde had tried to employ it to kill her, not suspecting that, the naiads having exchanged it for the one they had given her to put in its place, its fatal virtue would only act on Pigrieche, and that she would suffer the death that they had destined for her.

Meanwhile, the King, informed of the accident, of which he could not imagine the cause, went to the place where that misfortune had just occurred, and although he ought only to have sentiments of execration for the mother and the daughter, he did not think he ought to refuse to visit that disloyal wife in the state she was in.

Scarcely had he cast his eyes on Pigrieche's corpse than he was informed of Richarde's despair. Although the generous Prince should have repented of always having been so good, he was still sufficiently so to be touched by a spectacle that would have found any other heart than his insensible.

But he was never insensible to the unfortunate, and, not content with feeling sorry for his wife, he did not neglect anything to bring out of her faint a scoundrel whom he would have one better to strangle. I do not know whether his compassion even went so far as to mourn Pigrieche, without understanding the cause of her black metamorphosis.

Richarde finally recovered the usage of her senses, and found herself in the helpful arms of her generous husband. Far from being touched by so much kindness, she pushed him away furiously.

"Now you're avenged," she told him, "and I'm punished for all my crimes."

Good and Better, who did not think that speech signified anything except that the death of the daughter had turned the mother's head, forgetting the actions that merited that creature being as wretched as they had rendered her culpable, immediately hastened to reassure her. He assured her that he had forgotten the past, and that, to soften the pain caused to her by the loss she had just suffered, he would have more kindness for her than ever; in sum, that he would neglect nothing that might efface the memory of her misfortunes from her mind.

But Richarde, whom the loss of everything that had been dear to her in the world had cast into the ultimate fit of despair and fury, more irritated than grateful, repaid the King for his compliment according to the merit of his puerile generosity.

"You still don't know me, feeble monarch," she said to her spouse, with movements of rage that made the spectators tremble. "You're unaware of all my crimes, but since I have the misfortune of not being able to consummate that one I had meditated, I can at least give myself the satisfaction of informing you of it and assuring you that the only consolation I could receive in that state that I am in would be to have the pleasure of recommencing to torment you, your daughter and your son-in-law."

Then she detailed all her crimes, not forgetting, above all, that of the fatal attempt of the candle, which had cost the life of her dear Pigrieche.

"But I've always been unlucky," she continued, "and I've never undertaken anything against your daughter that has not become fatal to mine. Now that I've finally succeeded in depriving myself of her, by the same means that I thought would raise her to the throne, it's time to follow her, and I want, finally, to render you a service by sparing you the trouble of punishing me or the shame of pardoning me."

With those words, the furious woman, seeing an open window, launched herself through it.

As the story of so many black deeds had rendered the spectators motionless, she found no obstacle to the justice she wanted to render herself. The King cried in vain for someone to help her. In any case, what help would they have been able to give her? The place from which she had just precipitated herself was so high that she was broken to the extent that her corpse scarcely appeared to be that of a human being.

In spite of all the horrors of which Richarde had just declared herself culpable, the King was touched by her death; but as that streak of compassion only came from the excess of is natural goodness, the tender impulse soon passed, and he even felt obliged to render thanks to Heaven, which had delivered him from his dangerous enemies.

Fatal as that catastrophe had been, it was incapable of interrupting for an instant public joy and the delight of the young newlyweds.

Richarde and her daughter were enclosed promptly in the same coffin, and those two monsters, who were buried without pomp, were so promptly forgotten that in less than four days, no one had any more memory of those Megaeras than if they had never existed.

Meanwhile, in spite of the pleas of Perfect and Lisimene, the King, having lost his taste for sovereign power, put it in their hands, and renounced without regret the grandeurs that had attracted such terrible misfortunes to him, to which he had needed nothing less than the protection of the aquatic nymphs in order not to succumb.

He chose for his retreat a château not far away from the royal city, inviting his children affectionately to give him the pleasure of seeing them often. They had no need of that invitation to acquit that just duty with joy and to render themselves worthy of his goodness.

Not only did the new King often go to obtain the advice of his father-in-law on the fashion of governing, but he also went there to enjoy the pleasure of his conversation, and the Queen, his wife, accompanied him on those journeys.

The young monarch soon succeeded in making himself considered as the model of Kings; combining the mildness of Good and Better with the art of making himself feared, and respected and loved as much as he was feared.

Perfect and Lisimene enjoyed the delights of their kingdom for a long time, where they never forgot, as you might imagine, to give the the their benefactresses the naiads and gnomides evidence of the most ardent gratitude, by erecting temples to both, and having inscribed in the annals of the Empire everything that might serve to render their memory immortal and hand that memory down to our century.

SF & FANTASY

Adolphe Alhaiza. *Cybele*

Alphonse Allais. *The Adventures of Captain Cap*

Henri Allorge. *The Great Cataclysm*

Guy d'Armen. *Doc Ardan: The City of Gold and Lepers; The Troglodytes of Mount Everest/The Giants of Black Lake; The Abominable Snowman*

G.-J. Arnaud. *The Ice Company*

André Arnyvelde. *The Ark; The Mutilated Bacchus*

Charles Asselineau. *The Double Life*

Henri Austruy. *The Eupantophone; The Olotelepan; The Petitpaon Era*

Barillet-Lagargousse. *The Final War*

Cyprien Bérard. *The Vampire Lord Ruthwen*

S. Henry Berthoud. *Martyrs of Science; The Angel Asrael*

Aloysius Bertrand. *Gaspard de la Nuit*

Richard Bessière. *The Gardens of the Apocalypse; The Masters of Silence*

Chevalier de Béthune. *The World of Mercury*

Albert Bleunard. *Ever Smaller*

Félix Bodin. *The Novel of the Future*

Pierre Boitard. *Journey to the Sun*

Louis Boussenard. *Monsieur Synthesis*

Alphonse Brown. *City of Glass; The Conquest of the Air*

Émile Calvet. *In a Thousand Years*

André Caroff. *The Terror of Madame Atomos; Miss Atomos; The Return of Madame Atomos; The Mistake of Madame Atomos; The Monsters of Madame Atomos; The Revenge of Madame Atomos; The Resurrection of Madame Atomos; The Mark of Madame Atomos; The Spheres of Madame Atomos; The Wrath of Madame Atomos* (w/M. & Sylvie Stéphan)

Jean Carrère. *The End of Atlantis*

Félicien Champsaur. *Homo-Deus; The Human Arrow; Nora, The Ape-Woman; Ouha, King of the Apes; Pharaoh's Wife*

Didier de Chousy. *Ignis*

Jules Clarétie. *Obsession*

Jacques Collin de Plancy. *Voyage to the Center of the Earth*

Michel Corday. *The Eternal Flame; The Lynx* (w/André Couvreur)

André Couvreur. *Caresco, Superman; The Exploits of Professor Tornada* (3 vols.); *The Necessary Evil*
Gaston Danville. *The Perfume of Lust*
Camille Debans. *The Misfortunes of John Bull*
Captain Danrit. *Undersea Odyssey*
C. I. Defontenay. *Star (Psi Cassiopeia)*
Charles Derennes. *The People of the Pole*
Georges Dodds (anthologist). *The Missing Link*
Charles Dodeman. *The Silent Bomb*
Harry Dickson. *The Heir of Dracula; Harry Dickson vs. The Spider*
Jules Dornay. *Lord Ruthven Begins*
Alfred Driou. *The Adventures of a Parisian Aeronaut*
Odette Dulac. *The War of the Sexes*
Alexandre Dumas. *The Return of Lord Ruthven; The Man who Married a Mermaid* (w/P. Lacroix)
Renée Dunan. *Baal; The Ultimate Pleasure*
J.-C. Dunyach. *The Night Orchid; The Thieves of Silence*
Henri Duvernois. *The Man Who Found Himself*
Achille Eyraud. *Voyage to Venus*
Henri Falk. *The Age of Lead*
Paul Féval. *Anne of the Isles; Knightshade; Revenants; Vampire City; The Vampire Countess; The Wandering Jew's Daughter*
Paul Féval, *fils. Felifax, the Tiger-Man*
Charles de Fieux. *Lamékis*
Fernand Fleuret. *Jim Click*
Charles-Marie Flor O'Squarr. *Phantoms*
Louis Forest. *Someone is Stealing Children in Paris*
Arnould Galopin. *Doctor Omega*; *Doctor Omega and the Shadowmen* (anthology)
Judith Gautier. *Isoline and the Serpent-Flower*
H. Gayar. *The Marvelous Adventures of Serge Myrandhal on Mars*
Louis Geoffroy. *The Apocryphal Napoleon*
G.L. Gick. *Harry Dickson and the Werewolf of Rutherford Grange*
Raoul Gineste. *The Second Life of Doctor Albin*
Delphine de Girardin. *Balzac's Cane*
Léon Gozlan. *The Vampire of the Val-de-Grâce*
Jules Gros. *The Fossil Man*
Jimmy Guieu. *The Polarian-Denebian War* (2 vols.)
Edmond Haraucourt. *Daah, the First Human; Illusions of Immortality*
Nathalie Henneberg. *The Green Gods*
Eugène Hennebert. *The Enchanted City*

Jules Hoche. *The Maker of Men and His Formula*

V. Hugo, P. Foucher & P. Meurice. *The Hunchback of Notre-Dame*

Romain d'Huissier. *Hexagon: Dark Matter*

Jules Janin. *The Magnetized Corpse*

Gustave Kahn. *The Tale of Gold and Silence*

Gérard Klein. *The Mote in Time's Eye*

Fernand Kolney. *Love in 5000 Years*

Paul Lacroix. *Danse Macabre; The Man who Married a Mermaid* (w/Alexandre Dumas)

Louis-Guillaume de La Follie. *The Unpretentious Philosopher*

Jean de La Hire. *The Fiery Wheel; Enter the Nyctalope; The Nyctalope on Mars; The Nyctalope vs. Lucifer; The Nyctalope Steps In; Night of the Nyctalope; Return of the Nyctalope*

Etienne-Léon de Lamothe-Langon. *The Virgin Vampire*

André Laurie. *Spiridon*

Gabriel de Lautrec. *The Vengeance of the Oval Portrait*

Alain le Drimeur. *The Future City*

Georges Le Faure & Henri de Graffigny. *The Extraordinary Adventures of a Russian Scientist Across the Solar System* (2 vols.)

Gustave Le Rouge. *The Dominion of the World* (w/Gustave Guitton) (4 vols.); *The Mysterious Doctor Cornelius* (3 vols.); *The Vampires of Mars*

Jules Lermina. *The Battle of Strasbourg; Mysteryville; Panic in Paris; The Secret of Zippelius; To-Ho and the Gold Destroyers*

Maurice Level. *The Gates of Hell*

André Lichtenberger. *The Centaurs; The Children of the Crab*

Maurice Limat. *Mephista*

Listonai. *The Philosophical Voyager*

Jean-Marc & Randy Lofficier. *Edgar Allan Poe on Mars; The Katrina Protocol; Pacifica 1, 2; Robonocchio; Return of the Nyctalope;* (anthologists) *Tales of the Shadowmen 1-13; The Vampire Almanac* (2 vols.)

Ch. Lomon & P.-B. Gheuzi. *The Last Days of Atlantis*

Camille Mauclair. *The Virgin Orient*

Xavier Mauméjean. *The League of Heroes*

Joseph Méry. *The Tower of Destiny*

Hippolyte Mettais. *Paris Before the Deluge; The Year 5865*

Louise Michel. *The Human Microbes; The New World*

Tony Moilin. *Paris in the Year 2000*

Michael Moorcock's *Legends of the Multiverse*

José Moselli. *Illa's End*

John-Antoine Nau. *Enemy Force*

Marie Nizet. *Captain Vampire*

Charles Nodier. *Trilby and The Crumb Fairy*

C. Nodier, A. Beraud & Toussaint-Merle. *Frankenstein*

Henri de Parville. *An Inhabitant of the Planet Mars*

Gaston de Pawlowski. *Journey to the Land of the 4th Dimension*

Georges Pellerin. *The World in 2000 Years*

Ernest Pérochon. *The Frenetic People*

Pierre Pelot. *The Child Who Walked on the Sky*

Jean Petithuguenin. *An International Mission to the Moon*

J. Polidori, C. Nodier, E. Scribe. *Lord Ruthven the Vampire*

P.-A. Ponson du Terrail. *The Immortal Woman; The Vampire and the Devil's Son; The Police Agent*

Georges Price. *The Missing Men of the* Sirius

René Pujol. *The Chimerical Quest*

Edgar Quinet. *Ahasuerus; The Enchanter Merlin*

Henri de Régnier. *A Surfeit of Mirrors*

Maurice Renard. *The Blue Peril; Doctor Lerne; The Doctored Man; A Man Among the Microbes; The Master of Light*

Restif de la Bretonne. *The Discovery of the Austral Continent by a Flying Man; Posthumous Correspondence* (3 vols.); *The Fay Ouroucoucou* (2 vols.)

Jean Richepin. *The Crazy Corner; The Wing*

Albert Robida. *The Adventures of Saturnin Farandoul; Chalet in the Sky; The Clock of the Centuries; The Electric Life; The Engineer Von Satanas*

J.-H. Rosny Aîné. *Helgvor of the Blue River; The Givreuse Enigma; The Mysterious Force; The Navigators of Space; Vamireh; The World of the Variants; The Young Vampire*

Marcel Rouff. *Journey to the Inverted World*

Marie-Anne de Roumier-Robert. *The Voyage of Lord Seaton to the Seven Planets*

Léonie Rouzade. *The World Turned Upside Down*

Han Ryner. *The Human Ant; The Superhumans*

Louis-Claude de Saint-Martin. *The Crocodile*

Frank Schildiner. *The Quest of Frankenstein; The Triumph of Frankenstein*

Nicolas Ségur. *The Human Paradise*

Pierre de Selenes: *An Unknown World*

Norbert Sevestre. *Sâr Dubnotal: Vs. Jack the Ripper; The Astral Trail*

Angelo de Sorr. *The Vampires of London*
Brian Stableford. *The Empire of the Necromancers (1. The Shadow of Frankenstein; 2. Frankenstein and the Vampire Countess; 3. Frankenstein in London); The Wayward Muse; Eurydice's Lament; The Mirror of Dionysius; The New Faust at the Tragicomique; Sherlock Holmes and The Vampires of Eternity; The Stones of Camelot* (anthologist) *News from the Moon; The Germans on Venus; The Supreme Progress; The World Above the World; Nemoville; Investigations of the Future; The Conqueror of Death; The Revolt of the Machines; The Man With the Blue Face; The Aerial Valley; The New Moon; The Nickel Man; On the Brink of the World's End; The Mirror of Present Events; The Humanisphere*
Jacques Spitz. *The Eye of Purgatory*
Kurt Steiner. *Ortog*
Eugène Thébault. *Radio-Terror*
C.-F. Tiphaigne de La Roche. *Amilec*
Simon Tyssot de Patot. *The Strange Voyages of Jacques Massé and Pierre de Mésange*
Louis Ulbach. *Prince Bonifacio*
Théo Varlet. *The Castaways of Eros; The Golden Rock.; The Martian Epic* (w/Octave Joncquel); *Timeslip Troopers* (w/André Blandin); *The Xenobiotic Invasion*
Pierre Véron. *The Merchants of Health*
Paul Vibert. *The Mysterious Fluid*
Villiers de l'Isle-Adam. *The Scaffold; The Vampire Soul*
Gaston de Wailly. *The Murderer of the World*
Philippe Ward. *Artahe; Manhattan Ghost* (w/Mickael Laguerre); *The Song of Montségur* (w/Sylvie Miller)

Victor Margueritte. *The Bacheloress; The Companion; The Couple*

MYSTERIES & THRILLERS

M. Allain & P. Souvestre. *The Daughter of Fantômas*
A. Anicet-Bourgeois & Lucien Dabril. *Rocambole* (stage plays)
Guy d'Armen. *Doc Ardan: The City of Gold and Lepers; The Troglodytes of Mount Everest/The Giants of Black Lake; Doc Ardan: The Abominable Snowman*
Cyprien Bérard. *The Vampire Lord Ruthwen*
A. Bernède. *Belphegor; Judex* (w/Louis Feuillade); *The Return of Judex* (w/Louis Feuillade); *The Shadow of Judex* (anthology)

A. Bisson & G. Livet. *Nick Carter vs. Fantômas* (stage play)

André Caroff. *The Terror of Madame Atomos; Miss Atomos; The Return of Madame Atomos; The Mistake of Madame Atomos; The Monsters of Madame Atomos; The Revenge of Madame Atomos; The Resurrection of Madame Atomos; The Mark of Madame Atomos; The Spheres of Madame Atomos; The Wrath of Madame Atomos* (w/M. & Sylvie Stéphan)

Félicien Champsaur. *Homo-Deus; Nora, The Ape-Woman; Ouha, King of the Apes*

Jules Clarétie. *Obsession*

V. Darlay & H. de Gorsse. *Arsène Lupin vs. Sherlock Holmes: The Stage Play* (stage play)

Harry Dickson. *Harry Dickson vs. The Heir of Dracula; Harry Dickson vs. The Spider*

Séamas Duffy. *Sherlock Holmes in Paris*

Alexandre Dumas. *The Return of Lord Ruthven* (stage play)

Paul Féval. *The Black Coats (The Parisian Jungle; Heart of Steel; The Sword-Swallower; 'Salem Street; The Invisible Weapon; The Companions of the Treasure; The Cadet Gang); Gentlemen of the Night; John Devil*

Paul Féval, *fils. Felifax, the Tiger-Man*

Louis Forest. *Someone is Stealing Children in Paris*

Fortuné du Boisgobey. *Two Crimes*

Émile Gaboriau. *Monsieur Lecoq; The Casebook of Monsieur Lecoq*

Arnould Galopin: *Harry Dickson: The Man in Grey; Harry Dickson: Tenebras*

Goron & Émile Gautier. *Spawn of the Penitentiary*

G.L. Gick. *Harry Dickson and The Werewolf of Rutherford Grange*

Léon Gozlan. *The Vampire of the Val-de-Grâce*

Georges Grison. *The Heads that fell in Paris*

Paul d'Ivoi. *Around the World on Five Sous* (w/Henri Chabrillat)

Paul Lacroix. *Danse Macabre*

Jean de La Hire. *Enter the Nyctalope; The Nyctalope on Mars; The Nyctalope vs. Lucifer; The Nyctalope Steps In; Night of the Nyctalope; Return of the Nyctalope*

Rick Lai. *Shadows of the Opera: Retribution in Blood; Sisters of the Shadows: The Curse of Cagliostro*

Etienne-Léon de Lamothe-Langon. *The Virgin Vampire*

Steve Leadley. *Sherlock Holmes and The Circle of Blood*

Maurice Leblanc. *Arsène Lupin vs. Countess Cagliostro; Arsène Lupin vs. Sherlock Holmes (1. The Blonde Phantom; 2. The Hollow*

Needle); The Island of the Thirty Coffin; 813; The Many Faces of Arsène Lupin (anthology)

Gustave Lerouge: *The Mysterious Doctor Cornelius* (3 vols.)

Gaston Leroux. *Chéri-Bibi* (stage play)*; The Phantom of the Opera; Rouletabille & the Mystery of the Yellow Room; Rouletabille at Krupp's*

Maurice Limat. *Mephista*

Jean-Marc & Randy Lofficier. *The Katrina Protocol;* (anthologists) *Tales of the Shadowmen 1-13; The Vampire Almanac* (2 vols.)

Richard Marsh. *The Complete Adventures of Judith Lee*

William Patrick Maynard. *The Terror of Fu Manchu; The Destiny of Fu Manchu*

Michael Moorcock's *Legends of the Multiverse*

Frank J. Morlok. *Sherlock Holmes: The Grand Horizontals* (stage play)*; Sherlock Holmes vs Jack the Ripper* (stage play*); Sherlock Holmes, Fantômas, Lupin, Raffles and More: The Spanish Plays* (stage plays)

Jean Petithuguenin. *The Adventures of Ethel King, The Female Nick Carter*

P.-A. Ponson du Terrail. *The Immortal Woman; The Vampire and the Devil's Son; The Police Agent*

Georges Price. *The Missing Men of the* Sirius

Charles Rabou: *The Secret Bureau: 1. The Secret Bureau; 2: The Brothers of Death*

Antonin Reschal. *The Adventures of Miss Boston, The First Female Detective*

Norbert Sevestre. *Sâr Dubnotal vs. Jack the Ripper; The Astral Trail*

Eugène Thébault. *Radio-Terror*

P. de Wattyne & Y. Walter. *Sherlock Holmes vs. Fantômas* (stage play)

David White. *Fantômas in America*

Pierre Yrondy. *The Adventures of Thérèse Arnaud of the French Secret Service*